THE IMPORTANCE OF PAWNS

CHRONICLES OF THE HOUSE OF VALOIS

KEIRA J. MORGAN

With gratitude to three people without whom this book would not exist.

Roberta Rich, my invaluable mentor

Oscar Humberto Lopez Valdez, my wonderful husband

Jan Henry Morgan, my inspirational mother

Copyright © 2021 Keira Morgan

The Importance of Pawns

Keira J. Morgan

www.kjmorgan-writer.com

author@kjmorgan-writer.com

Published 2021, by French Renaissance Fiction/

Fiction de la Renaissance française

Ottawa, ON, CA

613 701 2856

ISBN 978-1-7773974-0-1 (ebook) Mar 2021

ISBN 978-1-7773974-1-8 (paper) Mar 2021

Cover design by Jenny Q at Historical Fiction Book Covers.

Cover created from the following paintings both in the public domain and made available under the Creative Commons license.

Portrait of Queen Isabella of Bourbon (1602-1644) c. 1620 by an unknown painter (Formerly attributed to Juan Pantoja de la Cruz); and Portrait of a child of the House of Redetti c. 1570 by Giovan Battista Moroni.

This is a work of fiction. All characters, organizations, and events portrayed in this novel are either the products of the author's imagination or are used fictionally.

AUTHOR'S NOTES

1. American English is used throughout this book.
2. Lyon, the French spelling of the city spelled Lyons in English, is used through this book.
3. Names and titles present challenges to authors. First, royalty and nobility have many titles, all of which they use as names. Second, as they change their status, from a count to a duke for example, their titles change. To keep it simple, I generally ignore this change for minor characters. For my main characters I cannot, since it is important for the story. So when Louise changes from a countess to a duchess it is not an error, it is an important increase in her status. **If you become confused, check back to the list of principal characters.**
4. I provide endnotes and a glossary of terms for the words I expect to be less well known.
5. In the Afterward you will find an explanation of canonical hours and the difference between the Julian and the Gregorian dates.

PRINCIPAL CHARACTERS AND AGE
(WHEN STORY OPENS)

Queen Anne de France (37)

Queen of France, **also Duchess de Bretagne,** wife of King Louis and mother of Princess Claude and Princess Renée.

King Louis XII de France (52)

Husband to Queen Anne, father of Princess Claude and Princess Renée, divorced from Jeanne de France, **Formerly Duke Louis d'Orléans.**

Princess Claude (15)

Elder daughter of above, betrothed to Duke François d'Angoulême. **Becomes Duchess Claude de Bretagne, then Queen Claude.**

Princess Renée (4)

Younger daughter of above, has Baronne Michelle de Soubise as Gouvernante.

Baronne Michelle de Soubise (34)

Also known as Michelle de Saubonne, widow of Jean IV of Parthenay l'Archimbault, Baron de Soubise. **Gouvernante**[1] **to Princess Renée.**

Countess Louise d'Angoulême (38)

Widow of Count Charles d'Angoulême, mother of Marguerite [married to Duke Charles d'Alençon] and Duke François d'Angoulême. **Becomes Duchess d'Angoulême.**

Duke François d'Angoulême (20)

Son of Countess Louise de Savoy, betrothed to Princess Claude, heir presumptive to King Louis XII of France. **Becomes King Francois 1.**

Mme. Jeanne de Longwy (29)

Baronne de Pagny et Mirebeau, natural daughter of Count Jean d'Angoulême, stepdaughter to Countess Louise d'Angoulême. **Gouvernante to Princess Claude.** Later, Countess de Bar-sur-Seine.

Countess Françoise de Tonnerre (45)

Françoise Rohan-Guéméné, widow of Louis III de Husson (d.1508). Gouvernante to Princess Renée.

MAP OF FRANCE CIRCA 1500

SHOWING BRITTANY ON NORTH-WEST

4 JANUARY 1514, EARLY AFTERNOON

CHÂTEAU DE BLOIS

Countess Louise d'Angoulême

COUNTESS LOUISE D'ANGOULÊME appraised her reflection in the fine Venetian mirror her son, her marvelous François, had given her for her holy days *étrenne*[1]. Was it not just like him to give her the costliest gift he could find? And who would pay for it? Putting the problem aside, she turned her head this way and that. Were those gray hairs in among her glossy dark blond locks? Did she have crow's feet fanning from her wide gray eyes? The perfection of the image from this latest invention was perhaps not an advantage to an older woman. Impatiently she put it down.

When would that Agnez arrive? It was unsuitable that a woman of her rank should be kept waiting by a servant girl. She paced once more around the perimeter of her suite's presence cham-

1

ber, running her fingers over the thick Flemish tapestries that absorbed the chill from the stone walls. She reminded herself that she had done very well to parlay King Louis's favor into this suite of three rooms, despite the overcrowding at the Christmas court. It had taken some effort on her part, but despite Queen Anne's enmity, she had even charmed the king into furnishing the rooms. When she arrived early in December, she had come accompanied only by her bed and clothes chests.

Louise threw herself into a folding leather chair in front of the hissing fire. The crowned L & A for Louis and Anne emblazoned on the fireplace hood drew her eyes. How the emblem irritated her! Well, there was always some fly in the ointment, she thought. When her son was king, she would order those initials replaced immediately.

A knock rattled the door of her presence chamber. Finally! When her gentleman usher pulled it open, the queen's maid, Agnez, sidled in. She bobbed a curtsey. "You sent for me, Countess?" She twisted her hands on her apron.

Louise did not rise. "The court is rife with rumors that the queen is sinking and will not last the month. Be it true?"

Agnez's chapped lips twitched into a knowing smile, and she gave a jerky nod. "The queen be mortal ill. She will be passing right soon."

Louise nodded. It was as she thought. Queen Anne was dying, and much sooner than anyone had expected — if Agnez's words proved true. Though there was no reason to doubt her. On past occasions she had earned her pay. But it was too irritating. Queen Anne's illness was just another difficulty! She still had not approved her daughter's marriage to Louise's son. They had been betrothed for years and would be married already, but for Queen Anne's unrelenting opposition. Not that plain, fat

Princess Claude with her ugly limp and mousy hair was the match Louise would have chosen for her magnificent François, but what choice did she have? King Louis was her son's guardian, and he insisted upon the marriage. Too bad he couldn't control his stubborn wife — or did not choose to. At least Claude was wealthy, and soon would be richer since she was heiress to the duchy of Brittany when the queen died, and it was just one of Claude's dower lands.

"Baronne Michelle was with the queen all morning." Agnez brought a finger to her lips, muffling her words. "She will not last but days."

It took Louise a few seconds to understand Agnez's mumbled words. When they finally sank in, Louise barely concealed her worry. There would be no wedding if the court was in mourning. "You are certain?"

Agnez's chin bobbed. "Oh, yes. I was scrubbing the floor, so I heard the whole." She frowned. "There was more."

"Yes?"

"She said—"

"Who said?"

"Mme. la Reine said—" The girl fell silent.

"Tell me, child. I will not bite."

"She'd not leave Brittany to the Princess Claude. Goin t'leave it to the Princess Renée."

"By the shoes of the Blessed Virgin!"

Agnez fell to her knees. "I'm s-s-sorry."

The countess realized she was glaring at the girl. "There, there, wench, calm yourself, you surprised me. That is all. Stand up."

3

Louise forced herself to speak coolly. She pointed to the ale, "Pour yourself a tankard. Now, what else did the queen say?"

After she took a swallow, Agnez snuffled through her nose. Hands gripping the mug, she said, "You be not angry, be you, Mme. Louise?"

"Not with you, girl. You have been useful and the more you tell me, the better I will reward you." That should open her lips. Hopefully, it did not encourage her to embellish her tale.

"You'll not like it, Mme. Louise."

Louise's gray eyes snapped. "I do not blame you for the words of others, girl."

Agnez pushed wisps of greasy hair back under her cap. She spoke in a singsong as if quoting: "The queen said, 'The Countess d'Angoulême is no more pleased about the marriage than me. She don't like my daughter and agrees to it only to please the king since he's pow'rful and rich... 'cause she's greedy. Let 'er find out that Brittany won't go to Claude and see how fast she ends the 'trothal.'" Agnez slowed to a stop.

Louise did not doubt that Agnez had repeated the queen's words. Though Louise's face burned, she controlled herself. "Was there more?"

The girl shook her mob-capped head.

Louise stood. "You have done me good service, Agnez. Continue, and there will be more like this." She tossed her a bag of small coins.

Catching it, Agnez scrambled into a curtsey. "Thank 'ee Mme. Louise." She almost ran from the room.

Louise paced the parquet floor for some time before regaining her temper. That the queen was correct about her opinion of

Claude and the marriage was irrelevant. That the Queen called Louise avaricious was insulting but unimportant — another example of a rich woman despising a clever one for her lesser means and greater talents. That the queen planned to disinherit Claude of Brittany was unacceptable.

As Louise moved about her rooms, she stopped to caress the soft Flemish tapestries, the glowing frames on the paintings by Botticelli and Raphael, and the tooled leather covers on the books she had taken from the great library. Was Claude worth marrying without Brittany? Her dowry also included Milan — the single richest state in the West. She was the best dowered heiress in Europe. But King Louis had lost Milan, and who knew if he would recover it — or be able to hold it. So, what was it worth? Yet her son valued it more than all Claude's other domains and was determined to regain her birthright. It was an obsession of his. To Louise it was a chimera, but she would do anything for her son. What made men so eager to fight, to become storied warriors, wasting their wealth and risking maiming and death?

Louise shook her head to rid it of these unwelcome thoughts. As she passed Botticelli's painting again, she paused to gaze at it. Venus floated to shore on a scallop shell while three Graces danced on the grass nearby. Its perfection usually restored her sense of order. Today it did not work its magic. Why could not the actual world be so orderly? Brittany was too great a prize to permit the queen to bequeath it away from Princess Claude.

MICHELLE DE SOUBISE stood over the table cluttered with flasks and packets of remedies. When she opened the stoppered bottle of valerian, its woody odor penetrated the close air in Queen Anne's bedchamber. She measured a dose.

When Michelle put the cup to the queen's mouth, Anne wrinkled her nose. They eyed each other. She opened her lips and swallowed. "You know I do not like medicine."

"It is not a medicine, Milady. It is a restorative, to ease your pain." Michelle's voice was low and reassuring. Never would she admit to the queen that she gave her medicine. Queen Anne abhorred everything to do with doctors, blaming them for her children's deaths.

"You always have a pacifying answer." The queen smiled faintly, though pain lines creased her brow.

Michelle smiled back, repressing her sorrow. It was like pressing her tongue on a chancre to watch over the queen as she weakened and shrank. Although Queen Anne was only thirty-seven, she looked much older. Already her cheeks were sunken, her skin yellow and tight over her cheekbones and jaw. Only her enormous amber eyes fringed with long dark lashes hinted at her once great beauty.

Queen Anne should be in bed, but she would not stay there. A month ago, she had been bustling about, and still refused to admit how ill she was. So, she was resting fully clothed in her favorite armchair, her feet raised on a footstool. She shivered.

Michelle felt the queen's forehead. It was clammy, despite the heat radiating from the logs crackling in the fireplace of her vast bedchamber. Michelle crossed to the four-poster bed, the heavy canopy dressed in the queen's colors, to pluck up an ermine coverlet. At least this new part of the Château de Blois was well-sealed from winter's frigid draughts. The wainscoted walls insulated by the queen's favorite silk tapestries brightened the space. Returning to her, Michelle draped the soft fur over the queen's knees. Queen Anne winced.

"Bring those braziers close, Agnez." When the chambermaid finished the sooty task, Michelle smiled a thank you.

"Stop bustling about, Mme. Michelle. Your fussing disturbs me." The queen sounded querulous, a sign of her ill health.

Michelle sank to a stool beside the queen and smoothed her overskirt over her knees. "Would you like me to read aloud or to write a letter, Mme. la Reine? Or…?"

"Not yet." Queen Anne leaned back and closed her eyes.

As the queen's *dame d'atour*[2], her highest-ranking lady and only real friend, probably even closer than her husband, she was privy to Queen Anne's deepest secrets. Perhaps only her confessor knew more. So, they both knew she was dying, although the queen had yet to admit it. But she had little time left and many hard decisions to make. Talking about them would help, Michelle thought.

The queen's voice disrupted Michelle's brooding. "The king keeps pressing me to agree to a date for Claude's marriage. Now that she's turned fifteen — and her monthly flowers[3] have begun — he has become insistent. And after I am gone, I cannot prevent it. But what will I do about Brittany? How can I leave it to Claude when she is betrothed to Duke François?" She turned her head to Michelle, even that small movement sending a flash of pain across her face. "So, what do you advise, my wise friend?"

Michelle puffed out a breath of relief. Here was the opening she had been waiting for. Yet she was irritated, too. Brittany, always Brittany. "Dear friend, although I have waited to say so, it is time to turn your thoughts to your eternal life. Look at all you have already achieved for Brittany. Our homeland is now rich and peaceful. Please trust that our Savior knows best. Turn your thoughts instead to final matters: the future of your daughter,

Renée, the last dispositions you must make of your worldly goods, and your last confession."

"Do not rush me out of this world, Mme. Michelle." Queen Anne's voice cut sharp as a rapier. "You may not consider the future of Brittany one of my important final matters. I do." She straightened in her armchair, flinching again. Michelle guessed that her *renes* pained her much more than she would admit. "Listen to me."

Those were the last words she spoke. The next moment she was writhing in agony. Ordering Agnez to bring two men servants to carry her to her bed and send for Dr. Nichel, Michelle managed to get the queen to swallow a dose of willow bark tisane laced with opium.

AFTER THE QUEEN'S sudden relapse, Michelle sent a page flying to King Louis. By the time he arrived, Queen Anne was sleeping heavily from the dose of pain medicine.

King Louis, face lined with sorrow, stood at the foot of the queen's bed, staring at his wife's waxy face. She lay pale as a corpse under her embroidered coverlet.

Michelle touched her forehead. "She experienced an excruciating attack of the renal stone[4] and is still fevered, but less so."

Queen Anne stirred and began a high-pitched mumble.

This was a worrying symptom. "Agnez, fetch a jug of the filtered, cold water." Michelle ordered. She poured a measure of clear water into a bowl, set two stoppered bottles on the worktable, added a measure from each to the bowl, and stirred. A fresh herbal aroma cleansed the stale air.

King Louis perched on the edge of the chair. "What are you preparing?" He leaned forward to sniff. "It smells of flowers."

"It is a mix of lavender oil, spirits of alcohol and pure water — to reduce her fever and freshen her. She will sleep more calmly."

"From what does she suffer?" King Louis insisted.

Knowing him, she believed he would prefer the truth, She said, "I can list her symptoms, but is not your question: will she recover?"

"I shrink from any hint that she will not, yet...." He squared his thin shoulders. "The unsugared pastille then." He stared at the floor.

"Her humors[5] are imbalanced. For some time, I have suspected a bilious humor from the sour odors of her urine and breath, signs of a renal disorder. The agony she suffered today suggest stones have lodged in the renal passages. Only our Savior can give a certain answer, but I know no remedy. My treatment today only served to reduce her pain."

"Why did you not send for my principal physician to attend her? Is Dr. Loysel not learned?" King Louis sounded like an inquisitor.

"You know Mme. la Reine detests physicians. I have been ministering to her since she lost your last child two years past. She is resting quietly now, Sire, as you can see."Michelle strove not to sound defensive. "Dr. Loysel will bleed her, purge her, and prescribe stinking curatives of bats blood and snake excrement." She sniffed. "The queen has neither the strength nor the blood for such remedies. My treatment — willow bark tea mixed with a drop of opium — reduces her pain and allows her to sleep." She picked up her notes from the bedside table and offered him the note pad — leather-bound scraps of vellum held together by string. "I have recorded all my treatments."

King Louis swallowed and glanced at the notepad. "I must know she is receiving the best... the correct... treatment."

"To be sure, the queen must have the best care." Michelle hesitated. People could accuse even noblewomen of witchcraft these days and then torture and burn them at the stake for small acts. Whenever anything went wrong — a failed harvest, a sudden hailstorm, an outbreak of plague — the burnings started. With the queen so ill, Michelle would be safer if an infirmarian attended her. "Princess Renée's infirmarian, Dr. Nichel, has seen her. But perhaps your Dr. Loysel, should attend her instead."

King Louis considered. "It is true that my wife blames the doctors for our infants' deaths. And we both trust you...." He chewed his lower lip. "But I must be sure. She is precious to me." He leaned over Anne and dabbed away a drop of sweat on her brow.

Michelle said: "Send for him, Sire. Let us hope he knows of cures of which I am unaware." It was prudent to have him present. It should quell the inevitable rumors.

The king rose, still troubled. "I shall. Although I doubt he.... I have observed that my wife improves most in your care."

"You are kind, Your Grace. In truth, the queen's recovery lies in the Lord's hands."

4 JANUARY 1514, LATE AFTERNOON

CHÂTEAU DE BLOIS

*C*ountess Louise d'Angoulême

In the Countess Louise's presence chamber, crimson drapes blocked the icy late afternoon chill that would have penetrated through the mullioned window. She played tarocchi[1] against herself as she awaited her daughter's arrival.

When her gentleman usher threw the door open, Louise hurried to Marguerite and stood on tiptoe to kiss the duchess on both cheeks. Then she took a step back to admire her. With her smooth olive skin and dark eyes, Marguerite looked remarkably like her late father and every inch an Orléans. Her dark hair was tucked back into a golden snood. Today she looked elegant with her coloring enhanced by the dark-green bodice, checkered red and green overskirt and matching great, red sleeves. God be praised, Marguerite did not have the beaky nose that made François look like a bird of prey.

"Bonjour, ma fille. Did you attend the queen this morning?" Taking her arm, she led her to a leather chair near the fireplace.

Marguerite rose from her curtsey and answered, "I was reading my stories aloud to my godmother and my cousin." So like her. She favored her father's side, too, in her poetic talents, so unlike Louise's practical nature.

She pulled a chair close to Marguerite and sat. "Have you been enjoying the Christmas court?"

Marguerite's eyes sparkled. "It is delightful to be at the center of things again. Alençon is so provincial and my mother-in-law disapproves of my writing. And it is always a joy to spend time with you and François. And with people who read and write. Who talk about books and ideas."

It was true, Louise thought. Though the royal court was a barren wasteland compared to her cultured court at Romorantin — whenever the king permitted her to live there. Only fourteen years separated her daughter and her, and people said she looked young enough that they could be sisters. Among the queen's ladies there was a greater age range.

She said, "Have you spent time with your brother?" Marguerite brightened. They both adored him.

"He dances with me at every ball. I see him in the afternoons composing love songs." She snickered. "They are very bad; the kind full of 'love' and 'dove' and 'lips and wine' and 'mine and thine.' But his voice is melodious, and his eyes are soulful, so the ladies swoon."

They both chuckled. They had been watching him lure damsels since his first growth spurt shot him taller than they.

"I hope he has been taking care with his choice of hussies to bed," his mother said. "I worry about him."

"He does not have to choose harlots, Maman, with all the court ladies willing to accommodate him."

"Do not be an innocent, my dear. It is not only the sluts who are diseased these days."

Marguerite looked worried. "I hope he is careful."

"He will join us for dinner. He went with the hunt today." Louise picked up the tarocchi cards from the table and shuffled them as she arranged her words. "Have you seen his new armor?"

Marguerite fussed with the red velvet oversleeves of her gown, refusing to meet her mother's eyes. "He is the best jouster in France. A good suit of armor is not a waste for he will be safer. He will not lose it being tumbled off his horse." Then she sighed. "Is he badly indebted again Maman? Every time I see him, he is wearing another gaudy doublet or extravagant hat. And he gambles for the highest stakes." She met Louise's eyes. "Have you seen his helmet decorated with peacock feathers?" She giggled. "I know it isn't a laughing matter, Maman, but the thing is absurd."

Louise understood her daughter's attitude. She found it hard to deny her son, her precious César, the luxuries he needed to shine. Especially now that he was heir to the throne. Yet her husband had left enormous debts. They still threatened to engulf the estate almost a decade later. And the dowries for his illegitimate daughters, not to mention Marguerite herself, had added to the burden.

"I have arranged an excellent marriage for Souvereine. Or I shall, if I can find the dowry."

"I see." Marguerite became serious.

"I need your help."

"What can I do?"

"The betrothal to Claude. We must secure it immediately. The queen is dying. She must be persuaded to agree before she does. François does not care. I need your help to persuade him." Louise reached out to take Marguerite's arm.

Before Marguerite could reply, there was a knock on the door. It flew open. As the gentleman usher bowed to François, servants from the royal kitchens slipped in carrying steaming dishes that scented the air with meaty aromas. They placed the covered dishes on the wooden buffet against the room's end wall, while menservants set up the sawhorses and a pine board. Her chamberlain moved the folding chairs from the fireplace to the table as the servers prepared the board with a white linen tablecloth, napkins, silver gilt plate and Venetian glasses from the buffet. Within moments, they transformed the space into a charming dining chamber.

Marguerite and Louise greeted François with hugs. Louise kept a grip on his hands. "I swear, son, that beak of a nose serves you as well as their muzzles serve your bloodhounds. You have arrived at the perfect hour." She marveled, as ever, at his remarkable luck. When he was still in her belly, the holy hermit, Francis de Paule, promised her that her son would become King of France one day. At the time it seemed impossible. Had not Queen Anne just borne a dauphin? Now Louise believed that the holy man — who had lived his entire life as a poor hermit no matter what three successive kings of France had offered him — was a saint. Had not Queen Anne lost every one of her sons while Louise's César thrived?

It was like old times having both her children with her. François and Marguerite sparkled brighter than the crystal and their conversation was spicier than the dishes: cygnet roasted with savory herbs; onions and Jerusalem artichokes; pigeons stuffed with larks in sweet current sauce; and plaice and lamprey with mustard greens and pepper sauce. After their second course of sweet biscuits, candied fruits, blancmange, salad and brandy wine, they moved their chairs back before the fire.

She did not want to change the mood, but their debts hung over her like the sword of Damocles. The constant struggle to stave off parsimonious King Louis's demand to take control of her finances drained her. It had been going on since her feckless husband had died, leaving Louis as guardian of her children. Any solution was better than to ask him for money. But they needed an extraordinary infusion of funds, and soon.

"Children, there is nothing I am more reluctant to discuss than the state of our finances, but I can avoid it no longer. My chancellor has brought the accounts for this quarter. François, we are drowning in debt." She let her words settle.

They stared at the birch logs crackling in the fireplace. Strips of white bark curled like promissory notes before flaring red and turning to ash. Flames licked the three logs that formed the tent-shaped fire. It burned blue at the base and leaped in orange and yellow tongues. Occasionally, smoke puffed into the room, bathing them in an acrid cloud. Louise coughed, disrupting the ghosts of everlasting debt that harried her. "What would you have me do, my César?"

François, sleek in a new velvet doublet and form-fitting silken hose, pushed himself up and stalked the room like a caged panther. He was silent, but Louise had learned patience. Finally he said, "What is the problem, Maman?"

"Do you want to see the accounts? Shall I call M. de Saint Gelais?"

François grimaced. "No. No. But... perhaps I could approach Seigneur de Ganay for an increase in my allowance."

"You could." They both knew that the last time he'd asked, he had received the Duchy of Valois. And a warning: this was the last grant. From François's tone, Louise knew he did not expect to succeed. "How do you think he will answer?"

François banged his fist on her wooden prie-dieu[2]. "S'Bones!" It was so unexpected Marguerite and she both flinched. Louise heard an edge of panic in his voice. "What would you have me do?"

"It is time to press Princess Claude to settle the date for your marriage. Tell him, Marguerite."

His sister tucked her arm into the crook of her brother's and matched her footsteps to his. "Like you, I have been spending time in Princess Claude's court these days. She has grown into a delightful girl, brother, who listens well and answers intelligently. She is witty but never cruel, plays the lute well and discusses the latest subjects without putting herself forward. Her presence is calming, and she has good judgment. Yet she can be merry. The qualities of a good queen." As she broke the confidence she had pried from the princess's naïve heart, Marguerite dropped her eyes. "When I tell her stories of your childhood, she listens as if I am talking about Sir Lancelot and she imagines herself as Guinevere. You are fortunate, brother. Like all the damsels at court, she is enamored of you."

He sighed. "I met Princess Claude out riding today. She may be good-natured, but you cannot deny she is as plain as a post. And she limps, like her mother. Perhaps like her, too, she cannot bear living children. I have not been sorry that the queen keeps us from marrying — even if it is because she detests our family." He looked down at his sister. "You know why I have been present so much at her court these days, and where my heart has been leading me."

Louise stepped in. "Son, it is not a question of hearts. Royal persons do not marry for preference. Be grateful she is French, rich, of excellent temperament and wishes to please you." As he continued to pout, her voice sharpened, "Enough of this nonsense, François. You have already made public vows before the court and the Estates General[3]."

His face paled at the irritation in her voice. She straightened the lace edge of the chemise under his doublet and patted the row of golden buttons on his chest, as if gentling a nervous horse. Sweetening her voice, she said. "I will speak to King Louis. You will persuade the princess to obtain her mother's consent. The queen is likely to die within days. Yet we need you to marry Princess Claude by Easter."

He said nothing but looked sulky. He was skittish these days. Would he obey?

AFTER MICHELLE OVERSAW Princess Renée's bedtime rituals, she hurried to Queen Anne's suite. Though the atmosphere was subdued, several of the queen's ladies-in-waiting played cards and gossiped in her outer chamber. They pressed the baronne to join them, but Michelle refused, careful not to give offense.

"The queen asked me to make her a tisane this evening. If she does not require me for long, I will join you." She waited until they began their next hand before slipping away.

When Michelle entered the queen's private rooms Queen Anne had already retired, although her bed curtains remained open. She leaned propped up against her pillows.

"My back aches as if someone was stabbing it with daggers. I cannot possibly sleep," Queen Anne turned her head towards Michelle. Her troubled face was pale as milk.

Michelle ordered servants to set up screens around the bed and to bring braziers and candelabra to trap the warmth inside.

"I shall prepare you a willow bark tisane to ease your pain."

The queen shook her head.

Michelle examined her expression. "Is something bothering you, Mme. la Reine?"

"Bring a stool and sit by my bed."

Michelle complied. They sat in silence for several minutes before the queen spoke. "My daughter, Claude, came to talk to me after Vespers[4]."

Michelle had not seen the princess since they returned from their ride that afternoon. Princess Claude had her own small court in one wing of the Château with her gouvernante, demoiselles-in-waiting, and household. Mme. Jeanne, Countess Louise's married stepdaughter, had been Claude's gouvernante since her birth. The appointment had surprised Michelle since the queen and the countess detested each other. But Princess Claude had been born at Countess Louise's domain of Romorantin because of plague at Blois. King Louis had been away fighting in Milan and appointed Countess Louise's stepdaughter when he returned. The wily countess knew how to coax him.

Queen Anne twisted the rings on her fingers one after another. "Claude pleaded with me to permit her to marry Duke François this spring. Before Easter."

Michelle sent a silent prayer for Claude heavenward. "What did you say?"

"I asked her why she wanted to marry him."

Finally. The marriage was so hateful to the queen that she had long since forgotten to consider her daughter's sentiments. At first, Michelle had understood. Princess Claude was only six when the king and his advisors confronted the queen. But at fifteen, the princess was past the age that many princesses married. "Did she have a good reason?"

Queen Anne contemplated her embroidered emblem on the canopy. Michelle followed her gaze. The divided shield combined the ermine tails of Brittany on one half with the golden fleur-de-lys[5] of France on the other. Above it sat a royal crown. The thick, golden cord of the Cordelières, the women's order founded by the queen, wrapped around the crest. Michelle understood. The emblem symbolized the joining of Brittany to France, the union that tormented Queen Anne.

Queen Anne closed her eyes. "Claude said she did not want to go to a foreign country where she would be lonely and ill-treated. In truth, she said much more." Michelle saw tears brimming under her eyelids. "She said, 'Maman, I have seen foreign brides come to our court. Most are scorned and isolated; mocked for their odd ways. I am fat, and plain, and have a limp. If I marry outside of France where I am unknown and do not speak the language, I will also be treated unkindly for I am not charming, and I do not learn languages quickly. Even if I am queen and bring my great dowry. Here, Duke François will treat me with respect. So will the court and the people. I will live where I am loved, and I will be content.'"

Queen Anne's lips quivered. "Claude knows what is required and understands that happiness is not the lot of royal women. I doubt she will be happy with Duke François, but she chooses him for sensible reasons." Pulling a handkerchief from her sleeve, she blew her nose. "When I left Brittany at fourteen to marry the stranger who had conquered my duchy, I prayed daily that none of my children would have to suffer such a fate. I hoped—"

"Shush, shush, shush," Michelle murmured, capturing the queen's fluttering hand. "Enough talk." She stood. After bathing the queen's reddened eyes with cool lavender water, Michelle persuaded her to swallow some willow-bark tea, and rest against the sturdy pillows. But the queen pushed away the jellied broth Michelle offered next.

When Queen Anne spoke again, she had calmed. "When Louis and I married, I prayed we would have many sons so that when we chose husbands for Claude and Renée, we could consider their wishes as much as their duty. The Lord has not granted my prayers. But I will no longer oppose this marriage. I gave Claude my blessing."

Michelle said a quick, silent prayer of gratitude. Conflict within the royal family unsettled her — and everyone at court. She was about to say so when the queen spoke again.

"But I cannot permit Brittany to become part of France, Mme. Michelle. I cannot. Claude has an enormous dowry already with Milan from Louis and with my French counties and baronies. I must bequeath Brittany to Renée. Although if Louis discovers my plan, he will do all he can to prevent me."

Michelle crossed herself, picturing the troubles the queen was stirring up. Nine years before, Anne had quarreled furiously with Louis when he betrothed Claude to François without her consent. This row would be equally fierce and — as with the previous fight — Michelle was sure Queen Anne would lose. No matter what Queen Anne believed, most Bretons would not celebrate. The people of the country and cities of Brittany had rejoiced at the betrothal of Princess Claude and Duke François. They saw the marriage as a guarantee of the end to the wars that had destroyed families, reduced their homes to burned-out shells, and their fields to wasteland. Her elder brother, Jean, crippled during the French-Breton wars, had sent a jewel-encrusted crucifix to Queen Anne to celebrate the betrothal. Michelle fingered the beads of her rosary, praying her stubborn friend would reconsider before the least whisper of this plan escaped.

"Calm yourself, Michelle." Queen Anne ordered. "I see I trouble you. But you must promise to keep my secret."

Could Michelle keep such a secret from the king? Her late husband and his family owed him everything. She was part of that family, as were her three growing children who lived with them. And yet she owed as much to the queen.

Queen Anne's voice was urgent. "I need your help."

Her loyalty won. "I promise."

The queen said. "I do not understand. You are Bretonne. When Duke François marries Claude, those avaricious d'Angoulême will destroy everything Breton in their haste to gouge every last *denier*[6] they can from *my* duchy." She sounded forlorn. "Do not you care about what will happen to our duchy?"

"May I speak plainly, Mme. la Reine? Though my words may displease you."

The queen flushed. "You are the only person in this court whom I trust. I cannot promise to be pleased, but I assure you I value your candor."

Michelle leaned close to Queen Anne. "Brittany must not suffer another war. If you succeed, it will lead to war with France. And though I was very young, I can never forget. We sent twenty men from the estate to the battle of St-Aubin-du-Cormier. Only five returned. My older brother was bedridden for over a year afterwards. Maman, my sister-in-law, and I nursed his wounds. The worst was his pus-filled stump. It would not heal." Tears stained Michelle's cheeks.

"I never forget either," Queen Anne whispered, "But I *must* make one last attempt. I must speak to Seigneur Robert de Fleuranges. Send to tell him I wish to see him tomorrow. You know it is urgent."

5 JANUARY 1514

CHÂTEAU DE BLOIS

aronne Michelle de Soubise

MICHELLE HID her surprise when Seigneur Robert de Fleuranges limped through the door; he had been whole of body when last they met. At twenty-three, only three years older than Duke François, he was one of the few favorites of both the king and the duke. He had already made himself a name for his reckless courage. He held a silver lion's-head cane that he twirled in his right hand with a courtly flourish, wielding it now with a sword master's skill as he swept a bow so low his nose almost met his knee.

A smile curved Michelle's lips. "Always the charmer, Seigneur. I am delighted to see you." The strategic location of his hereditary lands — straddling France and Flanders — made him a perfect

envoy from Queen Anne to Regent Marguerite of the Netherlands. Yet when he learned of the service the queen wanted
from him, Michelle doubted he would feel pleased.

They crossed the marble floor of the queen's private chamber to
the enclosed area where she sat, their footsteps muffled by the
viola music drifting through the room.

Queen Anne, wrapped in a loose robe over her night rail[1], sat
near the blazing fireplace, the back of her armchair stuffed with
cushions. An ermine robe covered her lap and her feet rested on
a large footstool. Once again, she had insisted on rising even
though it had drained her. Today her eyes looked bruised,
mauve pouches under them.

Michelle noticed Seigneur Robert shrink, as if shaken by her
aged appearance, but he recovered before he reached her side.
His compliments as he bowed and kissed her hand were as
extravagant as ever.

Queen Anne began with gossip. "I heard that the upstart Duke
Charles Brandon has set his sights on Archduchess Marguerite.
And she reciprocates. What a scandal. He is but a jumped-up
bourgeois that King Henry of England has raised to the
dukedom of Suffolk."

Seigneur Robert reddened. "No truth to it at all. Mme. la
Regente was furious about his advances. She would never
consider such a misalliance."

"Well, that is a great relief. A closer alliance between England
and the Imperial Flemish provinces would displease us. What
about the young Duke of Burgundy's betrothal to King Henry's
sister? Might Mme. la Regente be open to considering other
possibilities?"

Seigneur Robert raised his eyebrows. "Their betrothal continues with no change. Princess Mary is reputed lovely as a rose — and excellently dowered. Why do you ask?"

"How well dowered?"

"To the tune of 200,000 livres. Is there a reason you ask?"

The queen ignored his question. "Why would his family press for a dowry in coin, rather than lands? Is it true the New World is not as profitable as is claimed? Does my husband know this?"

"Naturally, Your Majesty."

"Seigneur Robert, I have an urgent and confidential letter that must be delivered to the regent. Would you undertake this confidential task for me?"

Michelle held her breath, but Fleuranges hesitated only momentarily. "Majesty, I am yours to command. Naturally, I have a few matters I must address with His Majesty before I am able to depart. May I know the service I am to undertake?"

Queen Anne did not answer at once. She appeared to be considering.

"In the eventuality that Mme. Marguerite asks for clarification or wishes to negotiate a point. I presume you would wish me to settle minor points without having to refer all details back to you." Seigneur Robert's suggestion slid as smoothly as butter into the silence.

Could Queen Anne accept she would not have the luxury of time to negotiate? Michelle wondered.

At last she nodded. "As you say. I propose a betrothal between Princess Renée and Duke Charles, with Brittany as the princess's dowry."

Seigneur Robert seemed staggered, but quickly recovered his poise. He said, "Your offer may persuade both Mme. Marguerite and the Duke's grandfather. Both Austria and Aragon have wished for… this… alliance for years."

His *sangfroid* impressed Michelle. She thought the queen's pasty smile was genuine for she said, "I perceive you are the perfect courtier for my task. Naturally, this is a confidence between us until I receive Mme. la Regente's reply. The king must not know."

"Naturally." Seigneur Robert bowed acquiescence.

Michelle was uncertain what she had expected. Unlike her, he owed his loyalty solely to King Louis. Why had he not resisted more?

"When will you depart?" Queen Anne shifted in her chair. Her suffering was evident to Michelle. It was time to end this audience.

He counted on his fingers. "Today is the fifth. I require four days. With your permission, by first light, January tenth, I shall leave."

"We will have the documents you need and will see you then to discuss the final arrangements."

As Michelle accompanied him to the chamber door, she wondered how such a dangerous secret could be kept at this leaky, gossipy court.

AFTER THE AFTERNOON MEAL, the privileged few were invited to join the royals in the adjoining private salon for the second cover. Michelle, Princess Renée, Princess Claude and Madame

Jeanne entered first and moved away from the doorway. Inside, servers offered guests trays filled with jellies, creams, shelled nuts, exotic fruits and crisp biscuits. The rich sweets were presented on the new porcelain trenchers recently introduced from Italy. Michelle eyed the new dishes doubtfully. They looked beautiful, but too delicate for Renée to manage.

The rush that poured in like a cavalry charge delayed Countess Louise and Duchess Marguerite. Soon Michelle noticed Duchess Marguerite signal her mother with a slight jerk of her head. Within moments, Countess Louise and the duchess herded Princess Claude into a quiet corner as successfully as a sheepdog with an errant lamb. Taking Princess Renée by the hand, Michelle inserted herself into their circle. As they arrived, Duchess Marguerite was saying, "Mme. Jeanne mentions you visited your Maman, Princess Claude? How is our dear queen?" Marguerite slid her arm around the princess's shoulder, caressing the shorter, younger girl. Claude beamed up at her as if addressed by a fairy queen.

Nonetheless, Princess Claude's training stood her in good stead, for she replied with dignity. "She is much as she has been." As Marguerite pressed her for more, she could not hide her happiness. "Maman agrees that Duke François and I shall marry before Easter—." Pausing, she added with a rush, "and she will speak to Papa today. Please say nothing until I say you may." She flushed with guilt, for she had a tender conscience.

They crowded her like a pack of scavenging dogs. The countess squeezed Claude's hands. "We are delighted." Her voice oozed like liquid honey. "Look, here comes your betrothed now." She signaled to him.

Michelle watched François swagger towards them through the crowd of courtiers, arm-in-arm with Seigneur de Fleuranges. Duke François's dark locks were covered with an ostrich-feathered hat, and she would hazard he rouged his rosebud lips. To Michelle he looked an utter popinjay in his gold brocade doublet with matching breeches, out of which thrust a codpiece[2] so large it made her want to laugh. Princess Claude's eyes, however, glowed as she gazed at him. Poor girl, she was entranced. Seigneur Robert could not compete with the showy duke, despite his extravagant outfit and wondrous silver cane.

Duchess Marguerite smiled. "We are honored by not one peacock, but two."

Seigneur Robert flicked his lion's headed cane, offered her a dapper bow, and raised her hand to his lips. "Gracious Duchess, what a pleasure! Your voice enchants the ear and your presence outshines all the other Muses."

The duchess's laughter tinkled like water in a fountain. "Flatterer. Enough. Congratulate your friend," she said.

"Of course. Why?"

"The queen has approved his marriage to Princess Claude. You see before you the next Duke de Bretagne."

Poor Claude. Betrayed so quickly by her idol.

"But I tho—" He concealed his confusion as he swiveled to bow to Princess Claude, but not quickly enough to escape the falcon eyes of Countess Louise.

"We startle you, Seigneur Robert. Why should you be?" Countess Louise's question cut through the air, sharp as a stiletto.

"You mistake me. I am simply surprised to be included in the family secret."

"Why should you think it a secret?"

"Because I had not already heard it, Madame." He turned to François, who was still dazed. "Nor had your son. Nor did Mme. la Reine mention it when I visited her earlier."

Countess Louise looked as startled as François. It was he who said, "Why did *she* want to see you?"

De Fleuranges recovered. "Milord, I always greet my king's beloved wife when I come to court." His eyes sought Michelle's. As she turned away, she felt Countess Louise's cold, gray eyes following her, her nose twitching like a bloodhound hard upon a scent. What did the countess suspect?

6 JANUARY 1514

CHÂTEAU DE BLOIS

aronne Michelle de Soubise

As Michelle watched the king's doctor examine the unconscious queen, she guessed Dr. Loysel also recognized the queen was dying from his request to meet her in the queen's library. She doubted he would want the responsibility of treating her. Ministering to a dying queen could be dangerous. Dr. Loysel — Principal Infirmarian to the King, robed in his gown as Senior Professor at the Sorbonne — his pale blue eyes veined with red and his thin hair slicked to his skull, spoke to her as if he were the Grand Master of a great order speaking to an uninitiated adolescent. "Though her symptoms are contradictory, I diagnose an overabundance of black bile caused by a malfunction of the excretory systems. An overabundance. Yes. She winces when touched between the ribs and hip, an indication of blockage in the renes. A sure indication. Yes. Her cutis is yellowing, indicating that her *urinea* is not draining as it should. The *urinea* is not draining. Not as it should. No. Therefore, my dear young lady, I grieve, yes, grieve, I must conclude, yes I infer she is beyond earthly help, yes, that her best hope lies in the hands of our Savior. At most, I recommend purging and bloodletting. You would be capable of carrying out that procedure, hmm, carrying that out?"

Michelle forced herself to adopt a subservient tone, keeping her eyes lowered. "As you say, Dr. Loysel."

The good doctor rose. "Then we are agreed. You shall manage here, Mme... uh... Madame. I must hasten to the king. His Majesty will be inconsolable when the queen leaves this earth. When she ascends, yes. It causes me much worry, yes, great anxiety, for he is by no means a healthy man. No, by no means. I must prepare for his needs. Must prepare, yes." He tapped his heels together and bowed in Michelle's general direction. "Thank you, yes, thank you for your—" And he was gone.

Michelle watched him go, her mouth a determined line. It was one thing to fear that the queen was dying; it was another to hear a professor from the Sorbonne agree. Yet what cruelty to suggest purging or bloodletting when such treatments could not possibly cure her. She needed time to make peace with her end, prepare her last testament and say her last goodbyes. And remedies that reduced her pain.

It was time to insist to the queen that she make her final preparations. Michelle fought back tears as she kneeled by her friend's bedside and said, "Dear Madame, you can wait no longer to put your affairs in order. It will not be long before you pass from this world into a better one."

The queen lay as still as a wax effigy. When she spoke, her voice was no louder than a breath on the wind. "So... it is come." Her hands clung to her mother's rosary with its tiny crystal reliquary that contained a precious thorn from Christ's crown. "Thank you, dear friend. I am so tired, Michelle... and I long for the pain to end. Yet I cannot rest."

She turned her head toward Michelle, eyes pleading. "Louis is not well. I pray for him, for his health... Still, you have cared for our daughter, Renée, from the moment of her birth... You are her second mother. Will you promise.... Will you stay with Renée? Until she grows to womanhood?"

"I swear it." Michelle kissed her fingers and reached out to touch the queen's face. Losing the queen was going to be a hard, a terrible loss. She had been pushing away the thought of parting from Princess Renée too, each time it forced itself into her mind. Renée was closer to her than her own children.

Tears slid down Queen Anne's face. "I did not fear you would refuse. Yet I am so grateful."

"It would break my heart to leave her, Mme. la Reine." Michelle pressed a fist against her breast. "But will the king agree?"

"I shall inform Louis it is my wish. Once I am with God, I cannot be certain he will do as I desire, but he loves me. I will have him swear on my rosary." Her voice grew feebler.

"Thank you, dear Madame. I shall educate her as you would wish."

Pain flitted across the queen's face.

"You need something for the pain. It is time to—"

"I have one more subject we must discuss... alone."

"Only if you drink this. And we must not talk long." Michelle added a few drops of pain mixture to watered wine. Then she raised Queen Anne until she could drink from the goblet. The queen took several sips.

"Finish it, Your Grace," Michelle insisted.

Queen Anne grimaced, but she swallowed several times. "Done."

Michelle lay her back against the pillows. Her lips were bluish. "I worry about my girls. About Louis. He is not well." She paused to recover her breath. "If he dies while the girls are underage... Renée is still so young... who will protect their inheritance? And he is so determined to make Brittany French that I cannot trust even *him* with Brittany." The last came out almost as a wail.

She stopped, panting. "Although I leave a great estate, I cannot name those I trust as guardians, for it would lead to endless litigation — perhaps even war." When Michelle protested, the queen frowned. "We both know it is true. When Louis was Duke d'Orléans, he went to war against his sister-in-law for the regency of her brother."

Michelle nodded reluctantly. It was true.

"So, I must appoint the person whose claim is least likely to be disputed."

The baronne nodded again.

"Therefore, I shall name Countess Louise d'Angoulême as their guardian."

Michelle reeled. The countess and Queen Anne loathed each other. Until today, Queen Anne had used every twist and turn to avoid leaving even the duchy of Brittany within her grasp. And now she was proposing to leave the entire inheritance of both her daughters under her guardianship. The queen and she had despised Countess Louise as a manipulator who charmed men — and King Louis in particular — into giving her whatever she wanted. After her husband died, she had hoodwinked King Louis into believing she would collapse if he separated her from her only son. She had even persuaded the parsimonious king to settle her and her household at Amboise at his expense.

She knew the queen had seen her recoil, but Queen Anne continued to stare at the devices on the canopy over her head. "Yes, she has always been my enemy. But Mme. Louise will be Claude's mother-in-law. Duke François is her favorite child and he will be king when Louis dies." Her whispery voice hardened. "Therefore, the countess should have no incentive to steal from Claude's estate... since it would be stealing from her own son and grandchildren. By making this disposition, my fortune should remain intact for my descendants, since they will also be hers. And as Duchess de Bretagne in her own right, Claude can protect her inheritance once she marries. I shall make it her duty to guard her sister's inheritance, even though I cannot name her guardian since she is not yet of age. Claude and Louis must promise a half-share of my estates for Renée's dowry. I will make Louis swear to guarantee Renée's rights...." She gave a long sigh. When she spoke again, she sounded exhausted. "Do I reason well, Michelle? It is the best I can do...." Her voice drifted away and Michelle could hear a rattle in the queen's chest.

Michelle's eyes filled with tears. She did not argue, although she thought there could be no worse choice than Mme. Louise who loathed Michelle almost as much as Queen Anne. Would she keep Michelle as the princess's gouvernante? She could not imagine how she and Mme. Louise would ever agree on Mme. Renée's upbringing.

Queen Anne's voice was hardly more than a whisper. "Send for Mme. Claude. I must speak to her. Then the king.

She was failing rapidly. Michelle crossed herself. "Mme. la Reine, now that the Lord has made His will known to you, you must rest! You promised you would, rather than wasting what little strength you have." As her fears increased, Michelle's voice sharpened.

The queen's lips were gray. "I will. Just fetch them: Claude. Louis. The notary. Countess Louise. I promise I will rest after they leave." Her whispery voice dwindled, and she closed her eyes.

PRINCESS CLAUDE ARRIVED after Matins[1] determined to keep a vigil while her mother slept. She resisted all Mme. Michelle's efforts to dissuade her from her night watch. After the third attempt, the baronne gave up. "If you stay, shall I retire? I have not slept in a bed for three nights. Send a page if there is a change, or if you wish me for any cause." Her shoulders sagged from exhaustion.

Claude kneeled on the prie-dieu near her mother's bed. Alone in the enclosed area surrounding her Maman, lit only by the braziers heating it, she prayed desperately for her mother's recovery. The sacred music flowing from her mother's chapel choir, chanting at the far end of the queen's dim, chilly bed chamber, added to her grief.

After a time, her father entered. He hugged her when she rose and kissed her forehead. He wiped at the tears that rolled down his cheeks. "I see you, too, wish to be close to her," he said. "I will not interrupt your prayers.

35

He went to the far side of the bed. She could hear him pull an armchair forward. After she threw some sandalwood incense onto the braziers she returned to her prayers. Quiet settled back into the room. The choir continued its dirge. The brazier crackled from time to time, sending out whiffs of acrid smoke, scented now with aromatic spice. Occasionally Claude's mother shifted and moaned on her high bed.

Claude repeated her rosary endlessly. Out of the darkness, she heard her mother's voice. "Dear husband. It warms my heart to find you beside me." Sounds of kissing followed. Claude thought it was her father who wept. Her mother spoke again. Claude had to strain to hear. "I have news to please you, husband. I promised our daughter, Claude, to support her marriage to Duke François. I thought to tell you sooner, but..."

"Was she pleased?" Papa's voice sounded husky. "What changed your decision, dearest love?"

Had he forgotten she was here? Claude wondered.

Then she heard her mother sigh. "Claude spoke of the... discomfort she would feel... were she to leave France. She feared being treated... unkindly since she could not learn another language quickly." The queen's voice weakened. "She feared being mocked because she's crippled and... plain."

Listening to her mother, Claude cringed. She sounded like a sniveling child, unable to face the least hardship. What were a few harsh words compared to all the grief her mother had borne? Both her parents had died before she was twelve. Her younger sister had died a year later. Her allies had abandoned her; she had lost a bitter war and had been forced to marry the victor. Every son she bore died a few days or months after birth. And yet Maman soldiered on, never giving up her fight to maintain Brittany's independence. How would she ever find the courage to save Brittany's independence if she did not even have the mettle to live anywhere but France?

The silence grew. Claude heard her father's loud sniffles as he forced himself to stop weeping. Claude was choking on her own swallowed sobs, burying her face in the skirt of her harsh brocade gown and almost missed his next words.

"Thank you, *ma Bretonne*, for your approval. It is a gift." The thickness in his voice blurred his words. "I love you."

"Yes, Louis, I know..." Maman coughed and coughed and coughed.

Give her some watered wine, Papa. It is on the table beside you, Claude shouted at him in her head. She did not dare rise now and show herself an eavesdropper.

When her mother finally caught her breath, her voice rasped. "When we married, I had been living in France for six years and was accustomed to the country. Besides, I was never gentle, like Claude.... I fear she will not make a good duchess for Brittany."

Claude froze. She sank to the floor, as winded as if her mother had just punched her in the stomach. It was one thing to fear that her mother did not trust her with Brittany; it was another to hear it from her lips. Curling into a ball, she wrapped her arms around herself, unable to pay attention to the voices that rumbled on. Then she heard her name.

"Claude will not mind. Nor oppose me." Her mother's voice trailed off. The bed creaked as she moved.

"Maybe she would not. But I would, and so would Duke François. And Mme. Louise. Brittany must remain part of Claude's dowry. You cannot change that now."

Her mother fell into another coughing fit. Papa shushed and murmured until she had calmed. He said, "Let us not quarrel, my love. We must not waste our precious time together."

"Promise me! Mme. Michelle will continue as Renée's gouvernante... Promise that Renée will receive her portion from my estate."

Her father's voice sounded as soothing as syrup. "Of course, my love. It shall all be as you desire. No more, my love. Rest."

"Just one more thing." Her mother's voice was scarcely more than a hoarse whisper. "Promise me you will marry again.... Quickly. You must have a son."

The noise of a chair scraping on the floor warned Claude to stay as still as a hunted rabbit. Then her father, sounding — what — angry? No, distraught. "You are making it too hard, my love. I cannot think of such a thing, Do not push me beyond endurance. Please." His voice broke.

But Maman was relentless as only she could be. "Yes, Louis. You must marry and have a son for France. Promise me, Louis." Claude heard her sob but did not believe her tears. "I failed you. But you must not fail."

Claude clamped her hands over her mouth. Maman would do anything, anything, to deny François the throne... and to keep Brittany independent. It was not love for Louis and his lineage. Only Brittany's independence. She felt hot with rage, and still she did not dare reveal her presence.

After Vespers, Michelle walked from the chapel to the queen's chambers. Wood smoke from the kitchens scented the crisp evening air. As darkness fell, the faint glow on the cloudless western horizon signaled the close of what had been an unusual, sunny day.

King Louis hunched beside the sleeping queen his chin prickly with gray stubble. He did not move, even when Michelle touched the queen's chilly forehead and lifted her limp arm to feel for the beat of her life force. It was weak and irregular. For several minutes she observed the faint rise and fall of her breath and the bluish pallor of her skin.

Sinking into a curtsey, Michelle waited for the king to acknowledge her. He rubbed his reddened eyes. "Yes, Baronne?"

"Sire, it is time to call the queen's confessor. She must make her last confession."

She did not think he heard, or perhaps he did not wish to believe her. "Your Grace, it is time. Shall you send for Queen Anne's confessor, or shall I?" When he still stared at her blankly, she reached out to shake his arm. "The queen's confessor, Majesty?"

At her touch he roused, and tears spilled from his red-rimmed eyes. He pushed himself up, using the arms of the chair like an old man, and gazed down on his wife's still face. He looked every one of his fifty-one hard years.

Clamping his rosary in one hand, he kissed Queen Anne's withered cheek. His love for his wife was palpable. "Send for me once her confessor has left. You know how precious she is to me." He still stared at the immobile body on the bed. "Lord, forgive me, but why? Why are you taking her from me?" His voice breaking, he shuffled away. At the screens he turned and said, "I will send for her confessor."

Her confessor slid into the queen's room carrying the sacramental vessels. Silent on slippered feet, he glided to the foot of her bed and kneeled. Although he was a man of God, Michelle became rigid when she saw him. He was a harbinger, his rites the pathway to lead her mistress from them. Although she should be grateful that her lady would no longer suffer, that she would join those who loved her, and rise to glory, Michelle did not want to lose her. How would they go on without her?

CHÂTEAU DE BLOIS

rincess Claude de Valois

IN THE DARKEST, coldest hours of the early morning just before Lauds[1], when owls hoot, witches ride and blood runs thinnest, Queen Anne breathed her last. As the chapel bells tolled the queen's passing — thirty-seven solemn peals, one for each year of her life — King Louis, Princess Claude and Princess Renée led the procession to St. Calais Chapel. There, they heard the first mass for the dead sung by the powerful voices of both the king's and the queen's choirs.

Claude felt her mother's spirit with them for the duration of the mass as the chaplains called upon the Saints, the Holy Spirit, and their Savior, to receive her soul. By the time the choir sang the closing prayers and the priests had given them leave to depart, they were all encased in their personal shells of sorrow.

"Tomorrow would have been our fifteenth wedding anniversary. Why, Lord?" King Louis's voice was raw and tears streaked his cheeks. He lurched down the aisle like a mechanical figure. A gentleman of his bedchamber walked on either side, holding an arm to steady his wavering path.

Her swollen face obscured by her black veil, Princess Claude, also unsteady on her feet, leaned upon Mme. Jeanne. After her mother had breathed her last, when Papa had finally risen to his feet, he turned to her and said, "We will conduct her mourning in black as is the Breton custom. She would want that. Tell her Master Chamberlain I have ordered it."

Claude watched her young sister, four-year-old Renée, walk beside Baronne Michelle. Renée had been subdued during their vigil, sleeping much of the time and saying her rosary, guided by Mme. Michelle. When she became restless, the baronne had removed her from the room, but they returned quickly. She was with them at the end. When would her little sister understand that Maman was gone forever? When would she?

MICHELLE WAS desperate for some time alone. She decided to walk in the back gardens. In this cold, with the night already fallen and the wintery gardens leafless at this time of year, she thought it unlikely she would meet others. She bundled her woolen cape over her gown, closed it with a broach, and then pulled her hood over her headdress, tightening it around her face until the fur tickled.

Her leather-soled shoes crunched on the curving gravel pathways. The low bushes of the new Italian gardens, laid out in the geometric patterns so favored by the queen, were blanketed in the coarse cloth that would soon encase her departed friend. It would protect *them* from death. Denuded of color in the pale starlight, the bushes matched her somber mood, their dark sinuous forms slinking like the serpent in the Garden of Eden. Her lantern cast a lean flickering shadow before her. As she trudged through the dark landscape, wet snow deadened the small sounds until all she could hear was the sloppy splash of her feet on the winding path.

Tears rolled down her cheeks. At the far end of the gardens she came to an iron bench and sank upon it, sobbing until her first wave of grief passed. It was a relief to have the privacy of this deserted garden in which to release her sorrow.

She was so absorbed in her own mourning that she did not hear the footsteps. When she felt the arm wrapping around her shoulders, she shrank back and screamed.

The person who held her flinched, but murmured, "Shush, shush, shush, it is only me, Claude."

Michelle snorted, shocked into an involuntary chuckle, and gulped back her tears. "M-Mme. Claude? W-w-what are you doing here?"

"I came out to be alone, but heard weeping. It sounded so sad I felt a need to offer consolation." Princess Claude pitched her voice low so it would not carry in the crisp night air should others be listening. "Would you wish to share your sorrow with me?" she added, offering her a handkerchief.

Michelle took the offered cloth and blew her nose. As she composed herself, she became aware that the girl's body was quivering. "We are both grieving the same loss, are we not Mme. Claude?" she said, taking the princess's closer hand in hers.

"I did not think Maman would actually... I cannot believe it yet." The last word was swallowed in tears as the princess broke down. In tears herself, Michelle put her arms around the weeping girl, and they rocked together, their tears mingling. They stayed that way for some time.

Michelle calmed first. Finally, the princess's tears became snuffles and hiccups. Fumbling in the pocket of her cape, Michelle pulled out a wrinkled cloth and wiped the girl's face. With a tearful chuckle, she said, "Now it's my turn to offer you a cloth to mop your face. But it is not as nice as the one you gave me."

Mme. Claude straightened and blew her nose, and then said, "You are a great comfort, Mme. Michelle."

"Do you want to talk about it, Princess? Is it losing your Maman whom we both love that you grieve? Or is there more?"

In the flickering light of her lantern Michelle saw the girl's chin wobble, but she did not break down into tears again. "When I think about Maman, I feel a huge pain in my heart. It hurts so much—" she stopped and swallowed noisily, "that she died disappointed in me." Her voice quivered, so that it was hard to distinguish her words. "It hurts that she disliked Duke François so much even though she agreed to our marriage." She blew her nose again. Michelle thought she had finished, but then she spoke, her voice hardly above a whisper. "But that she did not trust me to take care of Brittany is the hardest thing." She dissolved into the tears she could no longer repress.

Michelle rocked her as she continued to sob. Even though her friend had just died, Michelle felt herself flush with anger, for she knew Claude was correct. Why did Anne cause her daughter so much pain? Mme. Claude was a gentle girl. "Why do you think that?" Her voice was soft. She felt the girl shake her head.

"I heard her."

"Wha— How... how painful." Stunned for an instant, rage swamped Michelle next. She took a deep breath and struggled to regain her control in order to understand why Anne had wounded her daughter so... so cruelly. "What exactly did you hear her say?"

"I wish to dower Renée with Brittany." But before that, I could tell from the way she looked away from me when she talked about needing to be strong-minded to be the duchess."

It could not be worse. "Who was she speaking to?" She was not at all sure the princess would answer, but thought she would feel better releasing the poison in the words from her body.

"Papa." After a beat, she continued. "He said that as King of France he could never allow Brittany to pass to France's enemies and that Brittany would be safer and richer with France, anyway."

She stopped crying and leaned against the baronne's shoulder. They sat quietly, each tangled in her own thoughts. Michelle seethed. She wanted to shake the queen for her obstinate conviction that hers was the only solution for Brittany. Finally, Mme. Claude said, "It hurts that not only am I plain and clumsy, but that my Maman who I love so much, d-d-did not believe me worthy of her trust."

Michelle's heart went out to her. She must change the direction of her thoughts. It was not good for her to wallow in self-pity, though her mother had been harsh. "Princess Claude, you are sweet, smart and gentle. Also, well-read, witty and one of the richest and best-dowered princesses in the world." She hesitated a moment, feeling disloyal to her departed friend. Hoping both Anne and Claude would forgive her, she stiffened her resolve. But Anne had been wrong, and her daughter needed Michelle's reassurance now. "Hard as it is for me to say, for she has just left us, I thought your Maman was wrong about Brittany. We argued about it many times. I am Bretonne too, and I agree with your Papa. You must make up your own mind, but I believe our home needs peace. You will bring us that, I pray. None of us has everything we want, nor did your Maman. Come, I am feeling chilled. Let us return inside and pray for her."

The princess gave her one last squeeze and straightened. "Mme. Michelle, you are the kindest person I know. Thank you so much."

"Dear, Princess, you flatter me. You are both kinder and gentler. And we shall keep each other's confidences, yes?"

TEN HOURS EARLIER, Countess Louise had bolted upright as the clamor of tolling bells burst into the pitch black of the curtained bed. For a moment she had wondered where she was. Then she felt the strong comforting arms of her dear Jean and heard his sleepy voice murmuring: "It must be the queen. She must have died."

For a moment, Louise worried. What if they were looking for her at the Château? Would there be gossip when she could not be found? No one knew that she and Jean de Saint Gelais were secret lovers, and she intended to keep it that way. She would invent an explanation as she returned, was all. Problem resolved, she lay down again, pulled the coverlet over her and curled up beside Jean's warm body. He folded her into his arms, snuffling her hair that fell in a long braid over her naked white shoulder. She gave a throaty murmur of pleasure but pushed him away before he could get too eager. She had more important things on her mind.

"By Our Lady! You must be right, *mon amour*. So, she's dead. Why else would the bells make such a clamor at this hour?" She stretched. "Her just reward for so many years of trying to keep my son from the throne. And now he is another step closer. Just as the holy hermit, Francis de Paule foretold. He said my César would become king." She never tired of repeating it. Just to make it more sure, she crossed herself. "It's so lovely and warm here, yet I must hurry back — and with no one the wiser." As she considered how best to manage it, she frowned and then rubbed the lines from her forehead.

Sliding her legs over the side of the bed, she complained, "Is not it just like her to die at such an inconvenient hour. I shall have to steal in by the postern gate and hope no one is roaming about down there."

"Not likely so early, in this cold, with all the commotion inside." Jean slipped an arm around her slim waist, trying to pull her back into his bed.

She slapped his wrist lightly. "No time for that, naughty man. I must return before I am missed."

She grabbed her chemise from the floor where he had tossed it the night before. "I probably will not be able to slip away for a sennight[2] or more, *mon amour*. There will be many ceremonies — and her testament to be read."

As she dressed — first stockings, next front-tied corset, then chemise—she smiled to herself. After dropping a sheer partlet over her head, she fitted it discretely over her shoulders and upper breasts, admiring their firm whiteness. Soon she could afford the kinds of fabric and jewels to display her body as it deserved. Just two days ago the queen had astonished her by asking her to be guardian of the two princesses and administrator of their vast estates and huge income should anything happen to the king. She shook her head in wonder once again, as she tied the overskirt at her waist, recalling the scene. Queen Anne had even begged Louise's forgiveness for past slights. But enough of that. She gave the sleeves a quick tug. Yes, they should hold to the bodice. She struggled into it and called Jean to get himself out of bed to pull the cords tight. She must get back to ensure no one tried to change those delightful testamentary arrangements.

"You watch, Jean," she said. "I shall be richer than Queen Anne one day. Soon. When my son is king, we will never again live in the penury we have had to suffer because of my husband's foolishness and *his* father's misfortunes."

After giving him a quick kiss, she tossed a drab olive cape over her clothes and pulled down the hood to cover her face. Before she tied a short, sharp poignard at her waist, she tested its blade, then disappeared down the narrow back steps. At the bottom, she waved briefly to her lover. Now she hurried along the dark alley with her lantern. The crisp air fairly tingled with adventure.

CHÂTEAU DE BLOIS

*B*aronne Michelle de Soubise

The morning after the death of the queen everything was in a muddle. Instead of breaking their fast in the queen's rooms as they usually did after returning from the mass at Nones[1], the queen's household took their morning meal with the rest of the court in the great dining hall. The stocky, silver-haired Principal Lady of Queen Anne's household invited Michelle to join their table. Normally composed, Michelle's hands trembled as she served herself from the platters offered to her by kneeling pages.

As Michelle was leaving the main dining hall, the Principal Lady, spots of color flaming in her cheeks, took her into an alcove. "It is only right, Baronne de Soubise, that you take charge of preparing the queen's chamber for mourning."

Since preparing the queen's chamber for the mournful elegance of her lying in state involved coordinating many sensitive and highly placed persons in each of the offices of the Queen's household, yet had to be accomplished with haste, it required great diplomacy. As the queen's principal secretary and *dame d'atour*, Michelle had expected to be asked, but she had not expected the Principal Lady's air of suppressed agitation.

Michelle said, "I am honored... but is there a problem?"

The Principal Lady sniffed. "Mme. the Countess d'Angoulême arrived this morning set to take the responsibility. When I demurred, she said that as first lady of the court after the royal princesses, it was her right. Such arrogance. I told her that since she was not a lady of the queen's household, I did not consider it appropriate to appoint her. She is not head of the queen's household yet."

"The queen is not yet cold, and the contending for status and power starts already. I am grateful you warned me." Michelle gave her grieving companion's hand a sympathetic squeeze.

As Michelle went to the queen's apartments to begin the arrangements, she pondered her next steps. Countess Louise had been so subtle in her attacks while Queen Anne lived, Michelle had not expected the countess to assert herself so soon. Would she limit herself to criticizing all Michelle's preparations? Set about turning the rest of the queen's former ladies against her now that the queen, her protectress, was gone? Or would she choose wilier methods to discredit her? It might be wiser to allow Countess Louise the honor of readying the queen's chamber for her lying in state, since she would be responsible for Princess Renée's household before too long.

Then, drawing upon her own Breton stubbornness, she stiffened her resolve. Her dear queen would want *her*, not Countess

Louise, to prepare her for her last public appearance. She would not permit herself to be intimidated into foregoing this last service for her friend.

LOUISE CROSSED herself as the mass for the dead concluded and then glided from the St. Calais chapel as the Vespers service continued. Always wearing deepest mourning, she had attended masses assiduously since the queen died.

The guard at the door of Princess Claude's suite was reluctant to disturb her. Only when the countess raised her voice to insist that Mme. de Longwy would certainly wish to see her did the door finally open. Her stepdaughter glowered, but reluctantly permitted her to enter. Stepchildren were always a problem, Louise reminded herself, though she prided herself on having married Mme. Jeanne well.

Her stepdaughter put a finger to her lips. She gestured to the sobbing princess who huddled on a cushion near the fireplace. "She's eaten almost nothing since her mother died," Jeanne breathed. "All she does is attend mass and curl up in a corner with her mother's rosary and weep."

Louise shook her head. "What have you given her to calm her?"

"She will take nothing."

"By Our Lady, Jeanne, what nonsense. She needs a calming tea. Send a maid to my chambers to fetch my box of special teas for calming the nerves. My maid will know which one." Without waiting for the maid to return, she walked to the fireplace and rattled the simmering kettle on the hob. "We will set her to rights in no time."

Kneeling beside the sobbing princess, she said, "Mme. Claude. You will injure yourself if you continue in this intemperate way. You are soaked from your tears and cramped from cowering on the cold floor. Take my hands and rise, lest you injure yourself."

As Louise expected, the princess obeyed her order although she had to insist. On the third repetition, she stood, reached down, took Claude's hands and tugged. Unable to resist the stronger will, the princess let Louise haul her to her feet.

By the time Mme. Claude's maids had changed her gown, added onyx jewelry and placed a black veil on her head, Louise had prepared her tisane.

"No, No," Claude pushed the cup away. "I cannot swallow anything."

"Just sniff it. It contains mint leaves and honey — two flavors known to settle an uneasy stomach." It also contained hemlock — though Louise would never say this — just enough to soothe nerves without putting the girl to sleep. "It will soothe your agitation. There, does it not smell delicious? Go ahead, take a sip." Really, the girl was as obedient as a spaniel puppy. She finished the beaker. Louise regarded Jeanne over the princess's head. For shame, she thought. All that Jeanne needed was a little determination. What was her problem? "Once you have eaten a portion of bread and meat, you may visit your mother in her rooms if that would comfort you."

Jeanne frowned, but Mme. Claude, said, with a catch in her voice, "Yes, I would like that."

Turning so the princess could not see her expression, Louise gave Jeanne a triumphant smile. "Eat then, child," she said.

As the princess obediently took the plate, Jeanne murmured, "I do not know how you manage it, Mme. Maman. You have a gift. I could not get her to stop crying."

Louise patted Jeanne's arm. "Experience, daughter. You must learn to be firm."

As the bells for Sext[2] faded, Michelle stood at the foot of the bed in the queen's apartments. The late queen's bed, its new frame soaring like the nave of a gothic cathedral, was fitted with a black brocade canopy. A foot-wide border draped the canopy on all four sides. Upon each border were sewn three black-edged shields with her emblem. Above the soaring frame, three towering black crosses held the canopy in place. Queen Anne, looking impossibly tiny, lay on the cloth of gold coverlet that draped over the vast state bed. Her body was wrapped in an ermine mantle, her crowned head propped on pillows. The hand of justice and the scepter rested in her hands, their tips reposing on the golden coverlet. She would have been proud of how well she looked, Michelle thought, and it would have been important to her.

With only a sleeveless over-gown over her black mourning robe for warmth, Michelle shivered in the chilly room and hugged herself. Unthinking, she arranged the queen's robes to cover her feet so they would not feel the chill. Sniffing back tears, she shook her head. The queen would never feel the cold again. Her tears slid unchecked down her cheeks as she turned away.

Mme. la Reine no longer needed her and never would again. The emptiness overwhelmed her each morning. It was true she still had Renée to care for, and her heart bled for the child, but

Renée was more bewildered than broken-hearted. It was they — her father, sister and Michelle — who suffered.

She kneeled in prayer at the prie-dieu, staring at the crucifix on her rosary. The prayers rattled from her lips automatically, and she murmured them so quickly that she completed them in less than one quarter of a ring of an hour candle. She did not budge when she heard footsteps behind her.

Trailed by Countess Louise and Mme. Jeanne, Duchess Claude crept into the mourning chamber. She clutched the rosary that her mother had tucked into her hands like a talisman before she slipped into her last sleep. Tears staining her cheeks, the princess stumbled to her late mother's bedside and sank to her knees, pressing her precious rosary to her lips. Mme. Jeanne kneeled beside her and murmured her beads.

Countess Louise paused beside Michelle. "I have not yet had a moment to compliment you for your excellent work on the late queen's mourning chamber. It has met with complete success. Everyone praises it to the skies. The late queen appears to be resting at peace."

Michelle seethed. Was she supposed to simper with delight at this compliment? How unfitting her timing; how insensitive her words. The queen was younger than Countess Louise, and yet she lay here in state while the countess still lived and was assuming her place.

Countess Louise chattered on, seeming to Michelle as if she were almost rubbing her hands together, so pleased she was with herself. "I, too, have been busy. The clothiers who fitted the Duchess for mourning will prove useful when it is time to organize the wedding of my ward and my son." She rambled on as if Michelle and Claude were not at prayer, not grieving. "My son and I have consulted. François is eager to marry as soon as possible. It will be a comfort to my ward, Duchess Claude. She is bereft."

Her callousness infuriated Michelle. This was not the time or place for the conversation. And she was acting as if the princess belonged to her now. Yet the king was still alive, though he was grieving too. Would she take the same proprietary view of Princess Renée?

Michelle spluttered, "Duchess Claude is not your ward, for her father still lives. You may have forgotten that I was present, Countess, when the queen prepared her testament and that I, too, witnessed the document. The queen was making provisions 'in case' something happened to the king, not while he lived."

The smile froze on Louise's lips, and she raised her eyebrows. "By Our Lady, Baronne, what has got into you? I am concerned for the well-being of the duchess, my future daughter. As you can surely see, she exhausts herself with grief. I but do my duty as a loving mother. Why would you stand in the way of my easing her suffering? Would you wish to harm her?"

There, the countess had done it again. Michelle felt she had been put into the wrong. She replied, "Of course she is grief-stricken, Countess. Her mother has just gone to our Lord." Crossing herself, she said, "She must be allowed time to mourn, as is natural when a daughter suffers such an irreplaceable loss. I hope you do not plan to interfere with that."

Duchess Claude raised her eyes from her beads, gave them both a stricken look, and then burst into sobs and fled, shadowed by her gouvernante. Michelle felt ashamed. The princess was correct. They should not be quarreling in this room. Humbly she went and kneeled again at the prie-dieu.

Countess Louise took the princess's abandoned place, her expression remote. Examining the countess under her eyelashes, Michelle sensed satisfaction emanating through Louise's poorly simulated grief.

She reminded Michelle of an attenuated, ancient crone with her stark black-and-white robe, her nacreous flesh, her black, gable hood with its slice of white linen coif. It seemed to Michelle there was a shadow beneath Louise's skin, as if she were under-painted in a gray wash. Her pale lips moved soundlessly, like a puppet's. Michelle hoped she was saying the decades of the rosary, not casting spells. Louise's outline blurred as if she was behind a pane of thick, bubbled glass. It conjured a memory.

One day the queen and some of her ladies had been visiting Maître Jean Bourdichon in his studio in Tours. Michelle stood beside him as he showed the queen a miniature he had painted for the queen's great Book of Hours. Recognizing Michelle's interest, he pointed to one of the succubae. With the light at one angle she saw a crone, but when she followed his instructions and moved her head a few inches, the whole image shifted. Then she perceived within the same form a young, beautiful and dangerously seductive woman. She shuddered. The maître chuckled and said that women were the very devil.

Now Michelle watched, filled with an inarticulate rage as Countess Louise leaned closer to the queen's body and touched Queen Anne's sacred hand. Michelle could not bear it. How dare she!

She recalled Mme. Louise's words when Dauphin Charles-Orland died. "Dear Queen Anne, what a tragedy to lose a son, especially an heir you have not seen in over a year. I can only imagine your grief, for I could never bear to part from my son for so long."

Michelle clenched her fists and hissed, "Why do you touch the queen? Her body is as sacred in death as in life!"

The countess drew herself up, outrage in every rigid line of her body. "Who are you to question me, Mme. Michelle? I know you for a traitor to France. Did you not encourage Queen Anne to forswear Princess Claude's betrothal to my son? You do not have Queen Anne to protect you any longer. And soon I shall be guardian to Princess Renée."

Her accusation bit as sharp as ice on a frigid morning. That it was untrue was irrelevant. The countess believed it — or pretended to. How long had she been waiting to show her enmity openly? How far would she spread this dangerous gossip?

The guards in the corners of the mourning chamber shifted at the disturbance. Michelle heard the clank of armor and rattle of swords loosening in scabbards. Reminded of the sacredness of her surroundings, Michelle fell silent.

She confronted the bitter truth that she was behaving foolishly. She had lost more than her liege lady, confidant and closest friend. Of course Countess Louise bore her malice. Michelle had been the queen's friend. Queen Anne had chosen to make her *dame d'atour*. King Louis had selected one of his favorites, the late Baron de Soubise, Sieur Jean de Parthenay l'Archimbault, to become her husband. A widower, he had been happy to remarry. The queen had favored her new husband's family, even though Michelle had not asked. It was the way of the world.

Now forced to think like the countess, she realized that Countess Louise considered it deliberate conniving on Michelle's part. In a similar position she would have used it so, in Michelle's opinion. Now that the queen was gone, she felt it safe to attack Michelle for she was vulnerable. While the king still lived, she should be secure. But he had been ailing for years. No one had seen him since the queen's death. He had loved his wife dearly. How would the queen's passing affect his health?

What would happen when he died? She had more to trouble her than simply how to comfort and protect Princess Renée over the coming months. Suddenly Michelle was afraid. It focused her. "Please forgive my plain speaking."

Countess Louise stepped back. "You are overwrought. I accept your apology and forgive your outburst — this time. I shall return with the Duchess Claude later when we can be assured of privacy." She twirled and left, her skirts swirling.

THREE WEEKS LATER, as January drew toward its close, in the early morning dawn, Michelle held Princess Renée's hand as King Louis, Duchess Claude, and the young princess gathered in the great hall of the Château de Blois. To hold back her tears, Michelle stared above her at the barrel-vaulted ceiling of midnight blue adorned with golden crosses. Through the shimmer of tears in her eyes, it looked like stars shining in the night sky. The king and queen had hosted many great events here — including the meeting of the Estates General in which King Louis had betrothed his daughter to Duke François — the event that had so embittered Queen Anne.

Now, behind them, the entire court gathered to witness the encoffining of the queen's body.

To vaunt his love for his late wife one last time, the king gave Queen Anne's Breton guards and herald the central ceremonial roles. As the queen's choir sang a Magnificat, Brittany Herald, in his tabard emblazoned with the Breton coat of arms, removed the crown and symbols of the queen's power. Then her gentlemen ushers lifted Mme. la feu Reine, still resplendent in her coronation robes from the bed. Michelle closed her eyes as they lowered the dead queen into a lead coffin. Sealed, the lead coffin was placed within a wooden coffin. She winced at the hollow sound as the lid closed forever. She would never gaze upon the queen again. Much as she tried to recall her living face, the wax death mask had already hazed her image of the living lady. *Sic fugit memoria.*

The queen's company of Bretons had the honor of carrying her cloth-of-gold covered coffin to the gun carriage that waited at the main doors of the château. Immediately behind, Brittany Herald followed with her standard of fleur-de-lys and ermines. The shuffling king led them in procession. Poor man. How lonely he must feel. How much he must resent seeing the young arrogant dauphin, Duke François d'Angoulême, with Princess Claude, now Duchess de Bretagne. Duchess Claude blushed even in her grief as she walked beside her betrothed, who would marry her only for her wealth. A son was the only way to keep the young jackanapes from the throne. Michelle wondered if the king would heed the late queen's plea to marry again.

As Michelle, holding Princess Renée's hand, followed the coffin down the steep stairs, the whispers that trailed behind them like crystalline puffs of breath in the chilly air reminded her that Countess Louise was not alone in envying her position. The procession accompanied the coffin through the ancient lower court of the château. A cloud of mist rose over the close-packed bodies of the mourning citizens of Blois, who had filed through the ancient narrow gates. Crowds squeezed together, doffing caps, many in tears, for she had been popular for her generosity. A path opened to the Church of St. Sauveur. The Bishops of Paris, Limoges, and Bayeux said mass; Queen Anne's confessor pronounced thirty-seven praises of their late queen in his funeral oration, one for each year of her life. For Michelle, it was a bitter reminder that yesterday would have been her thirty-eighth birthday.

Finally, the cortège began its slow journey to Paris. It would stop for services at Orléans, Étampes, and Notre Dame des Champs outside Paris. Michelle had made this journey many times with Renée, Claude and the queen. This would be the last time.

The second night, inside the walls of Orléans, Michelle returned with Princess Renée from the mass for the queen to the château that guarded the bridge across the Loire. It was dark; icy winds blew the falling snow into their faces and obscured the slippery cobblestones. Even with fur-lined boots and mittens, Michelle's toes and fingers tingled.

Princess Renée was acting silly. She paid no attention to where she was walking but ran in circles, her face skyward, trying to catch snowflakes on her tongue. Renée was carrying the angel-winged rag doll Michelle and she had made and brought to every mass.

After each service Renée said, "Maman is in heaven now, telling the Virgin to pray for me." It comforted her in a way nothing else did. It had become their ritual. When they returned to her room, she placed her doll in its coffin and they prayed together, often discussing what happened after death.

Now the child began to run on the steep, icy street. Suddenly, she fell on her back, her arms flying wide. There was a muted thunk as her head struck the cobblestones. Stunned, she slid down the glassy slope. She let out a wail. The ladies-in-waiting rushed forward, awkward and clumsy on the dangerous pitch. Some fell to their knees to comfort the princess.

In the confusion, no one noticed that the angel-doll had flown from Princess Renée's arms. The ladies-in-waiting settled her and made sure the princess had not injured her head or broken any bones and then returned her to her feet.

But now Renée became frantic. "Angel-doll! Where is Angel-doll? You must find Angel-doll!"

Everyone searched the street and the side streets as the princess became more hysterical, tears freezing on her cheeks. The doll was nowhere to be found. Michelle worried that Princess Renée would become ill in the night air, but any suggestion they continue without her precious talisman sent the child into another paroxysm.

Wringing her hands, one of the ladies-in-waiting sobbed, "I believe she went to join your Maman in heaven." It was inspired.

Princess Renée's wails turned to hiccups. "Is it true? Is that what happened, Mme. Michelle?"

What should she say? Miracles happened often enough. And Angel-doll had vanished. Crossing herself, Michelle kneeled beside the wide-eyed girl. "I do believe she is correct, my darling. Make a sign of the cross and let us return to our room to praise Our Lady."

16 FEBRUARY 1514

BASILICA OF ST. DENIS

aronne Michelle de Soubise

SUNLIGHT PASSING through the great stained-glass windows of
the Basilica of St. Denis imbued its vast interior with shades of
lapis lazuli and crimson. Thousands upon thousands of candles
laced the immense candelabra hanging from its ceiling. But the
ceiling was so high that it was lost in deep shadows, and the
candle flames glittered like stars in the night sky. The echoing
of sound in the enormous space added to Michelle's solemn
sense of the sacred. Immersed in the exquisite choral music,
Michelle's excellent Latin also allowed her to find solace in the
prayers of praise composed for the occasion and the traditional
words of the mass. Kneeling in the dim interior, she was
grateful for the Lord's gift of time that had blunted the sharpest
edges of her sorrow in the weeks since Queen Anne had died.

In the prolonged and extravagant rituals of her lying in state, the masses for the dead, the funeral feasts and processions, the many somber services on the long journey from Blois to Paris and on to Saint Denis, King Louis had wanted everyone to share the intensity of his grief. On the slow winter trip, Michelle had striven to keep Princess Renée occupied and warm, so the princess did not brood over the loss of her mother. All this had helped them grieve.

The highest prelates of both French and Breton churches conducted this last, long, solemn ceremony. Finally, the queen's coffin was lifted, carried to the vault below the high altar and lowered into its burial chamber. Then her household faced its saddest duty. Beginning with the Grand Maître, each principal officer kneeled and released their symbol of office. When it came to Michelle's turn, she let fall the queen's wardrobe keys and scribal pen. As they clattered onto the coffin below, she could not restrain her tears.

When the last household officer had finished his sad task, Brittany Herald stepped to the head of the Queen-Duchess's open vault. He waited until all eyes were upon him. Utter silence reigned in the vast edifice, broken only by the occasional cough, the hiss of the candles, and the twitter of the few birds who had not flown south. Brittany Herald had a magnificent voice, deep and sonorous, trained for years. Thrice he called, "The very Christian Queen of France, Duchess de Bretagne, our sovereign lady and mistress is dead. The Queen is dead." The final time, his voice broke. "My... queen is dead."

The organ crashed into the *Te Deum*. The great bells tolled. Michelle heard bells from the neighboring churches take up the peals, a mournful tocsin rolling in waves to wash across France toward Brittany announcing the departure of her well-beloved lady. For the rest of the world, life would move on. For those of the late queen's household, the bells signaled an unwelcome end. What would become of them now? Michelle shivered. Queen Anne had appointed her gouvernante to Princess Renée. How long would the king live to honor his wife's testament?

The royal party led the procession to the main doors. The day was as cold and gray as Michelle's mood. Standing outside with Renée's hand in hers, as they waited in the Basilica forecourt for their carriage, Michelle saw the papal envoy whispering with King Louis's chancellor. Watching the two men together, Michelle crossed herself, her spirits lifting a trifle. She took it as a sign of God's benediction. This reconciliation would have pleased Queen Anne, who had been hopeful when Pope Leo was elected. Since he was a Medici, she had hoped he would favor France, for Florence had long been a French ally. Healing the rift between King Louis and the papacy had been one of her deepest desires.

Michelle turned to Duchess Claude. "Do we share one litter for warmth to the Hôtel des Tournelles, or do you ride, Duchess Claude?"

"Do not call me duchess!" A moment later, Duchess Claude quavered, "I am sorry I snapped."

Duke François slipped between them and bent his head to Claude's. "Do you ride with me, Duchess?" His voice was as smooth as honey.

She took his arm, her eyes brightening. She answered Michelle, but her attention stayed with her betrothed, "I shall meet you in my apartments."

Princess Renée pouted as she watched them walk away together,

Michelle did not reprove her for showing her feelings. Her charge's dislike of the duke was obvious. Though she was jealous, she was also an astute judge of character.

MICHELLE AND PRINCESS Renée played fox and geese while they waited in Duchess Claude's suite for her to return. As first lady of the court, Duchess Claude now occupied her late mother's chambers in Paris's ancient royal palace. It was furnished and arranged exactly as the late queen had always preferred it, and because of this, Michelle found it uncomfortably filled with memories.

She had mentioned as much.

Duchess Claude had shivered and agreed. "Sometimes I feel that Maman's spirit is hovering over me."

"Why do not you refurnish it with your own pieces?" Michelle had suggested.

Mme. Claude had resisted. "I do not want to cause a fuss. It does me well this way."

When the duchess returned from the funeral, her cheeks pink, she walked with more spring in her step than she had in weeks.

Her cheerful mood encouraged Michelle to renew her suggestion. "Mme. Claude, let us redecorate this suite with furnishings of your choosing today. We can make an expedition of it. Shall we visit the storerooms? There you shall choose a bed and chairs, a desk and tables, cushions and chests and hangings. We can go to the library, afterwards, and choose books until the porters set everything in place. It will be an adventure."

The brightness faded from Claude's eyes. She sank into the armchair in which Michelle had spent too many hours nursing the late queen.

"I have not the strength to choose." Her sigh seemed to come from the bottom of her heart. "Comforting Papa is my only solace. He is as sad as I am. Taking part in Maman's funeral rites, speaking with all the mourners, going to the masses and dinners consoled me. Now what will I do?" She wiped her nose on her sleeve.

Michelle handed her a clean cloth. "It will cheer you to change the furnishings. You will feel less mournful in rooms filled with your own belongings, arranged as you prefer. Do this for your health!"

"I have no time. Soon I ride with Papa as he used to do with Maman. I must call my maids to make me ready." Michelle doubted this was true, but she did not challenge her. Duchess Claude was too diffident to order them to leave, but neither would she wish to argue. Michelle felt it necessary to insist. It was for her own good, after all.

"If you prefer, Mme. Jeanne, Mme. Renée and I can take care of it for you. Mme. Jeanne will know what to choose. You can make changes when you return if you are not pleased. You need to lift your spirits. I speak as a healer, you understand."

The duchess burst into noisy tears and threw herself onto her mother's bed. "Everyone pulls and pokes at me," she wailed. "Sometimes I feel like a criminal being executed. One with horses chained to each limb. Each horse is pulling in a different direction... and my legs and my arms are splitting from my body... and I am bleeding... and screaming." She scrunched with her knees humped under her on the bed, arms over her head, sobbing hysterically.

Princess Renée jumped up from her game, gave Michelle a look of horror, ran to the bed and flung herself, wailing, upon her sister.

Blessed Virgin in Heaven! Crossing herself, Michelle could only speculate about what had provoked such a storm. Sending a maid for sweet wine and biscuits, she rubbed the princesses' backs, shushing and soothing until they calmed. Once they had both quietened, she sent the younger girl back to her suite with Mme. Jeanne.

Michelle perched on the bed and said, "Tell me what is troubling you, Duchess Claude. If I can serve you, be sure I will. If not, speaking of it will relieve you. You know your words shall stay between us."

Duchess Claude sniffled. Michelle handed her another handkerchief. Wiping her eyes, she moaned, "No one can help. People are just being k-k-kind. Mme. Louise wants me to call her Maman, but I cannot. It would be betrayal. I call her Maman Louise, but even that feels false, though I can endure it."

She blew her nose again. "I should not say this, but she nags. This morning, she repeated that I should a-a-ask Papa to choose a date for the wedding, but I do not want to marry yet, Mme. Michelle. Papa would not agree, I know. When I said that, she pulled down her mouth in that disapproving way she has and said, 'Well, if you do not wish to wed my son....' It made me feel t-t-terrible, but also angry. 'I said, Maman Louise, yes I want to marry him, but it is too soon. I am too sad about losing Maman. What if I cried in front of the guests or on our wedding night? And custom says I must wait one year.' She stopped pushing me then. I do not think she had ever heard me say nay to her before. Mayhap she believed I dared not." Tears leaked from her eyes again. "In truth, if she insists, I do not dare."

She threw herself into Michelle's arms. "When people's keys rattled into Maman's vault today, I wanted to run away. And when Brittany Herald's voice cracked, I cried again. Maman is truly gone now. I will never see her any more!" She wailed the last word, working herself into hysteria once again.

Michelle did not want to slap her, which must be her next step if she did not calm. She chose a fresh approach. "There, there, Mme. Claude. You will see your Maman again in heaven. Remember that and hold to it. But you terrified Princess Renée. For her sake, dear one, you must pull yourself together. Your mother would expect it of you." There was truth to that. She reminded the duchess that Brittany Herald was on his way now to Nantes with her mother's heart in its golden receptacle.

"Mmhmm. That is a consolation. Maman's heart will be with our grandparents in their crypt in Brittany. I have memorized all the inscriptions on her reliquary — on both sides of the outside and inside." Her sniffling subsiding, Mme. Claude straightened up and wiped her face with the damp cloth.

Relieved she was calmer, Michelle asked, "Would you like me to speak to Mme. Louise. She must stop fretting you. I could suggest we ask your father to postpone your wedding." Trying to lighten the girl's mood, she said, "I doubt I can do much about your calling her Maman Louise. Speaking from experience, I would say it is the price one pays with mothers-in-law. Be relieved if you find it is no higher." She did not add that she expected Claude would find it much higher, for the court snickered that Duke François chafed under his mother's thumb. "But if you wish, I could suggest the countess wait until after the wedding."

Duchess Claude gave a sad chuckle. "Please do not propose that to her. But I would be grateful if you and she talked to Papa. I begin to avoid Duke François, for each time we meet he asks if I have settled on a date. Even today. When I say no, he teases, claiming I do not wish to join my destiny with his. Ever since he learned from somewhere that Maman hoped to leave Brittany to Renée if she married the Duke of Burgundy, he pretends I am delaying because I would prefer to marry the duke myself." Her eyes shone with tears.

Michelle resented Countess Louise's callousness in pressuring the grieving duchess. Had the countess teased Seigneur de Fleuranges into spilling Queen Anne's planned secret mission to Regent Marguerite? And if it were not he, who was the talebearer? Countess Louise would have confided in her son, of course. Knowing them, they would hold a grudge.

"What else is troubling you?"

The duchess shook her head. "Nothing else."

Michelle decided not to probe further; she'd progressed further than she'd expected.

"Why do not you and one of your ladies look at furniture and decide what you would like for your chambers? I will speak to the countess and arrange to see your Papa."

Duchess Claude gave Michelle a watery smile. "I see through your schemes, Mme. Michelle. You will have me change the appearance of these rooms willy-nilly in the name of my health. Fine, and I shall take Renée. She always lifts my spirits."

Countess Louise swept past her ladies-in-waiting so quickly they did not have time to scramble from their cushions, and then retreated to her inner sanctum, ordering her gentleman usher not to permit anyone to disturb her. The prolonged funeral ceremonies for the late queen were finally over, but

Claude and her intimates would still be sobbing and wailing. The countess's apartments in this rackety old Hôtel des Tournelles were her only haven for, by Our Lady, she really could bear no more.

She had barely settled into her chair and picked up her playing cards when Lady Blanche knocked and poked her head into Louise's private chamber.

"What is it?" she asked coldly.

"Mme. la Baronne de Soubise presents her regards. She wishes to consult you about the Duchess de Bretagne."

Checkmate. Louise recognized she could refuse neither the person nor the excuse. "Show her in, my dear."

She did not stand but gestured Mme. Michelle to seat herself on a footstool near the fireplace. "Mme. Michelle, I did not expect your company." She put the painted tarocchi cards into their carved wooden box. They fit precisely.

"Beautiful playing cards."

Louise stroked the intricate flowered design of the top card. "A gift from my nephew of Savoy. It is an Italian set."

The baronne lifted the top card, examined the twisting design, and said, "Exquisite. I hear you are an expert player." She returned the card to the box. Louise snapped the lid shut.

"A few of us enjoy playing. It becomes more popular all the time. The Italians are always inventing new games."

From her pouch, Mme. Michelle withdrew a small packet wrapped in lovely cloth, that she presented almost as a tribute.

Obviously, she wanted something. Louise opened the wrapping and discovered a painted tin within which nestled freshly made candied violets. How delicious. The baronne had learned her tastes and spared no expense.

"I am surprised by your visit. How may I serve you?"

Mme. Michelle chose instead to speak of the magnificence of the late queen's obsequies, asked after Louise's son and daughter, and inquired of her health. Only after completing these formalities did she show her hand. Then she was blunt.

"The Duchess de Bretagne has spoken to me of her marriage. She is bereft after losing her mother and wishes to delay her wedding until her year of mourning ends. She asked me to convey her wishes to you so that together we could beg the king to heed her plea."

Louise stiffened. "Why does she not approach me herself? I will soon be her maman-in-law. Or ask my stepdaughter, Mme. Jeanne, to do so? Surely either of us would be more suitable?" She saw Mme. Michelle bristle. What did she expect? If Mme. Michelle could be blunt, so would she. It pleased her she had offended the baronne. Duchess Claude should have come to her.

Now Mme. Michelle tried tact. "Mme. Jeanne is unwell today, and I was the inadvertent recipient of Mme. Claude's anguished outburst. To calm her, I offered to speak to you myself."

Louise sniffed. "Why does she not speak to King Louis herself? He is her papa."

"She considers that we, as her father's contemporaries, will have greater success than she would. To him, she is a child, not yet ready for adult responsibilities. Nor is he ready to discuss her marriage. It only recalls his painful loss to mind."

Gracious, listen to her now. So circumspect. Louise thought she must have drawn blood. What a pleasure to bait her. How far could she go? "She is young, indeed, and blind, if she believes her father and I are of a similar age."

"It is your experience and astuteness in negotiation that she compares to the king's, Countess. Please forgive my inelegance in so poorly relaying her compliment." The baronne lowered her gaze to her hands.

Louise gloated. She is rattled. But enough. "Baronne, could you explain the problem more clearly? I fail to understand."

Michelle said, "Naturally, Mme. Claude is eager to marry Duke François. It has been the desire of her life. She does not wish to withdraw from her betrothal. But rather than marrying before Easter as planned, she wishes to wait until next Epiphany or thereafter before wedding. She believes her father would agree if we speak to him on her behalf."

"I see. The poor child grieves. The king, too, of course." Louise did not change her expression as she uttered these banalities. So, the child wished to wait a year? Well, her son and, indeed, her entire family needed Claude's dowry now. How fortunate little Claude did not dare approach her father without her. Louise knew she was adept at persuading the king to her way of thinking. "What date does she propose? Epiphany itself? Does she have other conditions? For we must approach him once only, do you not agree?"

They dueled verbally as they worked out the details. They would go together to the king. Louise would request the interview — which she did immediately — and would be the principal speaker, since she was Claude's future mother-in-law.

By the time the king replied with an appointment for the 21st — five days later — Mme. Michelle had already left Louise's rooms. The Countess smirked as she sent a page with the information to the baronne. Mme. Michelle was naïve to believe her presence could prevent Louise from swaying the king.

THE KING'S chamberlain bowed the baronne and Louise into the king's private study. Like much of the chilly, old palace of Tournelles, it was so cramped it did not even have a fireplace. For warmth he made do with a brazier, fingerless mitts, and a fur-lined robe. The two women shivered on the window seat while King Louis sat at his desk that faced a tapestry-covered wall. He continued to read. After signing a document, he handed it to the chamberlain and turned his chair towards them.

"Mme. Louise, Mme. Michelle, good morrow. How may I serve you?"

They started to rise, but he motioned them to stop.

"You know I've no time for idle ceremony in private."

They were accustomed to his abruptness. "My condolences, Sire," Louise said. "The funeral rites—"

"I do not wish to talk of it, Mme. Louise," King Louis snapped. "If you have come to condole, you may leave. Or do you have some purpose? Declare it, for I am immersed in state affairs."

She hesitated. The king was in a foul temper. No wonder Mme. Claude was reluctant to approach him. She adjusted her words. "Dear Cousin Louis, let me not waste your time. Mme. Michelle and I are here to petition you on behalf of your elder daughter. Our children were to marry before Easter—"

King Louis was already shaking his head.

Louise dropped to her knees and reached for his hands. "Listen to me, Cousin. I agree, before Easter is too soon. We are all bereft. But let us not wait long. Spring. Think of spring. You are the Father of Your People. After this long, sad, cold winter — this tragic, mournful time of loss — you, your people, we, need a season of hope. Something to cheer us, to renew our faith, after this heartbreak. You witnessed the depth of your people's woe over the past tear-soaked weeks. Their sorrow during our beloved queen's funeral was palpable. Even now Paris wades in grief, as do we all. Help us recover, Father!"

She released his hands and held up her palms in prayer, a maiden begging to her God. This time he took her hands between his, and they clung to each other.

Louise sneaked a glance at Michelle, who was staring at her, mouth agape.

Smiling secretly to herself although she kept her expression soulful, Louise continued, "We both know France will be safer the sooner she has an heir."

He nodded, his eyes hooding and a smirk flashing across his face. It was an odd reaction and Louise tucked it away to mull over later as she continued her plea. "If Princess Claude is like her beloved mother, she will prove fertile. Why not give France a reason to celebrate once more? Let our two families become one, gracious Sire. Allow our beloved children the happiness they have awaited so long!" Running her tongue over her half-opened lips, she gazed into his eyes, her expression soft and longing. He had not had a woman in months, she was certain. He was putty in her hands.

The king pulled his gaze from her mouth and addressed the baronne, his voice gruff, "What say you, Mme. Michelle? Is this what my daughter wants? Would my dear wife have agreed?"

74

"No, Sire. I have spoken to Mme. Claude. She does not wish to marry until the mourning year is concluded, although of course she is your obedient daughter and will do as you command."

Her words infuriated Louise, who would have turned the witch to stone had she that power.

King Louis hemmed and hawed. "Yes, yes. So, she wishes to marry. We should wait a year, it is true, until the strict mourning period is over. My wife deserves that. A year is not long. But Claude is young and hasty." He sat back, rubbing his clean-shaven chin with his hand, pondering.

As Mme. Michele stared, Louise covered her mouth to hide her delight.

The baronne began to say something, but the king interrupted her. "The English war is going badly. Brittany and Normandy have suffered much from coastal attacks. I imagine Duke François believes he could do better if he were in charge of Brittany. Is that it, Mme. Louise?" He thrust his chin forward, glaring at her.

"Never, Sire. He is a novice in the art of war. You are a crafty, experienced warrior." Always curious about affairs of state, she tried to provoke a revelation. "Are you concerned about an alliance between England and the Empire?"

"No. No, I am not. Now, listen to me. I administer Brittany. I intend to keep it that way. If you wish a rapid marriage, the dauphin needs to accept this. Do you understand me?" His sharp eyes appraised Louise.

So, he suspects my motives. "Sire, whatever you — and Duchess Claude — decide will be agreeable to me and my son." She added for good measure, "I trust it will never become necessary to play a role in your children's upbringing." Louise wondered if she had gone too far when his mouth twisted wryly, but he made no comment.

She caught the baronne giving her a sour look. She obviously felt betrayed. Louise did not care. Only the king's opinion mattered. And King Louis was looking thinner and frailer than ever. When he shifted in his chair, he winced. Without his dear Anne to keep him alive, he would not survive a year. My César will not have long to wait, Louise thought.

"Well, you have taken me by surprise, but now I ponder it, I see benefits." He harrumphed. "I am prepared to consider it."

Louise shot the baronne a triumphant glance. Michelle opened her lips, probably to counter her arguments. To distract her, Louise trod on Michelle's foot hard with her sharp heel as she rose. "My son will be eternally grateful, Sire." Curtseying, she added, "I thank you from my heart on behalf of the young couple."

"It pleases me to make my daughter happy if I can. I have one or two concerns. I shall reflect on the matter and speak with my daughter." He turned back to the papers spread on his desk.

"*Adieu*, Sire." Baronne Michelle was quick to take his hint.

Not so fast, Baronne. "Concerns? Perhaps I can help you resolve them." Louise could not leave it like this. If he spoke to the princess, he would learn she had misled him. Then the marriage might never come about. Besides, best to strike the iron when it was glowing red.

"Well, I would have conditions."

"Please confide in me." Deliberately arranging it that Mme. Michelle stood at the king's back, Louise sat down again and smiled, looking as innocent as a choirboy. "Whatever I can do. As her future maman-in-law, it would be my place to organize the wedding with her, if you were to agree. Naturally, it will be a pleasure as well as a duty to obey all your requirements."

He turned to her. "Humph. I have no time for this. Affairs of state.... Still. Perhaps it would be best to be done with it.

"First, it will not happen before Easter. May — I think May. After the court moves to St. Germain-en-Laye as we always do. That is a suitable location, private enough that it would not be scandalous. We will still be in deep mourning. I cannot — will not — interrupt my mourning for a state wedding, and the funeral has been such an enormous expense. No new clothes. The court shall dress in the same clothing as were used for the funeral — in black. No feasting. No celebrations. Minimal expense."

Louise wished she dared sneer at his stinginess and stalk from the room. What a miserly skinflint the old knave was! All this to save the cost of a proper wedding for his daughter and her glorious son. Instead she said, "I understand, Your Majesty. Your feelings do you credit. I shall advise her." She made her voice tremble with emotion and the king lapped it up. With her ready agreement to his conditions, she won him over.

The baronne tried to interject, but the king did not seem to hear her. "Thank you, Ladies." He bowed. "I give you leave."

In the hall outside his rooms, Baronne Michelle drew herself up to her full height. "That was ill-done, Countess. A one-month postponement is not in keeping with the spirit of our agreement."

Louise smiled into her stormy face. Baronne Michelle was going to look quite a failure when she spoke to Mme. Claude.

WHEN SHE LEARNED of the new date for her wedding, Duchess Claude became as limp as a monthly cloth. She shrugged when Countess Louise urged her to persuade her father to permit colors at her wedding rather than funereal black.

"I prefer black," she murmured. "We are mourning Maman."

Since it was the extent of her mutiny, Mme. Louise did not insist further. Instead, she relieved the duchess of the responsibility for organizing her wedding and furnishing her future household. When Mme. Jeanne argued, pointing out that the task fell into her purview, Louise frightened her stepdaughter into deferring to her authority. Duchess Claude drooped as spring drew near and the date approached when the court would leave the gloomy old warren of a palace in Paris for the country delights of St. Germain-en-Laye.

On fair days Michelle went riding with Princess Renée in the countryside outside the city. Fresh greens appeared in the fields, and spring foods came into city markets. The week before Easter, the Lord blessed them with soft weather. By the end of the week, the streets had dried and even the stink of Paris lessened as fresher breezes found their way down the Seine River and wafted through the city gates to the gardens within. On Holy Tuesday it rained, as if to match the somber events of Christ's crucifixion.

Michelle spent Holy Thursday reflecting on her sins of omission and commission. Kneeling, eyes on the crucifix on the wall, she examined her conscience. It was a painful process, for she could no longer evade the subject she had been avoiding since the queen's death. God had allowed Queen Anne and all her sons to die. Yet He allowed Countess Louise and her family to prosper. He permitted abuses and laxity in His Church and among His priests. Goodness was not rewarded; and evil was not punished. She feared she had lost faith in the Lord's justice, and now she despaired of God's mercy.

The more she meditated, the more disturbed she became. Madame Louise had been envious of the queen and cruel to her. She manipulated the king, and Michelle did not believe she wished well for him. The countess had betrayed Duchess Claude over the delay to her marriage date to benefit herself and her son. She was unkind to Princess Renée in countless small ways — and of all her faults that unkindness bothered Michelle the most.

RATHER THAN MOVE with the court to St. Germain-en-Laye, Louise was removing to her small court at Romorantin and she was so cheerful it was hard to hide. She offered many spurious reasons, but in truth, even though Claude brought the family a fortune, Louise had no desire to attend the shabby wedding of her magnificent son to his dumpy bride with her ugly limp.

She strolled through Duchess Claude's overcrowded suite and supervised her packing. Here and there she picked up objects that caught her eye: leather-bound books in their jeweled book boxes, butter-smooth marble statuettes, Venetian glass goblets on golden trays, the late queen's silver-gilt dinner service. Louise caressed them, and those she coveted most, she set aside for her own suite. Those to go to St. Germain-en-Laye for the ducal suite she replaced for packing.

Princess Renée giggled with a companion. Their giggles rang bright amongst the subdued voices. The whole gloomy lot of demoiselles and ladies-in-waiting surrounded the duchess and the baronne as they embroidered altar cloths or sewed for the poor. Renée made herself a nuisance, bumping into walls and people and furniture as she galloped about on her hobby horse. The servants doing the packing merely tried to avoid the romping children, but Louise raised her eyebrows and barked at the princess.

Mme. Michelle gave Louise a measuring look, rose, and took Princess Renée's hand. "Let us walk in the gardens," she said. "It will be more agreeable and if you are not underfoot, it will be easier for everyone."

Duchess Claude jumped to her feet, ignoring her mother-in-law. "I will come, too. Ladies, you may join us or go to your rooms as you wish." On their way from the room, the duchess — who had not recovered from the insult of Mme. Louise's refusal to attend her wedding — said to Michelle in a low voice, "In truth, it will be pleasant to be free of Maman Louise's company. She and Renée grate on each other's nerves." She gestured to the glare the countess directed at Renée, who frolicked like a tumbling hound, as their demoiselles scattered like dandelion puffs in a breeze.

The swish of their skirts rebuked Louise as they swept from the suite. She glowered after them. The baronne's presence irritated her more each day. The princesses clung to her too much. Michelle also interfered with affairs in Brittany. When she entered the duchess's rooms today, Louise had overheard Mme. Michelle offering to write replies to the Breton Chancellor for the duchess as she used to do for the late queen. They had changed the subject as soon as they saw her, for Claude knew she misliked Mme. Michelle.

When Louise spoke to her son about the problem of Baronne de Soubise, he said they should tread carefully since the king favored Mme. Michelle's late husband's family. She suggested to the Maître d'hôtel in charge of accommodations at St. Germain-en-Laye that he move Mme. Michele further from the royal suites, but he would not do so without the duchess's permission. When she suggested it to Claude, she shook her head, her voice syrupy.

"No, no, Maman Louise, that would be impossible. She is like Renée's mother now. I would never distress my little sister by separating her from Mme. Michelle." She even chuckled. "Besides, you do not know Renée if you think it would succeed. She would simply find Mme. Michelle and slip off to stay with her. Why would you suggest it?"

Louise said, "I am not one to judge, as you know, but sometimes my heart goes out to poor, little Mme. Renée. Mme. Michelle is so strict with her. The other day, when the princess wanted to bring a sweet puppy to her room, Mme. Michelle forbade it and sent her off with a servant when she argued."

A puzzled frown flashed across Claude's face. A moment later she smiled. "Oh, yes, now I remember. A puppy from the hunting kennels. It was tiny. Too young to leave its mother. Renée has her own dog in her rooms."

As if the thought popped into her mind at that moment, Louise said, "Mme. Michelle could have returned it later rather than refusing the child a simple pleasure and punishing her."

"She could have, I suppose, but the mother hound would have been distressed. Besides, Renée is willful. She must learn to obey. Maman would have required her to do so, and Mme. Michelle follows Maman's precepts." Her lips quivered.

By Our Lady, the girl was a rabbit. She would be in tears if Louise persisted. Irritated, Louise dropped the subject. That baronne was wily. She had hoodwinked the king and queen for years. Yes, the baronne was well-educated — but her superior ways did not impress Louise. No doubt her teaching skills were excellent, but Princess Renée required only to write and read

French, have perhaps a smattering of French history and litera-
ture, and enough Latin for her prayers. The rest — Mme.
Michelle's knowledge of Greek and Hebrew and her vast herbal
knowledge — were excessive. There were many more suitable
to teach Princess Renée to play instruments and extemporize
poems, including her daughter, Marguerite. Louise did not
forget Mme. Michelle's rudeness in the late queen's mourning
chamber. Nor did she like the baronne's increasing influence
with Duchess Claude. Even her stepdaughter, Mme. Jeanne said
pleasant things about her these days. By the Virgin's teats, the
court would be better without her.

18 MAY 1514

ST. GERMAIN-EN-LAYE

*B*aronne Michelle de Soubise

ON HER WEDDING DAY, Duchess Claude sat up in Michelle's bed and pushed open the heavy curtains surrounding them just as dawn painted the horizon with streaks of apricot light. A draft of cooling air entered.

"What will it be like?" she whispered.

"Your wedding night, you mean?" Michelle was surprised the duchess would ask her. "You have not spoken about it with one of your cousins or with Duchess Marguerite?"

"They are too old." Her cheeks were rosier than the morning sky.

"And I am not?" Michelle could not keep the amusement from her voice. She had been her mother's friend; the others were closer to Duchess Claude's age.

Mme. Claude gave Michelle's shoulder a little shake. "You know what I mean. You are like a mother... or an aunt. Someone who will not make fun of me in my absence. And will keep my question private." She kneaded her hands together.

It had been years since she had reassured a young bride. Claude's mother had not needed reassurance, for when Queen Anne married King Louis it had been her second marriage. "Your question takes me back to my first marriage a long time ago, when I was a young girl about to marry my cousin, whom I scarcely knew." Michelle pushed back the coverlet from under her chin. She lay on her back, listening to the susurration of the wind in the trees outside their window. It reminded her of her girlhood in Brittany and the sound of the sea breaking at the base of the cliffs when she woke.

"I did not know you had been married twice." Duchess Claude's voice dragged Michelle back to the present.

"Yes. My first husband died campaigning in Italy at the battle of Fornovo. I was with your Maman in Lyon awaiting his return. She retained the widows of all her Breton soldiers in her service. Most remarried, but I refused."

"Did you care for him so much then?"

"No, dear one." Michelle did not wish to discourage her on her wedding day, and, in truth, she had not disliked him, but nothing about the marriage had made her wish for another. She wed in haste, because her betrothed was eager to join up when the Duchess Anne's new husband called a levy from her estates. He had obtained places for her and her mother in the duchess-queen's court so they could accompany him. Michelle would never forget her ignorance and his hurried groping under her night rail that wedding night. She would not wish upon any young girl the dry thrust and sharp pain that was her first experience of the marital act.

"I simply enjoyed the freedom of living as a widow in your mother's household more than I did life as a married woman."

Resolutely, she turned her attention to the duchess's situation. "Your husband is experienced, which is not news to you. Although you may have found this hurtful," Michelle checked Claude's expression, but Claude was keeping close guard on it, "It will stand you in good stead tonight, for he will probably be gentle." She paused a moment. Her virginity was likely Claude's strongest appeal to him. "If he is not — if he is hurting you or being hasty — ask him to go slowly and remind him you are inexperienced... and innocent."

Michelle reflected a moment before her next comment. Deciding it was suitable, she added, "We will prepare you well. You will wear a silk gown; your lovely long chestnut hair will be loose, and your clean, fresh scent will arouse him."

Duchess Claude wrapped her arms about her sheet-covered knees and leaned her face against them, hiding it from Michelle's view. She winced and shifted. Her weak left hip, the source of her problem, must ache, Michelle deduced. It made her left leg a little shorter than the right.

"Say that you want to please him and that you need him to teach you what he likes. That should persuade him to take his time. Can you do that?"

Claude was quiet and Michelle wondered if she would answer.

Without lifting her face, she finally said, "Yes."

"Good." Michelle was not sure what to say next. She decided to be direct. "Do you know what is going to happen?"

"I have seen horses and dogs rutting."

It was hard not to chuckle, but she managed. "Men are somewhat different from animals.... He will expect you to lie on your back. Likely, he will lift your night rail rather than remove it, although he may take it off or ask you to. If he does, encourage him to remove his nightclothes as well. Remember, he is your husband, and your duty is to obey, so you must do as he requires."

Obedience was the first duty taught to girls, Michelle knew, but Claude was a wealthy princess who brought him great riches and power. She deserved the best in this marriage. "Never forget, you are his wife, and you may encourage him to enjoy the experience with you. To get you with an heir, he must come to your bed often.... Are you listening?"

Claude nodded, her head still resting on her sheet-draped knees.

Did she feel frightened or excited, or some of both? "Do you feel any stirrings?"

Duchess Claude did not answer.

"It is good if you do," Michelle said, "and it is quite normal to picture yourself and him naked together."

The girl said nothing, though her breathing quickened.

"Before you climb into bed, I will give you an ointment that you may rub on your private parts. Once on your back, you must spread your legs wide so he is able to penetrate you. He will show you how and where. The ointment should ease his ability to do so. He may use his fingers to help. All is permitted between a husband and wife, so if you can relax and enjoy the sensations, do so. Ask him what you can do to make the experience pleasurable for him. He may show you... or not. He may talk... or not. Are you following so far?"

Another rustle and a hand crept into Michelle's. "Yes."

"We are almost done. He will lie on top of you and ride you, and you will probably find it somewhat painful the first time or two. Do not worry. It rarely lasts long. Once he has finished, he will probably make some sort of noise, a groan or gasping, and relax onto you. He may ask if you liked it. Always say 'yes.' After that he should fall asleep fairly quickly." Michelle fell silent.

Duchess Claude sat beside her, saying nothing. After a prolonged silence, Michelle said, "What? No questions?"

"No, I do not think so." Duchess Claude's voice sounded strangled as she choked out her words. "You have explained it clearly, dear Mme. Michelle." Running her fingers under her nightcap, she added, "I am not so afraid now. It does not sound terribly difficult."

Michelle restrained a chuckle. Poor sweetie. "No, Duchess, it is not difficult." Reluctantly, she came to the part she least wanted to mention, for she expected the duchess would find it embarrassing. It was not something she had needed to face, but royalty must. Taking a deep breath, she said, "I must remind you of one more thing you may have forgotten. You are a royal princess, and he is the dauphin. This marriage is important to France and to your father as king. There will be witnesses to the consummation in your room."

Duchess Claude made a small hissing noise. "No... you are right, I had forgotten." Then she surprised Michelle. "You are correct, it is normal for royal women." Still, her voice trembled.

Her voice gentle, Michelle said, "It will not be as bad as you may fear. Madame, your mother, told me she forgot about them once the bed curtains closed and her husband put his arms around her. She did not even see them, for they were behind screens — as they will be in your case — and the chamber is enormous."

Duchess Claude's hand squeezed Michelle's and released it. "Thank you. Already I feel better."

Glad she had spoken, Michelle put an arm around her. "Insist that François treat you gently. You deserve it. You are a precious prize. A sweet, generous, good, gentle person who brings him an enormous dowry. He should fall at your feet in gratitude and make sure you enjoy every minute of your night."

At that, the duchess laughed and hugged her. "No wonder Maman loved you and that Renée does too. So do I. Let's get up now."

Since Countess Louise had chosen not to attend her son's wedding, Duchess Claude asked Michelle to join her as she dressed. Princess Renée and she fussed over Duchess Claude as the maids bathed her, arranged her hair, and dressed her. They took turns brushing her shining chestnut hair until it glowed like burnished autumn leaves. Then they watched as her dresser wove strings of pearls into the tresses that fell loose to her hips. Next, they convinced her to display the delicate white lace of her sheer linen chemise, to brighten her black gown with its white satin underskirt, and to twist strands of her mother's famous pearls around her neck. They pinned her mother's precious rosary to her overskirt. In her hands she carried the treasured *Book of Prayers* her mother had given her as a child.

Michelle embellished Princess Renée's overskirt with opals, pinned nosegays of colored ribbons to her bodice, hung the pearl rosary that was her mother's gift at her neck, and added a string of pearls to her somber French hood. Their maids added touches of cinnabar to their pale cheeks and kohl to their eyebrows and lashes. Adorning Claude and primping took their minds off the significance of their black clothing.

Just before Nones, the king and Princess Claude led the procession from the château to its small private church. A light breeze sweetened the scents of the lilac bushes, lilies of the valley, forget-me-nots, and bright red poppies that bloomed along the well-traveled gravel path. But King Louis, who was attired in unrelieved black, insisted that everyone at court, including the servitors, match his dress. As the somber wedding party wound its way to meet the soberly clad bridegroom and his small party of groomsmen, Michelle speculated once again on the d'Angoulême family's reasons for persisting with the wedding despite the shabby arrangements and the bride's obvious reluctance. Their finances must be in dire straits.

A small group of courtiers clumped at the church doors. They clearly had not dared refurbish the clothing they had worn at the late queen's funeral. After the couple made their vows in subdued voices, everyone entered to hear the wedding mass. The king had forbidden removal of the black bunting and banners in the church or the banqueting hall. Despite her absence, however, Mme. Louise had found a way to elude his bleak decree. She had ordered the church wreathed with May flowers, tactfully chosen of royal mourning colors. Even King Louis could not disapprove since they came from the château gardens. The fragrance of violets, lilacs, and lilies lifted their spirits. Michelle felt a rare moment of appreciation for the absent countess when she saw smiles tilting the lips of the bride and groom. Once the simple mass had concluded, the company repaired to the similarly bedecked great hall for the wedding meal, the only festivity to celebrate the couple's wedding.

The king had refused the newly married couple the traditional days or weeks of celebration. Like Louise, Michelle agreed with her uncharitable opinion that his prohibition resulted less from grief than from parsimony. He probably begrudged the cost of feasting and jousting for the hordes of their relatives because he envied François's youth. Besides, the expense of a wedding coming so soon after the extravagance of his late wife's funeral must be too much for his penny-pinching ways. Since becoming king, he had prided himself on his thrift and boasted regularly that his many wars had enriched rather than impoverished his countrymen and had inflicted no damage on French territories. Or so it had been until two years ago. Then God had punished his pride. Michelle believed he felt worse about the damage to his treasury than the lost battles inside France. His delight at the death of Pope Julius had been positively sacrilegious.

She herself was most distressed about the invasions from England into Brittany. In a naval battle off Brest, the English sank their greatest ship. Then the French lost the battles of Guinegate and Therouannes to England and the Holy Roman Emperor. Michelle had heard rumors that ever since the queen's funeral Louis's ambassadors at the English court had been negotiating with England, *Grâce à Dieu*. She shook her head to stop her speculation and returned her thoughts to the present.

Duke François — hailed as Duke de Bretagne — led his bride, now Duchess of Valois and Angoulême as well as of Brittany, to the head table. He sat on King Louis's right and placed his new wife on her father's left. When Duchess Marguerite came to sit beside the bride, Princess Renée refused to move and insisted Michelle stay beside her. With Renée threatening a tantrum, Duchess Claude ignored her new husband's glower. Placing

Duchess Marguerite beside François, she said, "I prefer to keep my sister happy and, as it is my wedding day, I shall have *one* thing as *I* please." Her words created an awkward silence among those who heard her.

CLAUDE LAY wide awake in the semi-gloom, listening to the intimate snuffles and rustlings of the large man beside her. They reminded her of the sounds her puppies made as they slept stretched out in her bed. A warm sensation invaded her, and she had an urge to cuddle him as she did them, but she was uncertain he would welcome it. But she could not resist running her fingers through his thick hair. Murmuring softly in his sleep, he rubbed his head against her hand, stirring a frisson in her heart and loins. Resting her fingers in his soft curls, she stilled. Moments later he rolled away, wrapping himself in their silk coverlet. Like the silk tester overhead that created a warm nest, it was embroidered with their combined coats of arms: hers a white swan and an ermine with a ducal crown and his, a crowned salamander. Their coats of arms were quartered with their combined duchies of Valois, Angoulême, Brittany, Burgundy, and Milan. The five huge territories seemed weighty responsibilities, and she wondered idly how many they would be allowed to govern now they were married.

She lifted her naked body to cover herself with the linen sheet and woolen blanket. A smile flitted across her lips. François had insisted on removing her night rail. Mme. Michelle had been right; she had not minded her deflowering. François — she blushed thinking his name, but she had the right to call him that now — had been gentle and taken his time, and she had almost enjoyed the experience. Crossing herself, she prayed fervently he had, too. By the time they coupled the first time, she had forgotten the witnesses in the chamber. They had coupled three times more, and so, yes, François must have liked it very much.

The beautiful man beside her shifted, stretching a leg. She turned her head towards him, desiring to slide a hand down his arm and feel the silky hair. Her hand hovered, sensing his warmth. Still, she chose not to disturb his sleep, even though she wanted to see whether the sheets were properly stained. She also wanted to clean her private parts and use the close stool. To distract herself, she reached for the beads she'd hidden deep under the pillows and began a rosary, begging the Virgin for a son.

The distant clatter of footsteps in the stone corridor reached her ears. They neared, a mixture of armored footwear and leather boots. Claude was struggling to decide whether she should rouse her husband when he jerked awake.

"What? Oh, yes, you... Good morning, Wife." He leaned over and kissed her mouth.

How truly surprising! How lovely. Was this what married people did? Before she had more time to reflect, a sharp knock rattled their wooden door. She heard it creak open as they stared at each other.

"Cover yourself well, Wife." François grinned. "You have no time for more." Sitting, he pulled the sheet over his naked groin.

From the noise on the other side of their bed hangings, it sounded to Claude as if a delegation were shuffling into their room. Then a hand flung open the bed curtains and King Louis's face appeared. Claude shrank into the pillows and wished she could pull the sheet over her head.

Her father laughed. It sounded crude to her ears. "I see your blush, Daughter. All is well. I did not leave the room last night until I was certain this young man had done his duty." He clapped François on his naked shoulder. "I believe you pleased my daughter. I am proud of you, *Son*." He emphasized the last word for everyone to hear.

Claude glimpsed her husband's eyes narrow the way they did when he was making an abrupt decision — the kind of decision Maman Louise would call rash. Before she could say a word, François threw back the sheet and leaped from their marital bed displaying his splendid, naked body. A chorus of gasps and clapping covered the bawdy comments that rang out. François towered over his liege lord, his superb physique emphasizing the king's scrawny stoop.

He grabbed Louis's hand, dropping to one knee. "My liege, a boon."

King Louis, although at a disadvantage, did not lose his composure. "Ask. Then we shall consider."

"As stipulated in our marriage contract, I am Duke Consort de Bretagne, while Claude is Duchess in her own right. But you have retained management of the duchy since the death of your late wife."

Her father became rigid, always a bad sign. Why was François doing this? Several times during their short betrothal she had warned him it was unwise to press Louis. She knew her father well. When the time was right, she would talk to her father herself. He could be generous, but he was François's opposite. He would rather wear old clothes and invest in merchant ships than sport the latest fashions and owe his patrimony to money-lenders. This public confrontation would infuriate him. She clamped her eyes onto her new husband's bold, beloved face, trying to send him a frantic message. Her father would release the income from Brittany to them, but he needed time.

"Sire, perhaps you believe Claude is too young to rule alone. I am older and will rule with her. Naturally," François added, waving one naked arm grandly as if this resolved everything, "the rights to the Duchy will revert to her sister if the Lord fails to bless us with heirs. After you order the Estates and Parlement[1] de Bretagne to invest us, we shall immediately go to Brittany for a joint coronation." He remained on his knee.

Claude's eyes flew to her father's face. They had all signed their marriage contract only the day before. Did François believe her father would alter its terms after only one night? If he believed this bedding so precious that Papa would relinquish control of Brittany, he understood nothing of his uncle's frugality. She closed her eyes.

"Son, this is neither the moment nor the... apparel," Louis guffawed, though his eyes glittered as he raked them over his son-in-law's nakedness, stopping at François's shriveled pintle, "in which to present such a request. Since you have, my answer must be not at this time. We are pleased to greet you and leave you until you have attired yourself more... shall we say adequately. Good morrow to you both." He pulled his hand from the young man's and strode from the chamber.

His chattering entourage scrambled behind, voices rising and heads craning to gawk at the red-faced duke, who turned his pale buttocks to the crowd. His valet hurried to offer a brocade robe, blocking his master from prying eyes while Claude's two maidservants scurried into the bedchamber.

François glared at Claude, who huddled under the thin sheet. "You promised me that your father would give me Brittany! You said it was just a matter of our marriage. You lied to me!" He clenched his fists, his eyes slits. In a daze, Claude watched his chest heave, wondering what he would do, her wits numbed.

Screwing up his mouth, he spat at her. "You promise me just to hasten this marriage! You repellent, lying cripple! Do you think I would have married you one minute before I must, if not for Brittany? Scheming—!" He pinched his lips together, and then stormed from the room, fumbling with the belt at his waist. The duke's valet scrambled after him. Her maids backed away from the bed, carefully avoiding her eyes.

Claude was shocked mute, her ears ringing with his terrible words. Wiping her face with the sheet, she heard her own voice speaking as if it came from far away. "Leave me, please. I shall rest longer."

Tugging at the tester curtains, she tried to pull them closed and gave up. Rolling over, she pulled a pillow over her head, but could not block the echo of François's cruel words. Clutching her mother's rosary, biting her lips to smother her sobs, she hugged the pillow as if it were her only friend. She stayed there until her tears subsided.

Eventually she pushed away the pillow, struggled to a sitting position, wiped her eyes with the sheet, and sniffled. She was a married woman now, and so she must pull herself together. This was not a tragedy. Her husband had made an unreasonable request of his liege lord and blamed her when he was refused. Though he had wounded her with cruel words, he had not beaten her. In her mother's rooms growing up, she had heard married ladies whisper similar stories every week. Only, she had not thought to face it so soon. She was a royal princess. She would not shame herself by giving way or showing reddened eyes in public.

19 MAY 1514

CHÂTEAU DE BLOIS

aronne Michelle de Soubise

THE MORNING AFTER THE WEDDING, Duchess Claude's husband stormed off. Michelle was not privy to the cause of Duke François's flight, but she admired the duchess for her dignity in the face of this humiliation. Indeed, she acted as if his childish behavior was normal. Despite Duke François's abrupt departure, his sister, Marguerite, would not admit her brother's behavior was insulting. Within two days, she forsook them for her mother's court at Romorantin.

As the days went by, awkward silences fell more often whenever Duchess Claude entered a room. Still, she did not utter a word of criticism of her husband. But each day she rose later, ate more, and walked more slowly, signs to Michelle of the pain she held inside. She was becoming undeniably chubby, which was bad for both her health and her appearance.

Duchess Claude ignored the gossip and pitying glances for two weeks. Finally, on the last day of May, she announced her court would move to Blois. When she told Michelle, and that she and Renée would join her, Michelle said, "This is a decision that pleases all of us."

Still, it required two more weeks of Michelle's determined attention to bring smiles to Mme. Claude's face. They went riding each morning, played endless games of Fox and Geese with a chattering Renée, taught her the simplest moves in chess, and walked in the gardens. When Mme. Jeanne arrived from Romorantin without her stepmother, Michelle was truly grateful to greet her. The duchess needed her trusted gouvernante.

A few days later, Michelle found Mme. Jeanne ripping the heads off roses in the garden. Placing a comforting hand on her back, she said, "Mme. Jeanne, is there anything I can do to relieve your distress?"

The duchess's gouvernante hesitated. Michelle understood her reluctance. Although friendly, they had not been close before. Nonetheless, in the months since the queen died, they had come to rely on each other as they spent more time together. But Mme. Jeanne was furious and, as Michelle knew, had no other confident. Michelle led her to a secluded bench. There, Mme. Jeanne whispered the cruel words that Duke François had flung at her mistress. Michelle's heart ached for the duchess. Commiserating together over Francois's spiteful lie, they drew closer.

This sunny June morning, Mme. Jeanne stayed abed with a painful tooth. After their customary morning ride and early mass, Mme. Claude, Renée and Michelle descended as usual, with their entourages, to the gardens where summer flowers bloomed in pastel colors. Servants placed cushions for the ladies and demoiselles in the shade of the trees, their leaves the bright green of early summer. Instead of entertaining Princess Renée as they usually did, Mme. Michelle wanted to walk with Mme. Claude hoping to prod her to speak about the Duke.

Michelle and Queen Anne had nurtured a medicinal herb garden for years. Enclosed within a low border of yew, it was shaped like a large twelve-pointed star. Inside, flat stone paths separated each of the diamond-shaped beds that together formed a six-sided starburst made up of monkshood, nightshade, foxglove, hellebore, henbane, and castor oil plant with a central eye of poppies. Some were flowering; some were still in bud. It was a perfect spot for a stroll and a private conversation.

Michelle stretched like a cat. "Let's stroll in your mother's garden today. Otherwise I shall fall asleep."

As they moved away, Michelle heard Renée's voice raised in argument, and she gave a low chuckle. "Her stubbornness when I wish her obedience may annoy me, yet I recognize your mother in her when she pulls her eyebrows together and announces, 'I would not.'"

"She is more like our mother than I am. She has fire in her belly." Duchess Claude sounded wistful. "Perhaps Maman *should* have left Brittany to her. She would defend it as ferociously as Maman did. I do not have the same fighting spirit."

So she and Mme. Jeanne were right. Behind her brave front, Duchess Claude was despondent. Michelle said, "Sometimes second daughters are better as thistles than as roses. Since she is motherless, I believe Princess Renée is fortunate in her prickly disposition." As a princess, she was a pawn in the game of marriage alliances and would need all her obstinacy and pluck not to be crushed as she grew. "Yet I am certain François prefers sweet violets like you as a wife. He left in a tantrum, but he will return and appreciate you."

Claude would not be drawn. She sighed. "I've spent so little time in Brittany. Papa would not let me travel there with Maman unless he went too. We went only once and no further than Nantes. Maman was proud of how handsome it was. It was nicer than Paris, full of bustle and new buildings and a busy port. She showed me the university my grandpapa founded. It had his statues everywhere. But what I remember most is how people thronged around Maman." Her voice held a mixture of awe and envy. "They cheered and crowded around her wherever we went, trying to touch her. The way they treated her made me understand why she was so stubborn about Brittany. She insisted it was our duty to protect their ancient rights, for they had always defended us, the Montfort."

As they strolled, Claude constantly squeezed the fingers of one hand with the other. It was the only outward sign of her inner turmoil. "But Papa says my Bretons will be safer, and their rights better protected as part of France. Now that François and I are married, one of our sons will become Duke de Bretagne, *si Dieu le veut*. Then Brittany will become an appanage[1] of the French crown. Maman would be so angry. Yet, the Bretons who come to court from the Estates and the Parlement agree with him. I do not know what to think or who to believe. And François bedevils me to obtain the rights to administer my duchy from Papa." Tears formed in her eyes. She wiped them away with the back of her hand. "I do not know how he expects me to do that! You know I wrote to the Breton Chancellor asking him to support my request, and I asked Papa again just before we married, but François must wait."

"Are you sad or angry?" Michelle risked asking. Interrupting Claude might end her confidences.

Duchess Claude gave an odd little sound somewhere between a snort and a growl. "Both. And at both of them." She covered her face with her hands. "And guilty, and ashamed for feeling so angry with them. I am only a girl, after all, and they are men."

Michelle pursed her lips. This was the reason Queen Anne — Duchess Anne — had doubted her daughter's ability to hold Brittany. "In Brittany, women have a right to inherit if there are no male heirs. Your mother was the legitimate heir — as King Louis knew. He accepted her right to rule her duchy herself. You are of age and the legitimate duchess. You should have your full rights!" Michelle did not raise her voice, though she spoke emphatically. Duchess Claude had every right to be angry with both her father and her husband, for they were depriving her of justice. Yet Michelle did not advise the duchess to confront her father. She must conclude that herself. He would be as yielding as a down pillow compared to her mother-in-law once Duchess Claude had wrested control from him. And Countess Louise was a challenge that would intimidate even the most spirited young woman.

That thought led Michelle to her growing fear. Mme. Louise was trying to detach Princess Renée from her, despite the countess's promise to retain her as the princess's gouvernante. She said so to the duchess.

Duchess Claude twisted the gold and pearl chain of her mother's crucifix, a sure sign she was perturbed. "I wish Maman had not named Countess Louise as our guardian. Now that I am married she has no power over my estates. But if anything happens to Papa, Renée will be her ward and she will become administrator of her estates." Duchess Claude looked frightened. "Renée is entitled to half of Maman's Breton properties.

While Papa or I manage my duchy, we can guard her portion. But Maman Louise will make François pressure me to entrust it to them. And then she can do as she wishes. Yet I am afraid to resist her. Maman will be disappointed in me. But she left Maman Louise as guardian!"

When Duchess Claude spoke again, she sounded frustrated. "She should not have left her estate as she did. She should have left Renée as your ward."

Michelle had pondered the problem of Queen Anne's will many times. Although she too disagreed with its provisions, she wanted to comfort Anne's daughter. "She could not leave Renée as my ward, for I am not a blood relative. Perhaps she meant what she said. It was as restitution for her sins."

Duchess Claude raised her eyebrows. If the pious duchess found the explanation implausible, Michelle thought she was right to disbelieve it, too. She still hesitated. Words were potent. Once they had been spoken, they could never be unsaid.

"Do you fear she will take more than a fair guardian's share of Princess Renée's estate? Or rather that she will administer it to benefit her favorites rather than loyal Bretons as she should?"

Duchess Claude took her time before replying. "I should not say this, but I have no one else. I cannot even talk to Mme. Jeanne because Maman Louise is her stepmother. One of my maids came to me very upset in St. Germain. She said that when Maman Louise was ordering the packing of my rooms, she had many of my paintings, books and tapestries addressed to Romorantin. I said nothing to Duke François for he is very attached to his mother." She nibbled on her thumbnail. "If she had asked, I would have lent her the pieces. But..." Her voice trailed off.

❄

LOUISE OFFERED her cheek to her son. François kissed it without enthusiasm. Ignoring his sulks, Louise examined his flamboyant outfit. He wore a doublet of gold and black with excessively slashed sleeves and matching breeches fitted with an enormous codpiece. It suited his tall, athletic figure, and dashing, dark looks.

"Handsome outfit."

"This shabby thing? *Merci.*" After a long moment, he winked.

She hid the relief she felt at his reappearance. Doubtful about her welcome at Blois, Louise had moved to the apartments King Louis still provided for her family at the Château d'Amboise, for she had calculated that François was most likely to return there after he tired of his wanderings. She had been correct. How well she understood her son. It had been almost two months since he had slipped away from St. Germain-en-Laye without a word, shaming his new wife and infuriating the king.

Louise was furious, too, for he should have been charming his new wife into providing the dowry for his stepsister, which had been the reason for his hasty wedding. The delay was causing her embarrassment, and possibly the de Gaillard family would repent of the alliance. Seizing his hands, she led him to her favorite brocade-covered bench and sat beside him.

"My dear César. You are a picture of health! It has been much too long. Where have you been?" She kept her voice sweet with a hint of laughter in it.

"Here and there, Maman. I went to Alençon to hunt for a few weeks, visited my uncle in Lorraine—who sends his regards— and stayed with friends in Boisy." He thrust out his chin. "Then I traveled through eastern France, reconnoitering the countryside, visiting family and fostering alliances." He tried to pull his hands from hers. "Let me go, Maman, I am thirsty. Do you order up some wine?"

"My man will bring it, dear boy." As the gentleman usher obeyed, she lowered her voice. "Now tell me why you vanished after your wedding, leaving your poor little wife alone. I could not get a coherent story even from Marguerite, who came running to Romorantin to tell me you had enraged the king. It has taken all my charm to calm him."

François flushed. At that moment, the gentleman usher reappeared with a tray bearing a jug of wine, a plate of biscuits and two goblets. François rose, took the jug of wine, grabbed a goblet, filled it, and then quaffed the contents. As Louise dismissed the young servitor, her son went and stood, legs apart, with his back to the unlit fireplace. He refilled the goblet, swallowed its contents, and filled it once again.

Finally, he met her eyes. "I imagine you are somewhat irritated." He gave her a rueful grin, cocking his head. "Do you really want to hear what happened that morning?"

"I admit to a certain curiosity." She did not return his smile, though she found it hard. He was aware of his power over her heart, but she could be stern when necessary — as she was now. His dandified outfit proved he had once again been wasting money he did not have. Besides, she had some important information to impart, if he had not heard it already gallivanting around France. She waited him out.

"I admit I lost my temper that morning. Thing was, Claude had promised me the old man would make me true Duke de Bretagne, not just duke consort. When he came prancing in and chortled about us making bed sport and called me 'son,' I had the notion—I know, I know, these notions of mine—that it was the perfect moment to put it to him. I flung myself out of bed and said, 'Make me Duke de Bretagne now, Sire.'"

She shook her head. Not a wise approach — as she could have warned him.

"I reckon he took it ill to see me vigorous and young when he was skinny and old. What must he do but humiliate me — before his whole cursed, heretic-loving court!" His eyes rolled skyward, as if reliving the scene and he curled his fists.

"What did you do?" Her voice seemed to jolt him.

He took his time to answer, shuffling his feet. Avoiding her eyes, he said, "I did something ungentlemanly. Understand, Maman, I was boiling mad, Picture me stark naked, the room full of tittering courtiers. On the bed, my homely wife — his daughter — pitying me. And she had promised!"

An awkward silence fell between them. Louise did not help him. He must confess himself. He dropped his head and slouched. The silence lengthened. Louise allowed it to drag on. There would come a moment when he could endure it no longer.

"I raged at her, Maman," he whispered. "I called her an ugly little cripple. Said I had only married her because I was forced to." His face blotched a nasty, mottled red.

He feels thoroughly abashed, Louise thought, as he should. No woman would ever forget such insults, especially a homely little cripple like Claude. "Well, it was poorly done, son, for she is a good girl. That you were enraged is no excuse. I brought you up better than that. Fleeing like a little boy was worse. I cannot condone your behavior. I doubt King Louis will forgive you for humiliating his daughter, though I did my best to excuse you to him. And what about your duty to your stepsister? You seem to have forgotten that to marry the comptroller general's brother-in-law, she needs her dowry... and soon!"

He closed his eyes and sank onto a hard stool like a log collapsing to ash. Louise observed him in silence. It was painful to watch his suffering, but he must learn discretion. He would soon be king.

After a time, she took pity on him. "I do have some good news. Your wife was completely loyal. Not once did she complain of your behavior or repeat a word you said. Neither have I heard a peep from your servants or hers."

His eyes widened in relief.

She was irritated. "Did you not even verify they had maintained their silence? Have you not rewarded their judgment? That is beyond careless. It is culpably foolish. In future you must do better. Why else do you employ a confidential secretary and personal couriers? Nonetheless, you are correct to be astonished. It is quite a feat to keep secret such a juicy piece of gossip. Your wife is a jewel. You do not deserve her. She has protected your good name as much as possible. What should be your next step?"

"Return to her and beg her forgiveness? Explain I lost my temper and say I did not mean a word of it?"

"Yes. Make sure she believes you. Baronne Michelle has used your absence to ingratiate herself — and she is no friend to us. You had best make yourself charming to her also — and continue doing so." At his enormous sigh of relief, she shook her head. By Our Lady, the boy was much too sanguine. As if with this confession, all was now well. She smiled grimly. Her next piece of news would shake his composure. "Did you hear news of France's alliance with England while you were gadding about?"

He was leaning back now, relaxed, one leg bent at the knee and resting across the other. "Word is that the King of Spain and Emperor Maximillian have formed a new alliance. Why does not King Louis prepare for war? He is too old and weak to be king." Eyes flashing, he launched into his favorite complaint.

"Do not you wonder why our warrior king has become suddenly pacific?"

Her question caught him off guard and silenced him. Then he said, "You know something. Do you want me to beg?" He dropped to one knee, lifted her hand and held it to his lips. "Tell me, beautiful, intelligent, charming, Maman."

She kept him on tenterhooks a few moments longer. "I have learned that the king is negotiating a peace treaty with England. And... it includes a marriage contract."

"No! Between whom?"

"It is a well-kept secret. But I believe one party is King Louis himself."

Color drained from François's face as their eyes met. "That could be disastrous," he said.

"It could. Now do you understand why you must go at once to Blois and court your wife?

CLAUDE RETURNED from early mass to find her Grand Treasurer, Sieur Jacques de Beaune, waiting in her private cabinet. Although she had invited him, she fidgeted around the crowded room to gather her thoughts before sinking into the seat behind her oak desk.

"I feel somewhat awkward, Sieur Jacques." She was still learning the complexities of administering her estate. It would be best to admit it to the financial genius who had years of legal experience behind him. "I must find 50,000 livres to settle as a dowry on Mlle. Souvereine d'Angoulême. You remember she is Duke François's half-sister? Yes, of course you do. His family has arranged her an advantageous marriage — with Sieur Michel III de Gaillard, Seigneur de Chilly no less — so naturally she requires a substantial dowry. Which of my estates is the best able to... to make the sum available?"

The Sieur de Beaune regarded her sternly. "Madame Duchess," he said, his prominent Adam's apple bobbing, "In these cases, it is usual that the funds come from the lady's family estates. Should not the duchies of Angoulême or Valois supply the dowry?" He ran a hand through his thin gray hair.

"You know that the estates of the d'Angoulême family are heavily encumbered. The de Saint Gelais family, whom the countess favors, have administered them since the duke's youth. They have benefitted more from the relationship than, perhaps, they should have. Besides, the estate has already provided dowries for two of the count's illegitimate daughters as well as that of Duchess Marguerite. What estate can afford that, no matter how wealthy? As theirs is not. Mlle. Souvereine d'Angoulême has waited patiently for a suitable marriage. This is an excellent opportunity for her." Claude felt a needle of anger. "Besides, is it not my estate? May I not dispose of it as I choose? Maman provided dowries to those in need. I wish to do the same."

Sieur Jacques lowered his head. She accepted it as acquiescence. "You may dispose of your estates as you wish, or will be able to when you are eighteen, as specified in your mother's will.

However, your mother dowered girls of good family." Claude understood. He did not include bastards in that category.

"Could there be a better family than the king of France?" Claude did not try to restrain a slight snippiness. Different standards applied to the king's bastards. Souvereine was not a king's daughter, but she would almost certainly become the sister of a king. The thought saddened Claude, but she faced it stoically. She could see how much her father had aged in the few months since her maman had died.

Sensitive to future benefits, the Seigneur de Chilly had agreed to the marriage despite the stain on Souvereine's bloodline, but only if she came with a substantial dowry and the unspoken promise of a place at court 'when the time came.'

"As you say, Duchess." When de Beaune still hesitated, she realized he had more advice to offer.

"Tell me, Sieur Jacques."

"The Seigneur de Chilly is brother-in-law to M. Robertet. We both know that is the reason your mother-in-law pursues this alliance. Mme. d'Angoulême will be able to ensure the latter retains his office as Secretary of Finances when your husband becomes—" He coughed and did not finish. "M. de Chilly would wait for the funds or take a note against the d'Angoulême estate. There is no need to encumber yours."

Claude chose not to argue. "Nonetheless. This must be done. I am not disposing of lands; nor am I granting rights of disposition. I wish simply to reassign the proceeds in favor of the Sieur de Gaillard and Mlle. d'Angoulême and the heirs of their bodies. In default of heirs, the proceeds of the estate will revert to me. That is acceptable, I believe."

He bowed. "You learn quickly. I will examine the registry and recommend the least damaging estate to alienate under these conditions. I felicitate you on your wise solution for the dowry. Is there anything else I can do for you today, Duchess?"

She shook her head, and he rose. Bowing, he said, "It is always an honor to serve you and, when you wish advice, a pleasure to provide it."

Claude watched him leave. He thrust his chest forward and walked like an ostrich. She had a fellow feeling for anyone whose deformity caused them to waddle. Her heart warmed to his loyalty, even if he was overbearing at times.

She wondered how François would respond to the agreement she had arranged. In two years, she could assign the lands themselves, but for the moment she could not alienate lands without Papa's consent. She doubted François would want her to petition her father and King Louis would, for a certainty, refuse. Besides, her Grand Treasurer was correct, François should have used funds from his own estates rather than encumbering hers, so he should not complain at her methods. It was not really François's way to worry about acquiring debt. Had it been his mother who had insisted they fund the dowry from *her* estates?

Claude told him what she had done as they walked to his mother's apartments. He frowned but agreed he would intercede with his mother and persuade Seigneur de Chilly to accept it. He told Claude to let him tell his mother. She was relieved.

25 JULY 1514

LONDON

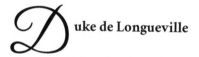

uke de Longueville

IN HIS PRISON suite in the Tower of London, the Duke de Longueville lounged in the window seat of the outer chamber. Bored, he was watching passers-by in the grassy inner court when a key rattled in the door and the French Ambassador to King Henry VIII's court stepped in. After sweeping a low bow, the duke trod across the carpet to greet him. He was always pleased to have company, especially of a compatriot. He took the ambassador's hands in his and pumped them with delight.

"My dear Ambassador, how charming of you to visit. What can I do for you? Do you have any news about the end of my insufferable incarceration on this inclement island? Have the terms of my ransom been arranged yet? Tell me it is so." He finally released the ambassador from his grip.

"Come, come, M. le Duke, you have not suffered terribly." The ambassador could not resist ribbing him a little, for the Duke was a man of remarkably good temper. "It is true you are housed here in the Tower of London. But this apartment is commodious, *non*? Was it not occupied by your noble ancestor, a previous Duke d'Orléans?"

The Duke—who had been imprisoned since the humiliating French defeat at Guinegate the year before—drew himself up straight as a halberd. "Ambassador, it is obvious you have never suffered the loss of freedom. It is true I enjoy the pleasures of charming company and luxurious surroundings. But I may not return to my beloved France. I am cut off from my family and friends, and I am under constant surveillance. It is not a noble way of life."

The ambassador looked suitably abashed. "Forgive me. Today, Duke, I bring a letter from your cousin, King Louis, who has concluded a treaty with King Henry. I will return in a day to receive your reply if that suits you."

The duke crossed himself. "The Lord be praised."

When he read the letter later, its content surprised him into a cynical chuckle. The king asked him—and he recognized the politely worded request as an order—to act as his proxy in King Louis's upcoming marriage to Princess Mary, King Henry's eighteen-year-old sister.

Louis to remarry? And he widowed a scant six months. To the most beautiful, nubile princess in the West! As de Longueville smirked, he grasped that the pressing need for an heir drove the king to this hasty remarriage. And although it was unstated, de

Longueville also understood that the king would secure his release and pay his ransom for this service.

Well-informed about the gossip of the English court, the duke shook his head dubiously. Princess Mary was beautiful and charming, but young. Reputedly delighted with her recent release from her betrothal to the Duke of Burgundy, rumor swirled that she was enamored of the king's low-born favorite, the Duke of Suffolk. Did King Louis know about the infatuation that was tarnishing her reputation? What kind of wife would she make for an old man?

He wondered, too, if the princess knew about Suffolk's notoriety. He was quite the social climber, using women to marry his way into wealth and aristocracy. The French ambassador had regaled de Longueville with the gossip about his wooing of the Regent of the Netherlands just a few months past. It was said he had compromised her sufficiently she would have to marry him.

Every treaty came with a price. As he calculated it, de Longueville dearly hoped that neither King Louis nor France would find the cost too high.

IN THE DOG days of August, Duchess Claude joined her father and husband in the courtyard of the Hôtel des Tournelles. Dressed in her formal regalia as reigning Duchess de Bretagne, she made her way to the waiting *chariot*, carefully avoiding the puddles from the recent storm. The vehicle would carry her and her father — robed in his blue velvet, ermine-collared cape — to the Parlement de Paris. She observed that her husband — handsome in his regalia as dauphin — looked sulky, as he so often did these days.

As the doors closed, the king said to his daughter, "Your mother was right. Your husband has much to learn before he will make an adequate king."

Duchess Claude chose not to irritate him by defending François. Papa was hiding something. He had told them only last evening they must attend the session of the Parlement today and refused to reveal anything about the purpose of the assembly. She speculated that it must be something unpleasant or upsetting and could not blame François for his irritation. Especially since it had taken ages the previous evening to organize their correct robes.

Heralds and the mounted Scots Guards[1] rode before them; mounted courtiers rode behind. The blast of horns and the ring of iron horseshoes on cobblestoned streets alerted the citizens of Paris that their king was making his way through the city. Always curious, people ran to line the narrow streets and hang from windows, slowing the procession to walking pace. Louis opened his shutter and pushed his head out. The stench hit the duchess like a solid wall, and the sting of ordure made her eyes water. She lifted the pomander ball that hung from her waist to her nose and inhaled its spicy aroma. Revived, she smiled and waved.

In the swaying royal *chariot*, the king rubbed his hands together gleefully. Since they were alone, she asked, "What will happen today, Papa?"

He glanced at her, hesitating. "The chancellor will make an important announcement at this morning's session."

"Do we have a role, Papa?" Duchess Claude clung to a leather wall strap to steady herself as the iron wheeled carriage rattled over the cobblestoned streets.

He cupped her cheek with his hand. "No, my dear. Just smile and nod as you do so well. You are our dearest blessing; the brightest jewel in our crown." He returned his attention to the crowds, touching hands and heads as he passed: his way, she knew, of avoiding further conversation.

The Parlement met in a low-ceilinged, dingy medieval chamber. Duchess Claude was last in the jostling procession behind her father and Duke François. Slowly, she made her way to the dais within the crowded space. A murmur like the buzz of insects on a summer day rose in the chamber as its members realized that there, sitting beside the chancellor, were the French ambassadors to the English court.

The chancellor waited while the heralds blew their trumpets. All eyes turned to him. At the king's nod, the chancellor spoke. "Today we announce a great success. With thanks to our great and noble king, Louis, twelfth of that name, Father of his Country, whose vision has brought renewed hope to his suffering people, and to the dedicated negotiating skills of our loyal ambassadors, the threat of war with England lies behind us."

The Parlement burst into cheers and applause. Clearing his throat, he shouted over the clamor. "In the name of King Louis, as Chancellor, I present to the Parlement of Paris for it to record, a treaty of perpetual peace between France and England." More cheers as the President of the Parlement came forward to receive the beribboned document. "To seal this treaty, upon its registration, a marriage shall take place, at the Église les Célestins in Paris, at a date to be announced, between the Princess Marie Rose, sister to the King of England, and our glorious King Louis."

The men of the Parlement rose as one body. The cheers, hoots, hollers and foot stamping lasted loud and long. Men slapped one another on the back, faces red, and foreheads sweaty.

Duchess Claude admitted, heart sinking, that it delighted them. The costly and dangerous war was over; trade with an important partner restored; the Channel reopened to shipping. And the king might beget an heir of his body. As a portrait of the future queen circulated, Claude recognized lust spring into men's eyes. She imagined she could read their thoughts: very fair, the young Princess Marie Rose; lucky Louis, perhaps a father again. Yes, splendid news for France!

The Herald King of Arms[2] blew another fanfare. Expectant silence fell. The Chancellor declared, "Further be it known that, the treaty being declared immediately in effect, the marriage of our beloved King, Louis XII, with the Princess Marie Rose of England will take place by proxy in England on a date approved by the Parliament of England, but no later than the end of October of this year of our Lord 1514."

Under lowered lashes, Duchess Claude glanced at Duke François, intercepting his glare. Stony-faced, she gave him a tiny shrug. Whether or not he believed her, she had been as uninformed as he about her father's secret. Probably her father had not wished to burden her conscience with keeping such an important secret from her husband.

Climbing the single step to his side, she kissed her papa on both cheeks. Under the hubbub in the room, she said, "I wish you every happiness, Papa. I know Maman begged you to marry again, so you but obey her command."

Her father put his lips to her ear. "I marry for duty, not pleasure. For a son. I miss your maman every moment of every day, Daughter." His voice was hardly more than a whisper.

Her eyes prickled. "I, also."

Their hands squeezed tight.

Louis stood, his arm around his daughter, and bowed in all directions. François stepped up to stand beside his father-in-law. The royal family stood united in appearance as the doors of the Parlement opened, heralds trumpeted the news from its steps, and cheers spread like waves in the streets and through the capital and across the kingdom. It did not make everyone who heard it happy.

IN HIS LUXURIOUS chambers in Greenwich Palace the Duke de Longueville, no longer a prisoner, sank into an armchair embroidered with the arms of France. Once the new Queen of France's retinue announced her departure from the wedding reception, he had left the dancing, as was his duty. He wished he could retire to the large canopied bed awaiting him, but he still had a duty to perform. No point putting it off. Calling his valet, he allowed himself to be stripped to his chemise and slipped into a fur-lined dressing robe and slippers. Then he sat at the oak desk while his man made up the fire. As his valet left, the Duke said, "Make sure there is a guard on the door and send a trustworthy messenger to take my letters to the ambassador's residence when I call."

Dating his letter, he began:

13 August 1514 in the 15th year of the reign of King Louis of France, Twelfth of that name.

Gracious Sire and Cousin,

Today I was honored to accomplish the task you set me. In the great hall of Greenwich Palace, in the presence of King Henry VIII and Queen Catherine, your Ambassador and the English court, in a ceremony conducted by Archbishop Wareham of Canterbury, you were married through my proxy to the gracious Princess Marie Rose Tudor.

I swore the required vows as did the princess, placed your ring — gold engraved with the lilies of France and Tudor roses — upon her finger, and the Archbishop gave the necessary blessings and proclaimed her your wife and Queen Marie of France. She makes a lovely queen.

It will please you that the Princess, your wife, declared herself bedazzled by the magnificence of your gifts: the outfitting of all members of the wedding party and the jewels for her as Queen of France. At the wedding banquet she professed herself most astonished that our clothing for the ceremony — mine as proxy for you as king and hers as bride — must match. The beholders were struck dumb with awe at the beauty of our new queen in the trailing gown you ordered of checkered royal purple and gold brocade, and they gasped at the kirtle of silver-gray satin sparkling with tiny diamonds with its matching shoes. Her ladies-in-waiting complemented her in their matching silver-gray satin gowns. Her hair, covered with your gift of a gold mesh cap, fell to her hips and glowed like a river of copper. It will please you that she wore the egg-sized diamond and pearl necklace you bestowed upon her, the so-named Mirror of Naples, and that she caressed this gift all day (Wherever I went, I overheard ladies oohing and aahing over its splendor).

My checkered purple and gold doublet and breeches, gold chemise, knitted purple silk hose and golden shoes compared magnificently with the attire of the English king and queen. [Please be apprised that I have returned them to the ambassador to be retained by the crown.]

The English, competitive as always, outdid themselves decorating the palace. The great hall was swathed in a cloth of gold, an arras of gold, and a frieze embroidered with the combined royal coats of arms of England and France. Flowers filled the hall, sweetening the air and the vista, while the music from King Henry's angel-voiced boys' choir floated over us from the balcony.

Before the commencement of the wedding banquet, the official bedding to confirm and legalize your wedding took place in the state audience chamber near the great hall. The state bed that is part of the new queen's dowry stood in the middle of the room, complete with her hangings, embroidered with her new royal arms that combine the French lily and English rose and her device, "La volonté de Dieu me suffit: The will of God suffices me." Let us hope she abides by it.

For the occasion I wore a doublet, red hose — one leg naked from below the knee — and red slippers. For discretion, I wore an elegant dressing robe over my outfit. When I entered, leading the dozens of required witnesses, I found Queen Marie sitting upright against the pillowed headboard. The ceremony had been arranged around the consideration of her great modesty.

When I stood at your bride's side and turned towards the guests in the room, the valet removed my dressing gown. Her maid lifted a discreet panel in her gown and rolled down her stocking. I lifted my naked leg, and kneeled so my leg rested beside hers, barely touching it. Then the maid covered both our legs with her gown's specially designed panel. Archbishop Wareham stood in front of us, blocking us from general view and blessed us at speed.

My chamberlain presented us each a glass of wine, and we remained thus, a few inches of hidden naked flesh touching discreetly, holding our goblets, while witnesses filed past and we received their congratulations.

At the ceremony's end, I removed my leg, donned my dressing robe once more, toasted the queen and bowed. 'Marie, Grâce à Dieu, Reine de France, King Louis deems himself most fortunate to marry the most beautiful princess in England, who will be the most beautiful woman in France. I envy him his good fortune. He has given me the delightful task of presenting the gifts to adorn his esteemed bride at your gracious convenience.'

The French ambassador organized and funded the banquet and the great dance that followed in the banquet hall of the palace. Chefs brought over from France, who had been working upon the dishes for the past week, produced the feast. The décor was equal to the magnificence provided by the English in the great hall. Thus, the honor of France was maintained.

I cannot say there is enthusiasm at the English court for the French alliance, although we have some supporters, among them the Chancellor, Archbishop Wolsey. However, he keeps his views hidden. I remain, Sire, yours to command. May God keep you in His holy care.

Louis d'Orléans

Duke de Longueville

For a time after completing this letter, he mused on the things he dared not write the king. He was not alone in his surprise that King Louis had remarried so soon. Still, duty was the lot of kings, and this treaty needed sealing with a royal marriage. He trimmed the candle, picked up the quill and addressed a second letter.

Ambassador,

This is for your eyes only. What I am about to tell you I have learned from a confidant within the English court. Among her intimates, it is well known that Queen Marie is enamored of Duke Charles Brandon and wished to have married him. When she learned she was to marry our king she is reported to have said, "What a miserable fate. To be forced to marry the sickly old King of France, who is whispered to be miserly and incapable, and sent to live overseas when my whole desire is to remain in England. And after I had escaped marriage to the Duke of Burgundy. But at least he was young — and potent." Her attitude towards me has been markedly cooler than it had been when she believed me incarcerated here for some time to come.

Since my release from the Tower we have spoken French, unlike our previous encounters, which were all conducted in her tongue. She appeared enchanted with the jewelry and admired it abundantly when we spoke during the wedding banquet; she does not seem aware that it forms part of her dowry. I suggest that more of the same will soften her attitude toward her marriage.

Other tidbits I picked up may be of interest. I heard someone in the retinue of Queen Catherine say that the moneys we spent might better have been laid out supporting our cavalry at Guinegate, so we have challenged their prickly English pride with our lavish wedding display. Also, the rapprochement between France and England displeases the Spanish. Archbishop Wolsey is on the rise; he was to be seen everywhere, fussing over details and sending servants off with orders.

The accompanying chest contains the clothing belonging to the Crown lent to me for the wedding and bedding ceremonies. I am returning it to you along with a request for a receipt indicating I have duly restored them to your care.

Please accept my thanks for your assistance in arranging my release. Are you informed of the date of my return to France? Farewell and may God keep you in His holy care.

Louis d'Orléans

Duke de Longueville

AT FIRST LIGHT the morning of the 14th September, the mile-long baggage train with its iron-wheeled cook wagons, commissary, tents, chests of clothing, chancery materials — everything necessary for the French court to function on the move — headed north out of Paris, creaking and clanking over the city's cobblestones and dirt streets.

A few hours later, on that sunny September day, the king married Princess Marie Tudor by proxy in the Église les

Célestins, the Orléans family church. As the guests emerged onto the church steps, the Duke de Longueville moved aside to permit the English Earl, who had stood proxy for Queen Marie, to take his leave with the rest of the English contingent.

Upon his return to court after his almost two-year absence, de Longueville had been shocked when he first saw King Louis. When they had last met, the king had been lean but spry, and full of his normal good humor. Queen Anne's death had aged him; now his spine curved; he leaned on a stick to shuffle along; and the lines on his thin face were as deep as crevices. He could not imagine that King Louis would measure up to the needs of his sprightly young bride. Could he even mount her to do his duty? Any red-blooded man would be delighted to give it a go. But what effect would the marriage have on the king?

Masking his lascivious thoughts, de Longueville bowed gracefully to the king.

"You've been most helpful, de Longueville. I will not say your incarceration was fortunate, but you served us well as a result."

De Longueville bowed. "I will not say I would be happy to do it again," his lips curled, "but I am pleased to have been of service. Your bride is both charming and exquisite — and her comportment is royal."

King Louis rubbed his hands together. "I did well to postpone my annual progress. I can combine the two trips since I have a duty to meet my new queen."

"Sire, you are a lucky dog who cannot wait to claim your prize." De Longueville gave him a nudge. "Never forget, I have ridden under your command. I well know your dislike of court protocol and your preference for country air."

The King and de Longueville mounted up and joined the courtiers traveling with them to meet Queen Marie. As one of the king's favorites and a close cousin, de Longueville rode beside the king.

King Louis said, "This is a perfect opportunity to travel through the north-east. I have not been up here since the troubles, and it is time to see how it is faring. You came back that way. How much damage has been repaired since the English and Imperial raids ended?"

"It begins, Sire, but slowly. Still, everywhere I stayed there was much enthusiasm for your great joust. Several times I was present when your heralds arrived announcing, 'a great tournament in honor of our gracious Queen Marie, to be held in Paris in November under the sign of Sagittarius, for it be the sign for battling and fighting and making friends among enemies.' All the younger knights vied amongst themselves for permission from their overlords to attend and challenged one another to prove they were the worthiest."

The king grinned. "I told my Grand Maître de Menu Plaisirs[3] to ensure it was bruited far and wide that there would be rich prizes allotted each day. The English cannot say I was too frugal." He sighed. "I may only watch though. Not only would it be the height of poor manners to compete, but I've accepted that I'm no longer capable of winning."

"After two years playing cards and chess, never allowed more than a gentle amble with the ladies in the woods when they went picnicking, I am in no shape to offer a challenge myself," the Duke replied, adding gallantly, "But you, Sire, should not disparage your skills."

King Louis punched his arm. "Do not lie to me, Cousin. I cannot abide flattery. You've been too long away if you've forgotten that." Staring straight ahead, he said, "There are few who give me a blunt answer these days. Tell me, does this young English king, Henry, like to be flattered? And what about his sister?"

Chastened de Longueville apologized. He was reluctant to talk frankly about Queen Marie, but the king's sharp rebuke warned him against courtly deceits. He took his time. "She is young, Sire, beautiful and accomplished — and is praised for her liveliness and charm. But she was her father's favorite all his life and expects such treatment... and makes her displeasure known if she feels slighted. She is a skillful horsewoman, appears healthy and she will be an elegant queen. We pray she provides France with an heir." As he gave his careful answer, he hoped the king could read into his message what he had not said. Queen Marie would want to outshine everyone in her new role. Not much more than a child herself, de Longueville doubted she would embrace her role as stepmother to young Princess Renée. Nor did he think she would befriend Duchess Claude, for Claude was only two years her junior, and neither pretty nor lively. She was unlikely to make friends among the older women of the French court; Most of all, he wondered how she and Countess Louise would manage.

King Louis nodded. "What more can I hope for? It's an arranged marriage. A son would be a great blessing."

As the days went by, the long journey on horseback with its constant jarring inflamed the king's joints and exacerbated his backache, and he became increasingly cantankerous. Yet he hurried himself and his cavalcade to jog along as if an enemy lay ahead that he must ambush. Finally, de Longueville told him bluntly that he would make a poor impression on his lively new queen if he could do no more than hobble and groan. He would do himself and everyone a favor if he took better care of himself. Chastened, Louis called for a rest until his pain had subsided, agreed to use a litter, take the baronne's pain preparations, and travel like a king rather than a military leader with a mission.

As they approached Abbeville where the French and English courts would meet, King Louis asked the duke, "What do you think Queen Marie will make of her new court?"

"Well, your court is more refined than the English court. Theirs is very young. They are always playing games, or dancing, or singing, or hunting. Or betting on cards, or competing at tennis, or bowls. Active, very active. Very competitive."

"Yes, you said she was lively. She will want entertainment, yes?"

"Their courtiers are much given to dalliance."

King Louis punched him lightly on the shoulder. "You old dog. We heard about your 'dalliance,' as you call it. I did not want your mistress among my wife's ladies. My queen's household must be above reproach, as was Queen Anne's."

De Longueville did not besmirch Queen Marie's name, despite his suspicions. Perhaps her heart belonged to another, but he was certain she had not been so foolish as to risk her chastity. Besides, she had been examined before she left England and he had heard no whisper of irregularities. "Queen Marie will behave as you wish, I doubt not. And I would not like my wife inconvenienced, Sire."

Ahead, the heralds sounded a fanfare. A captain of the guard galloped up and reared his horse to a halt. "Majesty, we near the gates of Abbeville. I sent a messenger ahead to announce your imminent arrival."

"Form us up, Captain. We may be at peace, but the emperor and his daughter, the regent, are displeased about this treaty and marriage… and Flanders is on the other side of the river."

De Longueville squinted to the east, checking for movement. He was also Vicomte d'Abbeville and proud of the prosperous town and surrounding area, his at present, although it had a long history as a prize of war. Most of the walled, modern town — built of red brick with stone-paved, sweet-smelling streets flushed regularly with water — was set on an island connected by high bridges to the French side of the river.

He surveyed the horizon. "We keep our territory well fortified. The Somme is at its lowest here. Excellent battlefield territory. Especially since it joins the English Channel downriver. But all is quiet since your treaties."

De Longueville lodged the king's court at his château within the town. When Queen Marie arrived with her English ladies and gentlemen, they would stay their first night outside the gates. Once she and the king married — and the king was eager — she would go to the king. De Longueville would be glad to have it over.

DUCHESS CLAUDE RODE with her husband on one side of her. Her sister, riding pillion[4] behind her groom, trotted on the other. The duchess wore an elegant riding outfit of royal-blue brocade that set her lovely skin and fair complexion off to advantage. She looked her best as she urged her palfrey forward, pleased she would meet the new queen on horseback. They streamed across the flat French countryside, their steeds gleaming in the fall sunshine.

Queen Marie's chamberlain had sent a message announcing her arrival that morning. At once, the dazzling procession to greet the English prepared itself to ride out as smoothly as the gears that operated the windmills peppering the countryside. In the distance Claude saw the richly accoutered English cavalcade approach, the banner of Queen Marie waving over it in the steady breeze that blew off the coast. A horn sounded. King Louis leading, their entourage formed up behind the French banner.

From her position in the front, Claude observed her father with jealous eyes as the two parties merged. She watched the new queen blow King Louis a kiss. Gallantly, her father reached out, caught her kiss, pressed it first to his lips, and then to his heart. King Louis cantered up beside Queen Marie and pulled his horse to a halt. He wore a red-trimmed cloth-of-gold doublet with crimson hose, shades that exactly matched hers. It was cut from the same bolts of fabric that he had sent to England.

"Dearest wife," the king lifted Queen Marie's hand to his lips, "you have captured my heart. I knew you would."

With her other hand, Queen Marie took the gold locket she wore and raised it to her lips. Claude presumed it contained his miniature, for she said, "You have been next to my heart since the moment we married, beloved husband. To be with you in person has been my dearest desire, and the manner of it has exceeded my greatest expectations." She dropped her hand to her heart.

Even though she knew the greetings were purely ceremonial, Claude could barely conceal the hurt she felt at the fatuous expression on her father's face. King Louis signaled Claude, Renée and François to come forward.

"Let me present those closest to my heart, for they are your new family. My daughter, Claude, and son-in-law, François, Duchess and Duke de Bretagne, Angoulême, Valois and Milan, and heir to the throne of France — until we have a son of our own." He patted Claude's hand. She knew her father did not see her as chubby and plain. His obvious pride in her salved some of the sting, and she greeted her new stepmother with a sweet smile, offering her hands.

Performing her role as principal hostess with regal grace, she said, "You are most welcome to your country, Queen Marie, good wife to my dear Papa. I wish you a long and happy marriage." Claude's low musical voice, her warmth and gracious manners masked her pain. Her mother was being replaced too soon.

Marie replied with becoming enthusiasm. Today, as French tradition required, her gown, styled in the French fashion, matched the king's colors. Although not the best color for her fair skin and Tudor red hair, nothing could detract from her youth and fresh beauty.

Impatiently, Duke François crowded his horse forward, pushed his wife aside and grasped Queen Marie's hands. Her horse sidled as he leaned out to kiss her cheeks. "I welcome you as my mother-in-law in the French fashion, with hearty delight." He caracoled his horse backwards a few steps, showing off his horsemanship.

Marie pulled her mare under control, flushed, and wiped her cheek with the back of her glove, saying, "I was not aware one greeted one's mother-in-law with such enthusiasm. I hope I do not have many sons-in-law."

Claude reddened, mortified by her husband's brash behavior. Her discomfort increased when her father barked, "No more nonsense, Duke François. Move aside." He motioned his younger daughter's mount forward. "Dear wife, it is my pleasure to present my younger daughter, Princess Renée. She is already becoming an accomplished horsewoman and resented my insistence she ride behind her groom today."

Queen Marie offered her hands to Princess Renée. "I was much the same myself. We shall ride together, for riding is my great pleasure."

Glowering at her Papa, Renée said in a rehearsed singsong, "Welcome to France, Mme. la Reine Marie; it is an honor to greet you in your new home." She released the gloved hands she had been offered and added, "I'm glad you told Duke François not to kiss you. He does it to all pretty ladies, and it is not nice for my sister."

Her remark surprised a laugh from the queen and king. King Louis said. "Like her late mother, she speaks her mind. She is in the right of it, so I shall not reprimand her."

Shrinking inside with embarrassment, Claude wished she could sink through the ground and disappear. To cover the awkward moment, she said, "So you are a keen horsewoman?"

Queen Marie said, "I am a passionate rider, so it delights me I share this pleasure with my new family. It enchants me that we meet engaged in our favorite pastime."

After a few more minutes of courtesies, King Louis announced their departure as custom required. Ordering the French contingent to turn, he urged her party to hasten to Abbeville where they would meet that evening. Their wedding would take place that very night, he told Marie, with a great feast to celebrate it. He lifted Queen Marie's hand. "For now we have met, my love cannot be contained."

Blind to her surroundings, Claude rode in silence, prey to foreboding. Already her father was infatuated with his beautiful bride. No doubt the new queen would be an adornment and her manners were polished, but Claude foresaw trouble, and not only with her own husband.

16 OCTOBER 1514

CHÂTEAU DE PONTHIEU

$\mathcal{B}$aronne Michelle de Soubise

MICHELLE'S HORSE trotted beside Duchess Claude's, close to the front of the party. Both rode side saddle. Beside them Princess Renée rode pillion behind her groom. They made their way towards the château, the early morning sun slowly burning away the mists until only wisps hung over the rivers and streams.

Ahead of them, King Louis leaned close to Queen Marie, who looked charming in a royal-blue and crimson habit with matching royal-blue boots.

Duchess Claude brooded. "My father is besotted. I have not seen him outside her company since they married."

Michelle answered, "You may not have noticed, but he has been outside her company, for this morning he ordered the Duke of Norfolk to return most of her people to England while we are away today."

Duchess Claude stared at her, eyes hopeful. "Nay, say you not so? Who is leaving?"

"Her principal lady, Dame Joan Guildford, for one. Her chaplain for another. All her ladies who cannot speak French. Only one or two will remain."

"'Zounds!" Duchess Claude raised her eyebrows. "They say the new queen has a temper. I doubt she will swallow that dish easily."

She did not ask where Michelle had learned this tidbit. That Duchess Claude had used a mild profanity, and that she had repeated gossip, indicated her shock.

Before Michelle could reply, Princess Renée piped up, "Sister, you should not use bad words. Mme. Michelle, why do you not reprimand her for saying a bad word?"

"You are correct, Mme. Princess. She should not, even when surprised. Although you, Princess, are impertinent to reprove anyone older than yourself and shall do a penance for your rudeness. However, perhaps she was praying. Were you praying, Duchess Claude?" Their eyes focused on the duchess, whose cheeks stained pink.

"Dear sister, you are correct. I shall say ten Hail Mary's as a penance. Do you think that is sufficient? I also ask Mme. Michelle to absolve you of your penance." The duchess restrained her chuckles.

Princess Renée examined her expression. "It is sufficient — if you are sorry. I have been listening, and I am not sorry that

Papa's new wife is losing her servants… except I was planning to learn English from them. Perhaps I should do a penance, too." She leaned against her groom and turned her head. "Mme. Michelle, will you find me an English tutor? It is a good thing to speak many languages."

"If you wish, yes. Tell us why you are not sorry her servants are being sent home?" It fascinated her gouvernante to learn what went on in the princess's reserved, intelligent young head.

She did not answer immediately. Finally, she said, "Tell you later. Maybe."

Michelle changed the subject and Duchess Claude, ever sensitive, followed her lead.

After her sister fell asleep, Duchess Claude returned to the departure of Queen Marie's retinue as if it were a canker she could not resist probing with her tongue. "Where did you hear that tidbit about the queen's people?"

"I overheard your mother-in-law telling Duke François as we gathered to saddle up in the courtyard. She was amused. Apparently, Lady Joan confided in her this morning, and asked Mme. Louise to pass the message to Queen Marie as soon as she could. Mme. Louise said she had promised… but she would find it possible only on the return trip."

"What did François answer?"

"He laughed and said it would be better if the queen had fewer of her people here. I moved away and heard no more."

A frown settled between Duchess Claude's eyebrows. "He will find it easier to approach her when she's surrounded by fewer English women, that is why. Especially Dame Joan. That one is a tartar." She sighed. "Well, perhaps better he flirts with my new stepmother than with my ladies-in-waiting. He cannot flatter the queen into…" Her voice trailed off.

"Dear Duchess Claude." Michelle reached across the space between their horses and took her hand. "He respects you. The rest are for bedding at most. Do not let them fret you. Only your children will inherit the throne."

The duchess raised her large blue eyes, bright with unshed tears, to Michelle's. "That is the path of wisdom, Mme. Michelle, not the way of the heart. It hurts to witness him being molded by others who do not appreciate his finer qualities."

Michelle burned with anger towards François and all amorous men of his ilk. "I pray every day he will recognize you, as we do, for the treasure you are."

As the women settled into the garden at the château, Michelle encouraged Renée to run off to explore with the younger children. She came back tired and hungry and snuggled beside Michelle on her pillow, her head in Michelle's lap. Michelle thought she was dozing when she said in a small voice, "I am angry that Papa married her. I hope it makes her sad that her ladies are being sent away. I would be sad if *you* were. Should I do a penance for that?"

Michelle hugged her without making it obvious. *Grâce à Dieu,* she thought, she trusts me enough to admit her resentment. "Dearest Princess Renée, your feelings are normal," she whispered, cradling the child in her lap. "You love your maman. It's hard not to feel your papa has replaced her. Is that it?"

Her head bobbed.

"It's natural you resent his new wife." Michelle rocked her, holding her close, trying to decide the right thing to say. Finally, she blurted the words closest to her heart. "I loved your maman very much, too, and I find it painful to see another in her place. But it is not your papa's fault. The laws of France say only a son may inherit the throne, so he needs one. Queen Marie seems pleasant, and she treats you, me, your sister and your papa kindly. That is important. Do you understand better now?"

Princess Renée lay still without answering, and Michelle did not insist. She could take her time to understand or accept. Michelle thought she was asleep when she heard a muffled, "Yes," and a sniffle.

Michelle said, "It is hard for you and Mme. Claude and all of us who loved... love your maman." Princess Renée quivered. Michelle added, "I am sure your father finds it hard too."

"No! He does not." Princess Renée reared to her knees to peer across the gardens to the dusty fields where the king and queen watched the cavalry maneuvers from the cover of an open-fronted tent. "Look at him, laughing and chucking her chin. He is being foolish." Her voice shook.

Michelle took her by the shoulders and turned her away. "Look elsewhere, sweetheart. Take your maman's rosary and say a decade. Your anger harms only you, not her or him."

The princess lifted her mother's rosary, kissed it, and began to murmur a Hail Mary. Michelle hoped the prayer would bring her solace, but she wondered where this ill-matched marriage would lead.

WHEN THE HOUR for departure neared, Countess Louise kept close to Queen Marie. She sidled her horse near the royal party as Queen Marie mounted her lively chestnut for the return.

The countess drew up behind the king — within hearing distance, but out of his line of sight. How fortunate she was that she had been blessed with sharp hearing. Louis brought his horse alongside Queen Marie's and offered her something with a flourish.

He said, "Please accept this gift. It cannot compare to your beauty or your charming habit, but I hope it pleases you."

Queen Marie, who appeared as fresh as she had that morning, fumbled opened the box in her haste. She exclaimed, "Husband! What an exquisite broach. How the sapphires and rubies flash." She angled it this way and that to catch the sunlight.

Leaning close, the king took it from her and pinned it to her low collar. "Shall we set forward? It is a long ride back." He led the cavalcade with Marie at his side. Countess Louise slid her horse into a space behind them and heard him say, "I hope the trinket will serve as a peace offering," his tone conversational, "for I have taken an action I fear will annoy you. So I remind you of your device." He pointed to the device embroidered on her palfrey's caparison: *The Will of God Suffices Me.*

Countess Louise bit back a grin.

"Not that I claim to be God, only your husband," King Louis added.

Elevating her chin, Marie straightened her back, as tense as a hooded hawk. "Husband, please do not keep me in suspense."

"Before we left this morning, I requested the Duke of Norfolk to return to England all those in your entourage who did not speak French. I have arranged to have your ladies replaced with Frenchwomen. You speak French delightfully, so you need not be served by Englishwomen."

Would she lose her temper with him in front of the court? Louise admired the queen's training, for she remained mute as she kneed her horse to a canter. The king and Louise hesitated only a moment before spurring their horses to her speed. They rode in silence for several miles. When Queen Marie spoke again, her voice was frigid. "I am disappointed, my lord husband, that you did not choose to discuss your decision with me beforehand."

Louise shivered, but King Louis merely chucked Marie under the chin. "My sweet, I had no desire to confront you. That Lady Joan of yours annoyed me. Interfering busybody! Who was she to insist on being present when I wished to be private with you? I had no mind to put up with a stranger in our marriage. The Countess de Nevers shall be your principal lady. As for the others, you do not need women who speak only English with whom to chatter secrets. I have selected the highest ladies in France to honor your rooms and keep you company. Give me a kiss, darling, and fuss no more." He leaned across and kissed her lips.

The gentle countryside rang with birdsong as the sun sank. The birds, like their party, were heading homeward, squawking and chattering as they readied to settle for the night.

Near Abbeville, Queen Marie slowed to a trot. "Husband, much as I do not wish to trouble you, I must request your help with a problem only you can resolve." Her tone held a touch of acid. "I intended to discuss it with Mother Guildford without annoying you, but you are now my sole support."

If she thinks to shame Louis, she is quite wrong, Louise thought. He is an old woman and thrives on gossip.

"Tell me. Your slightest care pains me."

Louise could not see the queen's face. "This is so awkward..." Queen Marie paused. "It concerns your son-in-law."

Fear clutched at Louise's heart. God's teeth, what had he done?

"He approaches me too closely, kisses me too frequently, and holds me too tightly when we dance."

A flash of rage burned like lightening through Louise's body. Curse the boy... and Queen Marie.

"The women of your court admire him, are enchanted by him. And he is delightful, of course, but he is too forward. Undoubtedly it is the French fashion, but I am from England. I find his attentions excessive." Queen Marie's voice halted abruptly. She reached out and clung to King Louis's arm like an ingenue. "Could you please ask him to treat me as a... a mother, not a maid?"

Louise seethed. She was certain the queen was using this as a ploy to punish the king for dismissing her attendants. How clever. And by setting him against his heir, she strengthened her position. It would work, too, for François had not been subtle in practicing his arts of seduction on Queen Marie.

The king patted Queen Marie's hand. His voice sounded rough with menace. "So, he has incommoded you! This is proof I chose wisely in removing your ladies, for it is better you inform me than anyone else. I alone can manage the young lecher. Do not give him another thought. If he dares trouble you again, speak to me at once. He shall know today that next time I shall banish him from court."

Louise fumed. Then she forced herself to regain her composure. This was no time to let her emotions overcome her. She would need to speak to her son and hatch a plan.

WHEN LOUISE SAW her son's furious expression as he entered her room that evening, she disbanded her card party. Sending her servants to bring bread, meat, and brandy from the king's commissary, she pulled François into her inner chamber, leaned against its closed door, and winced as he slammed a fist against the tapestry-covered stone wall.

"What has happened, my César? When I saw you as we returned, you appeared well." No point in irritating him with her foreknowledge.

"The king! That old windbag! May the Lord and all the Saints curse him! And his days on the earth be few and painful. May his time in the ninth circle of hell be endless!" François belched curses like a fire-breathing dragon, smoke shooting from its nostrils and ears, his face scarlet as a blazing fire. "The old bastard called me to a private audience... the... the... shag-eared... codpiece! Impotent old boar."

He sounded like a furious five-year-old child in a tantrum. She was hard-pressed to restrain her laughter, but that would only infuriate him more. "Yes, yes, you are in a rage. The king has insulted you and you want to take your sword and run him through," she soothed. "Now please calm down and tell me what happened."

François picked up a bowl of apples from a chest and then weighed the bowl in his hands as if to throw it. She snatched it from him.

"Enough! Grow up, Son. This is not your home, nor your bowl, nor your apples. Take hold of your temper and sit down." Her voice was steely. It had the desired effect. She moved toward the bedside table and poured two goblets of wine.

He steadied and seated himself near the smoky fireplace. She handed him a goblet and sat down on the bed.

"Now, tell me."

He swallowed the contents in one mouthful and wiped his sleeve across his mouth. "The king says his lovely bride has complained about my forward behavior. She does not like my excessive gallantry. I am to behave with more discretion towards her or I shall be banished from the court." He slammed the arm of the chair. It shivered.

Louise did not flinch. "Hmm. So, King Louis brooks no rivals with his pretty new toy. You had best beware, my son."

He leaped to his feet and paced like a lion in a too-small cage. "Why do you take his side?" He grabbed the jug of wine, poured another goblet, and downed the wine in one swallow.

She sipped her wine, eyeing him. "Rein in your temper, François. I did not say you had *behaved* badly, though that is how you chose to take my words. The king and queen have united over your advances because she is angry that he returned her people to England."

"How do you know that?"

"It is a reasonable conclusion." Louise thanked the Virgin for her quick wits.

"Well.... He said she said that 'I should treat her like a mother, not a maid.' Whatever that means."

"Do not be obtuse. It means you should treat her as you treat Mme. la Grande."

He lifted his lip in a snarl. "Do they not wish! What is she afraid of? That with me she will discover a man, not a limp noodle? I hear he has not been able to have her, and she remains as much a maid as when she arrived." He snorted, a sound as harsh as grit under a boot.

"Give thanks for that to the Lord, and the Holy Francis de Paule, who promised you would be king one day — and I predict it will be soon." Louise crossed herself and kissed her thumb.

"When I find her alone, I'll show her what a real man does in bed. Then she'll wish I were her husband, not that half-dead stick whose pintle is smaller than my pinkie and not even half as stiff." He bared his teeth.

What was the matter with him that he could not keep his prick in his codpiece? This was the one woman he should never touch! Rising in one fluid motion, she shook his shoulders. "You will obey your king and your mother. Leave the queen alone. Do you hear me? Otherwise, you will find your son, not yourself, on the French throne."

François's glare faded as her meaning sank in. But he snapped back. "Would not that put my thumb in your eyes, both of you." Then he stormed out.

AT DINNER in the great hall, Louise sat beside Duchess Claude at the high table, her son at his wife's left. His mother, observing the glitter is his eyes and his gaudy, heavily jeweled doublet and breeches, did not look forward to the evening. Duchess Marguerite sat on her other side, and beyond her, Princess Renée, with her ever-present gouvernante. As always, it annoyed Louise to see Baronne Michelle so elevated. Her exasperation grew as she examined the remaining seating arrangements at the high table on the dais. Queen Marie occupied the center of the table, her cloth of estate[1] above her, wearing the magnificent necklace set with the Mirror of Naples, one of the king's most spectacular wedding gifts. The few remaining members of the English retinue filled the places between her son and the queen. The Duke of Suffolk sat beside Queen Marie, craning his neck to speak to her. Beside the queen, the king's empty chair divided the table into two parts. After his active day, the king had chosen not to join them. On the other side of the king's empty chair, like a great divide, sat the castellan and his wife, followed by the cardinals, bishops, and abbots in their ranked hierarchy. As many of the court as could crowd the long tables from the steps of the dais to the far wall thronged the hall, hindering the servitors who attended the horde. The musicians in the gallery above added to the cacophony. Louise could hear Duchess Claude only by leaning her ear to the duchess's lips.

As the meal progressed, François, who was drinking heavily, made himself conspicuous by offering every dish he appreciated to Queen Marie. He sent a page to present it to her on bended knee with his compliments. The gesture was not objectionable in itself. When a guest sent one or at most two dishes, it was considered a delicate attention. But he repeated it over and over. In the crowded, noisy room, with insufficient servants and an excessive audience, it amounted to a provocation. Each time she turned to thank the sender, he lifted his wine goblet and toasted her.

As François offered each toast, Claude lowered her eyes, her expression carefully neutral. But Louise had no trouble imagining her humiliation, for she remembered her own. When Louise was first married, she arrived to discover that her husband's mistress was chatelaine of her new household, although the situation had hurt her pride not her heart. Count Charles had been more than twenty years her senior and a weakling besides. She had been required to marry him, and

Louise had never felt more than duty towards him. Poor Claude, it was far otherwise for her.

As she pushed her memories aside, her son's effrontery appalled Louise. Such heavy-handed tactics amounted to deliberately baiting the king. And with each new offering, plain Claude quivered afresh, her eyes filling though not a tear fell.

Louise said to her daughter-in-law, "You do well to pay no attention. He does it because the king reprimanded him."

Duchess Claude replied, "The person he annoys most, besides the queen, is the Duke of Suffolk. I believe he takes offense on behalf of the King of England."

Following her eyes, Louise glimpsed the Duke of Suffolk's expression as he stood to toast the queen. A vein throbbed on his forehead and his eyes had narrowed to slits. He deliberately turned his back to her son.

"M. François, why do you keep sending platters of food to the new queen?" Princess Renée poked her brother-in-law's shoulder hard with her knife handle. He jerked around, his hand flying to the dagger he kept scabbarded at his waist. Princess Renée was fortunate he had quick reflexes. Louise strained to overhear their conversation.

"What was that you said, little sister?"

"Why do you send so many platters to the queen? I do not think she likes it. She sends them all away untouched." Princess Renée's large brown eyes stared at him.

That was plain speaking. Good for the child! Though most ill-behaved.

"It is a courtesy." He flushed and kept his voice low. "To show that she is welcome in her new home."

"My sister would not reject the dishes if you shared them with her." Princess Renée said, voice matter of fact. "I think she would like it if you did."

Duchess Marguerite leaned past Louise and said, "Brother, do you recall our Savior saying we should allow ourselves to be guided from the mouths of babes, as he always permitted the little children to come unto him."

Louise nodded.

Meanwhile, Duchess Claude took Princess Renée's hand, "Little sister, come here. At once, please. Curtsey to the duke. It is not your place to offer advice to my husband. Now do you return to Mme. Michelle." Louise noticed she put something into Princess Renée's hand and then placed a finger on the child's lips.

The little princess nodded and returned to her place. Mme. Michelle spoke to her in a low voice, and Princess Renée's lower lip protruded. Louise curled her hands into fists under the tablecloth. The child was undisciplined; her gouvernante clearly could not control her.

BEAUMONT SUR OISE

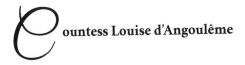

ountess Louise d'Angoulême

OUTSIDE, the sun shone in the brisk October morning. Because the king had fallen ill again, his court lodged in the old, gloomy — and overcrowded — royal castle in Beaumont sur Oise. As discontented as every other member of the royal court in the damp, musty accommodations, Louise huddled beside a glowing brazier. A shawl wrapped around her shoulders and a fur blanket tucked over her knees, she glowered around her one poky room. As she fumed, an order arrived — couched as a request — to attend the king in his private rooms.

Queen Marie, looking as demure as a country maid, sat at his bedside, eyes lowered, playing chess on the traveling board game of onyx and ivory that Louise had given them for a wedding gift.

The king lavished a besotted glance upon the girl and patted her knee. "There was never a queen in France that has behaved more honorably. See how she passes her time playing chess with me when I am so dull. She should be dancing and running about. Yet she sits with me playing cards and chess and checkers. She reads to me and plays music; truly she is an angel of mercy in my travails."

Queen Marie bowed her head, hands clasped in her lap, a tiny smile playing on her rosebud lips, like a little china doll.

"I am delighted she entertains you, Majesty." Louise curtsied, then said to the queen. "We, who love the king, value your ministrations to our beloved monarch."

"Well, well. Enough of that." King Louis said crossly.

Ah, so he did not want his young bride to think of him as a hoary old invalid, despite his words. He could say it; she could not. A foolish error on her part.

"I asked to see you for an entirely different reason. A flattering reason, dear Countess. The Duke of Suffolk was with me this morning."

Louise noticed Queen Marie flush and flash a nervous glance at the king. That was interesting.

King Louis gripped Louise's hands. "Twice, Countess, I have offered you excellent matches and you have refused. Do not disappoint me again. I reminded the Duke of Suffolk that he is a bachelor. When I suggested you would be a suitable wife, he was honored."

Because the king was watching Louise like a hawk circling its prey, she would wager he had not noticed the queen's muffled gasp. But she did. She would reflect on it later. First, she must find the way to protect her single state without offending the king.

Sinking to her knees, Louise said, "Sire, you are gracious to consider an old woman like me for such a noble match." She sought for the flattering words that meant never. Widowhood was the only status that allowed a woman to control her own life. "I fear I am past childbearing, and my health is delicate. As a devoted mother, I would despair at parting from Fr... er... our daughter, Duchess Claude. She is not always in the best of health and needs me." Good, that seemed to worry him. "My dearest ambition is to hold our grandchildren in my arms. I must stay with my dear Claude to support her. We cannot allow her to take any risks for France awaits a dauphin. Do you not agree, Sire?"

She looked through her lashes to judge her auditors' reactions. King Louis was frowning, his heavy eyebrows meeting over his jutting nose. Color had returned to Queen Marie's face, for she had paled when the king made the offer. Intriguing that the queen was so concerned about the Duke of Suffolk's marriage.

"Hmm," King Louis growled. "You raise an important issue. Nonetheless, the English alliance is close to our heart. Mayhap I shall consult my daughter. Baronne Michelle supported the late queen during her accouchements. Perhaps Claude will accept her care."

"You are always wise, Majesty," Louise said, hand to her heart. "You will do as you believe right. But in childbirth, Sire, there is no substitute for a mother's love."

When she stood to leave, the queen rose with her.

"Dear husband, I would play for you, yet my lute is in my chamber. I will call a servant to fetch it." Taking Louise's arm, they left the room.

In the outer chamber, the queen sent a servant on the errand. Releasing Louise's arm, she drew her to a window seat and sat close to her. Before she spoke, she scanned the room. Louise's eyes followed hers. The queen's ladies huddled on cushions near the smoldering fireplace at the far end of the room. Louise wrinkled her nose at the musty odor from the dingy tapestries on the stone walls. Judging from Queen Marie's expression, Louise guessed they shared the same opinion.

"Dear Mme. d'Angoulême, perhaps you will permit me to make a confidant of you?" Queen Marie pitched her voice low so it would not carry.

Louise nodded. Who would say no to such an offer?

"Since Lady Guildford returned to England, I am sorely in need of counsel. Although Mme. de Nevers is a distinguished lady, we have not warmed to each other. I pray you will accept the charge, for I need advice."

Louise hid her surprise. Did the queen not know she was Duke François's mother? She must. And this could be a dangerous role. But she could learn much and repair the harm François had done to his position. So, it was worth the risk. "It is an honor and, dare I say it, a pleasure, to serve you, Your Majesty."

Above their heads, the stinking pitch torches crackled in the wall cressets.

"It's an old castle from the English Wars," Louise apologized.

"We have many like it from our own civil wars," the queen confided. "I am used to them." She dropped her voice, "I honor your wish not to leave your native shores, for I, too, would have stayed in England, if I could. It was not to be, for my brother wished this marriage. If you would find it helpful, I will speak for you to the king, urging him to permit you to stay where you are needed." Her voice was breathless.

"Majesty, you are too kind. I would be grateful, for I do not wish to marry" Since Louise was certain the king would refuse nothing to his new plaything, this would immediately put an end to it.

Queen Marie's face lit up. "It is my pleasure. Ahh. Here comes the lad with my lute. *Adieu*, dear Countess."

What was the queen's interest in preventing the marriage? As Louise took her leave, she wondered at Queen Marie's innocence. Did the queen believe she would investigate no further? And search, too, for the influential person who wished to rid France of Louise's presence? Perhaps she would set Lady Blanche to making a friend of Mistress Mary Boleyn. She was known as a gossip.

The countess met François as he was on his way to the empty moat for a game of tennis against the Duke of Suffolk. She whispered to him that she had avoided an unwanted marriage and secured Queen Marie's confidence.

"Now, as long as you take a gentler approach in your flirtation with her, I predict our family will make a friend of her in no time."

"What technique would you suggest I use, Maman?" he jeered. "Offer to carry her cane and piss pot?"

Louise bit back a sharp reply. To take offense was to undo her good work. "There is no call to sneer, *mon César*. Try treating her like a young and beautiful aunt. Or like your sister. You may advance slowly if she responds."

Her son hung his head, suitably abashed, though he did not apologize. "Your advice is wise, Maman." He hugged her and went on his way. She accepted this was his act of contrition. Over the next few days of hunting and hawking, François's charming behavior to Queen Marie gave evidence he had put Louise's advice into practice.

A FEW DAYS LATER, about to set out on the last long stage to St. Denis for Queen Marie's coronation, young Princess Renée fell ill. Michelle sent Princess Renée's companions to travel under the tutelage of Mme. Jeanne, hoping the illness would not spread among the cavalcade. *Grâce à Dieu*, they would stop in St. Denis for several days.

While Renée dozed, Michelle prepared willow bark tea and added honey to disguise its bitter flavor.

"This is the medicine I gave your mother."

Anything her mother had taken was good, so Princess Renée swallowed the first dose without fuss. The same coaxing did not work quite as well with the oatmeal gruel. "Maybe you did give it to her," Princess Renée argued, "but I put it to you she refused it."

"Your mother was an excellent patient. She swallowed her medicine and food, if it was good for her, even if she did not like it."

"But she was growed up. I am not growed up, yet."

As Michelle made final preparations for the journey, she sent to the kitchens for thin gruel and mashed carrots with honey. Princess Renée whined about getting dressed, so Michelle permitted her to stay in her night rail, though she wrapped the princess's dressing robe over it and tucked her feet into socks and soft slippers. She added a fur-lined cloak and hood. In the courtyard, when Michelle ordered a manservant to lift her into the litter and she realized she would not ride, Princess Renée began to sob. As Michelle clambered in beside her, Princess Renée wailed louder, and then rolled over to bury her head into Michelle's shoulder.

As the day progressed, she worsened. Her fever rose, and she moaned that it hurt to breathe and that her throat felt scratchy. Michelle kept an arm around her and sang to her until the princess slept, wheezing and snoring. At times she moaned, calling for her maman. When Michelle bathed her forehead with lavender water, she remembered the days she had provided the same service for her mother. Later Princess Renée woke, and Michelle dosed her with gruel and with willow bark and honey tea.

"Maman Michelle?"

Tears prickled behind Michelle's eyelids. Never before had Renée called her Maman. "Yes, my sweet?"

"Am I going to die and go to heaven to see my maman?"

"One day you will, dearest Princess Renée, but an it please the Virgin and the Saints, not today or any day soon. You are not very ill." Hiding her fingers under the blanket, she crossed them.

Tears dribbled from under Princess Renée's closed eyes. "I feel dreadful bad. My throat burns whenever I swallow... and my chest hurts when I breathe." A phlegmy cough racked her thin body.

Michelle resorted to her strongest remedy: a sweet pastille made from honey, ginger, and lemon with a drop of hemlock. It soothed all pains. "Put this between your cheek and your gum and let it melt. It will soothe your throat. Do not suck it." As if she could resist, but she must try. It would give her something to concentrate on rather than her aches.

"Mmmm. 'Sgood."

"Just let it rest in your cheek. Do you want me to read you a story?"

"No... Maman Michelle? I do not want to go to St. Denis." Princess Renée's voice sank to a murmur.

"Why not?" Her heart sinking, Michelle feared it brought back memories of her mother's burial ceremony a few short months ago.

"I do not want to go to her cor'nation." Princess Renée's whisper vibrated like a rattle, and Michelle worried she would fall into another coughing fit.

"Hmm. Is it too soon?"

"Papa should not have made her que... eeen. He has no time for us anymore. He is always riding with *her*... talking with *her*... giving *her* presents." Renée's voice was clogged with phlegm, and tears ran down her cheeks. "He has forgotten my maman. And he does not love us anymore." Her thumb found her mouth, and she squeezed her raggle-taggle doll almost to death as she sobbed and spluttered.

Michelle rocked her, assuring her that, however it appeared, her papa loved her very much; that when people first got married this is what they did, but soon her Papa would return to normal, and Princess Renée should trust her to know. Soon her fever, the pastille, the overdose of emotion, Michelle's familiar arms, and the movement of their litter rocked her into a troubled sleep. Michelle, however, was not so sanguine as to believe she had convinced the princess. The king must visit his daughter to reassure her. She had failed Princess Renée, him, and Queen

Marie by failing to warn him earlier about the princess's jealousy. His ill health and new marriage were not good reasons to neglect his daughter.

At St. Denis, the Abbot came out fussing to greet them. "I have housed your entourage in my quarters," he said, "for it is the most suitable building for women within my monastery. Naturally, you will not enter the cloisters. I trust you will be comfortable." As he bowed them through the grand entrance and turned to leave, he added as if an afterthought, "And I have ordered only lay servants to serve you directly."

Michelle sniffed, irritated yet accustomed to the attitude that women corrupted the purity of the chaste religious. As if the lewdness of the clergy was not common knowledge and the source of mockery throughout the West. As they entered the Abbot's suite her exasperation increased. His rich furnishings — thick carpets, enormous gilt-framed paintings and life-sized silver crucifix — compared to the simple, stone-floored, whitewashed cell of the Blessed Francis de Paule was too striking to ignore.

The worldliness of the Abbot's palace offended her. True, kings often appointed younger royal sons and princes of the blood as the Abbots of St. Denis, and the Basilica had been the recipient of hundreds of years of pious offerings from France's richest peers, so she should not be surprised that the abode of the Lord's anointed rivaled the greatest royal palaces. But she still felt offended — and she was not alone. Even Queen Anne had shared her outrage at the complaisance of the highest ranks of the church hierarchy.

Michelle settled Princess Renée in her bed, invited Dr. Nichel to consult on her treatment, sent to the kitchens for fresh broth and pease porridge, and made a fresh decoction of willow bark tea. By then, the evening was far advanced.

Princess Renée lay in bed, but whined. "I am better. I want to get up."

"Tomorrow, Princess, if you are recovered. We will ask Dr. Nichel. He will come soon. Would you like me to read you a story while we wait?"

She frowned and shook her head.

Duchess Claude glided into the room on her way to Vespers. "Sister, I came to bid you a good night."

Michelle put up a hand. "Duchess, do not come closer. We do not know—"

"Claude, Claude. Come here." The little princess burst into noisy tears.

Gently, Duchess Claude pushed Michelle aside and sat at her sister's bedside. Michelle sighed and offered her Princess Renée's primer; its Bible stories were a source of delight for the Princess.

"Please send a message to Mme. Louise to attend mass without me. I shall stay with my sister," Duchess Claude said.

After mass, while Dr. Nichel was examining the princess, Louise barged into Princess Renée's rooms. "What is the matter with my ward?"

Princess Renée was not yet Mme. Louise's ward, but Michelle refrained from correcting her. *Grâce à Dieu* the king continued to live, as Michelle prayed daily he would. And that he sired a son.

Countess Louise glanced at Michelle. "Is something troubling you, Mme. Michelle? You appear to have swallowed something sour."

"I would advise you against approaching the Princess Renée because of the unhealthy humors in the air." When the Countess ignored her warning and leaned over the princess, Michelle snapped. "Also, King Louis is very much alive, Countess,"

Duchess Claude intervened. "Dearest Renée has caught a nasty grippe, Maman Louise. She has a fever, a sore throat, and her chest is paining her. Is it not so, my sweet?" She bathed her sister's forehead with cool lavender water.

Even though Princess Renée's face was swollen and her eyes puffy, she glared at the countess. Her voice phlegmy, she said. "Maman Michelle speaks true. I am not your ward." The effort threw her into a prolonged coughing fit.

By the time Michelle had dosed her with an expectorating cough syrup and more willow bark tea, Dr. Nichel had calmed Countess Louise with a discussion of the melancholic humor at the root of Princess Renée's malady.

The countess recommended bleedings and emetics. They listened, nodding attentively.

"Well!" she said when neither Michelle nor Dr. Nichel moved to obey, "I do not have a weak stomach. You may proceed."

Michelle said, "It is prudent to permit her recent treatment to act before commencing another. If you will excuse me." She turned and picked up her notes.

Mme. Louise came up behind her. "I wish to review the Princess's treatments," she said. "I will examine your notes, if you please." She reached to seize the notebook from Michelle's hands.

Michelle clutched it to her chest. "Pardon me, Countess. A record of treatments is confidential. It is a matter between the princess's medical staff and her father. I may not share it without the king's permission."

Mme. Louise's color rose, and she rounded on Duchess Claude. "If Mme. Michelle does not give me those notes at once we will all have reason to believe she is deliberately harming the princess."

It took Michelle a moment to register the countess's meaning it was so unexpected. Then she blanched with shock — and anger — at the dangerous accusation. As she turned to the duchess, her expression was scornful. Duchess Claude looked as shocked as she did. She began to stutter. Poor duchess.

"Mme. Louise, I protest—" Dr. Nichel intervened. He stopped when Countess Louise raised an eyebrow at him.

Michelle found her voice. "I make this decision on my own authority. Please do not involve the duchess or Dr. Nichel. If you wish to protest to the king, I suggest you return tomorrow. He will visit Princess Renée in the morning. Or if you prefer, I shall send for you when he arrives."

"Why do you say Maman Michelle is giving me bad things?" Princess Renée's voice rose hysterically. She labored to rise. Her face flushed with the effort and she struggled to breathe. Her voice hoarse, she wheezed. "I do not believe you. That is wicked. You are not nice to say that, Mme. Louise—." Racked by coughs, she stopped, fighting to breathe. Michelle and Dr. Nichel converge on the princess, intent on calming her so she could relax and regain her breath. They thrust smelling salts under her nose, applied salves to her chest and back, placed her under a steam hood, gave her soothing lozenges and took her pulse, finally relaxing themselves as her fit passed.

By the time Michelle recalled the confrontation and turned to apologize to Mme. Louise, still determined to refuse to release her treatment notebook that lay on Princess Renée's bed, the duchess had left. She raised her eyebrows at Duchess Claude. "Did your maman-in-law say anything before she left?"

Duchess Claude nodded. "She said, 'Tell Mme. Michelle that I shall certainly speak to the king about this. She shall hear from him tomorrow.'" She wrung her hands. "Of course her accusation is nonsense. Shall I—?" She looked frightened. "Do you want me to do something?"

Michelle thought Claude might faint if she had to speak to her father on Michelle's behalf or confront Duchess Louise. Besides, she was prepared to present her own case. If the king wished her to show her notes to Duchess Louise, it was his right. After Mme. Claude left, she sat by Princess Renée into the early hours. Before she fell asleep in the uncomfortable chair by Renée's bed, she thought she had been foolish to make a scene over the Treatment Book. It contained nothing secret. Still, Michelle believed in the principle of confidentiality. Unfortunately, she had enraged the countess. Had it been worth it?

5 NOVEMBER 1514

BASILICA OF ST. DENIS

*B*aronne Michelle de Soubise

QUEEN MARIE PAUSED inside the great doors of the Basilica of St. Denis and stood bareheaded in a sunbeam. At the vision of the queen's sapphire eyes, rosebud lips, and long copper tresses falling to her hips, a murmur passed like a wave through the enormous congregation. The soft sound took Michelle back to another coronation and another queen. Her eyes glazed with tears.

It had been the same season, ten years earlier. Queen Anne had stood there in all her glory, her chestnut hair flowing over her slight shoulders to her waist. She had looked like a goddess in her gown of white brocade and satin embroidered in the ermines of Brittany and the fleurs-de-lys of France. Her beautiful face with its enormous amber eyes, long eyelashes, and perfectly arched eyebrows, had seemed to glow. This had been Anne's second coronation as Queen of France, and she had carried herself with such grace and dignity that she seemed to float along the carpet.

Today, as it had been for Queen Anne's coronation, the air was heady with the floral scent of thousands of red roses and white royal lilies. Their sweetness competed with the pungency of musk and myrrh incense, the smoke veiling the interior in mystery. The many perfumes vied with the tang of human bodies. Even the scents reminded Michelle of Anne's coronation. Roses reminded her of Brittany and how much more valuable Queen Anne's contribution had been to France than the unstable peace offered by this wisp of an English queen. King Louis did not have many years to live. She doubted that King Henry would further François's dreams of foreign conquest by extending the alliance.

As choral music filled the air, Michelle clenched her fists. Behind Queen Marie and the Dauphin, Duchess Claude and Princess Renée led the parade down the central aisle of the Basilica. The Princes of the Blood — the Dukes de Longueville, Alençon and Bourbon-Montpensier, and Bourbon's brothers — followed them. Next came the Princesses of the Blood in their order of rank. So many of the princes and dukes who had followed her queen had fallen in King Louis's battles in Italy. The young and the brave lost, as her own husband had been lost... and her brother crippled. Michelle's thoughts slipped to Brittany again. She pictured its tranquil forests and sweet-smelling wildflowers, its seven sacred saints, and its mysterious great stone Calvaries. Why did Queen Anne have to die so young?

Michelle stood stoically, watching the endless ceremony. The Cardinal-Bishop of Limoges — who had married King Louis to Renée's nemesis in Abbeville — conducted this ceremony, too. When he robed Queen Marie in the regalia, the image of her late queen rose before her and she closed her eyes to control her emotions. She had attired Queen Anne's cold body, her spirit fled Heavenward, in this very regalia. In her last memory of her beloved lady, Anne's lifelike effigy was lying in state in this very Basilica. It was *she* who was wearing that crown, holding that scepter and rod. Only ten months previously. A piercing pain finally entered Michelle's consciousness. Opening her fists, she saw the red half moon imprint from her fingernails engraved into her palms.

The rest of the coronation passed in a blur. Michelle was relieved when it was over, and she could escape the chilly yet stuffy Basilica and its sad memories. When Michelle, Claude, and Renée stood together in the courtyard, Michelle heaved a great sigh. Taking Princess Renée's hand, she whispered to Duchess Claude, "Praise be that it is done."

"It could have waited until Queen Marie gave France an heir," Claude answered. "That is common practice. Papa did not need to rush this. He erases my maman more each day."

For Claude, the queen's entry into Paris the next day was even more painful than the coronation. She had driven with her maman, waving to the crowds as Lyon and Grenoble feted them with flowers, bunting, ribbons, and endless applause. The cheering crowds of Parisians lining the streets to greet Queen Marie — dressed in her coronation robes, and wearing her small crown, her long copper hair loose again like a bride — as she waved from the open carriage pierced Claude's heart like the thrust of a stiletto. The guildsmen and merchants of Paris marched in a square formation, carrying a cloth of estate high above their new queen. To add to Claude's pain, Duke François rode beside Queen Marie, leaning close to hear her and to make her laugh. Following in the next carriage, Claude looked on with jealous eyes.

Riding with Claude were Princess Renée and their gouvernantes, Mme. Michelle and Mme. Jeanne. Behind them, in the third carriage, sat Countess Louise and Duchess Marguerite.

Countess Louise bent her head towards her daughter and said, "I told Mme. Michelle she should not permit Princess Renée to attend the Entrée in this chilly weather for she has been ill and has not fully recovered. Observe how well my advice was heeded." Accustomed to agreement, she was preparing her litany of the baronne's many inadequacies.

"I imagine Princess Renée would have made a scene had she been denied." Duchess Marguerite was no stranger to Princess Renée's willfulness.

"She should learn to obey. Her gouvernante obviously does not know how to control the child."

"I doubt that any but her mother or father could control her. Mme. Michelle does admirably."

Countess Louise sniffed. Sometimes Marguerite could be *very* irritating.

As the procession wended its way, Queen Marie applauded the pageants, music, jesters, acrobats, poets, and stationary floats decked out to celebrate her coronation. As they approached Notre Dame Cathedral, one float stood out from the others. White cloth blanketed its entire surface and sheathed its front and sides like frosting. Hundreds of white fleurs-de-lys lay heaped upon the icy white surface. Sprays of red and white roses wove together through this sweetly scented bed. Their blooms looked as fresh as if they were growing in the lily garden and smelled as sweet. Singers dressed as shepherds and shepherdesses crowded the float. As soon as they saw Queen Marie, they burst into song, pointing to the garden,

What a lovely English rose has been newly planted

In the lily garden of France.

O how this heralds a glorious new era of peace

And love between our two realms.

Not likely, groused Duchess Claude silently, as she listened to the words. As if to punish her for her lack of charity, Queen Marie halted the procession, clapped her hands and insisted they sing the song again and again. As the procession jolted into motion, she instructed her guards to throw small coins as largesse. The same crowds who had so recently wept for Good Queen Anne now called, "*Vive la Reine Marie,*" "*Vive la Reine Marie.*"

Claude put her handkerchief to her lips to hold back her tears. Princess Renée muttered passionately, "I hate her."

Only Claude heard her over the shouts of the crowd. Putting a hand on her sister's shoulder, she whispered: "You must dissemble your feelings, Renée, as Maman did. Royal persons must show an amiable face."

When Renée turned and gave her a hurt look, shame flooded Claude's conscience. She had been blaming the people of Paris for their fickleness since the Entrée began. She leaned her lips close to her sister's ear and said, "Forgive me for reproving you. I am missing Maman, too."

18 NOVEMBER 1514

PARIS

uchess Claude de Bretagne

DUCHESS CLAUDE WAS HAPPIER than she had been since she married. Her husband was in his element, organizing the great tournament to celebrate the English alliance. In his enthusiasm, he showed no interest in other women and spent his few free hours pouring every insignificant detail into her ears. That day, his crew finished erecting the Arch Triumphant outside the Hôtel des Tournelles in the rue St. Antoine. It held aloft the four elaborate shields under which contestants entered their names and arms in one of the four categories of challenges to be held on successive days. As he described the whole successful enterprise strutting around her chamber chest puffed out, he reminded her of his sister's parrot when it was pleased with itself.

She had a harder time managing his mercurial temper when miserable weather arrived along with the great event. For four days sheeting rain and gusting winds turned the ground of the lists into a muddy marsh upon which carters poured cartloads of sand each morning — as hopeless an enterprise as pouring sugar into the sea — for each night torrential rains washed it away. Claude kept her laments to herself as these grains of sand that cost their weight in her gold trickled away into the Seine. And François? He ordered more, concerned only that his tourney should outshine every tale he had heard about English magnificence. Still, she was delighted for him that it was a success. He blossomed as martial music played and the crowd shrieked, as horses and men rode full speed at the tilt, fell injured and sometimes slain. Each day he seemed to gain in stature as praise for the tournament mounted.

MOST DAYS, Baronne Michelle left the tournament with Princess Renée as soon as the child squirmed in her seat, which usually occurred in the pause after the first pair of contestants ran their course — unless something exciting occurred like the jousters galloping dangerously fast and tumbling their opponent to the ground. Today, as they rose to leave, the king did too. He invited them to attend him in his suite. Princess Renée's face lit up like a sunbeam; she had not had private time with him for almost a sennight. Michelle's warning that Renée felt angry with him because she believed he was forgetting her Maman and that he loved only his new wife, not his old family, had shaken him. He made an effort to spend time with her these days.

Once his attendants removed his formal robes, King Louis sank to his bed. His legs trembled as if they were too weak to hold him upright. His wrists and forearms were skeletal. Michelle bit her lips to keep from commenting on his feeble appearance, grateful that he had taken to heart her reproach that Renée cried herself to sleep every night.

She offered him a biscuit and a goblet of wine from the serving dishes on his bedside table.

"No, Mme. Michelle, my stomach is too sour for such things."

"How long has your stomach been troubling you?" This hectic life of entertainment with his new wife was killing him, she thought.

His hand flew up. "No, Mme. Michelle. I will not permit you to physick me."

She sighed, "As you wish. I will send you a fortifier and mint pastilles to take morning and night."

As he rested, they played board games on the low table beside his bed. Princess Renée's favorite board game was Fox and Goose. They each set out a colored wooden goose on the wooden board divided into 63 curved trapezia that spiraled like a snail shell. Then they took turns rolling two dice and advancing according to the number they rolled. The winner was the one whose goose arrived first at the center despite the obstacles. Renée groaned when she landed on a tavern that sent her back the roll of the dice. She followed the maze her Papa's goose landed on that advanced him six squares and shrieked with delight when Michelle landed on a fox and had to go back to the start.

Michelle wondered who the fox was at court these days. Perhaps for each person it was different. For her, it was Mme. Louise. For the king, she thought it was Duke François. He had certainly annoyed the king recently. Or perhaps it was

Queen Marie, for she was the cause of the king's rapid decline.

After only two games, the king declared himself too tired to play. He asked Princess Renée to play the lute instead.

She picked up the instrument that lay on a cushion. "Do you like music, Papa?"

"I do. Music and poetry. Poetry set to music. Did you know your grandfather, my papa, was a great poet and musician?"

She sat beside him as he told her a story about his boyhood in Amboise. He fell asleep in the middle of it.

Renee looked at Michelle. "Why does he keep getting grayer?"

"His hair you mean? When people grow old that—"

"Not his hair. His skin. See." She patted his cheek. "It's not tan, or brown or pink, even where there's no hair." She leaned until her nose almost touched his cheek. "It is almost blue or gray. Not the right color."

He woke, probably from her breath warm on his face. She stared into his eyes. "Your eye is yellow."

He said solemnly, "Not brown?"

"One part is brown. And black. But the part around it is yellow. And red. Other people's are white. It does not look good. Like your skin. It is gray. Why?"

"Out of the mouths of babes. Why is that, Mme. Michelle?"

Princess Renée bristled. "I am not a babe."

"No, you are an observant princess." He pinched her cheek gently.

Michelle seized her opportunity. "Your Majesty, Sire, forgive me, but the life you are living is undermining your health. You are overtaxing yourself. I suggest bedrest without strenuous exercise. Follow the diet you consumed before this marriage: vegetables, sour wine, little meat with no fat, and no sweets. A tonic of herbs in the morning and a gentle walk daily. That is my recommendation. What does your chief physician say?"

"I do not ask him... or you." He frowned at her. "Hear me, Mme. Michelle. I am an old man with a delightful young wife who dotes on fine food, fine wine and lively entertainment. I intend to enjoy myself in her company... for the time that remains to me."

Michelle nodded, rebuked.

THE LAST DAY of the tournament finally arrived. When he woke to a clear and cloudless dawn, François shouted with relief for he was leader of the French team. When she rose, Claude sent him her blessing, grateful that the Lord had graced her husband's work with fine weather at last.

As the finest jousters of England and France attired in their best armor on their strongest destriers prepared to compete in the lists, heralds dressed in tabards of the royal colors sounded their trumpets. King Louis and Queen Marie appeared in the stands. The queen clasped the king's arm as she waved from the royal box. Sylph-like in a gown of silver tulle, she seemed to float at his side. The holiday crowds in the stands rose in a wave, shouting ear-shattering cheers. No one noticed Duchess Claude standing in the queen's shadow.

The remaining royal women — Princess Renée, Countess Louise and Duchess Marguerite — took their seats in the second row behind Duchess Claude. She admitted to herself as she looked out over the festive tournament grounds on which her husband had spent so much of their income that she resented this display honoring the queen's marriage to her papa. For his marriage, her father was spending enormously on a great and lengthy display. For his daughter's marriage to the dauphin, he had refused even a minimal celebration.

At both ends of the field, outside the competition areas, Claude could distinguish the colored tents that housed the myriad officials and staff necessary to manage the elaborate event: stable boys, grooms, and squires for each contestant; horse doctors, farriers, armorers, infirmarians, apothecaries and surgeons to treat injured horses and their riders; groundsmen to repair and maintain the field and tilts; organizers, administrators, and heraldic experts to set the order of riders in each joust; and the scorekeepers who kept track of winners and points.

Queen Marie reigned over the tournament; she would smile upon the winners, praise them and present them with their valuable prizes. Claude was secretly pleased that it would be Queen Marie who must deal with any awkwardness that arose, but she did not expect her husband to be its cause.

When François cantered onto the grounds, Claude was as astonished as everyone else. He was enveloped head to toe in jewel-encrusted golden armor. Including a golden helm! From the whoosh of indrawn breath that rustled through the jousting field and spectators' stands, not a single person had seen anything as magnificent — or as costly — before.

Once her first moment of surprise passed, Claude was quietly furious. How dare he keep such a costly acquisition secret from her? Forgetting her fear in her outrage, she turned to glare at Maman Louise. His mother was gazing upon her son as if she was watching Apollo come blazing to earth in all his glory.

"Did you know about this armor?" Claude asked. When she heard her voice, she surprised herself. She had snapped at her mother-in-law.

"He told me he was having it made, but I had not seen it." Duchess Louise answered her absently, her attention totally absorbed by the vision of her son.

Claude ground her teeth. He had told his mother, but not her. Yet who would pay for this gaudy — this vulgar — extravagance? Not his mother, that was certain! Listening to the buzz of admiration, she doubted herself. Did she have unrefined taste to see the new armor not as magnificent but as ostentatious? She stole a glance at her mother-in-law. It was clear Maman Louise did not agree.

Just then, the Duke of Suffolk rode onto the field for the English wearing workmanlike steel armor. The two dukes met in the center of the field and cantered side by side toward the royal box. As they arrived before the royal couple, François reared his horse onto its hind legs. As it dropped back to the ground, the partisan crowd let out a tremendous roar of applause. Duke François circled his great destrier in a tight figure eight, caracoling in acknowledgement while the Queen and Duke Charles waited, side-lined.

After finishing his display, François bowed to Queen Marie. Without giving the English Duke an opportunity to speak, his voice rang out. "Madame, *notre reine*, as leader of the French team, I beg to wear your favor to honor France." The French audience howled its approval, spectators cheering, whistling, and pounding their feet.

It was not well done. Once again, her husband was deliberately causing trouble.

Claude noticed Queen Marie blanch and shoot an agonized glance at the king. Why was François doing this? It had all been agreed upon beforehand. The queen would offer her colors to the Duke of Suffolk to honor the new alliance between France and England.

Duke Charles, his face brick-red and eyes narrowed dangerously, glared at François. As the noise abated, he signaled his herald to sound a blast. Into the spreading hush, the herald shouted, "Charles Brandon, Duke of Suffolk, leader of the English team, representing King Henry, eighth of that name, Sovereign of England, to celebrate the newly formed alliance between our nations of England and France, an alliance cemented through the solemn marriage between King Louis of France and Princess Mary Rose of England, now Queen of France, begs the honor of wearing the queen's favor."

The few English in the crowd — among them rowdy students from the English House who were studying at the University of Paris — cheered more loudly than their small numbers seemed capable of, causing scuffles to break out in the stands.

Claude's papa came to Queen Marie's rescue. Ordering another blast of the trumpets to silence the crowds, he sent armed guards running to quell the disorder in the stands and to expel the troublemakers. Champagne Herald's ringing voice amplified the king's shouted words. "Gentlemen! You each have right on your side, for our hearts belong equally to both. My dear wife, I suggest you offer Duke Charles the colors of England, which are the same as ours of Orléans: yellow and red. To Duke François, let us offer the colors and symbol of Brittany: black ermines on white."

"My dear husband, your solution is brilliant." From the enthusiastic kiss she gave the king, the crowd deduced she applauded his suggestion. Delirious cheers broke out.

For the second time in as many minutes, Claude was so furious with François that she might even have told him so were he there in front of her at that moment. She had not been this angry even when he disappeared from St Germain without taking leave of her. This time he had humiliated her in front of the whole tournament crowd. The entire court would know by the time the tournament ended. It would be common knowledge through the courts of the West as fast as couriers delivered mail. Pain mingled with her anger. Before her very eyes, François had publicly shown his preference for his stepmother-in-law over his wife.

Her cheeks burning, Claude handed the Breton black-and-white ribbons to the queen. Surprised, Queen Marie raised her eyebrows in an unspoken question. It was true Claude had been meant to offer the ribbons to her husband. Claude gave a slight shake of her head. The queen gave a tiny shrug and motioned Duke François to ride forward so she could pin them onto his surcoat. Waving him to move away, she waited until he did so before gesturing to Duke Charles. When the Duke of Suffolk brought his horse close, Queen Marie leaned forward, attached the red and yellow ribbons, and smiled into his eyes. Claude witnessed the warmth with which she bestowed the colors on the English duke. She could not blame Queen Marie.

The two team leaders bowed. Their stiff bows — as they bared their clenched teeth in a parody of smiles made them look like wild animals moments before attacking — poured further salt into her wounds. As they turned their horses and rode down the field to the exit, Claude's heart bled for her father. By quarreling over his wife, they shamed not only her but also him.

Yet Papa did not seem to take it so. Under the noise of the crowd, he shifted closer to her and growled, "Magnificent armor your husband is wearing, Daughter. I had not seen it before. It must have cost as much as one of my new cannons."

"He wished it to be a surprise." Keeping her voice steady, she found a diplomatic answer rising to her lips. *Grâce à Dieu*, her training had prepared her to conceal her own shock. "I had not seen it either." Aware of her mother-in-law's listening ears, she said no more. She would wager twice its price that he had not the funds for a set of Milanese armor, the best in Europe — and only the best would do for him. Milanese armorers had attended the Nantes fair, the Breton Chancellor had informed her in a recent letter. François had probably ordered his armor from them as they passed en route through Tours.

As the first joust got underway, her father rose, wincing as he leaned on two canes. He bent to Claude as he left. "Daughter, I advise you so you are prepared, I shall reprimand Duke François when he leaves the field. This time he has insulted both my wife and my daughter. I regret that it was necessary to marry you to him. Your mother was correct. He is insolent."

While he was speaking, Claude had worried that his voice would carry to her mother-in-law's ears, but now she understood. He had intended that she hear, undeceived by her pretense of deafness. As he straightened, he glared at Countess Louise. "Madame, you should be ashamed of your son. He is not fit to rule."

Because it was the last day of the tournament, Michelle and Renée stayed to see Duke François joust with the Duke of Suffolk in his gaudy golden armor.

As they galloped towards each other on either side of the wooden lists, lances pointed dangerously, Michelle's whole body chilled.

Duke François yelled, "*Montjoie Saint Denis*[1]!" pounding toward his opponent on his largest, fastest destrier, its head shielded with a protective iron *chanfron*[2]. As they neared, he rose in his stirrups, leaning forward in the saddle so his blunted lance changed its target. It no longer pointed at the Duke of Suffolk's round iron shield. Instead, it aimed at his vulnerable helm. The hooves of their horses thundered on the beaten earth as they cannoned toward each other. Only a thin, vibrating wooden pole separated their catapulting chargers. Neither veered.

Princess Renée buried her head in Michelle's skirts. Unable to watch the moment of impact, Michelle closed her eyes.

A crack like a bolt of thunder sounded as metal clanged and wood splintered.

Duchess Claude let out a little moan and gripped her hand until Michelle thought she might crush it.

"Who... was anyone hurt?" Michelle whispered her eyes still squeezed shut.

"*Grâce à Dieu*, no." Claude voice still shaking, she added. "Both men broke their lances but—," her voice dropped lower. "Oh no. My husband has lost his helm.... His golden helmet with its great peacock's feather, so he will be even more humiliated... and furious." She slumped against Michelle side, and Michelle staggered under the sudden weight.

"He will want another," she said. Then she added, in a voice so grim Michelle wondered if she had heard correctly, "And it will not be he who pays." Then she recognized that Claude had spoken her thoughts aloud without being aware of it.

Michelle opened her eyes and looked up to watch the scene. Both men had arrived at opposite ends of the barrier. Grooms and stable boys ran to catch their horses. Duke François was gesticulating and arguing with the officials. Michelle guessed that he wanted to run another course and was being refused.

When they saw Duke François at the banquet later that afternoon, he claimed it was pure chance he lost his helmet. "When we knocked together, the crash jarred the clasp on my helmet and unhooked it. By an unlucky chance for me — and a lucky one for Duke Charles — his broken lance caught in the hinge of my helm and pulled it sideways. Lucky for me I wore the best, for it sprang open. Otherwise I could have been pulled off, despite how well I was seated. That would have been a dishonor I could not endure." He shrugged. "They called it my loss, but it was a technical loss. I cannot win every time." He gave a great bellow of laughter. "Nine times out of ten is sufficient, is it not Wife? Or do you expect more?" To Michelle's ears, his laughter rang false.

By this late in the tournament, the English team and Duke Charles had won much more than Duke François and the French team. Today, in the last melée, a member of the French team — no one would say who — disguised an enormously tall and strong German soldier as a French contestant and brought him against Suffolk. Because they both began horsed, his team did not notice the remarkable length of the German's wooden sword. On tenterhooks, the spectators cheered and shouted like savages, betting wildly, as the pair battled back and forth, fortune favoring first one man then the other. After almost an hour, Suffolk triumphed to riotous cheers from the English university students. Despite their win, the English team, suspicious of the Duke's vigorous opponent, demanded an investigation.

Meanwhile, bettors who had lost sizeable sums erupted like volcanos, fighting almost as violently as had the contestants against the cocky English. Tournament guards plowed into them on their armored horses to rescue the young students, who then ran for their lives. But it wasn't long before the sergeants-at-arms suspected that the French team were fostering the uproar because during it, Suffolk's enormous, mysterious opponent vanished — leaving his outsized weapon behind.

Michelle heard King Louis mutter, "That big, spoiled fellow will ruin everything," and deduced he suspected that his son-in-law was behind the unknightly trick. Still, he hid Duke François's role in the incident when he spoke to the Duke of Suffolk after the fracas.

When the king dismissed Suffolk, his wife gestured the Duke of Suffolk to her side. She paled when she learned he had hurt his hand.

"It is nothing, a sprain, nothing more."

"Duke Charles, we are desolated!" She held out her hands. He refused to take them, kneeling instead. Blushing, she said, "King Louis informs me that you have put our French team to shame and you well deserve the champion's prize. We shall honor your win at this evening's closing feast. Please inform your team of our praise."

He placed his hand over his heart. "We have fought for you, for England, and for our alliance."

Seated beside Mme. Louise, who was watching them with avid eyes, Michelle felt uneasy. The countess wore an eager half-smile, reminding her of a cat teasing a mouse, all the while intent on its destruction.

✳

DUCHESS CLAUDE SIGHED. Monthly she met to review the accounts with Sieur Jacques de Beaune, Grand Treasurer of her household. She thought they had finished when he gave his inimitable throat-clearing cough. She knew all too well what it meant — he had a delicate subject to discuss. About to rise, she settled herself instead in the padded armchair in her private study. She loved this intimate room with its white-, blue- and gold-tiled floor. Mme. Michelle had been right. Surrounded by her favorite books, a comfortable desk fitted for her, and the cushions, tables and glassware she wanted, she felt more cheerful.

She sighed again, turning her mind back to the unpleasantness to come. Of late, delicate subjects almost always involved her husband or her mother-in-law. From her mother's household she had inherited this bald, aging financier with weak blue eyes behind a pince-nez, who knew everything about her estates and income.

"Madame Duchess," he said, opening an account book. "I must draw your attention to large loans now due, not authorized by you, that have been brought to me by the Lombards."

Her stomach lurched. She did not have large cash reserves; no one did. Since she had not borrowed the money, it must have been François. "Tell me. How much? By whom? To whom?"

"Duke François pledged to pay 10,000 *écus d'or* to the Lombards in Paris by the end of October. When he did not honor the bills, they came to me, knowing he was married to you. I have not paid, naturally, but said I would return to them with an answer by month's end."

"Do you know how he used the monies?" For once she was glad the man had been with her family forever. She did not have to ask him to keep the matter between themselves, though having such a secret mortified her. Again, indignation toward her husband swept through her.

"When the Lombard said he had required neither security nor an explanation due to the undoubted credit worthiness of the Duke de Valois et Bretagne, I investigated personally. Most of it paid for a suit of gold Milanese armor."

"I wondered how he financed it," she admitted. "It is splendid, and he looked magnificent. He outshone everyone on the field." They both knew he should not have encumbered her income without her authorization.

He probably did it as revenge for her father's refusal to crown him Brittany's Duke regnant. By the time King Louis announced late in October that he had decided to assign him the administration of Brittany — *hers* by right — François must have already authorized the payment. What a foolish risk to take, Claude thought. If Papa had learned of the transaction before he had given François her Breton income, nothing she said would have persuaded her father to agree. Yet even with that great increase in his income, he had not paid the debt. Still, she asked, "How do you suggest we cover the extraordinary expense?"

Sieur Jacques tapped his fingers on the desktop. "I have been reflecting. The *rentes* from the past quarter are fully allotted. The simplest items to reduce are those designated for charity."

She frowned at the suggestion.

"The amount set aside for books?"

She shook her head.

"Or the sums for gifts?"

Claude bit her lip. "What about the amount put aside for my wardrobe?"

"The cloth has already been purchased, Duchess. It would mean releasing seamstresses from your household. This is the most difficult time of year for them to find work, and Paris is far from their homes. The court does not return to the Loire Valley until the New Year. Nor would it cover the sum involved."

"No, that would not be right." Claude's eyes filled. "I cannot do that."

"I did not think you would approve."

She struggled with hard decisions. She might sell the loose jewels of Maman's she had stashed in her bureaus. Although they were valuable, she kept them for their beauty. And because running her fingers through them reminded her of Maman. It had been one of her few personal luxuries.

"May I make a suggestion?" Sieur Jacques spoke gently.

"Of course."

"You set aside a large sum for a war horse and bard[3] as an *étrenne* for your husband. I propose to use that sum to pay the debt. Your gift will be the armor he has purchased for himself."

As soon as she heard the proposal, she knew. "That is the correct solution. Please go ahead." It was the hardest decision she had made about François, and her heart hurt. It was hard to breathe deeply and there was a lump in her throat. She was not certain if she was sad or angry.

Sieur Jacques cleared his throat again. "I told the Lombard that in future he should require some security of the duke. Also, he should contact me when the duke came to him, but to be discreet; for it would be better if the duke were unaware we had dealings with his banker. It serves us to know with whom the duke has his dealings, does it not?"

For a moment she remained silent. It felt disloyal to discuss her husband with this man. Then anger shook her again. François had much for which to be ashamed. "Yes. After New Year's, when he realizes, perhaps he will be shamed into change, but until then it is a solution." She paused. The words she owed her treasurer stuck in her throat, but he had served her honorably. She took his hands in hers. "Thank you, my friend. My mother told me I would find no better Grand Treasurer than you. I never doubted her, and today you have shown me that she guided me well. You have saved me and the duke from embarrassment and from a quarrel with the king."

They both rose. He bowed deeply. "You are my liege lady. It is an honor to serve you."

Sieur Jacques pulled tight his fur-lined black houppelande[4] and departed. Left alone, Claude brooded. From the moment she had seen François ride up in his fine armor she had worried. He already controlled her share of Brittany's enormous ducal income, yet he was still acquiring more debts. What would he ask of her next?

7 DECEMBER 1514

HÔTEL DES TOURNELLES

aronne Michelle de Soubise

BARONNE MICHELLE SMILED at Duchess Claude's awed expression. "It is true."

"You could not have given me happier news." Duchess Claude jumped from her stool and hugged Michelle. Then she danced around her dressing room. "*Grâce à Dieu.* I am sooo delighted. A baby." She crossed herself. "When is it… he due?"

"I expect you to deliver about the middle of August. If God wills it so," Michelle crossed herself, "and if we recorded the dates of your last flowers correctly, which I am sure we did. And no, I cannot say whether you will have a boy."

The duchess's face fell, but she rallied with a laugh.

Michelle was sure Duchess Claude had seen midwives holding pendula over the bellies of expectant mothers in noblewomen's presence chambers. She wrinkled her nose. "Wise women and midwives will say that they can tell using a pendant or by the way you carry. I have not found it to be true, but expectant mothers often want certainty. Also, charlatans prey on women and say what they think you want to hear. Or what you fear. In truth, divination is magic, and some say it calls demons."

Duchess Claude cradled her abdomen, biting her fingernail. "You are certain it is true? I can tell François without fear I will disappoint him later?"

Michelle understood her hesitation. She had watched her parents' grief. All those infants who died so soon after birth. Hopes raised and tragic losses. She must fear she would share her mother's fate and carry sons who did not survive their babyhood. "It is always possible you may lose your baby early. But tell your husband anyway. Should you face such sorrow, you should not suffer alone. More important, give yourselves every moment to share this joy the Virgin sends you." He would rush off to tell his mother, Michelle did not doubt. It was a victory for the d'Angoulême family. She put aside the sour thought, determined to rejoice with the duchess.

Duchess Claude gazed about vacantly. The idea of a baby was still too new for her to absorb.

"Are your bubbies sore or enlarged? Does your gut feel tender? In the morning when you smell food, do you feel an urge to vomit?"

Her eyes brightened. "Ahhh," she murmured. "So that is why."

"Now do you believe me?"

She nodded and gave a small smile. "I should have guessed, for I have heard my ladies complain enough of those things. But it feels different when it happens to me."

"Is that not so often true? It only becomes real when it happens to us. This time it is not just that your flowers are late. You feel changes inside too, do you not?" Michelle wanted her to notice as her body altered. Only if she told her infirmarians quickly when she felt a change would they have time to solve any problems, God willing. But she did not want to frighten the girl.

Duchess Claude beamed at Michelle then. What a difference the news had made in her. Her countenance glowed pink, and her blue eyes sparkled. Michelle sent a quick prayer to the Virgin that Anne watch over her daughter and her unborn child.

She deserved this good news and the praise she should receive from her husband. "Shall I send for him? You will attend the banquet hosted by the City of Paris together, will you not? Or would you like me to call your ladies?"

Duchess Claude settled back in her armchair. "Yes, do send for him. He will be enchanted. And I do not want any of my ladies except Mme. Jeanne. She knows how to hold her tongue."

"There is one more thing we must talk about first."

Duchess Claude looked nervous.

"Nothing dreadful, Duchess Claude. It is about your intimate relations. You may continue until your sixth month. After that you must stop for the safety of the child. You may say so to the duke if he is nervous. But if you wish to stop before, tell him whatever you wish."

Duchess Claude blushed, the color rising above her low-cut gown all the way to her hairline. "But I do not wish to stop at all."

"That is excellent news for the future of the country," Michelle assured her, "but you must for the latter months." Michelle was relieved that they must interrupt their relations for five months, since she must wait until she was churched 40 days after the birth. When she examined Duchess Claude, the duchess showed no signs of the dreaded Italian disease[1] — or of the other illnesses that men brought to women — but Duke François had not reduced his lecherous ways. Duchess Claude was safer without his embraces.

At the banquet that evening, Michelle sat beside Princess Renée. Next to the young princess sat Duchess Claude. Duke François treated Claude as if she were made of the finest Venetian glass. He fed her from his own trencher, choosing the tenderest pieces of duck and pigeon, and the flakiest portions of whitefish and salmon. She blossomed under his care like a young rosebud in June, looking so pink and dewy that even King Louis, who each day looked more like a skeleton at the All Souls Day feast, gave his son-in-law a genial nod.

The trumpets sounded the fanfare for the second course, and the pages began their procession toward them at the head table. Its service took time, for the course consisted of twenty dishes including a salad and some fresh pears in sweet wine.

Princess Renée murmured to her sister, "Why is Duke François being so lovey-dovey to you tonight?"

Duchess Claude looked conscious. Michelle could almost hear her prepare a vague answer, but then Claude searched her sister's worried face. Princess Renée was direct, frightened... and always persistent. "Will you promise to keep my secret from everyone — except Mme. Michelle, who already knows?"

Princess Renée's lip protruded. "You told her before me?" Her voice dripped with heartbreak.

The clatter of platters as the pages served the king drowned Duchess Claude's chuckle. "No, do not try to make me feel guilty, Sister. *She* told me." She barely contained a giggle. "Can you guess?"

Princess Renée's eyes widened as she shook her head.

"Well, you must say nothing; nor even look surprised. Listen. I am going to have... a baby!"

"Ohhhhh," whispered Princess Renée. To keep her promise, she lowered her head over her trencher, pointing to the first dish the page offered. Fortunately, it was stewed eels, which Michelle knew she liked. Under the table, she clapped her hands. "That is wonderful, Sister! If we were not at this table, I would kiss you. I would even kiss Duke François." She perched her head to one side, "You may tell him that."

Duchess Claude's lips twitched. "He will appreciate it, I am sure."

Having done her duty by the dauphin, Princess Renée took an interest in the food whose spicy aromas now pervaded the surrounding air. She pointed to the roasted swan — presented with a gilded crown and feather-tips — and then chose a piece of the roasted boar surrounded by roasted turnips and pickled apples with greens. Michelle tasted everything that Princess Renée put on her plate before she did. Mme. Jeanne performed the same service for Duchess Claude.

The duchess and her sister finally ended their conversation when another fanfare of the heralds' trumpets announced the 'subtlety.' It was a massive replica in colored marzipan and spun sugar of the fabulous tournament just ended, complete with stands, tiltyard, caparisoned and armored horses, jousters with their standards and devices, and even a marzipan King Louis and Queen Marie distributing prizes in the royal box. As the musicians in the gallery played a march, the master guildsmen paraded their masterpiece on their shoulders before the high table and then throughout the entire hall. Like everyone else in the hall, Michelle was dazzled.

While servants cleared the main hall for the grand ball to follow, the city magistrates took the highest-ranked nobles to an exquisite antechamber hung with hunting tapestries, and warmed by fireplaces at either end. Here servers pushed their way among the milling guests with goblets of spicy hippocras, platters of comfits and sweetmeats, and trays of sweet wafers. Standing near the king, Michelle observed that he refused all the sweets, even a comfit Queen Marie offered him. He did accept a goblet of the sweet hippocras — pure poison for a stomach as delicate as his. Did Queen Marie want to shorten his life?

By the time they returned to the main hall, they found it transformed into an enchanted woodland filled with bowers of evergreens, aspen, myrtle, and holly bushes, among which wooden deer, fox, and rabbits peeked. Sprightly music played and she heard birds, cheeping and chattering. Michelle had to peer carefully among the leafy treetops to find the cages hidden high among the rafters.

When the Duke of Suffolk led out Queen Marie to open a stately pavane, Duchess Claude motioned for Princess Renée and Michelle to join her and Duke François beside King Louis. The music, shuffling feet, and waves of conversation, coupled with the distance granted them by their royal dignity, created privacy for the duration of the dance.

Gallantly, Duke François handed Duchess Claude onto the queen's vacant throne. The king threw him a puzzled glance.

Duke François winked. "Your Majesty, we bring you glad tidings. Your daughter, our beloved wife, is the precious vessel of a new life."

King Louis appeared bewildered. After a moment, the duke said, "She carries your first grandchild."

Michelle thought she glimpsed jealousy flash in King Louis's eyes. But it transformed instantly into joy.

"A grandchild," he breathed. "A grandson." Crossing himself, he lifted Claude's hands to his lips. "God bless you, my precious daughter. Your mother would be as delighted as I am."

Releasing her hands, he gazed at his son-in-law, his eyes damp. "My dear son, this is the best possible news. This evening you have pleased me... treating Claude as a husband should... and now you tell me I shall be a grandfather." He sniffed, pulled a handkerchief from his sleeve, and buried his face in the large piece of linen. His voice was thick when he spoke again. "When does this blessed event occur?"

François's cheeks flushed. "Naturally, we are informing you at once. Mme. Michelle says August, mid-August, an God wills."

Michelle repressed a smile. Did François think he sounded overeager announcing the news so early? With royal events of such importance, it could never be too soon.

"She must be treated like a delicate flower. No riding. Bed rest." Louis looked at Michelle. "I see you, Mme. Michelle. You must oversee her care. Ensure she is careful."

Michelle curtsied. "I shall do my best, Sire. I can only hope that she heeds my advice better than some of my patients." He had the grace to look amused.

"I shall order her to obey you," he said.

"She is her mother's daughter, Sire. She may appear meek, but she has much Breton blood."

King Louis chuckled. "Like you, I have known her all her life, so I learned that long ago." He gave his son-in-law a light punch on the arm. "I do not know if you have been married to her long enough to discover it."

Duchess Claude laughed, too, obviously delighted with the reconciliation between the two men she loved best.

Michelle wondered if she had been the only one to perceive the king's envy. King Louis would rather that it was his wife who was with child. Might it yet be so?

MICHELLE HURRIED to the duchess's suite, fearing the worst. As she entered, she saw Duchess Claude hunched in her favorite armchair near the fireplace, weeping and wringing her hands. A book lay splayed open on the floor as if she had thrown it aside. She was alone except for a maidservant who hovered in the background. Very strange.

Dropping her basket of herbs on the floor, Michelle hurried to Claude's side and peered at her skirts and the seat of her chair. No blood. Good. She turned to the maid. "Girl, bring me a clean cloth and cool water."

Then she dropped onto the stool beside Claude's chair. "Duchess Claude, what is the problem?" Michelle tugged the duchess's hands apart and held them.

Opening her swollen eyes, Duchess Claude stifled sobs turned into a loud wail. "Baronne! Oh, I do not know what to dooo..."

The maidservant brought the water.

"Take a deep breath, now release it, one... two... three... four... Another deep breath..." As she instructed the duchess, Michelle ordered the maid to fetch a table. Then she crumbled lavender flowers into the water, dipped the cloth and bathed Duchess Claude's face and hands, counting Claude's breaths until she calmed.

"That's better. Now, why are you so distressed?"

Duchess Claude looked as terrified as if Michelle had threatened her with hellfire. Her hands clenched, she squeezed her eyes closed, and pressed herself backwards into the chair as if trying to escape through it.

"It is not a hard question." Michelle murmured. "Are you in pain? Any nausea? Are you hungry? Do you want to sleep?"

After each question, Claude shook her head.

"What is it then?"

Duchess Claude opened tear-drenched eyes. "I w-was hungry earlier, but w-when my maidservant brought me a small beer..." Her voice trailed off.

"What happened then? Did the smell make you vomit? Has it happened before?"

Duchess Claude cowered in her chair. "Yes, the smell... it made me want to vomit.... So I sent it away.... I have not eaten since... though I am hungry." She paused so long between each sentence that Michelle was surprised when she continued and would not meet her eyes.

Michelle concluded that something serious must have occurred to frighten her, for when Michelle left her earlier, everything had been fine. After examining the girl's wrists and ankles, she said, "There is no sign of swelling. That is good." Claude did not respond.

Well, if nausea was the only symptom she admitted to, Michelle would begin with that. She said, "The best thing to eat when you feel nauseated is dry bread or toast. The best thing to drink is well-watered wine."

Duchess Claude looked at her blankly, as if Michelle had spoken in tongues and Claude could not understand anything she said. Her reaction was troubling. "Do you understand, Duchess?" Still she did not respond.

Michelle began to think that she might be in shock. Turning to the maid, she asked, "What happened just before the duchess fell into this state?"

The girl's voice quaked. "Ma'am, I didn't notice nothing particular. Mme. the Countess d'Angoulême left with her lady. Then the duchess told her ladies t'leave so'as she could rest and after a bit, she took on like she was when you came." It took work to understand the maid's garbled words. "So I sent for Mme. Jeanne... and she sent for you."

"Where is Mme. Jeanne?"

"I sent her away." They both turned toward the unexpected voice. Duchess Claude's voice wobbled, but her answer made sense. Michelle breathed a sigh of relief and motioned the maid to leave them.

"Tell me what happened with Mme. Louise." Then she waited.

Finally, Claude spoke. "I do not know who to b-b-believe. After you left, Maman Louise came to see me. She whispered that she had a confidence to tell me. She said that sh-she had wrestled long with her conscience because it would disturb me. Then she said… that Maman had t-trusted you, when she should not. That… that you made all Maman's sons d-die. All of them. When I said I could not b-believe it, she got that knowing smile of hers."

As Michelle listened, her ears began to ring as if people were clanging plague bells all around her until she could not think for the clamor. Duchess Claude droned on. "She warned me against trusting you… 'for the b-baby,' she said, 'if I did not c-care about my own health.'" Tears flooded down Claude's cheeks by the time she ended her recital.

Her years of experience came to Michelle's aid. By focusing on the need to calm the duchess's agitation, she pushed aside her own distress. If Duchess Claude became hysterical, she might well miscarry the child or make herself ill, either of which could convince Claude that Louise spoke true. How diabolical of the countess. "Close your eyes. Now breathe," Michelle said. "One… two… three… four. That's good. Keep breathing while I count."

After chafing Duchess Claude's hands, Michelle massaged the girl's head and face until her muscles relaxed and her breathing returned to normal. Then she said, "I want you to reflect a minute. You do not need to say anything. Would your Maman have kept me by her side for almost twenty years without noticing that I was harming her babies? Would no one in her lying-in chambers or during birthings have spoken out against me? You have lived your life at court, Duchess. Would there not have been gossip? Would a man as suspicious as your Papa have permitted me to stay with your Maman if there were a grain of truth to it?"

Duchess Claude rolled her head from side to side. "N-no. I should have thought of that."

Michelle continued the massage. "Mme. Louise frightened you. Did she tell you not to say a word to anyone?"

Duchess Claude's head wobbled an affirmative.

"Well, of course she did. She wanted you to feel alone and fearful, so you had only her to trust. No wonder you are so distraught." She sat down on the stool beside the duchess and took her hands. "May I give you some advice?"

Duchess Claude opened her eyes and nodded. She looked much more cheerful. "I do not know why I let Maman Louise cause me to doubt you. I am ashamed. Please forgive me."

"Do not blame yourself, Duchess Claude. It is one of our Lord's mysteries that when women are with child, they are subject to extreme and changeable humors. When you feel tearful or frightened, breathe the way I showed you until you are calm. Say a rosary. The Blessed Virgin sent us these methods to calm us. Now here are a few other things." She advised moderation in the quantity and variety of her food and drink, and to take mild exercise. "You must never permit bloodletting, purging, emetics or any such treatment without talking to me first. Your body does not like harsh treatments when it is in a delicate condition. I know many doctors prescribe such methods when women complain of nausea, dizziness, and cravings. But do not allow it."

Claude sounded worried. "But I am not good at refusing. Especially if Maman Louise orders me."

"Why do you not speak to your Papa? He knows that Dr. Nichel is the only doctor your mother trusted. Your Maman refused to see doctors when she was increasing. Ask him to order that Dr. Nichel or I should treat you."

"But what if Maman Louise persuades him she should take charge? You know how easily she persuades him to her way of thinking."

"Can you not tell Duke François that you trust only Dr. Nichel? And me? That you become terrified and hysterical without us? He can control his mother, even if your Papa cannot?"

Claude chewed her lower lip as she pondered this. Then she nodded slowly. "I can do that. He is so worried that something might happen to this child he frets whenever the least thing troubles my health these days."

Soon Claude was full of eager questions. "What exactly should I eat? How much is moderate?"

But Michelle did not indulge her long. After her excess of emotion, Duchess Claude needed rest. "I am leaving you some soothing teas. They will help. And one last thing. Never listen to women's tales of their bearing or birthing. I assure you, every woman who has birthed will have a terrifying tale to tell. And if you do listen, you must *not* believe them. Difficult as this counsel may be, it is my sagest advice. Now rest. See no one for the rest of the day."

Calming the duchess had calmed Michelle. Still, she needed a period of reflection. In the chapel, she prayed for guidance. This falsehood of Countess Louise's might well have created a breach between Claude and herself. What would she try next? And how could Michelle protect Claude — and herself — against the countess's schemes?

LOUISE and her son peeked through the curtained windows of her suite in Hôtel des Tournelles. As they watched, the English delegation emerged from the passageway, passed through the main gates, and then turned onto the narrow, malodorous Parisian street.

"Finally! They're off!" Duke François danced a little jig. "Never is too soon to see the Duke of Suffolk again. The king acts as if the sun shines from his arse. If he has not shaken the sheets with Mme. Marie, I will eat my new feathered hat." He tossed the extravagant object high into the air, caught it with one hand, twirled it on a finger, slapped it back on his head, and gave Louise a jaunty grin.

Louise did not smile back. "Start eating now. Though it does not look tasty to me... and when I think what it cost you not one month ago, I wish you would reconsider."

François took her by the shoulders and turned her to face him. "Are you telling me you are certain Suffolk has not played the two-backed animal with her?"

"Yes."

"How do you know? Why are you so certain?"

Louise tapped him on the chest. "You know she came to the king a virgin. She has told me that our king has not been able to perform his duty. Although he has tried. Repeatedly."

François raised his eyebrows. "You did well to winkle that secret from her. It is a matter of state. If she offers France a son, we will know he is a bastard."

"Not if the king recognizes him. And if she offers the king a son, what would you wager that Louis would reject him?" She moved away from the window and poured them each a goblet of wine.

"True. Well, I am not convinced you are correct." François ruffled her hair. Thank goodness she had not yet had it dressed for the day. "Queen Marie is a charming filly. Now that the Duke has gone, I have a mind to make a play for her again." Downing the wine, he changed the subject in his insouciant style. "Have you completed the arrangements and contract for Souvereine's wedding?"

Refusing to be side-tracked, Louise raised her voice. "Do NOT, François, do NOT seduce the queen. Surely you understand that if you were to get a boy on her, Louis would acknowledge him? Do you want to lose the throne to your own son?" Grabbing his shoulders, she shook him.

He was much taller and stronger than she. Catching her forearms, he swung her round. "Do not worry, Maman. I know how to prevent children. I have much experience."

She glared until he put her down. "You give no evidence of it. You have fathered several boys already! I know for I have paid for them."

François merely gave her a hug and kiss and left her apartments, whistling.

Louise rubbed at the frown etched into her forehead. She would not allow him to throw away his future on a tumble and a whim. She *would* not.

Pacing her room, she considered the possibilities. Louis was taking his time to die. It was most irritating. She had been pleased with Queen Marie at first, for her lively spirits had worn the king down and his rapid decline had been apparent to everyone. Recently though, he had taken to resting more. Marie, ever the dutiful wife, stayed at his bedside playing cards and chess. Too annoying. How risky would it be to prepare a tonic for Marie to give to him while she was away from court at her château at Romorantin for the Christmas season?

Did she dare hurry the king to his end? How could she accomplish it? A tonic was not realistic. She sank into a chair and steepled her fingers. Aha. Dried apricot pastilles with ground apricot pits. Four daily. The ideal solution. Upon further reflection, she decided perhaps it might not work. The king disliked taking medicine, so if she bribed a servant into adding new lozenges to his remedies, Louis would be sure to spot them. Then he would make a fuss to his infirmarian and all her work would be wasted. Sweets, then. Twice daily; after the second meal and in the evening. She could persuade Queen Marie to administer them without her even knowing. It would be much easier. Slower, unfortunately, but less likely to raise questions. Yes, it was the best plan. Anyone could eat one or two with no ill effect. And when he experienced nausea or fever, or an aching head and pains in his joints no one, including he, would think anything of it.

Now she could look forward to her departure even more eagerly. No one would comment on how Jean and she spent their time together. Here at court discretion was essential, and she missed his company. Besides, she must complete the arrangements for Souvereine's wedding. Although François, Marguerite, and their spouses could not attend, Souvereine's full sisters, their husbands and families would attend the late December ceremony.

The day before her departure, Louise brought the apricot sweets to Queen Marie, presenting them as an early New Year's *étrenne* for the king. "They are a favorite of his," Louise confided to the queen, "But he will enjoy them more coming from you. Offer him one after the second meal and another in the evening with his wine. Let us keep it a secret from King Louis until I return in January. I would like to surprise him myself." Queen Marie, who loved secrets and pleasing Louis, agreed.

Louise's carriage swayed and bumped along the frozen tracks towards Romorantin. Wrapped in fur blankets, with hot bricks on the floor warming the small space, she was cozy. She opened the curtains. Even in the winter, the scenery was enchanting. New manor houses and prosperous farms puffing smoke into the chilly air dotted the rich, peaceful countryside. King Louis's parsimony had benefited the country's farmers and merchants.

The dusting of pristine snow shining as white as beaten egg whites reminded Louise of her childhood home in mountainous Savoie. It sparkled in the sunlight, as bright as François's future. His wait could not be long now. He was itching to conquer Milan and assert his rights over the duchy included in Claude's dowry, but not yet under French control. It would be a splendid acquisition, but it would not be easy. At a minimum, he must make sure he left no enemies at his back. He would need allies. And a strategy. She leaned back smiling. She was good at that. And they would need diplomats. She considered which courtiers would make suitable appointments when he became king. Her son would appreciate her political talents. And he would repay her by giving her what she wanted.

Her hands curled into fists. One of her first projects would be to dislodge Baronne Michelle de Soubise, who was only a pawn in the game of power now. Except that she had her talons firmly sunk into Princess Renée's life. And now Duchess Claude had fallen further under her spell. They were as thick as cream these days. Claude was avoiding her, ever since she had insinuated that the baronne had harmed her mother's infants. Claude had not believed her. It had drawn her closer to Mme. Michelle. Much as Louise did not like to admit it, she had not handled that affair well. Well, she could do nothing about it now.

Reaching for the basket she had ordered the kitchens to pack for her trip, Louise put Mme. de Soubise out of her mind. For now, she allowed her thoughts to drift to Jean and their time together in Romorantin. It had been too long since she had last felt his touch.

HÔTEL DES TOURNELLES

DUCHESS CLAUDE CLAPPED her hands when she entered the ball-room of the Hôtel des Tournelles. "François, it is charming. I have never seen its like. And it smells like a pine wood."

François admired the transformation in the ballroom. "Queen Marie has altered it to her English taste. Look at the holly, ivy, and mistletoe draped everywhere, and the pine branches pinned on the walls. And the huge log in the fireplace. It must be an entire pine tree."

Pages dressed as shepherds strolled about carrying large bowls filled with a frothy brew. One approached her, sank to one knee, and held the bowl up.

"What is it?" asked Duchess Claude.

The page shrugged. "Madame la Reine ordered it. It is a posset, very English, that they drink at Yuletide. They call it 'Lambswool.'" The word came out as 'la soule'. He rolled his eyes. "It is made from roasted apples, beer, nutmeg, ginger and sugar." He raised his eyebrows. "Later, after the nativity play, she says we shall have large basins of water and children shall bob for apples."

"Well—" Claude looked doubtful but sipped it from the proffered ladle. "Mmmm. It is good. Try some François."

"Queen Marie, the woodland you have created is delightful." François practiced his charms on the queen when she came to greet them.

Claude curtsied, jealous of his admiration for Queen Marie. She had watched him stalking her like prey since she had arrived in France. Well-educated and skillful at flirtation, the queen had the beauty, intelligence and wit he admired in a woman. She was gifted with the confidence and beauty to make the seduction a challenge, yet morals easy enough to succumb to temptation — or so he obviously believed.

Claude knew well that many married court ladies were unfaithful to their husbands, just as their spouses were untrue to them. Her own husband was notorious. But she could not believe that Queen Marie would disgrace her royal blood.

When Duke François opened the ball with Queen Marie, Claude's father invited her to sit beside him on Queen Marie's throne. The couple shone as they performed the lively coronato and were flushed and breathless by the time it finished.

As he watched the dancing, King Louis said, "I am pleased to see your husband treating my wife as he should. He was overfamiliar when she first came to France, but his behavior improves. It is right that they open balls together when our conditions prevent us from participating." He reached for Claude's hand. "Besides, it gives us the opportunity to converse, an occasion afforded me far too rarely these days."

"You are rarely alone, Papa."

"Is that a criticism, Daughter? Careful or I will not regret how little time we have spent together." King Louis pinched her cheek.

Recognizing he was teasing, Claude smiled. "Forgive me, Papa. Even if true, I will say no more. It irritates me when those to whom I have confided our happy news immediately fuss over me when I have never felt better. It is clear you are delighted with your new wife." She did not like herself for grudging him his happiness. Yet each time she saw him laughing with Marie, it felt like another betrayal. Had it been so easy to replace her mother?

He patted her hand. "Never think I forget your mother because I enjoy Marie's company, Claude. When I am with my dear Marie, her youth and liveliness help me forget my aches and pains. But the moment I am alone, I remember what I have lost. Is it the same with you? Although the worst grief has passed, you do not forget your mother because you are happy with your husband, do you?" His eyes stared unseeingly at the coffered ceiling hung with the brightly colored banners of the noble families of France. "When a different cardinal enters my office, I miss Cardinal Georges and when another woman offers me advice, I miss your mother. I grow too old, Daughter, for I have outlived my dearest friends."

Claude rounded on him. "You must not leave us, Papa. Not me, nor Renée. Nor François. Though he thinks he is ready to rule," her voice dropped, "he is not. We need you. Selfish as that is." She covered her mouth with one hand. "Forgive me."

"You have a right to want your papa, child." He wore an odd, satisfied expression.

François and Queen Marie joined them.

"You were the best dancers in the room," Duchess Claude said. "Is that not so, Papa?"

"Husband, Duke François informs me that you and Queen Anne were notable dancers yourselves. I would have been enchanted to watch you." Queen Marie batted her eyelashes at the king.

"Be off with you, flatterers. My daughter and I are enjoying a comfortable chat." The king shooed them away.

As Queen Marie took François's arm confidingly and tinkled a laugh at one of his sallies, Claude's breathing shortened the way it did when her maid pulled the laces of her dress too tight. She hated to feel jealous, but she was familiar with his seductions. This was how they always started. Her husband charmed women into falling into his bed. Claude had seen it happen so often since she was a young girl that she knew the signs. She at least knew his flaws, and yet she loved him still. Hers was not some silly infatuation.

"You have not called Mme. Michelle, Papa?" Claude clenched her fists into tight balls to keep her temper. His bedchamber was as hot as a steam bath and reeked of foul odors and the sweat of too many people. He needed space and his room cleaned. Or so Mme. Michelle would say. Why was she not here?

He tossed and moaned in the bed. Claude leaned over, one ear close to his lips, struggling to untangle his words, garbled by whatever he had in his mouth. His breath stank, rancid and sickly sweet. "Marie did not wish to trouble her."

Claude spoke gently to the queen who was, she reminded herself, only two years her elder. "Queen Marie, Mme. Michelle is the person my family most trusts when one of us is ill. She has been with us since my parents married. May I call for her in your name?"

Queen Marie was rocking on the edge of her chair on the far side of the king's bed, her eyes flitting from Claude to her husband. "Dr. Loysel did not suggest it and he is my husband's personal physician." Had the queen emphasized 'my husband' or was it Claude's imagination? She did not think so.

"It is professional rivalry, for he is a university man and teaches at the Sorbonne. Her knowledge has all been practical since she is a woman. They have worked together many times."

When Marie hesitated, avoiding Claude's eyes, she steeled her voice. "Papa dismissed all other doctors and appointed the baronne as principal lady of my mother's bedchamber last January when she was mortally ill."

"But your maman died."

Claude said, "She died without suffering in clean and peaceful surroundings." She pointedly surveyed the noxious, crowded chamber, then locked eyes with the queen. "These conditions will only increase his ordeal without effecting a cure."

"Ooohhh. I do not know what to do... and I have no one to advise me. Why did Countess Louise have to leave the court at this time?" Queen Marie slumped, burying her face in her hands.

Ahhh. That was who had been advising the queen. Claude sighed quietly. So, her mother-in-law had caught another in her web of charm. Claude dropped to her knees beside the queen's chair. "I understand how heavily the responsibility weighs upon you. But, Queen Marie, I love my Papa and wish him to live as much as you do." Probably much more, but it would be unkind — and pointless — to say so. "Let me call Dr. Loysel to Papa's side and suggest to him that we invite Mme. Michelle. Papa will agree if you do. Please, support me. Will you?"

The queen nodded reluctantly.

Claude said, "You must show more enthusiasm, Queen Marie, or Papa will not agree. You are his wife. He will always support you. You must say, 'Yes, I wish it!' and your voice must be firm, the way mine was. Are you willing? If not, I shall say no more."

Queen Marie's gaze darted around the room. Claude guessed she desperately wanted someone to save her from a decision. Making her voice sympathetic, she said, "You were told not to trust Mme. Michelle, were you not? So it is hard to ask for her. I understand. But I trust her and so does Papa. If anyone asks, say I advised it."

Marie straightened. "Yes, I will do it."

They squeezed each other's hands. Not feeling so alone, Claude called a page. "Please send for Dr. Loysel. Now!" After he left, she blew a relieved breath.

MME. Michelle shepherded the last of the crowd of courtiers from the king's bedchamber. With Queen Marie's and Duchess Claude's support she had reduced the numbers in the king's inner chamber to three apprentice physicians, one apothecary, two nursing sisters and one priest, two maids and one manservant. At first the queen had demurred. She finally agreed after the baronne warned her that the larger the number permitted entry, the greater the risk of rumors. In unstable times when the king was dying, gossip led to idle speculation and created problems. Dr. Loysel was unhappy with the reduced numbers. She told him he could blame her if the king did not recover.

Dr. Loysel and Michelle agreed that he suffered from a disequilibrium of the sanguinary, hot, wet humor which had led to this debilitating attack of gout. They blamed his overindulgent living since he married. Because the apprentices who had just left had bled and purged him, Dr. Loysel reluctantly agreed to prescribe only a pastille to reduce the pain, fever and swelling. Made from the autumn crocus, its worst side effect was the diarrhea. Since Dr. Loysel had recommended another purge, he could not oppose the treatment once Michelle emphasized this side effect. She did not add that she would add a few drops of opium to help him sleep to avoid the nausea, cramps, and purging.

If the king recovered from this crisis, with a miracle he could recuperate, as he had previously. Then she would impress upon the young queen how essential it was that he follow a regime of gentle exercise, careful diet and plenty of rest — the lifestyle the late Queen Anne had regulated so well for him. But Michelle feared he was unlikely to survive.

After she consulted the queen and Duchess Claude, Michelle ordered the king's bedchamber set to order. Asking her companions to sit quietly, she had the servants place chairs near the king's bed. Then they arranged privacy screens, placed tables against the wall for his medicines, tossed applewood, bay leaves and rosemary branches into the fire to cleanse the air and cones of sandalwood incense to the braziers, swept the floor and removed the stinking close stools. Meanwhile, after preparing cool lavender water, she seated herself on a stool beside the king, and wiped his fevered face.

The king appeared unconscious while Mme. Michelle created order and tranquility in his chamber. After she refreshed his countenance, he spoke. "Thank you, Mme. Michelle. I understand why my late wife wanted you by her bedside. You have a way of enforcing obedience that many a battlefield commander would envy."

She smiled at him. "Coming from such a noted commander as yourself, that is a compliment I shall cherish, Sire. My next command is that you swallow this tisane and rest."

"I tremble and obey."

He waved his daughter to leave, inviting only his wife and Mme. Michelle to remain. Once the king slept, Michelle suggested the queen go to her room to rest. Before she left, she handed Michelle a box of sweets. "I have been giving my husband one of these after his second meal and each evening. If he wakes, please give him one for me."

Michelle took the painted cedar box. "What are they, Mme. la Reine?"

Her forehead wrinkled. "I am not sure exactly. A form of Turkish delight, I believe."

"He should not eat any sweet. It is the worst thing for his health."

Queen Marie brightened and said, her tone assured, "Oh, that cannot be. Mme. Louise gave them to me, saying they would be excellent for him. And she is a noted herbalist, you know."

Michelle took the box with a careful nod. "In that case..." she said.

As the queen swished out the door, calling her principal lady from the outer chamber to accompany her, Michelle sniffed the delicacy and took a small bite. "Dried apricot with something finely ground added to the paste. It tastes of almonds. Nothing could be worse." She did not know for a certainty that they contained ground apricot pits, but that was the most probable ingredient. Since they were a known poison, whoever had made them intended to harm the recipient. Mme. Louise had both the knowledge and the skill to do so. But to be certain, she would have to test the sweets. And for that she would have to confide in... in whom could she trust?

Michelle had heard rumors that people were plotting to kill King Louis. Some said that it was the English. Whisperers put it about that the new queen was at the root of it; the least of them saying she was killing the king through her excessive love of revelry. In Paris, louts in the street beat English merchants and students, and worse. Now her suspicions led her to the Countess. Should she say anything? And to whom? Sighing, she opened a new notebook to record the king's treatment.

When the king woke, should she confide her concerns to him if he was well enough? She did not want to worry him. But after her discovery of the apricot sweets, she could not doubt he was in danger. Would he believe her? Yet she could not allow him to continue to consume the treat without ensuring their wholesomeness.

King Louis woke in the darkest hours of the night, groaning from a painful attack of joint pain. She did not want to dull his senses before their conversation but, before everything, he was her patient. To help him sleep without the side effects of opium, she added drops of valerian to a soothing tea. With the tea she brought him fresh bread, which he grasped eagerly. After he had eaten, she said, "Sire, may I raise a concern?"

"Dear Baronne, of course."

"Sire, it is about your daughter, Renée."

"Well? Get to it."

She took a deep breath. "I have evidence—"

"Of course, you do."

"—that Mme. d'Angoulême plans to remove Princess Renée from my care."

The king said nothing. In the silence of the winter night, Michelle heard the coal crackle in the brazier behind them. Pine logs snapped and popped in the fireplace on the far side of the privacy screen. The residue of sandalwood hung in the air, masking the sour odors the king exuded. He did not answer for so long she thought he had fallen asleep again.

Finally, he stirred. "In her last testament, the late queen appointed Mme. Louise guardian to our daughter, Renée." Stating the unpalatable fact, his tone stayed neutral.

"She did. She also appointed me as Princess Renée's gouvernante and asked me — made me swear — to remain with her until she married. I took a deathbed vow." Michelle kept her tone neutral, too, as she stated these facts. The Lord, the Virgin and the Saints would not permit her to shirk her duty, nor would Queen Anne, for Michelle felt her presence urging her to persist. She was insisting Michelle hold to her commitment.

"So she did."

The king's voice sounded troubled. His closed eyelids bulged as if Queen Anne was near him, too. "Could you have mistaken Mme. Louise's intentions?"

"No." Perhaps he needed to be convinced? "I kept records of the various incidents, although I do not have my notes here. Shall I fetch them?"

Was that a sigh? "No. I have read the meticulous notes you keep. If you say you have records, so it will be proven."

The silence lengthened. After a time, Michelle rose.

"Do not leave," he said. "I am considering. So far, I have concluded only that I sail between Scylla and Charybdis."

She did not say that she had no intention of leaving. The skin under his sunken eyes looked bruised; his face was an unhealthy gray; and his breath shallow and wheezy. She felt torn. Her love for the princess was at war with her duty to the king.

"Sleep now," she said. "Often answers come when we allow ourselves to listen to the Lord during sleep."

Putting aside her concerns for the princess at present, she felt frightened for herself. How typical it would be of the countess to spread vile insinuations. Such as saying in her syrupy voice, "Do you not find it a strange coincidence that Mme. Michelle presided over the deathbeds of both the queen and king. And Queen Marie tells me she gave him apricot pastilles twice a day before he died. You do know how fatal apricots can be, do you not?"

SLEET FELL, the mix of snow and rain turning the cobbled streets to slush in Paris's city center. The unpaved streets in the poorer areas and outlying *quartiers* pooled into icy mud that slid down the hills into the Seine River, turning it into a frigid snake slinking through the center of the city. The dull splatter absorbed street noises. Even the myriad church bells sounded dense in the thick, brooding air as daylight faded to a leaden gloom. It was impossible to keep torches burning in the sodden atmosphere. By four o'clock that afternoon anyone with a choice huddled inside a home or tavern with windows well covered to keep every scrap of heat in and chill out. Even the homeless poor clustered together wherever they found shelter: under the arches of a bridge, inside an abandoned building, under a damp ragged tent, struggling to keep a scanty fire alight in a meagre fire pit. Only those with the most urgent need or most nefarious errand found themselves on the lightless streets of the city. None but the worst walked alone from choice.

Michelle remained on duty as the teams caring for King Louis rotated in shifts. Over the last days of December, he worsened. The few close to him recognized he was nearing his end, but the whole court felt the menace of uncertainty his demise would bring. Michelle's only goal was to reduce his suffering.

On the last day of the year, King Louis sent for Duke François. When he left the king's side after their private conference, Michelle had never seen the duke appear as solemn.

The queen, the duchess, and Michelle all bowed their heads or turned away to hide their wet eyes from him and one another. As Queen Marie and Duchess Claude sat each on one side of the king's bed, Michelle arranged his chamber for the inevitable to distract herself.

Menservants removed the screens around his bed, brought a table for the portable altar, and placed a bench for his family at the foot of his bed. A gentleman usher alerted his choirmaster that the choir would soon be required. When the duchess and queen left, Michelle brought Princess Renée to her father for his final blessing. She stood by his head, patting his face.

He asked, "Do you love Mme. Michelle?"

Princess Renée stood very still. "Yes."

He nodded. "I have written it down that Baronne Michelle will stay with you until you are grown up. Is that good?"

The princess clutched Michelle's hand convulsively. "It's essen'chal. You have to promise!" Her voice squeaked.

The king made a sign of the cross. "I promise."

"You, too." She turned to Michelle.

"I promise," Michelle said. Her eyes locking on King Louis's as she signed the cross.

In the rambling Hôtel des Tournelles, with its many dripping courtyards and dank corridors, Queen Marie and Duchess Claude consulted in grave tones. They concluded they must hold the traditional New Year's Eve celebration that evening, despite the increasing certainty of the king's passing, and their preference to cancel it. The celebration would diminish the gloom that had settled like a miasma over the court and dissipate rumors that the king had died. They informed the king that, with his permission, they would hold the New Year's Eve ball.

"Of course," he said, his voice weak, "I applaud your wisdom." He tried to lift his hand, but it fell back onto his coverlet. "God's Blood, but I'm a useless old stick. Would that I could open the ball with you, my sweet Marie."

She patted his liver-spotted hand. "Soon you will be well again, and we will dance."

"Do not humor me, my dear. I will do no more dancing. In hours or days at most, I will be in the arms of our Savior. I am ready. I regret only to leave you, my beloved ones." He closed his eyes, tired from his long speech.

The Grand Maître oversaw the whole affair. The great hall gleamed in the light from the hundreds of wax candles in the huge chandeliers. Banners in Louis's colors of red and yellow streamed from the high ceiling. Court ladies-in-waiting entertained in charming *tableaux vivants* followed by a lively ballet danced by a traveling minstrel company. Then court musicians played in the upper gallery, as Duke François and Queen Marie opened the ball. Afterwards, François and Marie circulated, chatting and laughing. The royal family stayed until a formal pavane was in progress and then slipped away, leaving their servants to ply their guests with wine, and their favorites to deflect questions about their absence. As a distraction, the royal kitchens prepared an exquisite repast. Guests pushed their way to the central tables in a most uncourtly fashion, scuffling among themselves to snatch the fruits, jellies, sweets, and delicacies that they so rarely ate. It all served its function. All but the most intimate of the monarchs' households were unaware of the unfolding events. The following day, exhaustion and ill-natured gossip continued to divert the court's attention.

IN THE COLDEST hour of early morning, King Louis's spirit slipped away. It fled so softly that Michelle was not aware of its passing. Only when the king's confessor rose, closed the king's eyes and began the prayer for the dead, did she realize the significance of the moment. She stood and took a hasty step forward to check that he had gone. The priest gave her an inimical look, and she stopped. He had more experience than she with death and no reason to wish to hurry the king's departure. Michelle overheard Duke François speaking gently to his sobbing wife. Good.

Queen Marie moaned, and so Michelle turned to her to offer comfort. "Can I bring someone to you, Mme. la Reine? Or would you like to go to your rooms? Or to the chapel first?"

Queen Marie looked around vaguely, seemingly lost.

Michelle had seen widows react this way many times. Taking her arm, she said, "You cannot believe it yet. That is normal. May I take you to your rooms and give you something to help you sleep? Your vigil has been long and has ended with a sad loss. You will manage better after sleeping." As she was talking, Michelle pulled the queen's arm through hers and walked with her through a back passageway. Queen Marie did not resist.

After she had left the queen to her maids, Michelle decided she needed time in the chapel before retiring. Upon entering, she heard muffled sobs. Standing just inside its door, she wondered if she should allow the mourner to grieve alone. Then she recognized the distinctive form of Duchess Claude.

"Do you wish company, Duchess?" she called softly. "It is I, Michelle."

A muffled sniffle, a brief silence, "Yes, p-p-please."

At the altar rail Michelle knelt beside the duchess who leaned against her and murmured, her voice catching, "A year ago we celebrated the New Year with Maman. Now both Maman and Papa have gone to our Father." She drew a tearful breath.

Michelle could not allow her to wallow in sorrow as she had after her mother's death. Claude must protect the child growing within her. "It is what he wished. He knew how to conduct himself to live longer. He did not do so. It is hard for us. But for

him, it is a release. Now he is with the Lord and your Maman."
It was small comfort in her grief. She put a consoling arm
around Duchess Claude.

"At least Maman loved him. Not another."

Michelle squeezed her shoulder. "This is no time for bitterness.
It is unlike you, dear Duchess. Queen Marie was an offering
upon the altar of state. You were afraid that might be your fate
as well. Do not blame her. Instead, bless your parents for your
escape. And remember you carry a child. It is your duty to stay
healthy for him."

1 JANUARY 1515, BEFORE LAUDS

HÔTEL DES TOURNELLES

 ueen Claude de France

IN THE TOWER oratory off the far side of her bedchamber Claude, dressed entirely in black with a black headdress ornamented in onyx, kneeled at her prie-dieu. Mme. Jeanne entered. Although she knew Claude was at prayer, Mme. Jeanne cleared her throat. Her mistress did not budge, and so Mme. Jeanne hemmed louder and kept coughing more loudly until her lady — now Queen of France — said, "What is it?" without turning her head.

"Forgive me for disturbing your devotions. Mme. Marguerite insists on seeing you. I told her you did not wish to be disturbed, but she said she came from the king."

Sighing, Queen Claude struggled to her feet. "You had no choice then, Mme. Jeanne." Wiping the tears from her face, she plodded into the bedchamber and settled onto her bed. "Invite Mme. Marguerite to enter."

The Duchess d'Alençon stumbled in the darkened room as she made her way to Queen Claude. "Mme. la Reine," she said as she rose from a deep curtsy.

Claude felt like an imposter. Her mother was Queen of France, not she. Except that her mother was dead. And now her father, too. Tears threatened to spill again. She bit her teeth together to maintain her control.

As Duchess Marguerite sat herself on a nearby stool and murmured condolences. Queen Claude pinned a small curve on her lips and blocked out the words by repeating a rosary to herself to preserve her composure. She had discovered the technique the previous year and it served her well. She waited for her sister-in-law to leave. But she did not.

"Mme. la Reine, although the king, grieves as you do, he must take up the reins of state. He asks me to beg for your support in an important duty."

Claude's heart sank. When François left her that morning, he had been firm that she was not to give way to grief. It would harm their child, he said. Obviously, he had enlisted his sister's help. "What does he ask?"

"The Dowager Queen Marie needs your help. She must go to the Hôtel de Cluny. The chamberlain will organize the details, but you must explain our French customs, so she understands what is required of her. Promise to visit her. That sort of thing." Marguerite was watching Claude. "My brother says you are the best person to help Queen Marie because you are gentle and careful of the feelings of others. And you are near her age. The change will be hard for her. And if you discover her plans, it will be helpful for him."

Claude appraised her sister-in-law. Marguerite would certainly spy for François. She and his mother did anything he wanted. She was probably spying for him at this moment. Well, she would not judge her husband or family, but she believed in keeping confidences. It was part of her code of honor. Still, Queen Marie must be suffering and alone. Her papa had been happy with her, and she had been kind to him. And Mme. Michelle spoke true. She had been a pawn in the alliance between England and France. Claude recognized her duty. She would do her best to ease Marie's worries.

She prepared to rise. "Yes, of course, I will obey my husband."

Later that day, Queen Claude arrived at the Hôtel de Cluny with the Dowager Queen Marie, called the Reine Blanche for she was dressed in white from head to toe. The Château — surrounded by high walls spiked with razor-edged fleurs-de-lys sharp enough to pierce the legs of anyone foolish enough to attempt a breach — was hardly a welcoming place. As was the French custom, it would be the Dowager Queen's home for the next forty days. As they entered, Queen Claude reminded her she must never leave the château grounds or receive male visitors while she lived here in seclusion.

Queen Marie was indignant. "Foolish rules. My reputation should be safe if I am accompanied by ladies and guards."

"It is the tradition." Claude was conciliatory. "And it protects you. If France is so fortunate that the Lord has blessed you with a child, no one would want the least doubt cast upon its paternity. For if a son, he would be the next king of France. If it is known that your seclusion is strictly guarded, you are safe and so is the kingdom."

Queen Marie pouted but said no more.

They toured her suite together. The living areas for her and her ladies were magnificent: a coffered-ceiling great hall, a presence chamber, a more intimate dining chamber hung with charming tapestries, a gilded chapel musty with stale incense, antechambers and inner chambers leading to her bedchamber, oratory, wardrobe, and privy. Anything she might require for sedentary entertainment was supplied: prayer books, and lighter reading, chess games, cards, board games, musical instruments, parchment, pens and ink.

Dowager Queen Marie exclaimed with delight when she saw the small private library lined with dark walls of books. On one wall, a large desk with a leather chair sat in front of a curtained window with many-branched candelabra on both sides. On the opposite wall, a fireplace warmed and brightened the cozy space.

"I am expecting to write many letters," she said. "Really, what else is there to do? At least this is a charming spot to do so."

Now that, thought Claude, is exactly what François would want me to explore. Who will she write to? What is she writing about? I shall not.

COUNTESS LOUISE'S cavalcade slowed to enter Paris through the St. Antoine Gate and pass the towering walls of the Bastille that guarded the city's southern flank. The horses, harnessed in tandem on either end of her litter, struggled through the narrow, icy streets. What a relief the Hôtel des Tournelles was so close, thought Louise. The trip from Romorantin had seemed so long.

She had fallen to her knees and praised the holy Francis de Paule when she read François's urgent missive. He was king! Just as the hermit had promised. François recalled her to court after he told her his thrilling news. And asked her to use her time to make a list of proposed appointments and urgent tasks.

François's Grand Maître d'hôtel bowed low before he led Louise to her new suite close to the king's. When she learned her son had assigned it to her so she would be nearby, she swelled with pride. Stopping only to attire herself as befit the king's mother, she hastened to the great hall.

When Louise presented herself at the entrance, the gentleman usher, bowing so low his nose almost touched his knees, informed her she had arrived the day King François was hosting a reception for the ambassadors to France and for members of his Grand Council. What good fortune.

He announced her, his voice echoing throughout the hall. "Countess Louise d'Angoulême, the King's Mother,"

"Maman!"

Her son, the king, clad in a padded jacket of the latest style, leaped from the throne on the dais. She stood stock-still, admiring him as he hurried towards her. Lifting her off her feet, he smothered her in a bear hug, and then took her arm in his. What a moment!

They promenaded together as he presented her to the most important ambassadors: those of Venice, Milan, England, the Holy See, the Kingdoms of Castile and Aragon, Flanders and other parts of the Holy Roman Empire — although of course she knew them already. She recognized François was presenting her to make his point that she was his representative and proxy.

They stepped onto the dais. François clapped his hands, producing instant silence. "You see beside me my honored mother, the Countess d'Angoulême, Louise de Savoy. Please know that when you speak with her, you speak with me, and when she speaks with you, she speaks with my authority." Well, that made it explicit.

The hall erupted in a thunder of applause. Bowing her head slightly left and right while the noise gradually faded, Louise considered her response. A quick, humble acknowledgement was best. "My gracious son, King François, honors me. It shall be my pleasure to acquaint myself further with each of you to learn your particular concerns."

After she and the king descended the dais, ambassadors swarmed them. She limited herself to praise for the late King Louis and discussions of plans for his obsequies.

The reception wound to a close. Louise squeezed her son's arm and smiled up into his comely countenance, swelling with pride. Under cover of heralds announcing the feast and the chamberlain opening the doors to the grand salon, she murmured, "You are brilliant, my César. You have a gift for ceremony. And your first appointments are sound."

He looked relieved. "Do you think so, Mme. Maman? You reassure me. Those honored seemed pleased."

Of course they did. And praising him was wise, as she had learned over years of mothering him. Not that it was completely true — after all he had just appointed his friend, the Seigneur de Bonnivet, as Admiral of France — but there was no point criticizing *faits accomplis*. It was time to take him in hand

and control his appointments before he became too independent.

He had appointed bumblers like her son-in-law, Duke Charles d'Alençon — just named second person in France and Governor of Normandy — ancient nobility of the sword to be sure, but useless. At least the Duke de Bourbon-Montpensier, whose dark head she recognized, was competent.

Like the parting of the Red Sea, everyone stepped aside to allow Majesty to leave the room first. It was her first time to experience the honor as they walked arm in arm. She felt exalted.

He disturbed her mood immediately by saying, "Now can we get on with planning for the war with Milan?"

Grâce à Dieu, no one dared approach them as they exited the chamber. "Talk like that should be kept until we are alone, *mon cher.*" She pinned a smile to her lips. "Men read lips and walls have ears. But there, once we have finished the appointments, your Great Council will be excellent — men of action and vision coupled with sound financial and administrative capability. That is what you need, and you will have exactly that. You will set out your grand designs and have the right men to make it happen. They will not fuss you with details — unless you choose. But enough, here comes your new Constable of France."

When the Duke de Bourbon-Montpensier bowed unsmilingly over her hand, her heart fluttered, but she crushed the sensation. François had appointed him Constable of France, an honor that had been in abeyance for almost twenty years. His expression was stern, however. She was surprised. Why no pleasure at the honor?

François hailed him, "Charles! Constable de Bourbon. Head of my army. And that will be no sinecure, my cousin. Prepare yourself for action. Come to me in private and we shall talk."

217

The Duke de Bourbon-Montpensier executed a correct bow without smiling. "As you require, Majesty."

François paused. "Constable, I expected more enthusiasm."

"I might have felt it, Sire, had you also confirmed King Louis's grant of my wife's rights to all her Bourbon-Montpensier lands."

The king put an arm around his shoulder, "Come, come, Charles, why should you doubt them?" and walked him away. Curious.

Sieur Antoine Duprat's bulky form filled the doorway. His small, deep-set eyes lit up as servants circulated with trays of cider and savory tarts. His girth revealed his predilection for food. He would enjoy the coming feast. He creaked a bow over Louise's hand. She intended to appoint Duprat as Chancellor of France. Officially then he would be Chief Magistrate and holder of the Great Seal, the most influential person in the land after the king. Unofficially, both he and she understood, however, that in reality *she* would hold that position.

She greeted the Secretary of Finances, one of the oldest men in the council — he had served both King Charles and King Louis — who glowered at Duprat's retreating back before bowing to her. He, at least, was an excellent choice. What a coup to have married Souvereine to his brother-in-law. Always best to be family to financiers when wars were in the offing.

"How is your charming wife?" she asked, "and your children?" Such men were always flattered by having their families remembered.

The next man she intended to appoint entered. Stork-like Sieur Jacques de Beaune had served her daughter-in-law's family for years. To divide his loyalties, she would persuade François to make him Inspector General of Finances. She expected advantages, by Our Lady, not the least being more information about Claude's Breton estates.

UPON ENTERING her daughter-in-law's antechamber, Louise pinched her nose at the heavy smell of musk incense. She should have known the day could not continue so well. At the far end of the room, the queen's ladies-in-waiting and maids-of-honor perched on cushions like a litter of puppies, busy with gossip and embroidery.

Near the fire, the queen's confessor murmured as Queen Claude, Mme. Jeanne, Mme. Michelle and Princess Renée fingered their rosary beads. Countess Louise approached the royal group on cat-silent feet, the thick Turkey carpet muffling her footsteps.

"Do you remember, Renée, riding with him this fall? He took you up on the back of his destrier." Queen Claude put an arm around her young sister. "It was on our trip to meet Queen Marie. You were bored riding with us in the litter."

Princess Renée wrinkled her forehead. "Mayhap. I might remember."

"I remember thinking how tiny you looked so high on Papa's great charger, yet so safe with his arms wrapped around you. All I could see was the top of your head and the bottoms of your boots sticking almost straight out. I could hear your voice, piping like a bird's and Papa's rumble. I was jealous. Do you recall, Mme. Michelle?"

"I do. It was a perfect time of year to ride through France, was it not? This is what I remember. The feel of crisp air. The smell of fresh cut wheat. The way the peasants stopped scything to watch us as we rode by. What do you recall?"

By Our Lady! Enough. Where was Marguerite? François did not want his wife brooding over her father's death, and so he had sent his sister to put an end to this maudlin pap. Clearing her throat, Louise stepped forward. She had to stop Queen Claude before she started another silly story.

"My dear daughter, here you are, sitting in the gloom, telling sad stories. This is no way to recover." Louise beckoned a maidservant. "Bring candelabra and light more candles. Remove that smoking censor, too, as you leave," she said, flapping her fan. "It is too much. In the chapel, in church, and here, too."

Louise poked the queen's confessor. "Do not think I misunderstand your disapproving frown, Father. But there is a time and place for everything." She plunked herself down on a stool in the middle of the group. "Besides, I have important topics to discuss."

As the king's mother, Louise considered herself the second lady in France, for Princess Renée was still a child — and her ward. When Princess Renée, popping her thumb in her mouth, stared at her with brooding eyes, she decided the child should go.

"Mme. Michelle, I do not believe the topic is appropriate for the young princess's ears. Perhaps you and she should leave us."

The gouvernante rose instantly. "I would be delighted, Countess. Princess Renée, curtsey to the king's mother. It is polite."

Michelle curtsied, too, but not quite as deeply as Louise thought she should, nor did she lower her eyes. Why did she not remove the child's thumb from her mouth? "This thumb sucking is an ugly habit, Mme. Michelle. I have pepper oil that could cure it within a day."

"Do you? I have treatments myself, but I prefer the princess to stop naturally, as she has in the past. Perhaps we should discuss it out of her hearing?"

Louise felt her cheeks flush, and she glared at the gouvernante. "Tush. You are making her soft."

Mme. Jeanne made agitated brushing hand motions to Mme. Michelle. Duchess Claude placed herself between Mme. Michelle and Louise and pressed a goblet into Louise's hand. "Have you tried this cordial, Maman Louise? You said you had an urgent topic to discuss?"

As the door closed behind them, the countess heard her ward say, "She's getting crosser every day, is she not?"

For a moment her anger almost boiled over, but she fisted her hands and began counting backward by threes, a trick she had taught herself as a girl in Mme. la Grande's court to ward off teasing and reprimands. It worked now. She calmed. She had erred in giving way to temper. Now it would be harder to obtain Claude's consent. "Please forgive my ill-humor, dear daughter, I should not allow that woman's insolence to irritate me." There, she had done it again. As Claude bristled, she brushed the subject of Mme. Michelle aside. "No matter, dear Daughter. Renée loves her."

Taking Claude's arm, she led her to an armchair. "You know better than to sit on cushions when you are increasing. Now, we have important matters to discuss — your dear father's funeral, your expanded household now that you are queen, and your sister's future."

SHELTERED WITHIN HER SABLE-LINED CAPE, Countess Louise called to the coachman who guided her equipage, "Drive me to the Hôtel de Cluny." She climbed inside and pulled open the curtains, eager to discover the mood of the city. She sensed apprehension in the cold winter air, as if the city hung suspended between the reigns of its familiar King Louis and its unknown young king.

Soon she arrived at the formidable entrance to the old château within which Dowager Queen Marie lived sequestered. Smoke billowed straight as arrows from its dozens of chimneys into windless blue skies. François wanted to know what Louis's widow was planning, and his wife had learned nothing. Time to use my wits, Louise thought, and see whether I still have influence with Marie.

"Never have I seen a lovelier widow," she said as she greeted the Reine Blanche, curtseying, but less deeply than before. After all, she was now higher in rank than a dowager queen. "You remind me of blessed Saint Anne in your austere garb."

"I have no aspirations to sainthood," Queen Marie answered, "nor any inclination to the convent. If I had ever any thoughts of it, these long, dull days in seclusion have proved to me I have no turn for a life of contemplation." Taking Countess Louise by the arm, she led her to the private library. "I have missed you. Sit with me. This is my favorite chamber."

"It is charming." Louise chose a seat of equal height to that of Marie's. "Tell me how you have been, my dear. It cannot have been easy for you."

The dowager queen plunged into a litany of her struggles in the days since her husband had died. It had been a shock to her how quickly her importance had plummeted. Accustomed to her position as the spoiled center of everyone's attention, life in a backwater did not please her. Louise played on her sense of ill-usage. Thus, she learned that Marie resented her struggle to retain the priceless jewels, the plate and the dozens of valuable gifts King Louis had bestowed upon her. Louise's sympathetic attention encouraged her to whine about her ongoing battle with King François's treasurer. "He keeps demanding that I return all my dear Louis's gifts — calls them the patrimony of France." She giggled. "Do not whisper a word to anyone, but I have already sent the Mirror of Naples to Henry as a peace offering."

"Why a peace offering? Are you at odds?"

"Not yet, but we may become so." She paused as if debating whether to say more.

"You know you can trust me." Louise leaned closer and patted Marie's hand.

It opened the floodgates. "Before I left, I made Henry promise that after King Louis died, he would allow me to choose my own husband. Of course, neither of us expected the king would die so quickly, Lord rest his soul."

"Umhum." Louise repressed a smile. If only you knew your part in it. You gave him his sweets each night.

"I fear he will not hold to his promise. Yet I would rather enter a convent — much as I would hate that — than marry against my inclination." Marie jumped to her feet, color rising in her cheeks. "The indignity of an old man's groping.... I can promise you, Mme. Louise, there is no possibility that I am with child. If that is the news you are waiting upon, your son can hold his coronation tomorrow!"

Louise rose and put an arm around the girl's shoulder. Even though she was delighted, compassion stirred her. She, too, had suffered bedding with an old husband. Although, *Grâce à Dieu*, not nearly as old as Louis. "Calm yourself, my dear. You will make yourself ill with all this agitation. Here, seat yourself again and drink this cup of wine. That is better." Once Marie was composed, she said, "You are certain you are not carrying a child?"

"I will swear on the Holy Bible. The king could not perform the act."

"Well, my dear, I can understand that you would not want to go through that humiliation again. As you know I have always refused to remarry. But you are young and childless. My children are my greatest blessing."

Marie covered her reddening face with her hands. "Drat my coloring." She laughed, "It is impossible to hide my blushes.

Louise laughed with her. "That is true, my dear. Who is the man of your choice?"

When Marie shook her head, Louise said, "Let me guess, the Duke of Suffolk, Charles Brandon."

Queen Marie's face blanched.

"No. No, it is not. Whatever gave you that idea?" But her hands flew to her face and her voice shook with agitation.

"There, there, Queen Marie, do not worry. I can guess because you have confided in me. You have not given yourself away to others, nor have I spoken of my suspicions." So much for François's hopes to marry her to one of his nobles. And to choose Duke Charles. That upstart! What was the Dowager Queen thinking?

"I have said nothing! And you will say nothing to anyone?"

"Of course not. And if you need help, I am always at your service."

There was nothing more to gain here, so Louise rose, gratified with the results of her work, and promised to visit the lonely queen regularly. I must tell François to have her letters opened before he sends them on, she thought as she departed. There will be much to learn.

HÔTEL DES TOURNELLES

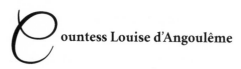

ountess Louise d'Angoulême

LOUISE HURRIED to the king's suite. Had it only been two days since she returned to Paris?

François toured her through his chambers. They included an intimate set of three tiny interconnecting rooms — a cozy library, a modest bedchamber, and a tiny privy complete with a close stool, a concrete tub filled with fresh water, shelves, porcelain basins and fluffy towels.

"This is one of the many charms of kingship," he said with a grin, inviting her to a seat in the library. He called his valet to serve them wine and sweet wafers. "No one is to disturb us. Not unless the palace is on fire," he instructed.

"Let's talk about Milan now that the Old Plodder is no longer weighing me down! I wish to conquer it by next year. Artillery is the most important item. Gaillot de Genouillac is our man. Fleuranges must organize the recruitment of the landsknechts-"

"Wait, wait, wait!" Louise spluttered wine, she was laughing so much. "Your enthusiasm is enchanting, *mon César*, but one thing at a time, I beg of you."

"We must start with the most important, no?" He was quivering like a bloodhound on a leash who had scented game.

"Yes, *mon César*, Milan. To succeed in Milan, you need arms and men, as you say. To acquire both, you need funds, yes? Also, to conquer Milan is one thing. To retain it is another. How many times did King Louis gain Milan only to lose it again?"

Still half laughing, King François glowered at his mother. "You know how to throw ice on a man's rising pintle, Maman. It is no surprise you are still unmarried despite all the offers you received. I am guessing you have suggestions to combat these obstacles?"

She made as if to toss her wine at him, "Such language — to your maman, no less." Each day she felt younger and more desirable. One day, perhaps, she *would* marry again.

"Be sure I do. I have been speaking with your Secretary of Finance. King Louis was a penny pincher, which irritated us when he ruled. But now—" She nodded as he rubbed a thumb and forefinger together. "Exactly. He left a healthy sum in the treasury. You start in an excellent position to purchase the best artillery your heart could desire. You have the experts to negotiate for whatever mercenaries you will need." She slowed, now choosing her words with care. "As to winning and keeping Milan, you could do no better than to follow the example of

Mme. la Grande before King Charles began his conquest of Naples. Neutralize with treaties all those who might oppose you. France has something each of them wants. Let us play them like fish on a hook so that when you make your move, you have no enemies at your back, and they will not combine to unseat you once you hold your prize."

He tapped his fingers on the arm of his chair. "It is a good plan — *if* it can be achieved."

"Do you doubt me, *mon César?* Did I not promise you from the time you wore short skirts you would be king of France?"

Continuing to tap, he said, "Where do we begin?

She numbered her list on her fingers. "First Flanders — and Imperial Burgundy for that matter. What can we offer the regent and the duke for an alliance? Second, we must renew our alliance with England. Third, an alliance with Venice so it does not attack. Fourth, you must make an ally of Pope Leo — which we need to do in any case to resolve the problems arising from the mess that King Louis left us. That is a catastrophe on the horizon. Fifth, it is essential to obtain Savoy's consent to the passage of your army. How is that for a start? Then there is the Dowager Queen. That is another whole problem."

François sat back, steepling his fingers, and raised his eyebrows. "What a discouraging list. Even old Louis's chancellor did not arrive with so much bad news."

"Speaking of chancellors, I propose Antoine Duprat. If you appoint him, we can make headway immediately."

"Fine." He was indifferent.

She masked her surprise at his instant agreement. But she had hoped to convince him and wasted no time handing him the proclamation.

He signed it with a flourish.

Well, that had been simple. Strike while the iron is hot. She went on to the problem of Burgundy — and the Baronne de Soubise. "Perhaps one part of the Burgundian solution would be a French wife for the Duke."

"With what else? An alliance? Or a pact of mutual aid if attacked by an outsider? Do you have a wife in mind?"

"What about Princess Renée? She is young to be sure, but as the queen's sister she is of sufficiently good birth." Louise watched, secretly amused, as her son spluttered.

He was so outraged he had trouble spitting out his words. "Maman! She is entitled to half of Brittany! What are you thinking!"

She enjoyed teasing him a little. "It could have been worse. If she had lived a little longer, Queen Anne proposed to betroth her to him and dower her with the whole Duchy of Brittany. Fleuranges told me."

"God's toes! Did she, by Christ!"

"Tut, tut, tut. She is dead, and it did not happen."

Patting his arm, she chuckled. "Take a glass of wine and calm yourself, son. Now hear me out. We would not dower her with Brittany, of course, but another royal appanage that would be more useful to him. Say Artois, or Berry. She is your sister-in-law. A great prize. And, he will be King of Castile one day so the marriage will take care of the threat along the southwest as well."

"Claude will not like it. I do not want her upset while she is increasing."

"We will say nothing to her until it is arranged — if it is. They may not be interested. And these betrothals of the young often come to nothing. How long was Claude betrothed to him herself? And to our Dowager Queen? Yet Claude married you. We could start by exploring their interest in an alliance. How is that?"

He agreed. That was all she wanted.

"Let us talk of something much more exciting. Your coronation and Grande Entrée into Paris." François's eyes lit up. He had decided ideas about what he wanted. But all the while Louise mulled over her approach to the Marqués de Gattinara, Regent Marguerite's ambassador to François's court. She was sure he would jump at an offer that included Princess Renée.

CLAUDE WAS both surprised and hurt when François named the Marshal of France as Grand Steward of her father's funeral in charge of the arrangements. She felt it as a slight, for her Papa had retired him after he first lost Milan and then was captured at Guinegate. The day after his ascension, her husband had invited him back to court and promoted him to Marshal. Though she refrained from saying so to her husband, this act worried Queen Claude. It felt like such a repudiation of Papa.

Princess Renée, Queen Claude and Michelle stood in an upper window as her father's funeral procession gathered and formed. From the house lent to them for the occasion, that faced the great square in front of Notre Dame Cathedral, she watched as the procession set out from the Cathedral, passing onto the cobblestoned Bridge au Mineurs to the left, on its journey to the Basilica of Saint Denis.

Hundreds of wailing beggars — gathered from the streets of Paris and kept in a ragged order by the sergeants and city watch — led the way. Heralds followed, shouting, "King Louis, Father of his People, is dead. King Louis, twelfth of the name, is dead." Claude's tears filled her eyes.

After them walked churchmen in their ceremonial robes, a splash of color. Archers and sergeants followed, placed there to separate the prelates from the university men who came next. Their placement was strategic; to keep the churchmen and academics separate to avoid their coming to blows over precedence. The Marshal, as Grand Steward, rode directly behind the 'men of the gown,' as the scholars were called. To keep an eye on them? Claude wondered. It increased her grief. How shameful that clerical and scholarly rivalry must be considered even at her Papa's funeral.

As the procession entered the bridgehead, each contingent squeezed and narrowed like a woman's waist as it was laced into a tight bodice. It slowed, stretched and lengthened into a long snake.

Finally. Black horses, caparisoned in black, pulled the closed carriage that held King Louis's coffin. It creaked along, its iron wheels clanking on the cobblestones. By the time it reached their window, neither Claude nor her sister could restrain tears. To comfort Renée, Claude put an arm around her shoulder. It eased her own pain a little, too.

Next, the wax effigy of King Louis in his coronation regalia — carried by the presidents of the four Parlements and the men of his Great Council — came into view. It was so lifelike she could not help but think it was the last time she would look upon her Papa's face. After it passed in a tramp and shuffle of booted feet, she shut her eyes to squeeze back the memories that threatened to overwhelm her. Not only of the happy times with her father and mother together, but of the previous year at the same time when they followed her mother along this same route to the same lonely destination.

Another square of priests passed, chanting prayers for the dead. Automatically Claude added her voice to theirs. By the time the sound of their voices had faded into the distance, along with the faint scent of incense and the tang of pitch torches, she had calmed. She opened her eyes. The procession had almost entirely vanished from view. It had been a meagre display after a shamefully short mourning period. Only ten days had passed since Papa had died. François said he did not want her to harm herself when she was carrying France's hope; explaining this was why he insisted on moving forward so rapidly. She wanted to believe him, but was finding it hard to do so. She would have to confess it and ask for a penance.

ON THE EVENING of King Louis's funeral, Michelle stood in the doorway of Princess Renée's large day room. The princess's rooms were draped with black crepe and mourning wreaths, like one of the gloomy paintings on the chapel walls. It was a mournful atmosphere for a child to live in. Countess Louise had commanded it — already exercising her authority as Renée's official guardian.

The young princess sat at the low table in front of the fireplace and dipped a piece of bread crust into her tankard of small ale. She sucked on it and then plopped the sodden mass onto her trencher. A nursery maid sat on a cushion beside her and tried to persuade her to swallow the crusts rather than spit them out.

"I cannot," Princess Renée whined. "My throat feels like it has a big lump in it. When I try to swallow, my throat closes and tells me it is going to gag." She made a sound halfway between choking and vomiting. Spittle ran from the side of her mouth. "Like that."

Wiping it away, the nursery maid, who half-gagged in sympathy, nodded. "Then you must not try more. Shall I ask Mme. la Baronne to come to you?"

Renée brightened.

Michelle stepped forward, her footsteps echoing on the uneven hardwood floor. Like the princess, she was in full mourning and wore a black brocade gown and a black French hood.

Princess Renée wrapped her arms around Michelle's waist, burrowing her face into her gouvernante's stomach. She raised Michelle's clove-and-orange-scented pomander ball to her nose.

"Is your belly bothering you, my little Princess?" Michelle brushed a hand over her forehead. She did not feel hot. "You do not seem to have a fever." Michelle spoke more to herself than to the child, but Princess Renée relaxed, perhaps because Michelle did, too.

"Not that kind of hot, sick feeling," Princess Renée said, pulling Michelle toward her favorite chair. "It is the kind of lump that makes it hard to swallow because I might cry. The kind that us'lly gets better when we talk."

Michelle nodded, glad Princess Renée trusted her. She sat in the wooden rocking chair as Princess Renée picked up the puppy that had wandered in. Michelle now lifted the little girl and the puppy into her lap, even though the Princess was getting taller and heavier all the time. Princess Renée squirmed until she was comfortable, her head snuggled against Michelle's left shoulder, her legs dangling towards the floor. She clutched the puppy between her chest and Michelle's.

"Tell me." Michelle expected her to ask where people went after they died. The princess surprised her.

"Why do people die?" She snuggled the puppy.

Michelle took a deep breath to repress her own rebellious anger about that very subject. "Well, that is difficult to know. Partly so we can receive the Lord's promise to redeem us. Partly because it is God's will. He calls us to Him. That is the most important reason. After that.... Well, people get old and sick or they are wounded in war. Or sometimes they eat injurious foods. What do you want to know, exactly?"

"Why did God want my Papa and Maman? Why both of them?" She gripped the puppy until it yipped in protest.

Why indeed? *Cui bono?* She did not have to look far to see who benefitted. Was that ill-natured of her? The apricot sweets might have hastened King Louis's end, but he still would have died within days. "Both your Maman and Papa were old when you were born. You know Claude is eleven years older than you are. And your Maman had been married before, so she was already twenty-two when she had Claude. She was thirty-three when she had you. That is the same age as our Lord Jesus when he died."

"And my Papa?" She squeezed the puppy again and now it yelped.

"Perhaps you should put puppy down, sweetheart. You are hugging him too tight. That is good." Michelle tightened her grip on the princess. "Well, like your maman, he had been married before. He was thirty-six when he married your maman, and he was already forty-eight when you were born."

"Why did God make them so old before I was born?"

"Are you feeling angry with God, little one?" So was she. And with Mme. Louise and Mme. Marie.

Renée sat up straight in Michelle's lap, fists clenched and cheeks bright red. "Yes. I am. Does that make me bad? Will I go to hell?"

Her poor baby. "No, my love. It makes you normal. We are human and limited. We cannot understand the Lord's inscrutable mysteries. Why He makes us suffer. When bad and painful things happen, of course we feel angry and we blame Him. God understands that... and loves you and will forgive you when you ask. Does that help?"

She did not nod. Michelle tried another way. "Both your Maman and Papa were sick and in pain. Do you remember that?" This time Princess Renée nodded a tiny assent. Michelle continued. "They did not want to leave you, but they were suffering, and God ended their pain. Now they are looking forward to seeing you again in Heaven when your time comes. Maybe you can remember that when you go to mass." Another tiny nod. "Until then, we must pray for forgiveness for our anger, and Lord Jesus surely will. He understands we do not know His divine purpose. As long as we find faith to believe He has one, we will regain our hope."

"Oh."

"I am sad and angry, too," Michelle confided. Princess Renée shot her a surprised look but relaxed against her.

How strange. In comforting her, Michelle had consoled herself. They did not speak for some time.

Then Princess Renée said, "Well if you are here, mayhap it will be all right."

Holding the child close, Michelle closed her eyes. She feared Countess Louise would do her best to separate them. Dear Lord, do not let her succeed.

11 JANUARY 1515, MORNING

HÔTEL DES TOURNELLES

ountess Louise d'Angoulême

"MAMAN," King François danced into Louise's suite and pulled open her bed curtains.

Like a cat, she awoke immediately. "*Mon César*! Why are you here so early? You have secrets! I can see it in your eyes."

As her maidservant scrambled from the pallet at the end of her bed, Louise pushed off the heavy coverlet and sat up. "Away with you, girl. Curtsey to your king and leave us. No, wait, bring small ale and fresh bread and for king — François, what will you have? — some meat. You heard him, girl. Quickly now. And be sure to knock before you enter."

"François, bring me the dressing robe lying across that chair. Not the black one, *mon César*, we are private. That lovely cream-

237

colored silk one. And the matching silk slippers." She slid lithely from the bed and kissed him.

Moving to the fireplace, she stirred the ashes. After he tossed on a couple of logs, she motioned him to sit on a nearby leather chair. Removing her nightcap, she draped her robe into elegant folds and said, "So, tell me all."

Her son gazed at her fondly. "I warn you, I am bringing you work. Work that will challenge even your skills."

She clapped. "There is nothing I enjoy more. What is it?"

"What say you to my coronation in Reims in two weeks?"

"No!" She sat back, beaming. "How did this come about? Tell me the entire story."

He laughed, throwing his head back so his dark curls shook like the mane of a frisky colt. "As you know, or perhaps you do not," he winked at her, "I have been visiting the Dowager Queen — to help her overcome her grief, of course." He grinned at the disapproving twist of her lips. "Do not worry, Maman. I have done nothing more than encourage her to stay in France. She is desperate to leave. She begs me to release her from the Hôtel de Cluny. Thus, she informed me that there was no possibility she was carrying an heir to France.

Louise smirked. "Wonderful! Though I am not surprised old Louis was incapable. How fortunate you failed to bed her." She had not told him about Marie's admission, concluding that it would come out soon enough, either in one of Marie's opened letters or because Marie would reveal it herself. Had Marie also confessed that she was determined to marry the Duke of Suffolk?

François rubbed his hands together. "She was reading a letter when I arrived. The one saying Brandon would be here soon. I prodded her. Kept offering her new husbands, like Duke Antoine de Lorraine. Well, we do not want her marrying her former beau, the Duke of Burgundy, do we? I have decided to offer him Princess Renée. She told me that the Duke of Suffolk was coming to take her back to England — with her dowry and the widow's portion agreed upon in her marriage contract. It will cost us a pretty penny." He brooded a moment but brightened as he returned to his story. "It was perfect. I convinced her it was a ploy on her brother's part to lure her back to England to marry her off to Burgundy once she was there. I played it up."

By Our Lady, he looked pleased with himself, Louise thought. "Clever, my son."

He puffed up like Marguerite's parrot.

"I did better than that, Maman. She broke down and told me all about her secret plan to marry Suffolk when he arrived to escort her to England. Begged for my support. Naturally, I agreed."

Louise nodded. "Excellent, my son." And it was.

"She fails to realize how much it suits us to remove her from the marriage market. Though it will cost us. And I would prefer the Duke de Lorraine. Now I will have to find someone else for him. She throws herself away marrying an upstart like Suffolk. Though the Tudors are parvenus themselves. She will find out soon enough that he is a libertine who will hop onto anyone with the correct parts. Lucky sod to joust with the king's sister. Will Henry let him live, I wonder? If she were my sister, he would hang at Montfaucon. It would amuse me to know he was dangling on the gallows for the crows to pick out his eyes."

MICHELLE TRAILED Princess Renée by a few paces; the child was in a lively mood by the time they reached the door to Queen Claude's inner sanctum. The queen's lady-in-waiting knocked, opened the door and announced them. Michelle heard her own name within the ripple of voices. As Queen Claude rose to greet her sister, Michelle curtsied to Mme. Louise, and nodded to Mme. Jeanne.

Princess Renée ran around the chamber, pretending she was galloping on a pony until Michelle warned her she must either quiet down, or they would return to her rooms. "There is nothing wrong with your desire to run. But this is not the place. When we visit an adult, we behave like adults. When we visit the Queen, who is going to have a baby we behave quietly, so she remains calm and does not upset the baby."

Renée stopped on one foot, sidled carefully to Claude, and took her hand. "How are you feeling, my sister, Mme. la Reine? How goes your belly sickness?" Her expression was so serious they all smiled.

"Much better, thank you."

Queen Claude took Michelle's hand. "You said that after three months the morning sickness usually passed. I conclude that I am three months gone, for the smell of food in the morning no longer sickens me. You are a wonder, dear Baronne. Your guidance has made me feel much safer, and your tisanes have eased the nausea."

Michelle observed Mme. Louise's frown. The countess rose and then sat herself beside Princess Renée, who had joined the queen's ladies-in-waiting around a sewing project.

"Princess Renée, let me teach you your stitches," she said.

Michelle sat with the queen while they talked about babies. She admired the baby clothes Queen Claude was embroidering for the infant. She and the king hoped it would be a boy and their heir. The whole time they spoke, Michelle felt Countess Louise's eyes boring into her, as if sending evil messages. Before she rose to take Princess Renée to her rooms, Michelle leaned close to the queen and murmured, "If anything should happen and I must leave the little princess, please remind her that God is her Savior and she can tell Him all her thoughts for He will listen and forgive her. Most important, she must never lose hope. Neither must you."

Queen Claude stared at her in astonishment. "Why would I need to give her such a message?"

"It is just a feeling. Mme. Louise does not want me here."

Queen Claude dropped her eyes to her lap but said, "I do."

Michelle said, "I may be wrong. I do not mean to worry you." She rose and called Princess Renée to join her.

Mme. Louise followed them into the queen's antechamber. In a voice only they could hear, she said, "I do not wish you to disturb my daughter-in-law with advice about her forthcoming child. She has doctors and midwives to advise her and I am an expert herbalist myself."

Michelle curtsied. "I shall inform Queen Claude of your orders."

A flush rose to the countess's cheeks. "You will do no such thing. I shall inform her myself."

Michelle curtsied again and left with the princess.

In the corridor Princess Renée said, "I do not like being with Mme. Louise. She pinches me."

"She does?" Michelle was horrified. "I did not know that."

"She never does it so people see. Even I do not see it. But it only happens when she is there."

Michelle was puzzled. "What does?"

"The pinching. That's how I 'duced it was her."

Michelle was shocked. It was clever of the little princess, but it was a dreadful discovery and she had no solutions. "Thank you, Princess, for confiding in me. I do not know what to do. I must think. Have you told anyone else?"

"No."

"For the moment, let it be a secret between us."

Princess Renée said in a satisfied voice, "I thought it was bad."

"It is."

They went to her chambers and dressed her in winter clothing to play outdoors. As Renée and a companion threw snowballs in the courtyard, Michelle considered Princess Renée's revelation. Mme. Louise was getting bolder and angrier by the day. She was also becoming more powerful. And she was the princess's legal guardian. What would she do next?

COUNTESS LOUISE ENTERED Reims Cathedral before anyone else as dawn was breaking on January 25th, 1515. On this day she wanted to be alone to breathe its holy air. From her vantage, she could overlook the high altar of this glorious cathedral where all the Kings of France had been crowned. She kneeled to pray. When she received a divine message as she meditated, she knew in her heart that it came from the holy Francis de Paule. The words were as clear as if he kneeled before her.

On this day of the Conversion of St. Paul, your son is being conse-
crated and anointed as I foreordained. For this you must hold yourself
grateful to the Divine Majesty, who amply repays you for all the
adversities and inconveniences that came to you in your early years
and in the flower of your youth. Humility ever bore you company, and
patience never abandoned you. Thus, the Divine Trinity in Their
mercy reward you.

How right that the saintly man should recognize her humility
and suffering. Mme. la Grande, her guardian, had striven to
keep her from her destiny by marrying her to a nonentity. But
God had rewarded her. Had He not sent death to each male who
stood between her son and the crown of France? Queen Anne
treated her with contempt, and so God had punished her,
choosing that all her sons should die while François flourished.
All just as the blessed Francis de Paule said, because she was
humble and patient and maintained her faith. She must prove
her gratitude. She vowed to endow many *Minim* foundations in
his honor. Louise crossed herself as she made this vow. It was
never wise to be miserly with the Lord.

Louise simpered as she looked around. She had arranged the
situation well. Of the royal family, only her son and she were
present today. His wife was in Paris, not well enough to risk her
health and their child's jolting on the road in the cold. Princess
Renée was too young to behave. Louise had dispatched the
princess and Mme. Michelle to Blois for the winter where the
air was healthier. Of course — conveniently — it meant the
baronne could not advise Queen Claude, for she was not
nearby.

While solemn music played, the peers of France, dressed in their
coronets and robes of estate, took their places, according to
their rank. Then François entered to the rolling sounds of the
organ and choir and Louise's heart fluttered. He was magnifi-

cent in his simplicity, clothed all in white with a simple white cloak. Alone, taller and more handsome than any man there, with his shining black curls uncovered, he looked like a God come to earth. He trod the scarlet carpet behind the highest clergy, as they paced solemnly in their golden robes, waving censors. Everyone fell to their knees and placed their right hand over their hearts. She kneeled at the front as he came toward her down the long aisle. The scene glimmered before her tear-filled eyes.

Throughout the ceremony, he bore himself magnificently, his bell-like voice ringing out his responses, his grip strong as he received the sword and scepter, his head steady as the crown of Charlemagne came to rest upon his proud head. Behind him, the huge jeweled golden cross glowed its blessing upon him. She had waited for this moment all her life. Her cheeks ached from smiling and she could not make herself appear solemn, try as she would.

Her son, King François, insisted she sit beside him as the feasting and toasting carried on well into the early hours of the next morning. It was a day they would relive together hundreds of times; the culmination, yet the beginning, of their dreams.

4 FEB 1515, MORNING

ABBAYE ST. CORNEILLE COMPIÈGNE

 uchess Louise d'Angoulême

As Duchess Louise's maids prepared her for the day, she pondered the best thing to do. First, she and King François must meet the Marqués de Gattinara, Regent Marguerite's ambassador for the Duke of Burgundy. The Duke should have attended François's coronation since he was her son's vassal for parts of Burgundy, which made him a peer of France. It was a studied insult. He was already so rich in lands and power that he probably did not wish to humble himself before someone he perceived as only an equal — and possibly an inferior. Was there any advantage in insisting his ambassador kneel?

This morning she felt exalted. She did. Taller. Stronger. More beautiful. As if she gave off emanations like those of her son's.

She was a *duchess* now. People must address her simply as Madame. If she had felt so elevated after the ceremony yesterday, how much greater must have been François's elation at his coronation. When the Abbot touched him with the mystical oil that consecrated him as king, she had heard a choir of angels sing. She tried to imagine how François had felt.

Lady Blanche, her favorite lady-in-waiting, arrived with Louise's best French hood, the one embroidered with dozens of pearls. After Lady Blanche fastened it, Louise invited her to join her in breaking her fast.

"The Marqués de Gattinara's entourage arrived last night after dark. We heard the bustle from our dormitory," Lady Blanche said as they ate. "The servants who made up our fires this morning said he brought over two hundred in his retinue. The abbey kitchens have been working all night to feed the influx. There is much grumbling."

She loved to gossip, did her Blanche. It was one of her attributes. "We trust that our Grand Steward will manage it with his usual aplomb." Louise would not permit such mundane considerations to bother her today. She and François wanted to negotiate an alliance with the Regent Marguerite. The alliance would protect her César's north-east as he advanced on Milan. Never lose sight of the goal, she reminded herself. So, there was no benefit to insisting upon the king's right to deference at this moment. She would say so to François before they met the Marqués.

The Archbishop, Abbot of the Abbaye St. Corneille, led the mass in the vast gothic abbey church with its ancient stained-glass windows. Then he led François to the abbatial chair in the wood-paneled Chapter House where they were holding this rendezvous with the ambassadors.

The Marqués de Gattinara and the nobles of his retinue bowed as they approached the French. François braced, like a hunting dog with its hackles rising.

"Our first duty," said the Marqués, his French strong with a Savoyard accent, "is to present humble apologies on the part of our lord, Duke Charles, for his unavoidable absence at your blessed consecration so recently held in Reims. As my first duty here, I offer vassalage for his fief as is your due." He fell to his knees before the king and placed his hands between the king's as he swore the required oath. Her son relaxed.

Clever of the duke to have his man swear. Honor was satisfied on both sides without the duke having to humble himself to François. Louise wondered whose idea it had been and suspected Gattinara. Her respect grew.

Gattinara suggested the three of them walk in the abbatial cloister gardens, under the winter sun. The interior court felt mild. Water splashed in the fountain and the glint of the sunlight on the carp in the basin charmed them as they pursued their conversation sitting upon the basin's edge. The background spray muffled their words. Louise and Marguerite, who were first cousins, had corresponded since their childhood when both had been wards of Mme. la Grande. Yet this was the first time she heard that the Regent was eager to embrace a French alliance on the Duke's behalf. She wondered at it and probed the Marqués, but discovered nothing.

The Marqués's next words startled her even more. "As a sign of indissoluble friendship and confederation, the Regent hopes you will accept Duke Charles's offer of his hand in marriage to the Princess Renée." Gattinara managed a courtly bow to King François even though he was seated. "As sister to your wife, Sire, and daughter of the late King Louis, it would do him great honor and make a solemn bond between us." Ambassador de

Gattinara's expression was slightly anxious, as if asking the greatest favor France could bestow.

How fortunate that both she and her son were adept at hiding their thoughts. It was much better that the Duke should propose the match.

François answered without missing a beat. "Our alliance with Flanders and Burgundy is equally important, for we are facing a delicate situation in the south."

The Marqués's expression became troubled.

François hurried on. "We value our sisters above all others, and this proposed marriage bond delights us. We agree in principle to betroth our sister Princess Renée to Duke Charles."

Gattinara did not reply immediately. "And this situation in the south?"

"The Duke of Sforza illegally occupies my wife's Duchy of Milan — to which I have a claim in my own right." For a moment, the king almost pouted. Louise guessed he was considering a *rodomontade* about his claims. She elbowed him. He continued: "As her husband, I am duty-bound to reclaim it, and I intend to do so within the year."

Gattinara frowned.

François was quick to say, "We do not look for financial or military support; simply the commitment that Duke Charles will not support young Sforza in any manner throughout any of his territories."

"Ah, I see. There is the problem of the Holy See, however. Duke Charles supports Holy Mother Church wholeheartedly. He will do nothing that counters her interests."

The ambassador's growing reluctance dismayed Louise. She broke in. "My dear Marqués, the rift between France and our Holy Father ended with the late king. And perhaps as a Savoyard yourself, you have learned that my half-sister will soon marry Pope Leo's brother?" His countenance cleared.

They agreed on the general principles of their alliance, although the details had still to be worked out. Louise kept to herself the news that her Savoyard brothers still bitterly opposed the papal match, considering it a misalliance with a parvenu. She was pleased with herself. They had taken another step towards Milan for François. And she had prepared her next move towards ridding herself of the baronne.

HEAVILY VEILED, dressed entirely in black, and wrapped in a black woolen cape, Duchess Claude rode through the narrow Parisian streets accompanied by a similarly attired Mme. Jeanne. It was mid-morning. Their horses slipped into the courtyard of the Paris home of Sieur Jacques de Beaune, now Inspector-General of Finances. They were expected. Grooms rushed to assist them to dismount.

The chamberlain hurried them up the steep stairs, through the elaborate entrance, into a private anteroom and closed the door behind them. Mme. de Beaune dropped into a court curtsey, profoundly gratified to receive them.

Claude was gracious but urgent. "Mme. Jeanne will be pleased to wait with you. I shall meet with Sieur Jacques at once."

Brought instantly to his presence, Claude was too nervous to glance at her surroundings. She threw back her veil and allowed him to help her to a seat.

Before she had a chance to speak, he said, "Please forgive my temerity in begging your presence here. I did so only because this meeting must be undiscovered. If we met at court or in another public place, I could not be assured that it would not be reported to Mme. Louise." He paused. "It may still be."

Queen Claude blanched. "Is it so secret, then?"

"I believe so, Mme. la Reine. The knowledge came to me in strictest confidence and I am deeply torn in conscience in sharing it. It is my deepest hope that it is already known to you. But my family has long served the Montfort de Bretagne I owe my loyalty to your late mother, an allegiance greater than to the royal service." Fear gripped Claude. She squeezed her hands tighter and tighter to hide her agitation. "Please tell me."

"A betrothal has been agreed between Princess Renée and Duke Charles of Burgundy."

Why she had not known? How was it that she had not heard even a hint of gossip? Sieur Jacques offered her a cup of watered wine. When she put the goblet on the table beside her, it rattled on the wooden tabletop. She needed two hands to steady it. "Please tell me the details."

Sieur Jacques was a blunt man and went straight to the point. "The tentative agreement was signed in Compiègne on February 4th, between King François and their ambassador, the Marqués de Gattinara. In return for a mutual alliance of peace and non-aggression, and assistance in case of attack by a third party, the Duke of Burgundy will betroth Princess Renée. The princess will stay in France until she reaches the age of twelve and be given a gouvernante fluent in Spanish and Flemish. She must learn both these languages."

"Does this mean Mme. Michelle will not stay with her?" Claude's voice quavered.

"Unfortunately, yes."

Claude moaned softly.

Sieur Jacques looked uncomfortable. Clearing his throat, he went on, "at twelve, the princess will travel to the duke's location for the formal marriage ceremony after a proxy marriage in France."

Tears trickled down Claude's cheeks.

"She will be dowered with the province of Berry and 100,000 gold écus. She will not receive any part of Brittany."

At this, color flamed in Claude's face and the tears dried on her cheeks. "This is the king's doing?" She was both dazed and furious. She thought she knew her husband. How could he be so cruel to her sister — and so greedy? Except... Renée's inheritance was not within his power to bestow. "No. Maman Louise!"

Her voice crossed that of Sieur Jacques, who said, "I believe the king's mother, was deeply involved in the negotiations."

Claude had never felt so outraged. "From whom did you learn this?"

Sieur Jacque looked uncomfortable. She wondered for a moment if he would answer. Then he said, "Chancellor Antoine Duprat, who took part in the negotiations. I trust this will remain between us?"

"Everything that has passed in this room will remain between us. As my presence here will remain between us, your wife and Mme. Jeanne. If it does not—" She stood. "Do you know who the spies are among my household?"

He shook his head. "I will do my best to discover."

"WHAT A MUDDLE!" Duchess Louise said. She climbed into the white-and-gold coach beside Queen Claude. Her words failed to hide her pride in all she and François had accomplished. "What a perfect, cloudless day. The chill will keep the odors at bay. *Grâce à Dieu*, the sun is shining on my glorious César for his Grande Entrée. I have dreamed of this day for years! And it will be as splendid as I had imagined." Today the city would celebrate the most fabulous, the most magnificent, the most brilliant *Grande Entrée* Paris had ever witnessed. King François had promised himself this, and she had made it so. What a team they were. She smiled at her mousy, crippled daughter-in-law. Fortunate girl to have married such a shining prince and to be able to present France with his children.

She peered around at the dozens of litters, horses, brightly colored garments, and crowds of excited spectators. Their litter was the most dazzling of all, as was proper. How delightful to be at the center of everything, here in the vast plaza at the Basilica of Saint Denis. It swarmed with robed and uniformed men — from cardinals and archbishops, to city counselors and guards; from the highest peers to 4000 beggars — everyone who was anyone, and those who were not. Slowly the *melée* sorted itself into a vast, splendid parade in which every corporate body in the city was taking part.

Tapestries, banners, and silken streamers hung from the balconies of houses, hostels, and taprooms. At each street-corner another church paraded its saint. Each guild marched, exhibiting its patron's statue. Louise glimpsed the university scholars strutting in their colorful robes as they turned corners along the route, and aldermen swaggering their batons to hint at their power.

In their litter they passed their time in talk for, although there was much to see, they inched past the endless crowds. The constant waving required of them was tiring. There was a trick to it, one must rest one's arm against a solid base, hardly moving one's hand, and never moving the wrist.

Queen Claude asked Louise about François's coronation and her investiture. Louise could not stop boasting. The coronation was the blessing of God upon her son, the culmination of her life's work. As was this outpouring of the people's love. Did Queen Claude not see this as a sign that France was ready for change, for renewal, for youth? Just as England and Castile had young rulers, so France was calling for youth.

Almost as if she did not want to hear Louise's opinions, Queen Claude interrupted her. "Look at that set piece! Is not that Phoebus rising from the sea? With actual water? Stop the litter so we can watch it longer! It is so clever."

"It is one of *my* ideas," Louise crowed.

Queen Claude used the pause to ask her about their meeting with the Flemish ambassadors.

Louise — to discover whether Claude had learned about her sister's betrothal and her plan to replace the baronne — asked Claude what she had heard. Claude was vague as always, and instead drifted off to another topic. "I heard Duke Charles did not attend the coronation as he should have. I was curious whether my husband was going to insist upon his rights and reprimand him, as Papa did."

Louise chuckled. "It worked out well. Neither side lost face. We met his embassy in Compiègne where Ambassador de Gattinara made full vassalage for the fiefdom. So, we informed them of my half-sister's wedding to the Pope's brother next week and invited their representatives to attend. Perhaps they knew already — although I doubt it. Everyone went away pleased, and it will ease the way for my son's war against Milan." That seemed to satisfy Queen Claude, and Louise breathed more easily.

The procession enchanted Louise. The king's Scots Guards, on their huge destriers, protected their litter fore and aft. Their very presence hinted at the damage they could inflict. Among these pressing crowds, who cheered incessantly for their gracious Queen Claude, daughter of their good King Louis, the jingling caparisons of the Scots Guards and the hot horsy smells were comforting. Surprising how popular Queen Claude was with the common riffraff.

Behind them Louise heard, "Three cheers for the king. Hoorah!! King François!" It rolled on like endless waves thundering on a rocky shore. She twisted to admire her son in his glory. Alone, huge, seated on his great white horse, more like a figure from myth than a living person — so grand and handsome. It had all been worth it, she thought, as she listened to the outpouring.

Crowds swarmed behind the procession as it made its way to Notre Dame. It helped that after the king passed, on low carts pulled by sturdy horses, almoners surrounded by armed guards, tossed numberless thousands of deniers — chosen because they were coins of the smallest denomination — so there was plenty for all. The almoners tossed carefully, high and deep into the crowd. Any scrambling occurred at the back and no one got hurt. It was a careful balance, since the armed guards monitoring the route were ruthless in ensuring order, as Louise had ordered beforehand.

IN HER SUITE at the Hôtel des Tournelles, Queen Claude cradled her growing belly, feeling isolated as she reflected on her conversation with her mother-in-law.

First, Louise had insulted her father, prattling on about how it was the time for young men. Did it not occur to her that perhaps Claude might not feel as delighted since it was her father who had died to make way for François? Or did Louise believe that her pleasure in becoming queen would outweigh her grief at losing her beloved Papa? Well, Maman Louise's mother had died young and her father had abandoned her to grow up with no one who loved her or whom she could trust above all others. So perhaps she could not understand.

Claude spent hours praying in her oratory, gazing at the beautiful Virgin on the wall as she held her mother's rosary. She must accept Renée's betrothal, for it was the fate of royal girls, but her sensitive soul balked over the plan to replace Mme. Michelle. She cried, imagining how she would have experienced the loss of Mme. Jeanne. It would be worse for Renée, for she was more reserved. It would shatter her little sister. The more Claude brooded, the greater her alarm about how Renée would cope with losing Mme. Michelle. In the past year, her sister had lost Maman and Papa. How could Maman Louise be so cruel as to separate Renée from her sister and Mme. Michelle too?

If she were not such a coward, she would prevent it. After all, Maman Louise had promised Maman that she would not separate Renée from her gouvernante. Claude prayed to the Virgin to thwart Louise's plan. She also asked for help to forgive Louise, but did not succeed.

After a week, Claude could bear her bewilderment no longer. She made an opportunity for her mother-in-law to inform her about Renée's betrothal and the new gouvernante. Inviting Louise to play chess in her presence chamber, while her ladies played cards, strummed lutes, and stitched embroidery, Claude painted an idyllic future of Renée, Michelle, the new dauphin and his gouvernante at Blois together just as her mother had wished while she, François and Louise went on royal progresses. Maman Louise did not blink. She nodded, smiled and added suggestions for the baby's gouvernante. It was clear her mother-in-law had no intention of revealing their plans for Renée's betrothal or new gouvernante. She must think Claude's opinion about Renée's betrothal was unimportant.

As she pondered the situation, she realized she could not allow it to happen. Much as opposing her mother-in-law caused butterflies in her belly, her Maman had wanted Mme. Michelle to care for Renée. She had bequeathed Renée half of her wealth and property. Claude could not abandon her sister just because she was afraid. It would do no good to speak to her husband. He had already agreed with his mother and, Claude admitted sorrowfully, he was under his mother's thumb. At night when he came to her bed, he talked on and on about how magnificently Louise was managing negotiations to make his dream of reconquering Milan a reality. He had signed the betrothal, too, yet he did not breathe a word to her about it. That hurt.

She was growing to know him. She could predict the way the situation would unfold. It had happened often enough already. He would make her extravagant promises. "Of course, no one will dismiss the baronne. Whatever gave you that idea? Maman, you are not planning anything like that? No, who would suggest such a thing? It is your imagination."

Then they would find someone at court Maman Louise disliked, blame her suspicions on them, and dismiss them. She would feel guilty for causing some unfortunate courtier to lose their position and income. And, at some later time, Mme. Michelle would still be dismissed. Better to say nothing to François.

Claude found herself becoming increasingly lonely and desperate. Who *could* she trust with this secret?

HÔTEL DES TOURNELLES

*D*uchess Louise d'Angoulême

KING FRANÇOIS CAME LATE to Louise's suite in the Hôtel des Tournelles, his eyes snapping and his cheeks flushed. He stormed about her chamber, lifting her precious gewgaws and snapping them down. She feared he would crush the delicate china.

"What has put you in this foul temper?" Louise snapped. "Calm yourself. I would acquaint you with the progress of our negotiations with the English ambassadors over the extension of our peace treaty with them."

"God's fingernails! Let Him send all thrice-cursed Englishmen — and women, too — to roast in hell!"

"Speak softly, Son, or leave me."

He threw himself into a padded armchair by her fireplace and ran his fingers through his hair. "That minx. That conniving harlot! Do you know what our sweet as sugar Dowager Queen of France has done? No, of course you do not! She has got herself secretly married! And bedded! Without so much as a by-your-leave." He hawked.

"Not in here, you do not expectorate, François!" Louise exclaimed. Then she added, "Queen Marie? By Our Lady, she did not waste time. It is her first day released from the Hôtel de Cluny."

He continued to fume.

"Well, you knew she intended to marry Brandon. You gave your permission." She offered him a goblet of wine. "Who brought you the news?"

He snorted. "The Duke of Suffolk himself. Proud as a cock on its dunghill. They had a secret ceremony in the Hôtel de Cluny chapel. The only witnesses were the English courtiers and the priest she had recalled. And he has bedded her. Did not waste any time playing the two-backed beast."

"Do not be vulgar, François, just because you are in a temper. Well, we look like fools. Not yet two months since her husband died, and she has remarried. It hardly seems legal. We will have to move quickly to satisfy King Henry that we had no hand in this misalliance before the gossip gets about. And they will have to have a proper ceremony, too. She is a sly one, no doubt about it. Good thing she is not your wife. But... let me think a moment. It may be good for us."

François tipped his head to one side, his anger cooling quickly, as usual. He sipped his wine, stretching his feet toward the fire as Louise pondered. Soon a cat-in-cream smile curved her lips. "I said we have been negotiating with the English?"

"Umhum." François's eyes brightened.

"They are greedy. They are demanding restitution of the dowager queen's entire dowry plus such jewels, precious stone, plate, apparel and other benefits that King Louis bestowed upon her during their marriage, as well as the cost of transporting her court and the convoy necessary to escort it to the coast for her return to England. Or a sum in lieu of 200,000 crowns. And, they wish to possess and administer her dower lands for the duration of her life."

François whistled. "They do not want much, do they?"

Louise twirled her wine goblet by the stem. "It is France's position that the jewels, precious stones, plate and apparel are the patrimony of France and must remain. We also are negotiating the restoration of Tournay in return for release of her dower lands."

Her cat smile clung to her lips. "When King Henry discovers that the duke and his sister have betrayed his trust, he will be furious. Our spies say he is a suspicious man with a temper to match his hair. Nor does he forgive and forget. I expect they will want to return as quickly as possible to placate him. So, their negotiators will need to agree quickly. That is to our advantage."

François's good humor restored, he rose saying, "Maman, it always does me good to bring my troubles to you. You have a way of turning failures to our advantage."

LOUISE HAD PERSUADED HER DAUGHTER, Marguerite, they should hold regular salons in Louise's presence chamber. They decided upon every Wednesday after the second meal between Nones and Vespers. For the first event, Marguerite proposed a debate on which was the higher art: painting or sculpture. Louise persuaded the court artist M. François Clouet and the sculptor M. Nicholas Chantereine each to present one side of the case. Their debate would set the tone for the evening and provide the theme and language for lively discussion. Their chosen artists selected illustrative pieces to furnish her presence chamber for the salon. Courtiers crowded to their first function.

Louise took pleasure in the debate between the artists, but she took an even greater satisfaction in circulating among the ladies and gentlemen and overhearing the elevated discussions that followed. The gratification of lifting the artistic tone of her son's court inspired her. To compare how two artists' used line to express spirituality, to contrast the capacity of sculpture and painting to lift Man to contemplate the Divine was good for the soul and the mind.

"Marguerite," she said, "Is this not what you intended when we planned this event? Does it not make you wish to continue?"

Her daughter cocked her head to one side and said, "To tell a truth I am not sure you wish to hear, I think many times the conversation changes when you pass within hearing. I, however, am seen as more light-minded, and so I hear more gossip. But it is a good beginning, and we shall continue." She gave her mother a wink. "As much for the chatter as the profound discussion. There is much to be learned from both."

She sauntered off to take the arm of the English Ambassador, who found her charming. Louise hoped Marguerite would learn some useful tidbits about English relations with Spain.

On the far side of the room her lady-in-waiting, Lady Blanche, was deep in conversation with her stepdaughter. Louise smiled indulgently. Marguerite was right. It was unlikely those two were sharing opinions on the effect of shadow on enhancing meaning in painting. Still, she did not doubt that their minds were the better for attending the event. She would question Lady Blanche later about her chat with Mme. Jeanne.

CLAUDE AND MME. Jeanne left early from Mme. Louise's salon. Claude always preferred the company of a few friends to the crush of crowds. Now that she was increasing, everyone accepted her excuses for retiring early. Since her husband craved liveliness and loud entertainment and her mother-in-law enjoyed taking first place at his court, perfect accord reigned among them.

After attending Vespers, Claude and Mme. Jeanne, followed by three or four of Claude's demoiselles, returned to Claude's suite. With a sigh of pleasure, Claude settled into her favorite armchair and accepted a cup of hippocras and a biscuit. Mme. Jeanne set up a backgammon table, and they began a game. After a few moves, Claude realized her gouvernante was distracted.

She leaned forward so her voice did not carry. "Mme. Jeanne, what is troubling you?"

Mme. Jeanne raised her light-brown eyes to Claude's, looking as guilty as a dog caught snatching a bone from the table. "Is it so obvious, then?"

Claude gave a tiny smile. "You have placed your last two pieces almost at random. And I have known you forever."

"When Lady Blanche and I were talking, she made a remark that I can hardly credit, and thus would not repeat. Yet she said it as if it were commonly known. And how would she know, except that Mme. Louise told her? And...." She was becoming incoherent.

Claude put her cup back on the table. It was not like Mme. Jeanne to become rattled. "Perhaps you had better tell me what she said?" her voice gentle. "And perhaps you should look at the board. Move a piece. Anywhere. It doesn't matter."

Mme. Jeanne slid a piece to a new position and hesitated. "I... I... well...." She stopped and began again. "Lady Blanche said, 'I hear that the Countess de Tonnerre is to be Princess Renée's new gouvernante, so I expect the princess's betrothal will be announced soon. Do you know when?'"

Shocked, Claude moved a backgammon piece randomly without replying.

Mme. Jeanne hurried on. "I pretended to be annoyed and said, 'You should not speak of it. It is a state secret. And I certainly know nothing about any announcement. These things often come to naught.' Then Lady Blanche whispered, 'You will not give me away, will you?' I promised to say nothing. But I decided I must tell you. For that is what I heard." She stopped speaking and moved another piece.

Claude's hands were shaking so much it was hard to keep up the pretense of play. Mme. Jeanne had given her the information she wanted — the name of the woman Duchess Louise had chosen to replace Mme. Michelle. But to learn it through court gossip! And to learn that the secret of Renée's betrothal was bruited about so publicly frightened her. She had not taken even Mme. Jeanne into her confidence, yet Duchess Louise's lady-in-waiting was tittle-tattling about it in public.

"You are very pale, Mme. la Reine. Should I have said nothing? I was worried. Shall I bring you something to drink… or…." Mme. Jeanne started to rise.

"No, no, no. Stay. You did right." Claude reached out to take her sleeve but drew back, unwilling to draw attention to their conversation. "So. The Countess de Tonnerre. Mme. Françoise de Rohan-Guéméné. I know her a little, for she served a time at Maman's court. She is a widow, is she not? That is all I really know…." She took a deep breath. "Let us keep on playing this game. Your turn, I believe. I had not intended to involve you in the problem — worse than problem, the predicament — that troubles me. Even now I hesitate for your own protection — for it may lead you into a serious quarrel with your stepmother and the king."

As she moved a piece, Mme. Jeanne' raised her eyebrows. "You make me think that Lady Blanche spoke the truth." When Claude nodded, Mme. Jeanne shook her head in disgust, "How stupid of her. What can I do to help, Milady?"

Her loyalty was almost too much for Claude's fragile composure. Bending close to the board, she warned, "Mme. Jeanne, you are taking a great risk. I cannot ask it of you. I may not be able to shield you, though I pledge to do everything in my power."

"Tush. Enough of that. Tell me what I can do?"

Gratitude almost overwhelmed Claude and she thought she should refuse. Then she reflected. She must have help. She needed information and someone in whom she could confide. And if she could not trust Mme. Jeanne, there was no one she could trust. "I wish to learn all I can about the Countess de Tonnerre without anyone suspecting my interest. Find people who know the family. Discreetly. You will know who among my equerries and chamberlains can be trusted. I will send to Sieur Jacques to learn what I can from him."

"Knowing my step-mother, she will quiz Lady Blanche about our conversation. If she learns I am asking about Mme. de Tonnerre, she is certain to ask me."

Queen Claude understood. "Ah yes. And what is it she would ask you about exactly?"

"Telling you about the Countess de Tonnerre."

"Was it a secret? You are so sorry, but Lady Blanche spoke of it so openly you assumed the queen knew. Did she not?" She gave Mme. Jeanne a limpid glance.

Mme. Jeanne breathed a small chuckle. "Of course, Mme. la Reine, you are right. I have nothing to hide. If anyone does, it is she.

UNLIKE FRANÇOIS AND HIS MOTHER, Claude felt no enthusiasm for the war to recapture Milan. France did perfectly well without the duchy. During Papa's reign too many of her family and friends lost fathers and brothers. Its expense had been her father's only extravagance. Worse, it had led to the dispute with Pope Julius and the Church, and that led to the interdict. Which had resulted in the bitterest quarrel between her parents she could remember. Aggressive wars wasted resources, brought cruel loss of life and created division within families.

But Claude did not share her opinion with either Louise or François. Indeed, she never discussed the war preparations with them or anyone. Her mother-in-law found her reticence on the subject ideal, for she reveled in advising her son and negotiating with foreign ambassadors. Since Claude disliked any form of conflict, this maintained their comfortable relations. She reaped the added benefit that neither her husband nor mother-in-law paid much attention to her activities.

Within days of her uncomfortably secretive meeting with Sieur Jacques de Beaune, she made sure they knew she reviewed the accounts of her estates regularly. Though they disapproved, she insisted with quiet, stubborn persistence and conducted them weekly. In the future, she would always have an innocuous reason to meet him. And she made more of an occasion of their meetings. The day they were scheduled, her chamberlain fussed to prepare the palace library. Servants built bright fires in the fireplaces at either end of the room, dusted and polished the long table and carried in her tall-backed chair piled with cushions. De Beaune's clerks arrived burdened with the great locked account books containing records of her estate finances and opened them before her chair.

Two weeks after Mme. Jeanne's discovery, she asked him what he had learned about the Countess de Tonnerre after his clerks withdrew out of hearing distance. As his answer, he placed a page in front of her. It detailed everything about her ancestry, which was satisfactory since she was a de Rohan, of a good Breton family from a branch not strongly tainted with treason.

"But in herself," Claude murmured. "What is she like? Is she willful? Difficult? Or compliant and biddable? Like Suzanne de Bourbon or like her mother?"

He smiled into his beard as if surprised by her comparison. "The reports I received provided more information about her health, appearance, and family than about her personal characteristics."

"They make all the difference," Claude said. "If she is biddable, I shall address her one way. If she is touchy and proud, I shall use a different approach. Is that not what you do when you negotiate? I am certain it is so." She studied his face.

He flung his hands apart. "*Touché,* Mme. la Reine. I am not accustomed to thinking this way about ladies. Please forgive my failure to foresee your need. I shall acquire the information you require."

Within the week he sent a messenger with a report. The lady, a childless widow, was a quiet person of retiring demeanor, soft-spoken and gentle. As evidence, he noted that she had returned to her father's home after her husband died two years previously, for her adult stepchildren made her unwelcome in the dower-house that was hers by right. She had not protested or taken them to the law.

Mme. Jeanne's sources confirmed the intelligence her treasurer had ferreted out; the countess was a timid little mouse. Mme. Jeanne added a few curious tidbits. The countess had a lovely singing voice, she was pious, and she was wealthy. Her stepchildren resented her because the old count had left her a fortune in jewelry and lands. Her father had married her to the count because their lands lay side-by-side, so Claude imagined that the timid widow must find her situation unpleasant, even though she lived in her parents' home.

Claude was in a quandary. Her goal was to bring the Countess de Tonnerre to court as rapidly as possible. Time was passing — too quickly. Soon François and Maman Louise would go to Lyon to prepare for the war, leaving her in confinement at Blois. Yet she dared not invite the countess herself. Because Duchess Louise was her sister's guardian, it was she who must offer the appointment. And Claude did not know if Louise had yet done so. Claude could not create a situation in which her letter crossed one from Duchess Louise, each of which invited the countess to court. It would raise questions and that would alert the Duchess. If she guessed that Claude knew her plans, she would change them. And cover her tracks more carefully.

Protocol decreed that the king's Grand Chamberlain, Monsieur du Bouchage must manage the delicate affair of a new gouvernante for Princess Renée. He was the oldest, wealthiest, stuffiest, most powerful *noble de robe* in France. Since he now rarely left his Château of Montrésor because of his many illnesses (he suffered from gout like Papa and kidney stones like Maman, poor man) how could she discover whether Maman Louise had asked him yet to make the appointment?

Claude consulted her gouvernante on this vexed question. "What do you think, Mme. Jeanne?" she asked after pondering the problem for more than a week.

"What about sending M. de Bouchage a letter of inquiry? That would be simplest," Mme. Jeanne suggested as they walked to a musical evening at King François's court.

"I have considered it, but he would report it to the king. Next, I thought of sending someone to him, but he would report that, too. Then, I thought of bribing someone in his household or finding someone who could bribe someone, but it is not worth the risk of discovery. Can you think of anything else? If not, I shall not fret about it further. It is not essential that I know."

Mme. Jeanne, whose frown had been deepening, relaxed.

A wave of guilt washed over Claude. She had been so relieved to share her burden that she had thrust the problem onto Mme. Jeanne. It was unfair. She must make up her own mind. François could not formalize the betrothal without her signature, but would she dare refuse to sign in front of the court and the foreign delegation? She tried to picture it and quaked. She could not imagine having the fortitude to do it.

How soon would the formal betrothal occur? She could not ask her husband or her mother-in-law. The regent's ambassador would know, of course. Francois's chancellor, surely. She had a gift for conversation. Could she extract the information from them? That would be the best way. She prepared a few conversational gambits for her next chance encounter with them and then wrestled with the other problem that tormented her conscience.

How could she continue to hide the danger from Mme. Michelle? She and Renée were the victims. The right thing to do was take Mme. Michelle into her confidence. Besides, Mme. Michelle always had the best ideas. She would come up with a solution. A wave of relief swept over Claude, until she realized that, even if she decided to impart the problem to Mme. Michelle, she had no safe way to inform her. Ever since Duchess Louise boasted she knew the Dowager Queen's every plan because her messages were opened and read before they were sent on, Claude had become wary. She no longer trusted that her mail was secure from her mother-in-law's eyes.

It was not as easy as she had hoped to lure either the ambassador or the chancellor into an indiscreet revelation without giving away her own knowledge. Weeks went by and she had not advanced. Many times, she wished she could confide in François, but he was so absorbed in his Milanese campaign and their coming baby that he did not notice her agitation or her restless tossing at night.

IN THE MORNING chill on the last day of March, Louise, the Duchess d'Angoulême, was cranky as she made her way to the Église les Célestins for the official wedding of the Dowager Queen Marie to Duke Charles. The marriage had prevented a rapprochement between England and Flanders and had created a rift between Henry and his sister and Suffolk, which were excellent results. But the negotiations for Tournay had stalled since the English no longer trusted Suffolk as their chief negotiator. Small wonder. By Our Lady, she would not trust him to negotiate a feast if everyone had agreed to the menu beforehand. He had fallen to the Dowager Queen like a house of cards. It was past time to get the troublesome couple out of France. This public marriage that would offend French opinion by its haste was another step.

Louise had even resolved François's resulting problem with the Duke de Bourbon. Since her son had promised the Dowager Queen as a bride for Duke Antoine de Lorraine in return for Lorraine's military support, King François now had to scramble to find another equally appealing bride. The Duke de Bourbon-Montpensier's younger sister was still unmarried so François offered her to Duke Antoine without consulting her brother. The Duke de Lorraine had been delighted; Duke Charles de Bourbon-Montpensier much less so. Louise had propitiated Duke Charles with promises of favors during the Milanese adventure to sweeten his acceptance of François's usurpation of his rights in disposing of his sister. Now marriage preparations were underway.

Louise pulled her fur-lined cape closer around her and glanced at the queen, whose bland, fat face she could see through the open curtains of the litter. François insisted Queen Claude be carried to protect their child. So, cloaked and hooded against the cold, they walked their horses beside her. Behind them, a few of his favorites formed a horse guard. Still sullen about being duped, François made loud, vulgar jokes about Queen Marie being "a well-ridden filly" as he and his friends chortled about "lusty nags," and "no neigh slayers here." Of course, Claude was never of any use in restraining him, and today was no exception. Acting as if she were deaf, Claude smiled, waved, and tossed alms to citizens in the street.

As they rode through Paris, François's temper sweetened as the people cheered him. He was smiling and waving graciously by the time he greeted the bridal couple at the church door. A solitary priest solemnized the quiet — yet public—wedding. The event served well enough for both Louise and Queen Marie. The marriage was now official, and the couple no longer risked Church penalties for fornication.

After the ceremony, the new Duchess of Suffolk curtsied to the King and Duchess Louise. "It is impossible to express sufficiently my gratitude for your support during these trying months. I will ever speak kind words of you and stand as your friend in England."

So I should hope, Louise thought, as she bowed her head slightly to Duchess Marie. "We are fortunate to have benefited from the joy of your presence here and look forward to a long and happy friendship once you return to England." The problem with princesses was simple. They had been indulged from birth and would have their way without considering the consequences. Marie would pay a high price for her unsuitable marriage. Being robbed of her dowry by her greedy brother, begging his forgiveness and pleading to return to England were only the beginning. "I believe you will depart soon?"

"As soon as King François sends our travel authorizations." Duchess Marie's answer was pointed.

Louise knew François was as eager as she for the couple's departure. Unfortunately, back in February, without consulting her, he had promised to help his Scottish allies negotiate a treaty with King Henry. Now he would not renege on his promise. Until he learned the English had signed the treaty, he kept delaying their permissions to leave Paris.

"I shall be your envoy to my son," she promised. "Begin your packing. This will resolve itself in no time." She kissed Duchess Marie on both cheeks, allowed the duke to kiss her hands, took Queen Claude's arm and swept from the church.

She wanted this greedy, feckless couple gone before they announced Princess Renée's betrothal. The English would not take that news well.

20 APRIL 1515, MORNING

HÔTEL DES TOURNELLES

 uchess Louise d'Angoulême

WHAT A MILKSOP my son can be! Louise thought, when Lady Blanche informed her that François had gone hunting early that morning. Anything to avoid telling Claude that Princess Renée would be betrothed that day. As Louise silently reproached him for his cowardice, she accepted she had never yet met a man who did not turn to jelly when facing a merited rebuke. Not about the betrothal, since it was the price of their alliance with Duke Charles, but because he had not told Claude sooner. He knew he should have.

Louise knew it, too. When François had wanted to tell his wife immediately after signing the agreement, she had persuaded him to wait. She explained she must locate a suitable replacement for Mme. Michelle, who had petitioned to return to private life at Parc Soubise after the deaths of Queen Anne and King Louis. At the time, he had not cared about the details and did not question her. But now that he had to face his wife, he was nowhere to be found.

Louise had worked closely with the French negotiators on the financial settlements. Princess Renée's dowry would comprise 100,000 gold écus and the Duchy of Berry in central France. Duke Charles was satisfied. The crown would retain her original Breton inheritance, which was worth at least twice the dowry settled upon her. Much to Louise's chagrin, the crown's lawyers insisted that Claude, as Duchess de Bretagne, must sign the betrothal documents because of the changes to the terms of Renée's Breton inheritance.

Louise argued, "As trustee for both Claude and Renée, I have the right to the income from all their property until they are of age and may dispose of it as I will."

The lawyers, members of the Parlement of Paris and *nobles de la robe*, were unimpressed by the queen mother and her arguments. "Two points we must make here. First, you are entitled to the income of minors, yes, but to their principal, no. In reallocating the income of Princess Renée's estate to the crown, you are affecting her principal. The Duchess de Bretagne must approve any such disposition."

They had not finished. "Second, Queen Claude is no longer a minor. Under Breton law and the terms of her mother's will, she is the duchess of the independent Duchy of Brittany. Therefore, she shall be treated as a *'femme sole'* in right of disposal of her income from the duchy. As its duchess, she must approve all changes to its principal." Try as Louise might, there was no moving them from this opinion.

Since she could not gain her point through law, Louise chose another approach. Aware of Claude's timidity and fear of conflict, she would confront her with the betrothal and its terms in public. Now that the moment was upon them, Louise was not looking forward to the event. Her daughter-in-law was bound to be upset at learning about her sister's betrothal in public. Louise would just have to crush her into acquiescence.. If she made a fuss, it would be an unpleasant scene, but it would not endure.

Claude and the Countess de Tonnerre were similar. They were both quiet, biddable little things. Life would be much more pleasant once this was done. Then she would no longer have to deal with the obstreperous Baronne Michelle.

When Louise arrived in the queen's chamber, she found utter confusion. Queen Claude still wore her shift with her under-skirt tied over it.

As soon as she saw Louise, she snapped, "Why am I ordered to appear in full court dress today? I was resting when Mme. Jeanne arrived, with orders from you. Orders!" She was quite unlike her usual self, and her large blue eyes sparkled with temper. "*She* said you had sent a message to her rooms that she and I were *required* in the great audience chamber immediately after Sext."

Louise had never seen her so angry. That message had been a mistake. Her best approach was to apologize immediately with suitable humility. "Forgive me, Queen Claude. In my eagerness to prepare for the day's events, I overstepped. I should have come myself to apprise you of the important occasion about to occur. Instead, I sent my stepdaughter in my place without providing her with sufficient information. I beg both you and she to forgive me." She curtsied to the ground and stayed in that humble position, schooling her features to contrition. In her experience, nothing was as effective as a fulsome apology to turn away anger. So it proved once more.

"Very well, Maman Louise, please rise. Explain to us the cause of this frenzy in our rooms?"

Dear, dear. Claude's voice was still icy, a bad sign. Louise reached out to take Claude's hands, but Claude shook free.

"Daughter Claude, will you not take a seat?" Louise seated herself. "It will be better if you send your ladies and maids away. I would explain, but for your ears only."

Queen Claude was still out of countenance. Louise could see that her earlier error had made her next task much more difficult. "As an essential part of the treaty with Flanders, the Regent and the Duke wished a marriage alliance with the Crown of France. The only available royal princess is your sister." Louise hurried on as Claude's lips thinned. "So, Princess Renée will be betrothed to Duke Charles of Burgundy as part of the treaty to be signed today. And, of course, your signature is required." As alert as a fox scenting the air, she awaited Claude's reaction.

"When was this decision taken to offer the betrothal of my sister?"

Claude sounded offended. Louise did not answer.

"Some time ago, then. Why was I not informed as soon as the subject was broached so that my views be considered?" Claude's voice chimed like brittle ice.

"Do you have any objections?" Offense was the best defense.

"It depends upon the terms of the agreement. When will my sister marry? Where will she live until then? What will be the conditions under which she lives? Who will have the care of her during that period? What is her dowry to be? Before I sign this treaty, I would have answers." Queen Claude's voice trembled. "I do not forget the sad experience of the present Regent Marguerite, who lived as dauphine at the French court from over ten years. When King Charles VIII broke his betrothal to her, she was returned ignominiously to Flanders like a used garment. I will have no such humiliation visited upon my sister."

Louise breathed a sigh of relief. Once Claude started questioning, she was doomed to lose. Her voice smooth as honey, Louise said, "There can be no fear the princess will be humiliated. Your sister will remain in France under the care of her gouvernante until she marries, at the earliest when she is twelve. She will not leave France until the marriage has been conducted either in person or by proxy. Her generous dowry has been set as the Duchy of Berry and 100,000 gold écus. You have nothing to fear for the care of Renée." Louise was pleased with her answer. While it was deliberately misleading, she had not lied outright which she could insist upon if Claude were to reproach her. "Come, are you reassured? Then let the maids continue your preparations."

Claude did not argue further. She allowed her maids and *demoiselles* to finish dressing her while Louise sat by. Her mind was elsewhere, and she gave vague, single-word answers to Louise's sprightly conversation. Louise took no notice.

At the betrothal ceremony Queen Claude behaved like a wooden doll, offering mechanical smiles and conventional responses to Ambassador de Gattinara; and signed where she was required without a glance. Mme. Jeanne who accompanied them was as stiff as she. They did not display the grace for which the French court was renowned; however, as King François observed *sotto voce* at the end of the formalities, Queen Claude had once again demonstrated her royal bearing, for she did not shame him with a public scene. Louise was relieved, too. Despite a moment of rebellion, Claude had proven herself a feeble opponent.

AFTER FRANÇOIS HAD LEFT her bed that night, Claude tossed and turned, unable to sleep. She had reproached him for having hidden Renée's betrothal from her, but only briefly and gently since nothing could undo it now. She must have faith that it would come to naught.

It had not been as easy earlier that day. It had taken every drop of her royal training to pretend to believe her mother-in-law's lies. Once she decided she must seem to capitulate to disarm her mother-in-law's suspicions, she had behaved with propriety. But inside she had made a vow. Despite her fear, she was going to do battle. She had spent little time in Brittany, but she was Breton as much as French. With that went a stubborn streak. She would protect her sister or perish in the attempt. Mme. Michelle *would* remain Renée's gouvernante.

At early mass that morning, she prayed to St. Expedite for forgiveness that she had not followed his example and acted as soon as she had learned of the secret betrothal Maman Louise had arranged for Renée. She vowed to procrastinate no longer.

Even though she exchanged letters weekly with Mme. Michelle and her sister, she had failed even to hint of the looming crisis. After breaking her fast, exhausted from guilt and lack of sleep, she settled at the desk in her withdrawing chamber. Her conscience was so cloudy she gnawed at the feathered quill and using the excuse of not knowing how she would deliver the letter to delay once again. Calling once more upon St. Expedite, she dipped the nib into the oak-gall ink.

Written by my hand, at the Hôtel des Tournelles

This 21ˢᵗ day of April 1515

Greetings to you my dear Baronne Michelle,

First let me assure you that all is well with me and with the infant I carry and with my husband the king and all here at the court. Since our Easter duty here is complete, and the city beginning to warm, and the château beginning to stink from its winter use, the court leaves by boat three days hence. We will travel first to Gien where we shall stay a sennight with my aunt, Mme. la Grande, if you wish to write to us there. In less than a month, si Dieu le veut, we shall be together again in Blois. It is my great desire.

Mme. Michelle, I cannot and must not delay any longer to inform you that yesterday, to my surprise and utmost distress, I was ordered to attend the formal betrothal of my sister to Duke Charles of Burgundy and to sign approval of the official documents. I made it clear that I would not agree that she leave France until she was of an age to marry. However, we both know that she is the ward of Duchess Louise and my consent to her departure is not required.

Much worse, and I ask your forgiveness for my cowardice in failing to reveal this earlier, my mother-in-law has formed the intention to replace your governance of my sister with that of Mme. Françoise de Guéméné-Rohan, feu Countess de Tonnerre. Please believe that I am not party to this and I have been seeking some plan to overcome Duchess Louise's purpose. I am ashamed to admit I have identified no solution, although I have learned that the countess herself is a meek and biddable woman — doubtless the reason the duchess selected her.

I beg you to apply your talents to this impasse. For my sister's sake and my own, I do not wish you to depart from my sister's life. It would be a cruelty to her, to me and to you, as well as an injustice and a great wrong visited upon you in consideration of the devoted service you and your family have given to me and mine. Both my parents call me from beyond the grave to combat this perversion of justice, and I shall stand strong in your defense. My late mother tied my hands of legal remedies until my sister comes of age at fourteen, since the wardship rests with Duchess Louise. Therefore, I beseech you to find an answer that will allow us to thwart the Duchess's intent without a legal confrontation that will give satisfaction to none but our enemies. May God keep you in His holy care.

Claude, Queen of France

Duchess de Bretagne

Rereading her missive, she wondered if she had been too humble, but decided that Mme. Michelle would understand her sense of guilt. Fussing over the wording was just another way to procrastinate. She folded it. Just before she sealed it, she added one more line. Then she sealed it carefully but wrote no name on its face. Ringing the bell that hung close at hand, she struggled to rise.

At the summons, Mme. Jeanne hurried in, arriving so quickly she must have been waiting just outside Claude's door.

"Let me help," she said, taking Claude's arm and pushing away the desktop to provide room for her protruding bump. When she saw the letter, Mme. Jeanne looked relieved. "May I take that for you?"

"To Sieur Jacques de Beaune's private residence in a black hooded cape at the dinner hour. Insist on seeing him personally. Instruct him he is to send it by private messenger, one he trusts with his most confidential documents, and that it is to be given directly into Mme. Michelle's hand. No other."

Mme. Jeanne almost forgot to curtsey as she hurried to leave, but paused when the queen spoke again.

"Ensure Sieur Jacques provides the messenger with a generous *douceur* — perhaps an *écu d'or* — on his return. And our gracious thanks."

AFTER THE CLOAKED messenger departed from the poorly lit back hall, Michelle stuffed the unaddressed letter into her underskirt waistband and slipped away to her rooms on Château de Blois's second floor. She sat on her bed, staring through the window. The scent of new earth and young greens wafted through it. It was late April, and the days were already warmer and softer. In the early evening sky, the horizon was fading to shades of pink and violet. Within and without the Château, the faint soothing sounds of work winding down as day slid into dusk created a mood of harmony. Yet the episode left her nerves jangling. It arrived like a scene from the time before Queen Anne had died, when important people sent her urgent, secret letters that ended, *Burn this letter.*

She lifted the crucifix on her rosary to her lips. The queen's letter this week had hinted of no troubles. An urgent, secret letter could mean only one thing: bad news. Breaking Queen Claude's seal, she unfolded the vellum that crackled under her fingers and glanced casually to the bottom of the sheet. Eyes widening, she clutched the document to her heart, then pulled it back to check again. It had not been her imagination: *Burn this letter once you have read it.*

She had to read it several times before she could believe the message. Duchess Louise wished to replace her with a different *gouvernante.* At first, she felt numb. After a time, she began to shake. More than any other feeling, rage rose within her, a fury so molten she felt she would blow apart. Not a person given to fiery anger, she was at a loss how to rid herself of the jolts of fiery rage that blasted through her. She paced her carpeted chamber like a caged tiger, pounding one fist into the palm of the other until the stinging hurt enough that she returned to her senses. Then she sank onto the chair in her room, and the pain she had been fighting overtook her. How could Mme. Louise part her from the child she had nurtured since her birth? How could she separate Renée from the woman the child now loved as her second mother? When Michelle thought about her child's grief, she had to wrap her arms around her body to keep from wailing so loudly she would bring the child running into her room.

She did not know how long she sat rocking before she calmed, but when she became conscious again, the sky outside was midnight blue sprinkled with stars. Her bones ached as she rose to kneel at her prie-dieu. She gazed a long time at the painting of St. Anne above it. Then she recited a rosary.

After she completed her devotions, she cooled her face with lavender water and put drops into her reddened eyes to clear them. Finally, she took the letter from the floor where she had flung it and read Queen Claude's words again. Rebellion struggled to choke her like a wad of coarse bread. Michelle pushed the feeling away. She would not let her emotions master her. By doing so, the duchess would win. Instead, Michelle would put her mind to outwitting Mme. Louise.

Michelle recognized how much courage Queen Claude had needed to oppose her husband and mother-in-law, even secretly. The law gave men complete authority over women. Only widows were excepted. Michelle believed this was the true reason the duchess had always refused to remarry. Only because Claude's duchy still kept its independence and she was its legal ruler, did she have any legal authority of her own.

Most courtiers thought Queen Claude a cypher, a timid little mouse, unwilling and unable to defend herself, much less anyone else. They mistook her physical infirmities for lack of moral courage and her pleasant nature for a lack of resolve. But Michelle knew her better. The daughter of Anne de Bretagne, she came from a long line of Breton lords who had maintained their lands against English and French invaders. True, the queen feared her mother-in-law, but this letter signaled that she was prepared to resist. Neither would Princess Renée allow anyone to impose upon her, young as she was.

The remnants of her emotional storm still soured her body and her outlook. She must change her focus before she could find solutions. With a start, she realized she was so late that the Princess must already have gone to bed. The child was undoubtedly distressed that Michelle had not come to bid her goodnight. After glancing in her brass hand mirror, to make sure she had removed the ravages of her outburst, Michelle went to Renée.

Putting a finger to her lips to silence the maidservant abed on the pallet at the end of the princess's bed, Michelle tiptoed to Renée's bedside. Holding a candle high, she pulled the curtain aside just enough to check that her charge slept. She did. Reaching inside gently, Michelle tucked some hair back into her nightcap and traced a cross on her forehead. The corners of Renée's lips curved into a tiny smile and she sighed. Love washed into every cranny of Michelle's body and with it a surge of faith that the Virgin would help her find a solution. For she must.

Returning to her room, Michelle sat in the window seat looking out toward the river. The night air was chilly now and cleared the cobwebs from her head. Questions rose in her mind. How would she know when she had identified a workable solution?

What were the criteria? As the familiar and beloved routine fell into place, she relaxed. Then she paused a moment to think of her father. He had gifted her with a fine education, insisting that even a girl deserved one. It had given her the blessing of an orderly method and a process for logical thinking. Tonight, she would list questions. What was the purpose of the solution? What did each person who was part of the problem want and need? *Nota bene*: Especially Duchess Louise; she wielded power so her desires and needs must either be accommodated — or circumvented. Were there examples from the past from which she could learn? Where else could she look for inspirations? She rose and found a wax tablet to scratch down ideas. Soon the task absorbed her.

23 MAY 1515

CHÂTEAU DE BLOIS

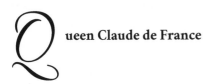

ueen Claude de France

AT SIX MONTHS, Claude already felt as big as a horse. She always had trouble walking because of her hip, despite the raised platform in her left shoe, but now she waddled like a duck. How could she feel like a queen when she looked like a goose? Her infant kicked within her belly, a sensation that startled her whenever it came. She knew she should not complain. She was carrying a child — a son? — for France, but sometimes it was hard to refrain. Still, today they were back home at Blois. When she reached the end of this long, painful walk to her rooms — her mother's rooms — she would see her beloved sister and Mme. Michelle. But she could not yet relax. Michelle had sent her reassuring letters, but without details since they must maintain discretion. Every day Claude had prayed to St. Anne and the Virgin that Mme. Michelle's plans would work. Finally, Claude would learn what they were.

The table in the dining chamber alcove glittered with plate and twinkling crystal. The queen had invited her guests to dine in her rooms.

"Mme. Renée, Mme. la Baronne de Soubise, Mme. Jeanne de Longwy." One by one they curtsied as Claude's gentleman usher announced them.

Princess Renée seemed more grown up already, although it had only been three and a half months since last Claude had seen her. She stared at Claude's protruding bump, a finger in her mouth. It was obvious she wanted to say something, equally obvious Mme. Michelle had told her she must not. Claude held her arms open and Princess Renée ran to her sister. As the queen hugged her, Princess Renée placed an ear to her belly and turned her face up to peer into Claude's.

"Darling Renée." Claude kissed both her cheeks. "Is there something you wish to ask?"

"Do you have a baby in here?" She rubbed her cheek against the silk brocade of Claude's underskirt.

"I do. A niece or nephew for you. You will be Aunt Renée in just a few months. What do you think of that?"

Princess Renée's eyes grew rounder. "Will I be able to hold it?"

"Yes, indeed."

Taking Princess Renée's hand, she said, "Let's go to dinner."

After her servants had cleared the meal away, Renée had gone protesting to bed and Claude had made an appearance among her ladies in her antechamber, Mme. Michelle, Mme. Jeanne and the queen settled into her bedchamber. Once Claude was settled in her armchair, Mme. Michelle and Mme. Jeanne sank onto stools facing her. Behind them, the immense white-plaster fireplace, had been filled with sweet-smelling roses from the spring garden. The scent reminded Claude of happy times with her mother and subtly lifted her spirits.

Claude could wait no longer. "You have a plan?" she said to Mme. Michelle.

Mme. Michelle nodded slowly. "But you must pick it to pieces. Both of you. There must be no holes, no mistakes."

They agreed.

She listed the questions she had asked herself and the requirements she had set. "The most restrictive," she said, "is that it must cause no gossip. How could I arrange a solution that would cause no one to gossip after Mme. Louise announced I had been replaced by the Countess de Tonnerre? The only answer is — to replace me with the Countess de Tonnerre." Her eyes crinkled at the corners as she observed their outraged expressions, but she kept her voice serious. "You do not see this as an adequate solution?"

They were both spluttering and spoke at once. "No!" "Of course not!" "What are you thinking of?"

She did laugh then. "Would you like me to explain," and became serious immediately. "It will work, and I will show you how. First, consider the timing. When is it probable that Mme. Louise will implement her plan? I theorize she will wait until you cannot complain to King François. What will that require? First, Mme. la Reine, that you must not know it has happened. Second, that by the time you learn, you will be unable to change it because Mme. Louise will be Regent."

Claude felt too shocked to argue.

Mme. Jeanne said, "But, but, but..." before she stumbled into silence.

"Do you disagree?"

Claude sighed. "When you put it that way, no." Discouragement swept over her. The Duchess was wickedly clever. "So, is it possible to prevent it?

"Remember, this is only one idea. There are other possibilities, but I think it the most likely. And my solution would work for any of them. But it will involve deceptions and sacrifices. On your part and mine. Are you willing?" Michelle sat with her hands folded in her lap. She reminded Claude of a soldier awaiting orders.

Claude was not sure what she had been hoping when she asked Mme. Michelle to devise a plan, but she had not expected it to test her conscience. "What exactly will it require of me... and you?"

Michelle pulled a scrap of paper from the small purse that hung on a chain from her waist. She ran her eyes over the paper as if gathering her thoughts. "If you please, Mme. la Reine, at the start you may think that my plan is preposterous. Please listen to my entire idea before speaking."

Claude's spirits sank. Was Mme. Michelle's proposition going to be so outrageous then? "I agree," she said. She must be prepared to hide her disappointment. It would be wrong to hurt Mme. Michelle's feelings.

Mme. Michelle nodded as if she understood their fears. "First, you will write to Countess de Tonnerre inviting her to join you at Amboise as one of your ladies. At the same time, I will go to Blois and look for an hôtel very close to the Château, hopefully attached to the outer walls. Third, before you enter your confinement, you or Mme. Louise will appoint the Countess de Tonnerre as my replacement as gouvernante, and I will leave with my belongings. With no one knowing where I have gone, I will go to the house in Blois in secret. When you go into confinement, the Countess will take Princess Renée publicly to the royal nurseries at Blois. She will be Princess Renée's formal gouvernante and carry out the basic functions of supervising the princess when she rises and when she retires. However, during the day, she will bring the princess to my home where the princess will continue under my care as before. This can continue as long as necessary.

"By then the king will have left for Lyon and Mme. Louise will go with him. He may even be at war and Mme. Louise will be Regent. When your confinement is over, you will join the regent in Lyon while Princess Renée and the new prince or princess remain at Blois and the Countess can be that child's gouvernante, too.

"But as you see, it will involve persuading the Countess to accept the deception — and you, of course."

By the time Mme. Michelle had finished, Claude was reeling. She was not sure she had grasped the complete plan, but it might work! A little shoot of hope, like the first sprouts that hinted at spring, grew within her. She felt an urge to dance. The thought made her smile. She would look like a great, clumsy, dancing bear.

"Does that little smile suggest you like the plan?" Claude heard the wistfulness in Mme. Michelle's voice. Mme. Michelle was one of the kindest and most selfless people she knew. She was offering to give up both a high honor and valuable pension and courting malicious gossip to stay with Princess Renée — from love and loyalty.

Now Claude thought she might cry. She reached across the space that separated them. "Oof," she grunted as her belly prevented her from bending. "Give me your hands. Thank you so much. I feel hopeful again." She sniffled. "I am so relieved." Fumbling in her sleeve, she pulled out a handkerchief and blew her nose.

Mme. Michelle rose and threw the scrap of vellum in the fire. "Now ask me your questions, Mme. la Reine."

"How will I persuade the countess to agree?"

"From what you have said and what I have learned from those who know her, Countess Françoise is biddable. Mme. Louise has informed her she is to take the position of gouvernante, and her de Rohan family has insisted she accept so she does not dare refuse. But she is timid and has no experience of court or children. I am sorry for her. She must be frightened since she has completely the wrong character for the position."

"But still...." Claude still felt doubtful

"When you also invite her, she will feel doubly pressured, for her family will insist she please you. But you are offering a solution. By accepting your proposal, she satisfies her family and the duchess without having to fail. She will have the position and entitlements without the duties and I will help her. She retains the dignity of the office and, if she wishes, responsibility for your newborn child. I will act as her friend and support her in every way. You may tell her that to encourage her. It should not be difficult to coax her with so many reasons for her to agree."

Claude took a deep breath. She was being cowardly again. No path was without risks. For her sister's sake, she would make this work. "I have an idea that might help the plan work more smoothly," she offered tentatively. "There is an ancient, vacant house built into the walls of this Château that I can have repaired and enlarged for you, Mme. Michelle. It lies close to my mother's private retreat. Although it was forbidden, my friends and I used to play in it when I was a child. I shall make it known that by my express wish the countess is using it for Princess Renée's education because of the new infant. Its entry is already extremely private and I shall order it made more hidden, better fenced and securely gated behind a high privet hedge. Thus, when the countess takes the princess to you, she need never leave the château grounds. The house has the added benefit that its main gated entrance opens onto the street below the château, providing a discreet entrance outside the grounds. That way it will be much easier to keep the secret."

The three ladies glanced from one to the other, trying to identify other problems. Hitches could well arise, but the principle itself was simple. Allow the Countess de Tonnerre to hold the title but keep Mme. Michelle close by with generous access to Princess Renée. Then Renée would not lose the last person who had been in her life since her birth.

"We will make it work. And after my confinement...." Claude thoughts drifted to the sounds of her shrieks reverberating in the darkened chamber, and herself there without Mme. Michelle's reassuring presence. Breaking into a cold sweat, she forced her mind back to the present and pinned a smile on her lips.

"After my confinement I will come to Blois with Mme. Jeanne and my infant to bring him to the royal nursery. That will give me an opportunity to spend time with you before I join Mme. Louise." Claude was even happier at this addition. "But what about you, dear Mme. Michelle? When you resign your position, you will lose your stipend as gouvernante, your position at court and the luxuries of court living."

"These are material benefits. Duchess Louise believes they are important to me. But I value the love of the princess, the blessing of kind friends and family and the pleasure of teaching young minds." She blushed a little when she said this. "I hope that does not sound too pompous. And I am not fond of the gossip and jealousy of the court despite its benefits — the library, the music, the art — and some warm friends. These are enjoyable, but will I regret their loss? Not overly. And there are many advantages to not being at court." She did not enumerate, and Claude did not press her.

"Mme. la Reine, please remember, I could be wrong. Duchess Louise may have some other plan or timing altogether. Nor do I know what excuse she will use to dismiss me. It will be essential to be adaptable and react promptly."

Claude felt as if she had been doused with icy water. Did Mme. Michelle fear that Claude would not protect Princess Renée or her? "Do you believe there is danger?"

Michelle chewed her lip. "Nooo…. But we must be careful to say nothing to anyone outside this group. I have shared nothing myself."

Claude struggled to rise. "Please forgive me. I must still prepare for the king's *Grande Entrée* into Blois on the morrow." Immediately Mme. Jeanne and Mme. Michelle flew to either side of her, lifting her by the elbows. "You have given me much to consider, Mme. Michelle. I shall act as we have agreed. Your plan is excellent."

After Mme. Michelle left, Claude lay down on her bed. "Mme. Jeanne, please cover me, then leave me for an hour, no more. I must rest." Although she closed her eyes, Claude found that sleep eluded her. Before long, she recognized she had only one problem to solve: where would she find the courage?

291

✳

DUCHESS LOUISE WAS DELIGHTED with the success of the *Grand Entrée* into Blois. Although this was a much smaller town than Paris, the entrée had been, in its way, every bit as magnificent. The town folk who lived here were much of a kind: artisans and merchants who supplied — or retainers who served — the court, and the administrators and nobles with homes in the city. They had demonstrated their appreciation of their new monarch and his court with banners and tapestries, flowers and incense, playlets and poetry, song and dance, marching and music, processions and saints and so much more. Food and festivities fueled the lively mood, for few of the inhabitants of this lovely, clean town that lived tidily within its walls were riffraff or troublemakers. François mixed with the townsfolk who would have slapped him on the back if it were not *lèse-majesté* and flirted with the prettiest girls whose names he made it a point to learn. It would cause problems later, but that was for Queen Claude to resolve. *Grâce à Dieu,* it was no longer her problem. By the time they arrived at the château, he was in the best of humors. Now was the time to approach him.

Louise lured him to her rooms with the offer of a gift and sweets, two of his weaknesses. The gift was truly remarkable: a square-form table clock. He had never seen one before. She had not either until an itinerant Jew brought it to her in Paris; she bought it because it came from Rome, and so it had a double value for her son. They spent at least an hour poring over it together. Because she had insisted she learn how it worked, she could tell François. Its spring-driven mechanism was visible through the molded glazed windows that shielded all four sides. The top face had hour and minute hands made of blue iron, and a silver dial with Roman hours and Arabic minutes. The whole four-inch square clock was enclosed in an exquisite, gilt and silvered brass case with round ball-like feet, and it all fit inside a glass-topped leather case. While they admired the clock, they sipped sweet rosé wine and nibbled on *pavés de Blois* — layers of nougat, praline and chocolate — and *malices du loup* — a mix of orange-flavored almond paste, honey, and hazelnut with a hint of anise. By the time they had finished the inspection, he was clay in her hands.

"François, just one thing before you leave."

"Yes, Maman?"

"I have mentioned my problems with Mme. la Baronne."

"Yes? I do not remember, really." He sounded uninterested, just as she wished, and was still turning his new clock this way and that, admiring its wonders.

"Well, I have, since before Queen Anne died. You know Princess Renée is my ward and I administer her estate."

"Umhum." He was fiddling with the clock in its case, examining how the winding mechanism worked.

"Be careful with that. The Jew told me the biggest problem with these new clocks is over-winding the mechanism. Better to let it wind down than over wind. It—"

"Yes, yes, you told me."

Do not nag, she thought. "About Mme. la Baronne. I'm concerned she's been abusing my trust — advancing her own family members to her advantage and assigning them to Princess Renée's estates."

"Hmm. Well—"

"No, François, I do not need advice. I have been managing estates for longer than you. I am also concerned about pilfering, which I mention it because it is time to assign Renée a new gouvernante, and I have selected the Countess de Tonnerre. Have you any objections to her?"

He was still playing with his clock, but at her question he raised his eyebrows and then said, "No." He hesitated and added, "It will not upset my wife, will it?"

"Do not worry about Mme. Claude. I will speak to her."

His expression cleared. "Well, then, it is fine with me." He gave her a big, one-armed hug and kiss, and said, "Thank you for this magnificent gift and the *Grande Entrée*. You are the best mother a son could have."

She watched him leave with pure satisfaction. He would probably not even remember the conversation, yet she could honestly say she had received his approval.

CHÂTEAU D'AMBOISE

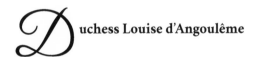 uchess Louise d'Angoulême

ANOTHER STEP ACCOMPLISHED, Louise thought, leaving the modern interior of the new St. Florentin chapel. In the sunlit courtyard at the Château d'Amboise, Duke Charles de Bourbon-Montpensier stood beside his sister, the new Duchess Renée de Lorraine. The newly married Duchess, her dark eyes narrowing with laughter, held the arm of Duke Antoine, as if she could not quite believe she had been lucky enough to marry him. Anyone could see she was delighted. The king stood with them, as handsome as always. He must be relieved that he and she had brought the wedding off despite the problems they encountered after Dowager Queen Marie's imprudent secret marriage. Duke Charles de Bourbon-Montpensier had taken offense when François offered his sister to the Duke de Lorraine without first gaining his approval. Perhaps he would have opposed the match if he had been given the opportunity. Did he have to provide too large a dowry? Was his objection that simple? Or was he envious of the king?

Louise turned away, putting the handsome duke's irritation out of her mind. This wedding signaled that their time at Amboise was drawing to its close, and Louise itched to forge ahead. The wedding had given them the perfect excuse to draw together all François's favorite *chevaliers d'honneur* who would be the marshals and commanders in the assault on Milan, along with the troop that was escorting them to Lyon to join the bulk of the army. Also joining them at the wedding were the Venetian ambassadors with whom she had sealed the alliance that was the last key to the expedition. She had arranged for the clerics who provided the administrative and logistical backbone to meet them here. High glory was fine, but without food, and the wherewithal to cook, serve, eat and clean up, and without water and beverages, medical supplies, clean laundry, dry powder, tents and blankets, and the wagons to transport it all, there could be no victory.

Today, François was in the highest of spirits. His huntsmen had captured a young boar twice the size of a normal male hog. For entertainment after the wedding ceremony, he had chosen a boar-baiting. Despite her objections, he insisted upon holding it in the central courtyard.

"Easier and more exciting, Maman."

"Think of the danger, *mon César*! There are too many people." As soon as she saw his eyes glitter, she knew she had erred. Danger was his meat and drink.

When she entered the courtyard, her heart sank. The barriers set up around the improvised field could not have been flimsier

— nothing more than the trestles that would serve as the bases for the tables later for the wedding feast. She thought she might stand inside an open doorway with Claude. That was when she discovered the doors were barred from the inside.

Ten of François's huntsmen prodded the boar into the temporary ring and waited for the order to release it. It snorted and pawed the ground in rage. The king and his companions cheered when they saw it and grabbed their weapons from their squires, who had gathered to hand them their short swords, daggers and lances. Once they had swarmed into the ring shouting and hallooing, enraging the beast further, François signaled his huntsmen to free the red-eyed beast. Yelling, tripping over one another, and jabbing the maddened animal with their lances and spears, the young lords entertained themselves gloriously.

The accident happened in an instant, as they always do. Yet, for Louise, watching it frozen to her spot, it seemed to last forever. The furious beast, maddened by its wounds and the attacks upon it, charged through an opening among them, raced away from its pursuing horde, and launched itself toward the flimsy barrier.

Out of nowhere, her César leaped in front of the rampaging animal, sword in hand. Louise clung to Claude, sending a frenzied prayer to the Virgin. What would happen if François was injured — or killed?

He impaled the slobbering beast with a single thrust of his sword. The swine fell dead at his feet.

Louise almost fell at his feet, too, but she had to support Claude, who had fainted in her arms. In the uproar that followed, someone lifted Claude from Louise's arms, and Louise tottered to a window embrasure where she shook for what felt like hours as the images replayed in her brain. What would have happened if he had missed his stroke? He could have died in front of her eyes. She had thought he would. As her fears for him passed, the anger set in. He had almost destroyed their future. All their plans. It had been a potent warning. In an instant, everything could fall apart. He could die in the coming war, for he would certainly lead in battles.

There was much she could not control, but one thing she could do. She had intended to wait until Lyon to execute her plan to dismiss the baronne, but she would wait no longer. Tonight, she would send for Mme. de Tonnerre. As soon as they left Amboise, she would replace Mme. de Soubise.

A FEW NIGHTS later Louise lay in bed, unable to sleep, consumed with her need to act. From the first, she had recognized she required the highest authority to coerce Mme. la Baronne to resign — so the dismissal must come from the king through his Grand Chamberlain, M. du Bouchage. Since he would insist upon authorization from the king and queen, she had prepared their letters. Now she had to make François and Claude sign them. As she lay in bed, she considered how to arrange it. François was no problem. She turned her mind to Claude.

Also, the man delivering the letter must be so important that the countess would be obliged to come immediately; someone who could intimidate a rabbit like her into obedience. It must also be someone traveling with them, yet whom the king could spare until they arrived in Lyon. Ah, of course! François's Maître d'hôtel — the Bailiff of Troyes.

For prudence, the letters could not include the details of the accusation in case they fell into the wrong hands. She would whisper the facts into the bailiff's ear to pass along to M. de Bouchage. It would add to his self-importance. Once she worked out these details, Louise fell into a dreamless sleep.

Next morning Louise dismissed her ladies and demoiselles to make their last preparations before setting out on the long journey to Lyon. They were so eager they rushed off without a backward glance. As they ran off, she called Lady Blanche. She had proven herself a useful conspirator in the past. Retiring to her withdrawing room, she swore Lady Blanche to secrecy and asked her to write letters as she dictated.

"François has written to his cousin, Mme. the Countess de Tonnerre, to induce her to drop everything to become gouvernante to Princess Renée," Louise said. "The letter has suggested the situation is dire and that only she is qualified."

Astonished, Lady Blanche dropped her pen.

"That's why you must keep this secret," Louise said. Lady Blanche bent her head over her slate and Louise smiled her cat smile. The countess must have been astonished to read how highly she was regarded at court for her rectitude and her skills with children, but in Louise's experience, flattery could never be too thick.

"Now, Lady Blanche, we will write the letters to M. du Bouchage. Use that slate." She pointed. "There will be changes before the wording is perfect. Date the first from Amboise on the 28th of June." She dictated and reviewed the letter until finally satisfied. Then Lady Blanche wrote it in her finest hand.

Monsieur du Bouchage,

Before my departure from Amboise, I decided and ordered a change to my sister-in-law's household.

I have charged the Bailiff de Troyes to leave from Amboise to bring thereto my cousin, the Countess of de Tonnerre. As soon as she arrives, she is to replace Madame de Soubise and, in her stead, to have the charge and government of my sister-in-law, Madame Renée de France and her house and goods.

I wish you and the said bailiff to understand that I am authorizing you to tell the said Madame de Soubise that it is my pleasure that she retire to her house with all those who are of her company, and that she leave the said charge to my said cousin.

Moreover, she is to provide an inventory of the jewels and goods that belong to my sister-in-law to the countess and you expressly require that it so be done.

Moreover, believe that which the said Bailiff will tell you as coming from me regarding this order. Fare thee well, Monsieur du Bouchage, may God have you in His holy care.

François

The King

She reviewed the final missive and was satisfied. The wording was clear and to the point. There could be no mistaking the meaning, yet if Mme. la Baronne persuaded them to permit her to read it, there was nothing specific of which she was being accused. Masterful!

Lady Blanche asked, "Are we done?" She was wilting, but Louise did not permit dereliction of duty.

"Not, my dear. We have still to write the queen's letter and mine. But the next two will go much more quickly."

Lady Blanche gave a long-suffering sigh.

"Enough of that." Louise sharpened her tone, and Lady Blanche straightened.

Louise reviewed her idea from the previous night. She would reuse the excuse she had given François many months before, that Mme. la Baronne wished to return to her home for the summer. As long as Claude did not read the letter, it should work. "This next letter will be signed by Queen Claude. Date it the 29th of June from Amboise."

Monsieur du Bouchage,

The King, my Lord, writes an order to you that my cousin, the Countess de Tonnerre, when she arrives in Amboise will replace Madame de Soubise and have the charge and government of my sister.

You will understand the wishes of my said Lord and me from the Bailiff of Troyes, which I beg you to believe. Farewell, Monsieur du Bouchage, may God keep you in His holy care.

Claude, Queen of France

Duchess de Bretagne

She reeled it off, for it was simple enough.

"Last one, Lady Blanche. It is easiest, for it is my own. Date this one from me on June 30th."

Monsieur du Bouchage,

The King and Queen have given a charge to the Bailiff of Troyes and to you to tell Madame de Soubise and those who have been placed in the service of Madame Renée by the said Lady of Soubise that they are to leave, as is she, and in her place Madame la Comtesse de Tonnerre is coming who will have the government of the said Dame Renée and of all her household. And the rings and jewels will be given in inventory to my said cousin, from which inventory a duplicate copy will be sent to the King. Please be warned that all this must be done at the same time.

The King and the Queen write to you that the said Bailiff will tell you more about all this matter, which you can believe. Fare well, Monsieur du Bouchage, may God keep you in His holy care.

Louise de Savoy

Duchess d'Angoulême

King's Mother

She revised all three letters. As she completed the third, she nodded with satisfaction. Their recipients would understand the implications and would conduct an immediate inventory. Mme. Michelle would have no time to prepare and she would be shamed. Louise had seen to that. Mme. Michelle would swear her innocence, but it was already too late. She should have treated Louise with more respect, more humility, more obedience.

"Thank you, that is all Lady Blanche. I will have the king and queen sign the letters."

Just then the bells calling Sext began to ring. What perfect timing. At mass today Claude would make the formal donation of her rights to the Duchy of Milan to the king. It was generous of her — another sign of her willingness to behave as a dutiful wife. But Louise acknowledged it was more than that. Claude loved her husband. This gift, like the clock Louise had given him, was chosen for his pleasure. Claude gave it to him because it was something he wanted and valued. Only she could give it to him — and he appreciated that she was doing so freely from love.

A twinge of guilt pinged Louise's conscience. Her daughter-in-law would feel distressed when she learned of the change of gouvernante, both for Mme. Michelle and for Princess Renée. It troubled her, for she cared for Claude. Still, the baronne was a dangerous influence. Louise hardened her heart.

AFTER COMPLINE[1], when Claude returned to her suite at dusk, her mother-in-law came with her. Within moments, one of the duchess's servants brought a tray of items that Duchess Louise had the maidservant place on a nearby table. Then Maman Louise offered her gifts: charming infant clothing and rattles, soft toys and ivory teething rings for the coming child; lovely dressing robes, night rails, books, games of chess and backgammon, and birthing charms for Claude's coming confinement.

"Oh yes, this letter, if you could just sign it," she added casually, giving it to her. Then she prattled on about how charming François had been as an infant, and how eagerly she awaited her first grandchild. Claude repressed a sardonic smile. She undoubtedly hoped to distract Claude into signing the document without reading it. But Claude had studied under careful teachers and had been administering her estate long enough not to be easy prey. Still, she preferred that Maman Louise believe she had duped her. So, she pretended a lack of interest in the letter as she read it surreptitiously.

It was addressed to M. du Bouchage. Claude gave no sign the name meant anything to her. She asked Maman Louise what it was about, her voice suggesting only the mildest interest.

The Duchess said, "Nothing really. Mme. Michelle wishes to visit her family for a time this summer, so I have made arrangements for the Countess de Tonnerre to replace her while she is absent."

"Umhum, that is fine." Claude nodded as if all were well and cleared a space on the table to sign. As the lines cleared from her mother-in-law's forehead, Claude knew she had been anxious. When she returned the signed letter and picked up one of the gifts at random to praise, Claude saw relief cross the duchess's face.

WHEN CLAUDE WOKE SHORTLY before Terce[2], she thought the castle was unusually tranquil. As her maidservant opened her bed curtains and sunshine flooded through the windows in her bedchamber, she asked her maidservant if it seemed quiet to her. The girl's stricken look told her something had happened.

"Send me Mme. Jeanne," Claude said.

When her gouvernante arrived, she learned the truth. The king, with Duchess Marguerite and Maman Louise, and their three courts had slunk off before dawn with the troop François had been training.

"I knew he would leave today. It was unkind in him to creep off without saying a final *adieu*," she said to her confidant, wiping her eyes. Yet she forgave him, for she understood. He felt guilty because he knew about his mother's plot. His stealing away proved it. He did not want to risk her asking him questions. But she said nothing to Mme. Jeanne as she readied herself for the day.

At the morning meal Claude invited Mme. Michelle to bring Renée to spend the morning with her ladies in her mother's gardens. While their ladies and demoiselles chattered, and her sister and companions ran about, they sat within the charming vine-covered gazebo — built for her mother — that shaded them from the sun and the eyes of their companions. Until today, Amboise had been so crowded that they had found little opportunity to speak alone. They had agreed that discretion would serve them best during Mme. Louise's time in residence. If she thought they were too intimate, she would become suspicious. Even now, Claude believed that Louise had left spies among her ladies.

"Last night, Maman Louise brought me a letter to sign inviting the Countess de Tonnerre to come and replace you as gouvernante," she said. "She told me you had asked to go home for the summer."

Mme. Michelle raised mocking eyebrows. "A visit to my family? I had not heard. How thoughtful she is." They smiled sardonically at each other.

"Did she say when I would make this visit?" Mme. Michelle worked the delicate embroidery in her hands without looking up.

"Not in the letter that I signed." Claude waited to see if Mme. Michelle would comment. She did not, so Claude continued, "I did not mention that two weeks ago I had invited the countess to keep me company during my confinement. I suggested she arrive in early July if it suited her convenience."

Still working her embroidery, Michelle said, "The repairs to the house you have so kindly provided for us in Blois are well-nigh complete.

"You are generous to provide such a perfect home. Several *nobles de la robe* own homes along the street upon which its front gates open, It is most private."

"It will be perfect — if the countess is amenable." Claude realized her words sounded ominous and added, "I am certain I will persuade her."

"I have no doubt." When Mme. Michelle spoke again, she was frowning. "I have another concern. I have had no opportunity to tell you that when Duchess Louise arrived here, she attached Mistress Michelle Gaillart to Mme. Renée's household as a senior *dame d'honneur*. It unnerved me. So I ordered a complete inventory of all Princess Renée's goods of value for which I held the keys: her clothing, jewelry, and shoes; her household plate, cutlery and table linens; her nursery and day nursery items, and her books and missals. After everything was noted and counted, we signed and sealed it, and I gave it into the keeping of her *Maître d'hôtel*. He has held the keys since then." She did not look up from her embroidery. The silence lengthened between them.

Some of the more obscure phrases in Duchess Louise's letter to the Comte de Bouchage became clearer to Claude. Louise had written something about learning things from the Bailiff of Troyes, which he might believe. Was it true, then, that her mother-in-law would deliberately prepare false evidence?

Michelle pulled a thick scroll from her bag of embroidery silks and pressed it into Claude's hands. "This is the inventory we prepared. You will see it is dated, sealed with my seal, that of the comptroller of Mme. Renée's Counting House and that of her *Maître d'hôtel*. I retrieved it from him today, telling him I would give it into your keeping. I asked him to verify with you later that you had received it and to authenticate the seal." She tightened her lips. "Like the comptroller, you may believe my caution is baseless. But the duchess must justify dismissing me since your family has long favored mine. What better excuse than theft and corruption." Her cheeks flushed with angry color.

Claude placed a hand over hers gently. "You must know I would never believe such a thing." She sensed she had said the right thing. She went on, "The letter I signed contained a curious phrase so vague it meant nothing to me. I believe you were wise to conduct the inventory to protect yourself. Take any other precautions you can. And you shall receive a stipend equal to that you received as gouvernante from my estates, for you must not suffer for your services to me and my sister." When Mme. Michelle would have protested, Claude stopped her. Then she continued, "Who is this Mistress Michelle Gaillart? Gaillart... The name rings a bell. Let me think.... Yes. I recall. Mme. Souvereine d'Angoulême married a Gaillart. How could I have forgotten? Her dowry came from my estates."

"Well, she is now in your sister's employ." Mme. Michelle pointed with her chin. "She is over there attired in purple velvet. I expect she is overheated, for she is certainly overdressed. You may wish to speak to her one day." Her fists clenched despite the brave face she was putting on.

Claude placed a hand over hers. "I am relieved Maman Louise has acted. I feared she would wait until I was confined. Like you, I am ignorant of the details, despite Maman Louise's promise never again to make decisions about Renée without consulting me."

"She promised your Maman I would continue as Princess Renée's gouvernante until she reached adulthood. But we already knew the value of her promises. And she is clever. What if I have misjudged, and she demands the countess take Mme. Renée to Lyon?"

Claude's heart sank. She clutched her mother's crucifix. Holding it, her Maman's spirit strengthened her. "Dear Mme. Michelle, calm yourself and breathe, 1-2-3-4, breathe, 1-2-3-4."

Mme. Michelle obeyed, smiling slightly to hear her own instructions offered back to comfort her. Claude said, "It is unlikely Maman Louise will want to burden herself with a child. But we have done all we can, so we will pray. Let us place ourselves in the hands of the Virgin."

CHÂTEAU D'AMBOISE

 ueen Claude de France

CLAUDE'S gentleman usher cautiously put his head through the door of her presence chamber and signaled Mme. Jeanne. After a whispered conversation, Mme. Jeanne approached Claude.

"The castellan sent to say that M. du Bouchage and the Bailiff of Troyes have arrived unannounced. M. le Maître d'hôtel expects they will seek an audience. He asks where and when you wish to receive them."

"So soon." Claude bit her lower lip, feeling anxious. Her mother-in-law's formidable presence seemed to fill the room as she sprang her trap. Had they guessed her plans correctly? Claude crossed herself, praying she had the courage to carry off her part.

"I shall meet them in the small audience chamber in one hour. Have M. le Maître d'hôtel send a light collation to their rooms." When Mme. Jeanne would have protested, Claude said to her, "I wish them to feel rushed."

Ignoring the stir of curiosity among her ladies-in-waiting and demoiselles, she rose awkwardly and retired to her bed chamber. Mme. Jeanne followed.

"I shall be ready," Claude said, willing herself to make it so. Sitting on a stool, she sighed. "I am as large and clumsy as an ox. A change of clothes will make no difference, but call my maid to tidy my hair and reset my hood. Perhaps add a pearl necklace."

"Would you like me to send for Mme. la Baronne also?"

Claude considered. "No. I shall see the gentlemen alone first."

When Mme. Jeanne seemed unconvinced the queen added, "Of course, you shall accompany me." Nodding, Mme. Jeanne called Claude's maid.

The guards pulled open the great doors of the audience chamber as Claude arrived, deliberately late. The gentlemen awaiting her bowed deeply. Claude greeted M. du Bouchage warmly, as was the eminent courtier's due, but his appearance shocked her. Already seventy-five when she last saw him at her mother's funeral, he had aged markedly since. Now his back was as bent as an archer's bow, and his long silver hair had thinned to wisps. He used two sticks to stand and shuffled when he moved.

She gave him her hands to kiss. "M. le Count, please forgive whatever service has brought you to us. Before we begin, let us provide you with a wheeled chair," she urged, "and a man to push it. We had one made for my father. It will be brought immediately. Usher, please see to it." When it arrived, she insisted he sit and make himself comfortable.

M. du Bouchage appeared somewhat taken aback by her concern. Claude knew, though, what it was to suffer from standing with aching bones. She would not permit a distinguished old courtier to suffer so.

She turned to M. le Bailli de Troyes. A greater contrast she could not imagine, for he was a burly man with a heavy beard and curly black hair. "Please forgive me for ignoring you, M. d'Inteville. I'm sure you understand."

Despite his appearance, he was a courtier. "Certainly, Mme. la Reine. Your compassion becomes you as it did your late, much beloved mother." She warmed to him despite her suspicions and invited him to sit as well so that M. de Bouchage would be at ease. Immediately, the atmosphere became more informal. To encourage the relaxed mood, Claude ordered biscuits and wine and had tables set beside each man. She then motioned the attendants out of hearing.

"Gentlemen, thank you for visiting. What has brought you here?"

The men eyed each other, hesitating. Ah, so they did not expect her to react well. She braced herself for an unpleasant interview.

"M. le Count, as the senior gentleman, perhaps you would do the honors?" she prodded.

"You wrote to me, Mme. la Reine," he said, unfurling the letter that her mother-in-law had required her to sign, "that I was to accompany the Countess de Tonnerre to Amboise where she would replace Mme. de Soubise as Princess Renée's gouvernante."

Claude nodded and answered, keeping her voice pleasant. "Yes, Mme. de Soubise goes to her family for the summer. She has served us well, and it is long since she has seen her children." Good, she thought, as the count shifted in his wheeled chair. That has worried you.

He cleared his throat. "Yes. Um... The Duchess d'Angoulême gave us an additional um... requirement." He squared his shoulders. So, he felt awkward, did he? As he should. "I am to require an immediate inventory of the princess's goods and jewels."

An angry heat infused Claude's chest. Mme. Michelle had been wise!

"Upon the installation of the countess, I am to dismiss all those persons who belong to the house of the baronne from Princess Renée's household and charge. The king's mother gave me — us," he glanced for support to M. d'Inteville, "to understand that you were aware of the situation."

Fighting her anger, Claude kept her voice even. "M. d'Inteville, she also spoke to you about the baronne?"

"She did, Mme. la Reine. In confidence. Said the baronne was feathering her nest and her family's, too, at the princess's expense. Gave us an inventory and said we'd find much missing in a new one. That you'd not be surprised. You knew the situation."

As he spoke, Claude took a deep breath to calm herself. Then, furrowing her brow, she sighed several times, each time more gustily, shook her head and 'tut, tutted,' in a low voice. As his accusations mounted, she dropped her jaw as if she could hardly credit his words, murmuring under her breath, "No, no, I cannot... I would never have... dear me... cannot imagine it."

Finally, he responded to her heavy hints and added, "Could have blown me over with a feather, though. King Louis trusted her late husband, the baron, and I knew him well. Would not have thought it of him. Or his wife."

Claude nodded. "I am pleased you say so." She gave him a relieved smile. "I find it astonishing that a woman so... so beloved and trusted by both my parents for many years... who has cared for my sister her entire life... could transform her character — and without my knowledge or awareness! I am shocked by these charges." She managed to look both sorrowful and disbelieving. "What think you, M. du Bouchage? Could my parents have been so mistaken about Baronne de Soubise's character?"

The count had survived many reigns by changing his opinions with each new current. He found the diplomatic words to avoid taking a stand. "Mme. la Reine, your parents and you have the greatest knowledge of Mme. la Baronne, naturally. The duchess may be mistaken, and it is our duty to so inform her if it is so proven. Nothing could be easier." He nodded wisely. "It is common knowledge that it is customary to conduct an inventory when a change of guardianship occurs."

Claude nodded. "True. True. Well, fortunately, it will be easily done. I hold a recent inventory of Mme. Renée's goods and jewelry, signed, and sealed by the princess's Maître d'hôtel and comptroller. It was conducted when Mme. la Baronne resigned that responsibility in early June. Will that be satisfactory?" She hid her satisfaction when the two men exchanged startled glances.

"Would you make us privy to the reasons for that change?" M. d'Inteville sounded hopeful. Did he truly think she would confirm his accusations?

"It seemed reasonable. Mme. Michelle planned to visit her family for the summer. When the duchess appointed a new lady to Mme. Renée's household it seemed opportune to make her responsible for the princess's wardrobe and goods during the baronne's absence. As I understand it, Mme. de Tonnerre will replace Mme. Michelle temporarily during her visit home."

The two men eyed each other, clearly unsure how to proceed. "Do you have a problem with that? Unable to control the quaver in her voice any longer, she sipped some wine from the glass on the table beside her.

They did not seem to notice, for they were consulting each other in low voices. In his most courtly fashion, M. du Bouchage assured her they could carry out their instructions using her inventory and were enchanted to do so, for it would ease their task.

When she spoke again, her voice was steady. "I am delighted to welcome the Countess de Tonnerre, for I had invited her."

By now she had recovered from the shock at the unexpected demand that Mme. Michelle remove 'all those persons who belong to the house of the baronne'. What persons were these? She knew nothing about Mme. Michelle appointing members of her family to her sister's household. She could hardly credit it, but she must investigate the charge. "I will look into this question of the appointments. I will not have her name or her family's reputation harmed without evidence. She has served my family well.

She placed her hands on her belly. "As I hope to present the country with an heir, *si le bon Dieu le veut*, my doctors require that I rest. And I must welcome the countess. I shall see you again before you leave."

As she limped from the room, Claude reviewed her performance. She had made it clear she trusted Mme. Michelle, yet she had done all the right things to assist them to carry out their instructions. They had every reason to report to Maman Louise that her orders had been fulfilled.

Yet Claude felt perturbed. What had the duchess uncovered? It was not uncommon for those in positions of authority to appoint members of their family to open posts. It was not wrong exactly... just somewhat underhanded. She would have to discuss it with Mme. Michelle and protect her if necessary. It would be a difficult conversation, perhaps even a confrontation. For a few moments, Claude wondered if she could go into confinement immediately and leave the task to Mme. Jeanne. Then she straightened. Of course she could not.

THE LAST TIME Claude had seen the Countess de Tonnerre was at her Maman's funeral. So, when she curtsied to Claude, she brought back sad memories. With her mousy hair, sallow skin, and widow's weeds, Countess Françoise carried gloom with her. Compared to Mme. Michelle, who dressed in rich colors and well-chosen accessories, she looked like a moorhen beside a swan. As the countess agreed with everything Claude said in a whispery voice, the queen understood Maman Louise's reason for choosing her as Renée's gouvernante. The poor woman. Strong-willed Renée would cow her within a week. Even with Mme. Michelle's help, Countess Françoise would find it hard to manage the château staff and the other children in her charge.

Mme. Michelle presented Princess Renée — who carried her favorite dog in her arms — to Countess Françoise. After her new charge left, Claude asked, "Are you pleased with your new appointment?"

Mme. Françoise turned a strained, anxious face towards the queen. "The princess is an active child, is she not? Headstrong?"

"She is. Loving and intelligent, but she requires a steady hand and strict rules, steadfastly applied."

Except for her writhing fingers, the countess sat as still as a statue. In her whispery voice, she said. "You know none of my children lived beyond babyhood." Her eyes filled with tears.

"I am so sorry." Claude's voice was gentle. She touched her baby, who was moving about, and sent a prayer heavenward. Too many women lost their children young, as had Maman.

Claude heard the catch in Mme. Françoise's voice. "I say this because I have no experience with children. I am deeply conscious of the honor the Duchess does me to appoint me gouvernante... yet I am afraid."

She was making Claude's task easy. "Do you fear you will not be able to control the princess? That she will resent you because you have replaced her beloved Mme. Michelle? Especially after her recent loss of her Maman and Papa? That you will not know how to manage her when she misbehaves?" Claude imagined and exaggerated all the fears she would have experienced in the countess's place. "Are you worried you will not be able to manage large numbers of children? Or that your new staff will take advantage of you?"

As the countess's face whitened, she felt more and more cruel. But she forced herself to continue. "Do you fear you will fail? Do you worry about what might happen if Duchess Louise were to learn of your failure and complain to your family? Are you worried your family will be angry?"

"Yes, oh, yes, Mme. la Reine." Mme. Françoise almost threw herself onto her knees before the queen. "You understand completely."

Claude felt like she was beating a puppy and hated it. It had been much easier letting other people do this kind of thing. And what if it did not work out after all? She would have caused the countess to suffer for nothing. Then she reassured herself. She was doing this to protect her sister. And it would be better for this poor woman, too. She could never manage Renée. "Well, I have a suggestion. It could solve your problem," she said.

Countess François looked pathetically eager.

"You must accept the appointment since it is wise to obey Mme. the Duchess. But Princess Renée is attached to Mme. la Baronne, who manages her very well. If you are willing…?" Claude suddenly thought the idea sounded preposterous and finished in a rush, "Mme. Michelle will continue to educate the princess while you hold the post of gouvernante and live at court."

When Claude began, the Countess de Tonnerre had appeared hopeful. Now her brow was clouded. "I do not understand. How can she tend the princess if she is not at court?"

"If I can show you, will you consider it?"

She nodded slowly. "But…"

Claude's heart sank, but she pressed on. "You would move to the main royal nursery at the Château de Blois. Mme. Michelle owns a house that accesses the château through a private entry. After early prayers each morning, you and the princess will slip off to her house. At Compline, you and she will return to the château. You may stay with Mme. Michelle or in my mother's retreat at Blois. I will assign it to your private use. A sous-gouvernante will manage the children and day nursery." Countess Françoise looked like a scared rabbit. Claude thought, I'm rushing her. She counted silently to fifty before asking, "What do you think of that arrangement?"

Countess Françoise's forehead was lined with worry. "Will not the servants notice and gossip when we are gone every day? What about…"

Her fears were swamping her. Soon she would baulk from fear alone. Claude did not want to order her if she could avoid it. She patted the space on the sofa beside her. "Come sit here beside me. You can do this. And you will be much happier. Most of the children return home for the summer. I will inform the household I wish you to take Princess Renée to my mother's private house daily for tutoring. Meanwhile, the royal nursery staff shall care for the few remaining children." As Claude explained how she would ensure that the Maître d'hôtel and head housekeeper took responsibility for super-vising the nursery and its staff, the countess seemed to settle down somewhat. Claude concluded, "And if anyone dares comment, you will say, 'Why do you wish to know?' or 'Why are you concerned?'" The queen could not imagine Countess Françoise sneering disdainfully at anyone, but gave her no chance to interrupt. "As soon as I leave my confinement, I shall return to Blois with the baby. Then everyone will focus on him… or her."

The countess brightened at the mention of her infant. As a final enticement, Claude added. "You shall become gouvernante for the infant. Would you like that?"

"Yes," she whispered. "A baby…" The countess looked as dazzled, as if Claude had offered her the crown jewels. "Mayhap it would suffice. But what about Mme. the Duchess? What if she discovers...?"

"Leave that to me." Claude forced herself to sound more confident than she felt. "Besides, she has already left for Lyon. She will be immersed in war preparations with my husband for months." When Mme. Françoise still looked frightened, Claude said: "I shall write to her that you are moving Princess Renée to the royal nursery at Blois. Mme. Michelle is already there ready to help you."

"Well...." As Mme. Françoise still shied, Claude's patience ran out. The baby was heavy, and the day had been tiring. She needed to lie down. And she must still speak to Mme. Michelle. Enough gentling this shying palfrey. "But if you do not wish to do this, you may resign the post. How is that?"

The countess lowered her gaze, teary-eyed. "I am sorry. I do not wish the appointment, but my family insists. I cannot..."

The kindest thing was to decide for her. "It is good of you to accept. Everything will work out, you will see. Your family will be pleased, so will Duchess Louise and Princess Renée. Mme. Michelle will prove a helpful friend." Patting her shoulder, Claude added, "Think how much better this will be than if you had the charge of my willful sister."

The smile that flitted across Mme. Françoise's face was genuine. "It is tactless to agree, Mme. la Reine, but I fear I could never control your sister."

It was evening before Claude invited Mme. Michelle to come to her bedchamber. The queen was resting in the armchair that had once been her mother's favorite when the baronne entered.

Claude noticed she had bitten her nails to the quick. How unusual for the baronne to display such a visible sign of anxiety.

"Dear Mme. Michelle, you must forgive the lateness of the hour. Events have outrun my plans today. I did not intend to keep you in suspense." Which was true enough. But Claude admitted she had been putting off this conversation. Mme. Michelle had stood her friend on many occasions. Just then the baby kicked her, and she recalled that Maman Louise had frightened her into believing that the baronne was a witch who had harmed all Maman's baby. Her mother-in-law was not to be trusted. So, her accusations about Mme. Michelle's appointments to Renée's household must be false, too. Even so, Claude must prepare the baronne to face her accusers.

"Is my unease so apparent then? I am failing as a courtier." Mme. Michelle produced a strained smile. "First, please tell me. How are the heir to France and his mother doing?"

Claude patted her belly. "We are both lively. But enough. I have much to tell you before you depart for Blois." She saw relief sweep across Mme. Michelle's face.

"So? The countess agreed? That is good."

"Yes. The few minutes Mme. Françoise spent with Renée convinced her she was not capable of controlling my sister. It made my job of persuading her to agree that you should keep charge of Renée much easier. Naturally she worries about the deception." That was one way of describing the countess's fears. "I assured her you would be her friend. After I promised to protect her from Maman Louise, she agreed." Claude decided she had said enough.

She could procrastinate no longer. A wave of exhaustion swept her, and she closed her eyes. The small sounds in her chamber soothed her; the swish of her maid pulling the bed curtains open, the snap of candle wax spitting, and the faint scent of roses in the vase in the fireplace.

Then Mme. Michelle spoke. "What is worrying you, Mme. Claude?"

There was no misleading someone who had known her since childhood. She opened her eyes "Tomorrow you must meet with M. du Bouchage and M. d'Inteville. They bring letters from the king and Maman Louise." Recalling their disappointed expressions, she smiled slightly. "Maman Louise sent the inventory that she wished them to use for the inventory of Mme. Renée's jewelry and household goods. They were startled when I told them you had not held the keys to her household since early June. Neither were they pleased we had a more recent inventory for them. I doubt they will reveal that information to Madame Maman." Still she put it off the unpleasant part of the conversation. "I thanked them for bringing Countess Françoise, whom *I* had invited to replace you during your *temporary* absence during your visit to your family this summer. I suggested they be circumspect when they presented the king's and Madame Maman's letters to you — unless they intended to accuse you publicly of misconduct."

"Is this what they came to say? You surprise me."

The moment had come. Her throat felt dry. She swallowed and clutched her mother's rosary tight between her hands.

"No," she admitted. "They came convinced that I believed you dishonest. They started to accuse you until I reminded them my parents held you and your husband in the highest regard. Then they recalled their admiration for your husband's family." Her voice hardened. "Loyalty is a value honored more in its breach than its observance." She swallowed again. "But they brought one troubling command."

"Yes?"

"Maman Louise ordered that all your family members appointed to Mme. Renée's household must leave with you. Since I knew nothing about it, I could not respond until you and I spoke. Can you inform me who and how many are involved so we can decide what actions we must take?"

Michelle clasped a hand to her cheek as if the queen had slapped her. Then she rose quietly and went to a far window. She stood staring out, her back to the room while silence reigned. Once again Claude noticed the many small sounds, but they were no longer soothing. She fought with her urge to call Mme. Michelle back and apologize. She must discover the truth of this matter for the baronne's sake — no matter how uncomfortable it made her.

After a time, Mme. Michelle returned and sat on the stool again. Her voice controlled, she said, "Mme. Claude, do you believe I would cheat your family to benefit from my position?"

"Of course, I do not. But such appointments are not uncommon. Nor are they inappropriate — in most cases. We both know that Madame Maman is looking for excuses to harm you. I ask in order to make provision so she cannot." Surely the baronne could understand that she was trying to help.

"I have made no secret appointments. Nor done anything to benefit my family. I never would." Claude shivered at the ice in her voice.

"In that case, I shall say no more." Queen Claude furrowed her brow. "I am sorry if you feel I have insulted you, Mme. Michelle. My intention was... well, I shall not repeat myself. But the duchess has accused you and you must be prepared to reply." She pushed on the arm of her chair, preparing to stand.

"Mme. la Reine, please do not rise," Michelle said. "I shall explain every appointment. Do you grant me leave to retire?"

"Granted, my dear friend."

The baronne curtsied, but her expression did not warm at Claude's words.

10 JULY 1515

CHÂTEAU D'AMBOISE

aronne Michelle de Soubise

AFTER HER INTERVIEW with M. de Bouchage and M. d'Inteville, Michelle did not return to her rooms. Her cheeks still burning, she held the scrolled letters from the king and Mme. the Duchess d'Angoulême in her shaking hands, undecided what to do. Much as she wished to crush them into a ball and throw them onto a blazing fire, she had promised to return them tomorrow at their final meeting.

After she dropped them in her room like burning coals, she slipped along the long halls and galleries of the château, slid through a small side door, and exited through a postern gate. The oversized iron latch screeched when she lifted it, and the heavy oak door slammed when she pulled it closed. She could not lock it from the outside either.

She tossed her head and walked off. The guards were diligent. She must burn away the anger that blazed through her. Eyes to the ground to avoid tripping over the uneven cobblestones or stepping into the stinking muck, she pushed through the market crowded with townsfolk and loud with the butchers, bakers, and brewers all shouting their wares. The everyday concerns of servants and housewives purchasing their goods helped calm her. It reminded her she needed to purchase a supply of oils and herbs. Since she was here, she made her way to the apothecary shop. It was located away from the noisy town center, in the quieter district where lived the suppliers of luxuries to the court, the soaps, perfumes, linens, silks and so much more.

The apothecary shop, with its mix of familiar odors — the dry scents of herbs, the powdery odor of ground bat's dung, the sting of antimony, the spicy aroma of pine and more mysterious fragrances — soothed her troubled spirit. Concentrating to recall what she needed since she had come without a list, she purchased the lavender flowers, willow bark and opium drops that she always used. By the time she left, her rage had dissipated. It left hurt behind.

Continuing her walk through the quietest part of town, she headed back toward the castle, as she faced her pain. She had served Queen Anne since she was fourteen and had been heartbroken when she died. If it were not for her promise to Anne to care for little Renée, she would have retired from the court at once. These accusations brought by King François stung. Those by Duchess Louise she dismissed with a toss of her head, though she would certainly repudiate them. And she regretted she had been so harsh to sweet Queen Claude, who was only trying to help her. In truth, she had been expecting to be dismissed ever since King François had succeeded to the throne.

By the time she returned to her rooms, Michelle had walked out her rage. She spent the next hours, until the candles guttered in the candelabra and dawn crept over the horizon, phrasing her letters to the king and the queen mother. She intended to avoid affront, yet she was determined to exonerate herself and her family. It was not easy to find the perfect words. She reflected upon each nuance and considered, too, its effect upon Queen Claude. It must also cause no harm to the two men her royal enemies had hidden behind.

She wrote first to the king.

Written in Amboise, 11 July 1515

Sire:

Most humbly I recommend myself to your good grace. I read the letter that it pleased you to write to Monsieur du Bouchage, in which you ordered him to tell me to release the person of Madame Renée and her goods to Madame the Countess de Tonnerre, and to retire with my suite to my estates.

Sire, at your advent, it pleased you to send Monsieur de Saint Marçault to me with written orders that it was your pleasure that I continue the charge the late King and Queen, her father and mother, had given me. You gave me your letters patent for the conduct of the business and the household of the said Madame Renée, to which charge, Sire, never have I caused you fault. And it disappoints me that when you were here, I did not understand your wish to replace me. I call it my greatest sorrow in all of this, those things Monsieur du Bouchage and Monsieur the Bailiff of Troyes said as coming from you.

These words will serve to remove me from this service for I desire more to dwell in your good graces in my estate than to serve here at your displeasure. I beg very humbly, Sire, that it pleases you to leave the estates to my family that it pleased you to give to us.

Please God that it be your will to recommend us and to keep us and our affairs in your good grace. Sire, I pray God to give you very good and long life.

Michelle de Saubonne,

Lady of Soubise.

The letter to Mme. Louise took more time, for she had to keep her indignation from spilling onto the page. Princess Renée was going to suffer because Duchess Louise would not tolerate any opposition. Moreover, the Duchess would spread calumnies about Michelle and her family because Michelle had dared argue with her about Renée's care. Her letter must be a model of diplomacy, yet full of compelling and indisputable details to defend her family from the duchess's false charges. She lost count of the number of times she cleaned her slate and started over before she was satisfied. But the candle stubs and her reddened eyes from their smoke told their own story.

Written in Amboise, 11 July 1515

Madame

With this letter I recommend myself most humbly to your good grace.

Madame, I have seen the letters that it pleased the King, the Queen and you to write to Monsieur du Bouchage, by which I am informed that it is the pleasure of the King that I charge the person of Madame Renée and her household to Madame, the Countess de Tonnerre, and that I retire to my estate with my suite.

Madame, I have always wanted to hear your pleasure and the King's in order to obey. I asked you before you departed hence, and it pleased you, Madame, to order me to continue in my charge. I had confidence in you and your kind words, which were the greatest hope that I had in this world. It has been the cause, Madame, which for many years has kept me from taking care of my own business, for I was never at my estates.

However, to obey the commandment of the King's and yours in all haste, as I have always done, I will go to my sister's house.

*Of the rest of the household in place, Madame, there has never been a man who was put there by me, except the late Monsieur de Soubise's two brothers to whom it pleased **you** to give the place of my other brother-in-law. The late Queen put him there, and he was the first servant in his Office, for before that my said Dame Renée did not have one. I have only one clerk of Office, whom the late King put there. The late Queen and the late King charged Mademoiselle de Vaucouleur to the said Dame Renée. There is, similarly, a girl that said late Queen baptized in the name of the said Dame Renée of those who came from Thunes, who always stayed with me and, at my request, was put in the estate during the past year, and there is only this one, who was also of the time of the said late King and Queen, as Sieur Jacques de Beaune and others know, for it was they who handled the estates.*

Madame, I have long wanted to declare the truth, and have it known to you. It has been the desire of all my life to serve Madame Renée, as it pleased the late King and Queen to charge of me, and it troubles me with all my heart that I am unable to show the King and you the pleasure I have had from doing this.

Madame, neither the Sieur du Bouchage nor Sieur the Bailiff de Troyes explained the King's or your wishes touching my family estates, which are in your gift.

I beg very humbly, therefore, Madame, as it pleased you to state at your departure, that it pleases you to keep me in your grace and that I may recommend ourselves to you. Madam, I pray God gives you a very good life and long.

Michelle de Saubonne,

Lady of Soubise.

Michelle rose from the hard chair and stretched before blowing out the candles. There was much she would have liked to say. But with what profit? Her family benefited more from royal favor than she would gain from justifying herself. Shrugging she knelt at her prie-dieu and asked God to provide her with justice, if that was His will. Then she fell onto her bed, still fully clothed and slept.

BEFORE HER INTERVIEW with the king's men the next morning, Michelle begged a few minutes of Queen Claude's time and thrust her letters into the queen's hands.

After Mme. Claude read them through carefully twice, she raised her eyes to Michelle's, feeling ashamed of her doubts. "As I always believed, there was not a word of truth in her accusation. Your explanations of each appointment charged to Renée's household are crystal clear. The only recent appointment she made herself, as well I know." She sniffed. "But I did not know that she had so recently asked you to continue in your position. As you say, since they were both here, they could have spoken to you directly, since they had each asked you to stay on as Renée's gouvernante after Maman and Papa died." It did not surprise her that her husband had avoided confrontation, but her mother-in-law's spinelessness startled her.

Claude brooded. Eventually she said, "I am puzzled about this part regarding your family estates. Are you concerned that your family will lose the Parc de Soubise?"

"I do not know what to believe any more." Michelle shook her head, her expression bemused. "When you said Mme. Louise intended to replace me, I found it almost inconceivable. Both my late husband's and my family have belonged to the Valois affinity for generations. I served your late mother as her *Dame d'atour*. I heard Mme. la Duchess swear a deathbed vow to Queen Anne that I would remain the princess's gouvernante. And then there is the love that I bear for the princess and she for me. Any one of these should have stayed her hand. So, when you ask, 'will the Duchess retract my husband's family estates because of her displeasure?' I no longer know."

"Sit," Claude said, "you are so white I am afraid you will faint." She reflected uneasily on what she knew about the harm done by her mother-in-law. She had certainly misled her about Renée's betrothal. Then there was everything that had happened with Dowager Queen Marie. Claude's ladies whispered that Mme. Louise had helped Queen Marie remarry in such unbecoming haste, so insulting to Papa and to France. She had certainly done her best to poison Claude's trust in Mme. Michelle. These were small acts compared to disinheriting a family. Yet now, when she was dismissing the baronne, she was trying to blacken the Soubise family name. Gossip would soon spread that she had done so because they had enriched themselves at the expense of the young princess. Mme. Michelle had good cause for her concern.

Claude's own fear of her mother-in-law increased. But it was her duty to reassure her friend. "Do not let this trouble you. For the time being, Maman Louise is much too occupied with the coming war in Italy. And your answer must prevent her from continuing with this charge." She signaled one of her ladies and ordered her to call a secretary. "I shall have a copy made before you leave this room. My ladies shall spread the truth to all their families. That is a start."

Once the copy had been made, Queen Claude initialed both letters so M. du Bouchage and M. le Bailli de Troyes knew she had read and approved them. As Michelle departed, she rose and walked her to the door so that all her ladies- and maids-in-waiting would see how highly she honored Renée's former gouvernante.

Michelle's second interview with M. le Count and M. le Bailli was short. After returning the king and the duchess d'Angoulême's letters, she asked them to read and initial her replies before sealing them with their official seals. "I am sure that you wish as much as I that we can all swear to the security of the contents when their Royal Majesties receive the replies," she said, though she did not believe they agreed. But they could not refuse.

She refrained from asking about the results of the inventory being conducted. She did not need to. Several of her friends had whispered to her in confidence that there had been several hasty meetings that morning to which Demoiselle de Gaillard had been called.

Instead, she reminded them she had stated she would leave for her sister's forthwith in her letter to Mme. d'Angoulême. "Thus, gentlemen, if we have completed this interview, I shall take my leave of you. My personal servants and I leave on the morrow at daybreak. There is much to do to organize my departure in such haste. The queen kindly lends me one of her teams and a carriage to make the journey." She curtsied and turned her back on them.

QUEEN CLAUDE STOOD beside the open door of the carriage in the courtyard as dawn broke over the horizon. The orange glow of the sky turned the river into a highway of fire. The distant rattle of iron wagon wheels and clatter of horses' hooves on cobblestones died away. Servants completed the final bustle of stowing the baskets of provisions, the portable desk with its writing supplies and the books they needed to occupy Mme. Michelle and her lady-in-waiting on the dusty drive. It should take less than a day if all went well, but it was always wise to leave early to allow for mishaps. Usually they would travel by river, but Queen Claude insisted on providing Renée's gouvernante with a team and equipage to keep in Blois.

She had informed her Master of Horse that the team traveling with Mme. de Soubise would not return to Amboise. When he questioned her, she practiced her advice to the Countess de Tonnerre.

Raising her eyebrows, she asked, "Do you have a problem with that?"

"Certainly not, Your Majesty."

"Good. That will be all. Thank you." She had smiled at him and turned away. It had not been easy. Her household was not accustomed to her giving orders without explanations, for she believed her people worked with better spirit when they understood the reason for what they did. But she, too, must learn, she had told herself.

"Your trip should pass smoothly," she said to Mme. Michelle. "The route should be dry, for there has been no rain for the past sennight. Mme. la Sénéchalle des Lancs says her bones do not ache so the dry spell will last another sennight." Her eyes crinkled and the corners of Mme. Michelle's lips curled. Mme. la Sénéchalle's bones were legendary.

Queen Claude pulled the baronne into a hug. Clinging to her, she murmured, "What did you say to Renée last night?"

Her mouth close to the queen's ear, Michelle answered, "I told her I was leaving this morning very early, but I would see her soon, *si Dieu le voulait.* But she must say nothing for now... and you would explain everything to her today. She loves a secret, so she settled down." Michelle held Claude a moment longer. Then, after kissing her forehead, she curtsied.

The valet standing nearby offered his arm for her to mount the step into the carriage. Claude could not bear to let her go. Until this moment she had not dwelt on her fear of giving birth without Mme. Michelle's reassuring presence. But now, as she watched her climb into the carriage to leave, her distress turned to panic. Her maman had lost almost every one of her babies. So many of her own friends had died giving birth. Tears flooding her eyes, she grasped the older woman's arm. "It seems hard that you will depart this way, going off to... um... with only your lady to accompany you. I wanted you to be here with me during my confinement. I may never see you a-a-gain."

Michelle pulled a cloth from her sleeve and patted Queen Claude's eyes dry. "Never say or think that, Mme. Claude. You will be fine and so will your babe. I will pray for you every day." She reached for Queen Anne's rosary that hung from Claude's waist and closed her fingers around its crucifix. "Trust the Virgin. And I will see you when the Lord permits, and when you can travel again." She curtsied once more.

Claude fought to pull herself together. She must do this for Renée. Wiping her eyes, she nodded and stepped back. "May the Lord bless your journey."

As soon as the carriage door closed, she trudged back up the stairs clutching her mother's rosary. She needed its protection now. Fighting the fears that threatened to overwhelm her, she made her way to the chapel instead of returning to her chambers. Maman Louise had not only deprived her young sister of her last trusted mother figure, she had also removed Claude's sense of security as her first confinement neared. Even if she had not been able to keep Maman's babies alive, Mme. Michelle had brought her mother safely through countless births. So many of her friends and the ladies Claude had known at her mother's court had died in childbirth. She would feel much more secure if Michelle were with her. The next weeks loomed long and dangerous. Lighting a candle, she kneeled and prayed to St. Margaret to protect her.

THE IRON-STUDDED wheels of Michelle's carriage clanked along the worn stones of the old Roman road. The body of the vehicle creaked on its leather straps, rocking Michelle as gently as a baby in a cradle. Their horses plodded at walking pace to keep their jolting to a minimum. The swaying had lulled her lady-in-waiting, seated on the opposite bench, to sleep. Their early morning departure had been too much for her, thought Michelle.

Although Michelle closed her eyes, sleep eluded her. The interior of the carriage glowed even with her eyes closed and the dark curtains pulled. Besides, the air was already becoming stale. The country sounds of cattle mooing and chickens cackling, birds twittering, and men calling to her outriders intrigued her. Popping her eyes open, she pulled the curtains back and leaned her head out. The rising sun dazzled over the tops of the distant trees almost directly ahead, so the landscape blurred into a silhouette. Squinting, she could make out the old road, long and gray, following the gentle curve of the Loire River. Beside them, the sun glinted on the river and the soft air already smelled fresh, scented with green things growing.

Leaning back against the hard cushions, she watched the passing scene while her companion snored like a lazy bee. Michelle's thoughts rose and sank, mimicking their rhythm.

Perhaps she should not have turned her back on the duchess's messengers at the end of the interview. She had kept her temper until then. Courtiers did not enjoy the luxury of revealing their thoughts. Reviewing her letters once again, she wondered if she had said more than was wise. Well, it was done now. Queen Claude had not advised her to water down her words. Her eyes filled at the thought of Mme. Claude. She had not admitted it to the queen, but she was worried about her upcoming childbirth. Not to be with Mme. Claude during her confinement was Mme. Louise's final cruel flick of the whip.

The sudden increase in the number of carts full of heavy stone, timber, and charcoal caught Michelle's attention, and she slid across the padded seat to the other side of the carriage and opened the curtains. They were passing a château that was under construction; it stood on the heights visible from the road. She could see the carts veering onto a dirt track to journey up the bluff towards it. Already the principal building facing the river had been completed, shining white in the sunlight. Elegant, modern, and charming. Like the d'Angoulême family itself. How beguiling they had been as they enchanted Claude into urging her dying mother to approve her betrothal. And Claude had been eager to join their family.

If Louise had not been so greedy, Claude would have continued to rely upon her, for Claude was gentle and trusting, and she had wanted so much to lean on someone after she lost her mother.

Mme. Louise had been impatient and had overplayed her hand. Fortunately for me and my little princess, Michelle thought. If Mme. Louise had waited until she was regent and the queen was with her in Lyon, she could have replaced me without Claude knowing until it had already happened. What a relief that the waiting was over. Resolutely Michelle turned her thoughts to the future. How long would it be before the countess and Princess Renée arrived?

THE BELLS for Nones had just ended when Michelle's carriage pulled through the portcullis into the courtyard of her new home. It was located in upper Blois tucked against the Château walls — the most prestigious section of the town. The narrow street that fronted it led directly to one of the defended town gates. Stables lined the opposite side of the street to service the private hôtels of the nobility and high officials of the royal household.

M. de Beaune fils stood in the courtyard to welcome her and show her through her new home while her Maître d'hôtel and lady-in-waiting managed the bustle of installing her household in its new residence.

She stood before the grand entry staircase, admiring its elegant curves. Craning her neck back, she looked upward to the patch of sky above the courtyard and the steep slate roofs high above her, for the house rose tall and narrow. The kitchens and store-rooms opened from the ground floor in front of her, but her guide motioned her to mount the stairs. Well, she would explore the kitchens herself another time.

When the double doors of the front portal were thrown wide to welcome her to the front hall that rose two stories high, she gasped. Light poured into the hall from the great paned window above her head. The grand stairway, leading to a balcony that stretched around three sides of the floor above them, faced them as they entered. From the ceiling high above them, a great chandelier lit the entire central entrance hall. Michelle felt dwarfed in its magnificence.

Michelle breathed. "I did not expect anything like this." The grandeur daunted her. It would grow on her, she supposed.

She was much happier with the day nursery. It was large and bright from the whitewash with tall front-facing windows. Painted rabbits and hedgehogs, swallows and owls, roses and daffodils, adorned the upper walls and capered over the ceilings.

"Did you think of this?"

"Madame la Reine ordered it."

The queen was the most thoughtful person Michelle knew. Already the room contained painted chests, probably filled with the dolls and games that Renée favored. She would have examined the room further, but laden porters arrived with tables, chairs and more chests.

Michelle's bedroom disappointed her when they entered. Though spacious, whitewashed, and well-appointed, it was dark despite the candlelight from its many standing candelabra, for it lacked windows.

M. de Beaune fils walked to the far half-wainscoted wall. He twisted a piece of the trim, chose a key from the many he carried, and inserted it into a keyhole. Picking up a lighted candle, he pushed a section of the wall forward.

"Follow me," he said., and pushed it closed behind them.

The whitewashed walls of the stone corridor extended for about six feet. About six feet high and about half as wide, it was not forbidding, but it *was* mysterious. A heavy wooden door barred its far end. Black iron hinges and a circular iron handle studded its surface. Below the massive handle, a keyhole stared at them like a giant eye. The young man offered Michelle a key and said, "Would you..."

Michelle gave him no time to finish. Inserting the key, she turned it. The mechanism moved easily. Grasping the enormous handle, she twisted it, pushed the door open, stepped outside and looked around.

As the queen had promised, she stood on the château grounds. Yet the entry to her house was well hidden by its corner location behind a tall privet hedge. Down a short gravel path she saw another tall locked gate.

"On the far side, a private path leads to Queen Anne's private retreat. Queen Claude has ordered me to provide keys to the Countess de Tonnerre when she arrives. Only you, the countess and the queen herself—or I in her absence—will have these keys." He gave her a set of keys on a heavy metal ring.

That night when Michelle entered her bedroom, it seemed welcoming and cozy. As she lay in her bed, Michelle already felt lighter as the weight of envy and court gossip lifted. Everything about the house was perfect. Already she was happy here, and she was certain Renée would be too.

CHÂTEAU DE BLOIS

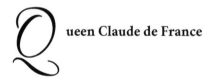ueen Claude de France

THE STURDY STONE walls of the Château de Blois glowed golden in the late afternoon sunlight. The moment it came into view from the queen's royal barge as it swept along the Loire River, Princess Renée began running up and down the narrow deck shouting, "I can see the castle, I can see the castle."

Mme. de Tonnerre followed behind her bleating, "Mme. Renée, you must be careful. Please do not run. Mme. Renée, a princess should never behave so."

The dozens of ladies crowded into the cabin smirked or exchanged speaking glances as they carefully avoided the queen's gaze. Queen Claude murmured something to Mme. Jeanne, who rose shortly after and strolled onto the deck. Next time the princess skipped by singing at the top of her voice, Mme. Jeanne called, "Mme. Renée, I would speak with you."

Princess Renée hesitated, skipped another step or two, and returned to her older sister's senior lady. "Yes, Madame?"

"Is that the correct way to address me?"

The princess pouted, but curtsied. "At your service, Mme. de Longwy."

Mme. de Longwy curtsied slightly in return. "Dear Mme. Renée. It is always a pleasure to witness your high spirits. Nonetheless, the deck of the barge is not the proper place either for running or raising your voice. Shall you, Mme. Françoise and I walk together? You shall point out the landmarks. After we dock you shall run with your friends in the castle gardens. How is that?"

AT ALMOST THE SAME MOMENT, the last of the baggage train carrying the household goods for the queen's court rumbled through the narrow streets of the upper town. Since early morning, the noble building had been in as much turmoil as an overturned ant hill. In the main courtyard, the Grand Equerry to the Master of Horse shouted orders to the grooms and carters who milled among the dozens of neighing, stomping, sweating horses, donkeys and mules that were harnessed to wagons and carts weighed down with every sort of baggage and foodstuff for the court.

By Nones, the Equerry of the Household Kitchens erupted into the courtyard, pulling at his hair in his distress at the disorder.

He was responsible for organizing the supplies, staffing, menus and food preparation for both the general household's and the queen's private kitchens. Shouting equally at the Grand Equerry, the wagoners and his Lord in heaven, he spread blame for the shambles as thickly as jam on toast.

As the day wore on, tempers frayed further. Keys were misplaced. Holders of the keys could not be found. Household staff disappeared when most needed, interfered with one another's tasks, and complained when essential bits unaccountably went missing. The Castellan, the Marshal de logis and the Grand Maître d'hôtel became more and more curt. Then word spread that the queen and her household had arrived.

SINKING with a grunt into the armchair that had been her mother's favorite, Claude winced. Her lower back and her right hip throbbed from the long walk to her bedchamber from the quay at the water gate. Even with the raised platform on her right shoe that made it easier to walk, the pressure on her hip worsened as her baby grew. She pressed the small of her back against the padded chair and groaned with relief as the pressure eased. When she saw Mme. Michelle, she would ask for one of her famous tisanes. Then her pain would vanish for a time. How pleased she was that she had come to Blois.

The bubble of exhilaration she had felt when the idea had first come to her returned. She had been kneeling at her prie-dieu, grieving the departure of Mme. Michele and gazing at Our Lady who held her infant Son. As Claude stared, tears glazing her eyes, the Virgin became surrounded in a glow of light. Then the idea popped into her head. Yes, Maman Louise could dismiss Mme. de Soubise as Renée's gouvernante and remove her from her sister's household. But Claude was queen. She could appoint whoever she wanted to her *own* household. If she wanted to appoint Mme. Michelle to it and keep her at Amboise with her, she could. It was that simple. The seemingly insoluble problem dissolved in front of her eyes and a whole new vista appeared.

And once she realized she could keep Mme. Michelle with her, she made a second leap. It was as if she had been blind since her maman's death, and now she could see again. She was queen. Once she had learned of Maman Louise's plans to dismiss Mme. Michelle, she had decided to thwart her. Sending Renée to Blois with Mme. de Tonnerre was a way to obey the duchess yet make sure Renée could continue to see Mme Michelle. But there was no reason Claude must stay at Amboise for her lying in just because Maman Louise had arranged it so. She had a choice. She could go to Blois for her confinement if she wished to. If she ordered it so, everyone would obey.

She took several deep breaths as the idea took root. It was like catching the first whiff of sea air when nearing the coast from inland. Then she felt light-headed and had to grasp the sides of the prie-dieu, for she thought she might faint. What would happen when Maman Louise found out? At the thought of her rage, Claude began to quake.

Then she remembered that Maman Louise was a long way away and could not easily return. Even if she did, Claude would already be in confinement, and it would be too late to change her location. So there was little she could do. The most she was likely to do was send a furious letter. But Maman Louise had a lot of more important things on her mind, so would she really? And even if she did, why would it matter? An angry letter would change nothing.

Claude examined the idea from every side. It would be better for Renée to have her only sister nearby, since she no longer had

Mme. Michelle as her gouvernante. Claude could manage her as Mme. de Tonnerre could not. It would be better for Claude to have Mme. Michelle nearby. She raised her eyes to the Holy Mother again. This time, Our Lady winked at her and gave a tiny nod. It was a sign she had her permission to act. Claude's heart filled with light. The Blessed Virgin had given her a revelation. She practically floated to her feet. But before she turned away, she lit a votive candle below the painting in gratitude.

Mme. Jeanne bustled into the queen's bedchamber. "Ah, it smells of summer in here. I told your servants to fill all the vases with roses." She peered down at Queen Claude. "Already your color is better. When you decided we must uproot ourselves and move to Blois, I had my doubts. But the change agrees with you." Twitching a light robe over the queen's knees, she checked that she had biscuits and hippocras within reach.

"I love it here. You and I passed much of my childhood here. And with Mme. Françoise and my sister coming here to the royal nursery, I realized we would all be happier if we were together."

"Now that I see you are well, with your permission I shall oversee the preparation of your lying-in chamber, Madame."

How easily some problems arranged themselves, Claude thought. She did not even have to invent an excuse to send her gouvernante away. "Could you please have M. de Beaune, fils come to me as you leave," she said,

When he arrived, she inquired whether Mme. Michelle had been satisfied with her new home.

"She claimed to be enchanted, Mme. la Reine and I believed her. She particularly admired the day nursery." His thin face lit up.

Claude was delighted. "Perhaps you will undertake one more task for me." She saw him flinch and smiled. "This one is much less time consuming," she assured him. "Mme. de Soubise does not know that I have arrived. Even if she is aware of the tumult here, she will expect Mme. de Tonnerre and my sister. Although Mme. de Soubise's presence is a well-guarded secret, I would like to see her this evening. Could you bring her to me unobtrusively? Without informing her I have arrived? I wish to surprise her."

Enveloped entirely in a long black cape, a hood pulled down to conceal her face, Mme. Michelle froze in the open doorway to the Queen's bedchamber. She appeared thunderstruck. Claude shot her a mischievous look and repressed a giggle. Then the baronne surged forward and sank into a deep curtsey.

Claude patted the footstool beside her chair. "Take off that cape and give it to the maid. Now, sit here."

As Mme. Michelle sputtered, at a loss for words, the queen reached out and took the baronne's hands in hers. "What fun to astonish you!"

The baronne was smiling too, though frown lines wrinkled her forehead. "I was worried. M. de Beaune would not tell me anything. But what are you doing here? I thought...?"

Claude lay a finger over Mme. Michelle's lips. "Shush. Just listen. I will explain. After I have finished, you may ask questions. Nod if you agree." She did not remove her finger until the baronne nodded.

"I have come here for my confinement. As of this moment I am appointing you my *Dame d'atour*. I wish you and your attendants

343

to move to the suite I have ordered prepared for you here in the château. I want you to attend me during my lying in. Do not worry, you will still give lessons to the Princess Renée as we have already planned. Mme. de Tonnerre will bring Renée to visit me in my lying-in chamber daily, so the three of us shall have time to amuse ourselves together. I promise Mme. Françoise will be delighted to give Renée into our charge —or perhaps I should say relieved — and glad to meet you." Laughing, Claude recounted various of Renée's escapades in the few days she had been in Mme. de Tonnerre's care.

"Then, after I am churched and depart for Lyon, I would like you to remain here at Blois to oversee the remaining children and the young *demoiselles d'honneur* of my court. I am certain we can persuade Mme. de Tonnerre that Renée should take her lessons and spend her leisure time with them." Their eyes met, and they burst into laughter.

By the time Queen Claude finished explaining her plan, Mme. Michelle's expression was serious. "Are you not concerned that Mme. Louise will be enraged when she learns of this."

Claude became thoughtful. "I shall regret it. But it is truly my decision to make."

"I commend you. You have cut the Gordian knot. It is an elegant solution. And it takes courage." Claude saw admiration in Mme. Michelle's eyes.

Claude blushed. She did not deserve such praise. It had taken her too long to face her fears. If her mother-in-law had not tried to dupe her over Renée, Claude was not sure she would have ever dared to challenge her. It was only when she realized how much she feared childbirth without Mme. Michelle that she had found it within her to defy Maman Louise. Now that she had done it once it no longer seemed as terrifying. She was sure she would not fall back into her old ways. For she was the queen.

A peaceful silence fell between them, and the sweet scent of the summer roses from Queen Anne's gardens filled the room.

FINIS

GLOSSARY

Appanage — is the grant of an estate, title, office or other thing of value to a younger child of a sovereign, who would otherwise have no inheritance under the system of primogeniture. Typically, in France it passed through the male line and when the male line failed, it returned to the royal demesne.

Bard — the bard is the term for a complete set of horse armor.

Chanfron — armor designed was designed to protect the horse's face. Sometimes this included hinged cheek plates. A decorative feature common to many chanfrons is a rondel with a small spike.

Cloth of estate — is a canopy-like arrangement of precious fabric above and behind a throne or dais.

Codpiece — (from Middle English: cod, **meaning** "scrotum") is a covering flap or pouch that attaches to the front of the crotch of men's trousers, enclosing the genital area.

Compline — end of the day, traditionally 9:00 p.m.

dame d'atour — was an office at the royal court of France. It existed in nearly all French courts from the 16th-century onward. The *dame d'atour* was selected from the members of the highest French nobility.

denier — or **penny** was a medieval coin which takes its name from the Frankish coin first issued in the late seventh century.

Étrenne — the practice of seasonal gift giving on New Year's Day and the gifts in the ceremonial exchange; the word is derived from the Latin word *strena*.

Estates General — in France under the Ancien Regime the Estates General was a legislative and consultative assembly of the different classes (or estates) of French subjects. It had a separate assembly for each of the three estates (clergy, nobility and commoners), which were called and dismissed by the king.

Fleur de lys — translated from French as 'lily flower' is a stylized design of either an iris or a lily that is now used purely decoratively as well as symbolically, or it may be "at one and the same time political, dynastic, artistic, emblematic and symbolic", especially in heraldry. It is particularly associated with the ancient regime French monarchy.

Gouvernante — the Governess of the royal children, recruited from the high nobility, oversees the education of the children of the royal couple, including the Dauphin. She is sometimes assisted by deputy governors. While the girls remained attached to the Queen's House, it was customary for princes raised by female governors to "pass to men" at the age of seven (the age of reason at the time) and to be placed in the care of a governor assisted by a deputy governor.

Grand Maître de Menu Plaisirs — The Controller of the Menus Plaisirs heard directly from the king what the plans for the king's personal entertainment were to be set in motion; by long-standing convention, he was a duke; although he was not a professional, it was up to him to determine how to carry out these plans. The Duke in charge of the Menus and Pleasures of the King was an important official of the court.

Humors — The humors were part of an ancient theory that held that health came from balance between the bodily liquids. These liquids were termed humors. The Four Humors were blood, phlegm, yellow bile and black bile.

Italian disease — Syphilis, introduced into Europe in the late 15th century. Its source is unknown, but it became rampant in 1494/95 after the start of the French-Italian wars. Known by various names, in Italy it was called the French disease and in France it was called the Italian disease. There was no known cure, though it was treated with mercury, it raced through the infected individual causing great pain. It was usually fatal.

Houppelande — an outer garment, with a long, full body and flaring sleeves, sometimes lined with fur.

King of Arms — The Ranking Herald. In France, A College of Heralds was organized in 1407, about the same time as in England it seems. It consisted of pursuivants, heralds and 12 kings of arms, chief among them Montjoye, followed in rank by Anjou. In the 16th century a number of kings of arms (Valois, Champagne, Dauphin, Normandie) and heralds (Guyenne, Angoulême, Lorraine, Orléans) were on the king's payroll and sent for diplomatic missions abroad.

Lauds — early morning, traditionally 3:00 a.m.

Matins — nighttime, traditionally 12:00 a.m.

monthly flowers — menses or menstrual period.

Montjoie Saint Denis — was the battle cry and motto of the Kingdom of France. It allegedly referred to Charlemagne's legendary banner, the Oriflamme, which was also known as the "Montjoie" and was kept at the Abbey of Saint Denis.

Night rail — the former term for nightgown.

Nones — the ninth hour, traditionally 3:00 p.m.

Prie-dieu — a piece of furniture for use during prayer, consisting of a kneeling surface and a narrow upright front with a rest for the elbows or for books.

Parlement — the most powerful was the Parlement of Paris, were judicial organizations consisting of a dozen or more appellate judges. They were the court of final appeal of the judicial system, and typically wielded much power over a wide range of subjects, particularly taxation. Laws and edicts issued by the Crown were not official in their respective jurisdictions until the parlements gave their assent by publishing them. The members were aristocrats called *nobles de la robe* who had bought or inherited their offices and were independent of the King. However, the king could force the Parlement to publish any law by arriving in person to hold a 'lit de justice.'

Pillion —a secondary side saddle behind the main saddle on a horse. A passenger in this saddle is said to "ride pillion". The word is derived from the Scottish Gaelic for "little rug", pillean, from the Latin pellis, "animal skin".

Renal stone — Kidney stones. *Renes* is the Latin word for kidneys. Queen Anne is believed to have died from severe kidney disease.

Sennight — a week

Sext — noon, traditionally 12:00 p.m.

Scots Guards — was an elite Scottish military unit founded in 1418 to be personal bodyguards to the French monarchy. They were assimilated into the King's Household and later formed the first company of the Royal Bodyguard. They survived until the end of the Bourbon monarchy.

Tarocchi — are cards for specific card games played with tarot (Italian *tarocco, tarocchi*) decks, that is, decks with numbered permanent trumps parallel to the suit cards. The basic rules, invented purely for gaming, first appeared in the manuscript of Martiano da Tortona, written before 1425. They became popular in France after 1494, the start of the French-Italian wars.

Terce — the third hour, traditionally 9:00 a.m.

Vespers — sunset, evening, traditionally 6:00 p.m.

AFTERWORD

APPENDIX 1 — INFORMATION ABOUT TIMES

Liturgical [Canonical] Hours

Already well-established by the 9th century in the West, these canonical hours consisted of daily prayer (liturgies) that were also used to refer to the time of day. Though the times changed throughout the day since they followed the hours of sunlight, I have used the following times as a rough guide. Often Lauds and Matins were combined.

Lauds (early morning) 3:00 a.m.

Prime (first hour of daylight) 6:00 a.m.

Terce, (third hour) 9:00 a.m.

Sext (noon) 12:00 p.m.

Nones (ninth hour) 3:00 p.m.

Vespers (sunset evening) 6:00 p.m.

Compline (end of the day) 9:00 p.m.

Matins (nighttime) 12:00 a.m.

Typical Mealtime Hours

In European courts at this time, it was typical that only two meals a day were served in the Great Dining Hall. They were provided to those who had the right to eat at the King's or Queen's table.

First meal, about 10: 00 a.m.

Second meal, about 4:00 p.m.

People at court often/usually went to mass before the first meal.

The Trouble with Dates

Until the adoption of the Gregorian calendar, introduced by Pope Gregory XIII in October 1582 (which occurred at different dates in different countries) the new year started on April 1. That is why those events occurring between January 1 and March 31 are often recorded in different years in different documents. Thus, for example, Anne de Bretagne's birthday, which fell on January 25, is variously recorded as occurring in 1476 or 1477.

We take the death of Louis XII on 1 January 1515 as significant. It would have been much less so in 1515, when the change of year was 1 April.

APPENDIX 2

APPENDIX 2 — FACTS AND FICTION

This is a work of historical fiction. Although I have attempted to stay close to the historical facts as I know them, I have made a few conscious deviations for the sake of my novel.

First, Queen Anne was ill for a longer period than I suggest. As it doesn't change anything important in the story and improves the pace, I have made the change. The second and very important change to the known facts is the suggestion I have made that Countess Louise d'Angoulême gave King Louis tampered sweets during his last illness. There is absolutely **NO** evidence that she **or anyone else** tried to hurry him out of this world. She was certainly happy to see him go and see her son on the throne, but I make no other claims against her.

Otherwise, all the principal characters existed, as did the rivalry between France and the Hapsburgs, the deep enmity between Anne and Louise, and Queen Anne's relentless struggle to maintain Brittany's independence.

For those who are puzzled, in France women were not permitted to inherit the throne because of a principle, called the 'Salic law' that stipulated that the throne must pass *patrilineally* to males only. Since Queen Anne and King Louis XII produced only daughters, Claude and Renée, the next male closest in patrilineal succession was François d'Angoulême.

A few additional historical details. Queen Anne of France was also Duchess de Bretagne in her own right. It was her life goal to keep Brittany separate from France. She did everything in her power to marry her daughter, Claude, to the future Emperor Charles V, who was also Duke of Burgundy among his many other titles. When it became clear that Anne and Louis were unlikely to have living sons, King Louis ended the betrothal and insisted Claude marry his presumptive heir, Duke François d'Angoulême. It became the sore spot in an otherwise harmonious marriage.

Queen Anne died on 9 January 1514, and King Louis XII, her husband, died close to one year later, on 1 January 1515. After Anne's death, King Louis married Princess Mary Rose [Queen Marie in France] who had demanded the right from her brother, Henry VIII, to marry whom she pleased when Louis died. Princess Claude, who became Duchess de Bretagne upon the death of her mother, was married quickly after Anne's death to Duke François d'Angoulême who became the next King of France. When he became king, François, who adored his mother, raised Louise to the rank of Duchess. She was instrumental in arranging his successful war against Milan in 1516.

Queen Anne and Countess Louise d'Angoulême were bitter enemies, yet in her will Queen Anne made Countess Louise the executrix of her estate and guardian of her children. Louise used her authority to enrich herself from Princess Renée's estate and treated Princess Renée badly.

The next question historians may raise is my treatment of the dismissal of Michelle de Saubonne, Baronne de Soubise. Baronne Michelle de Soubise was Queen Anne's *dame d'atour*, secretary, Mistress of the Wardrobe and closest friend throughout her second marriage [1499-1514]. Mme. de Bouchage was first official gouvernante to Princess Renée, but when she died, Queen Anne asked Baronne Michelle de Soubise to become Princess Renée's gouvernante. Historians believe that Countess Louise dismissed her once the countess became the princess's official guardian after the death of King Louis. The letters I use in this story are adapted translations from the letters that have been used for years to prove the above point. Most historians and biographers suggest that Princess Renée lived with Queen Claude until her death, after which she stayed with Marguerite, Duchess d'Alençon, until Marguerite married King Henry II of Navarre.

The ending of this novel is fictional. However, from my research, I have concluded that the current thinking, that the Baronne de Soubise was dismissed in 1516, and returned to her family home is incorrect. Although I do not have every fact necessary to prove my thesis, I present my evidence in 'Scandal at the French Court in 1515?' posted on my website, All About French Renaissance Women

FOR BOOK GROUPS

TOPICS & QUESTIONS FOR DISCUSSION

1. The people in the novel often suggest that events happen as God wills or that events must be left in God's hands. Do you think that the characters believe that they are unable to change their fate?

2. Various of the women in the book had arranged marriages. How did it affect their experience of marriage and of love? Did the couples love their partners?

3. Louise made a deathbed promise to Queen Anne to keep Mme de Soubise as Renée's *gouvernante*. Normally these vows were sacred. Why do you think Louise was so determined to remove Mme de Soubise from her position?

4. Who were the pawns in the story? Why do you think so? Did they remain pawns or did they take actions to influence their fate?

5. What kinds of power did the men in the novel wield over the women? Did they abuse their power? Do you

think that the novel portrays the relationship between men and women at the time realistically?

6. Why do you think Duke François was so determined to seduce Queen Marie when, if she had a son, he would have been replaced in the succession by the child?

7. Do you think it possible that Louise would have gone to the extreme of poisoning King Louis if she could?

8. How important was family to Claude? To Louise?

9. Why was Claude so reluctant to oppose her mother-in-law? What was she afraid would happen? What caused her to change?

10. How did you feel about the various women — Louise, Michelle and Claude — by the end of the novel?

Deepen Your Knowledge

1. Much of *THE IMPORTANCE OF PAWNS* takes place at either Blois and Amboise. Visit the official sites:

- to find out more about the Chateau de Blois, take a virtual tour of the Château's architecture
- to see what parts of the Château d'Amboise existed when Queen Anne lived there. (Go to the section on the history under the Valois which has drawings of the site at different time periods.)

1. Go here to learn more about Renaissance Clothing

1. Go here to discover more about French Renaissance food and feasts

2. To read more French Renaissance fiction, join Keira Morgan's official site to get **5 FREE classic French Renaissance novels** and keep abreast of stories, articles, book reviews etc. @kjmorgan-writer

3. To learn more about about the lives of Queen Anne,
   Queen Claude, Princess Renée, Louise de Savoie,
   Baronne Michelle de Soubise and many other French
   Renaissance women, visit Keira Morgan's research site
   at All About French Renaissance Women

If you have questions or comments you can leave them on her
site. She is always delighted to answer.

NOTES

PRINCIPAL CHARACTERS AND AGE (WHEN STORY OPENS)

1. *Gouvernante* — the Governess of the royal children, recruited from the high nobility, oversees the education of the children of the royal couple, including the Dauphin. She is sometimes assisted by deputy governors. While the girls remained attached to the Queen's House, it was customary for princes raised by female governors to "pass to men" at the age of seven (the age of reason at the time) and to be placed in the care of a governor assisted by a deputy governor.

1. 4 JANUARY 1514, EARLY AFTERNOON

1. *Étrenne* — the practice of seasonal gift giving on New Year's Day and the gifts in the ceremonial exchange; the word is derived from the Latin word *strena.*
2. *Dame d'atour* — *This* was an office at the royal court of France. It existed in nearly all French courts from the 16th-century onward. The *dame d'atour* was selected from the members of the highest French nobility.
3. Monthly flowers — menses or menstrual period.
4. Renal stone — Kidney stones. *Renes* is the Latin word for kidneys. Queen Anne is believed to have died from severe kidney disease.
5. Humors — The humors were part of an ancient theory that held that health came from balance among the bodily liquids. These liquids were termed humors. The Four Humors were blood, phlegm, yellow bile and black bile.

2. 4 JANUARY 1514, LATE AFTERNOON

1. Tarocchi — are cards for specific card games played with tarot (Italian *tarocco, tarocchi)* decks, that is, decks with numbered permanent trumps parallel to the suit cards. The basic rules, invented purely for gaming, first appeared in the manuscript of Martiano da Tortona, written before 1425. They became popular in France after 1494, the start of the French-Italian wars.
2. Prie-dieu — a piece of furniture for use during prayer, consisting of a kneeling surface and a narrow upright front with a rest for the elbows or for books.

3. Estates General — in France under the Ancien Regime the Estates General was a legislative and consultative assembly of the different classes (or estates) of French subjects. It had a separate assembly for each of the three estates (clergy, nobility and commoners), which were called and dismissed by the king.
4. Vespers — sunset, evening, traditionally 6:00 p.m.
5. Fleur de lys — the fleur-de-lys, translated from French as 'lily flower' is a stylized design of either an iris or a lily that is now used purely decoratively as well as symbolically, or it may be "at one and the same time political, dynastic, artistic, emblematic and symbolic", especially in heraldry. It is particularly associated with the *ancien regime* French monarchy.
6. Denier — or **penny** was a medieval coin which takes its name from the Frankish coin first issued in the late seventh century.

3. 5 JANUARY 1514

1. Night rail — the former term for nightgown.
2. Codpiece — (from Middle English: cod, **meaning** "scrotum") is a covering flap or pouch that attaches to the front of the crotch of men's trousers, enclosing the genital area.

4. 6 JANUARY 1514

1. Matins — nighttime, traditionally 12:00 a.m.

5. NIGHT OF 8 — 9 JANUARY 1514

1. Lauds — early morning, traditionally 3:00 a.m.
2. Sennight — a week

6. 9 JANUARY 1514

1. Nones — the ninth hour, traditionally 3:00 p.m.
2. Sext — noon, traditionally 12:00 p.m.

8. 18 MAY 1514

1. Parlement — of which the most powerful was the Parlement of Paris — were judicial organizations consisting of a dozen or more appellate judges. They were the court of final appeal of the judicial system, and typically wielded much power over a wide range of subjects, particularly taxation.

Laws and edicts issued by the Crown were not official in their respective jurisdictions until the parlements gave their assent by publishing them. The members were aristocrats called nobles of the robe who had bought or inherited their offices and were independent of the King. However, the king could force the Parlement to publish any law by arriving in person to hold a 'lit de justice.'

9. 19 MAY 1514

1. Appanage — is the grant of an estate, title, office or other thing of value to a younger child of a sovereign, who would otherwise have no inheritance under the system of primogeniture. Typically, in France it passed through the male line and when the male line failed, it returned to the royal demesne.

10. 25 JULY 1514

1. Scots Guards — was an elite Scottish military unit founded in 1418 to be personal bodyguards to the French monarchy. They were assimilated into the King's Household and later formed the first company of the Royal Bodyguard. They survived until the end of the Bourbon monarchy
2. King of Arms — The Ranking Herald. In France, A College of Heralds was organized in 1407, about the same time as in England it seems. It consisted of pursuivants, heralds and 12 kings of arms, chief among them Montjoye, followed in rank by Anjou. In the 16th century a number of kings of arms (Valois, Champagne, Dauphin, Normandie) and heralds (Guyenne, Angoulême, Lorraine, Orléans) were on the king's payroll and sent for diplomatic missions abroad.
3. Grand Maître de Menu Plaisirs — The Controller of the Menus Plaisirs heard directly from the king what the plans for the king's personal entertainment were to be set in motion; by long-standing convention, he was a duke; although he was not a professional, it was up to him to determine how to carry out these plans. The Duke in charge of the Menus and Pleasures of the King was an important official of the court.
4. Pillion —a side saddle placed behind the main saddle on a horse. A passenger in this saddle is said to 'ride pillion.' The word is derived from the Scottish Gaelic for 'little rug,' pillean, from the Latin pellis, 'animal skin.'

11. 16 OCTOBER 1514

1. Cloth of estate — is a canopy-like arrangement of precious fabric above and behind a throne or dais.

14. 18 NOVEMBER 1514

1. Montjoie Saint Denis — was the battle cry and motto of the Kingdom of France. It allegedly referred to Charlemagne's legendary banner, the Oriflamme, which was also known as the "Montjoie" and was kept at the Abbey of Saint Denis.
2. Chanfron — armor designed was designed to protect the horse's face. Sometimes this included hinged cheek plates. A decorative feature common to many chanfrons is a rondel with a small spike.
3. Bard —the term for a complete set of horse armor.
4. Houppelande — an outer garment, with a long, full body and flaring sleeves, sometimes lined with fur.

15. 7 DECEMBER 1514

1. Italian disease — Syphilis, introduced into Europe in the late 15th century. Its source is unknown, but it became rampant in 1494/95 after the start of the French-Italian wars. Known by various names, in Italy it was called the French disease and in France it was called the Italian disease. There was no known cure, though it was treated with mercury, it raced through the infected individual causing great pain. It was usually fatal.

24. 26 JUNE 1515

1. Compline — end of the day, traditionally 9:00 p.m.
2. Terce — the third hour, traditionally 9:00 a.m.

ACKNOWLEDGMENTS

No book is written alone. There are many people I wish to thank for their help and support.

Both my critique partner and mentor, Roberta Rich and my editor, Claire Mulligan, who have shaped this book through several iteration have been wonderful. Their hands lie heavy upon this work. I send a grateful thanks to the lovely group of experienced writers who gave useful commentary, kindly expressed, when I first exposed my book to the ears of others in February 2020, just before the pandemic locked us all in our cocoons.

I cannot bless enough my faithful and diligent proofreaders and beta readers, Rachel McMillen, Emerson Nagel, Carla Morgan, Jan Morgan and Carolyn Jakes.

If I named every person whose advice and suggestions, I have sought along the way this section would occupy pages, so I will stop here. To each one of you, I am truly grateful. Without all of you, this book would not be what it is.

Of course, every error of fact, imagination, grammar and orthography is mine alone.

ABOUT THE AUTHOR

Keira retired from training and management in the Canadian Public Service to begin a career as an author. She now has a home in and writes from Mexico. Her husband, two cats and two dogs keep her company.

Join Keira's mailing list to keep up with her latest, news, events, and posts. She will send you a **quarterly newsletter** if you choose. Keira welcomes comments and suggestions on both her KJ Morgan—Writer and her All About French Renaissance Women [https://www.keiramorgan.com] blogs. If you have an article to share, ideas for content, or ideas on improvements, write to Author@kjmorgan-writer.com

Follow Keira on any or all of her social media sites and on her Good reads and Amazon Author pages.

Facebook.com/kjmorganwriter

Twitter.com/KJMMexico

Instagram.com/RenaissanceFictionLady

Amazon Authors' sites

- Amazon USA
- Amazon Canada
- Amazon UK
- Amazon Australia
- Amazon France
- Amazon Mexico

Goodreads Author

61778957R00227